Praise for

Adult Onset

#1 NATIONAL BESTSELLER

Finalist for the Lambda Literary Awards'
Lesbian General Fiction Award
A *New York Times Book Review* Editors' Choice
A *Globe and Mail* Best Book
A CBC Best Book

"Impossible to put down once begun. . . . MacDonald . . . scans the parameters of parenthood with an unflinching gaze. Her depiction of the perils of everyday domestic turmoil can be harrowing as well as, at times, hilarious. . . . Since MacDonald's books have all been so extraordinary, it is impossible to rank *Adult Onset* against the others. Suffice it to say the novel is superb, a fine blending of fact and fiction, of remembered incident and forgotten history, a wonderfully written treatise on the power of the past to impinge on the present."
The London Free Press

"A complex, troubling novel that cuts with surgical precision into the sinew and muscle of family life." Sarah Waters, author of *The Paying Guests*

"What brings light for us readers is the sense of humour, self mockery and irony with which MacDonald gives shape to her dark message. With this penetrating and psychologically accurate novel this Canadian author gloriously adds herself to the company of her compatriots Alice Munro and Margaret Atwood." *Trouw*

"A brave and perceptive rumination on parents and parenting." *The Globe and Mail*

"MacDonald strikes just the right tone as she exposes the brutal undercurrents of domestic life." *The New York Times*

"There is barely a playing card's width between life and art in [*Adult Onset,*] an intricate, gripping novel that is also a master class in turning the personal into the universal through art." Brian Bethune, *Maclean's*

"Ann-Marie MacDonald has taken a big risk with *Adult Onset*. . . . [It's] raw, totally contemporary and deeply personal. . . . [MacDonald] explores the question of parental abuse and its origins with uncommon courage. And the whole thing has palpable authenticity." Susan G. Cole, *NOW* (NNNN)

"Remarkable. . . . A mile-a-minute exploration of modern life by a masterful author, who rides the fine line between fact and fiction." *The Vancouver Sun*

"At its core, *Adult Onset* is about what happens when we are unable to face the physical and emotional pain of our past head on, and how the chronic illness of trauma will haunt even the most insignificant moments of our days. . . . It is a high achievement for a writer to portray the persistent worry of avoidance in a way that rings true, and MacDonald has beyond succeeded. It is in this sense that *Adult Onset* is both a book that is difficult to endure, and one worthy of our praise and attention. . . . Many of us will see ourselves in the profound discomfort MacDonald has conjured, and though the narrative lends itself to frustration as a result, the book is an absolute triumph of terrifying authenticity." Stacey May Fowles, *National Post*

"A roller-coaster ride offering brief moments of serenity amid increasingly terrifying plunges into the darkness of Mary Rose's past. Suspense builds; surely, horror awaits. . . . MacDonald's book remains spellbinding throughout. It is impossible to forget, despite—or perhaps because of—an ending that leaves the reader exhausted and with no easy answers." *Quill & Quire*

"Big, troubling and brave. . . . Books like hers have a continental sweep." *The New York Times Book Review*

"She has again delivered a masterpiece." *The Globe and Mail*

"I binge-read this novel." Melanie Jackson, *The Vancouver Sun*

"Though all of Ann-Marie's works are very distinct entities . . . her third book has the same beautifully crafted descriptions and character-driven storytelling that readers have come to love." *Canadian Living*

"MacDonald's prose is always exquisite, and her humour sometimes subtle but always razor sharp." *The Chronicle Herald*

"A funny and frank look at what it means to be a parent and pursue happiness in the modern world." CBC Books

"A stunning and powerful work that will knock readers on their collective keister. . . . In *Adult Onset*, every character has depth, a story, nuance." *Post City Toronto*

"*Adult Onset* . . . transforms from an ordinary housewife domestic-saga-with-a-twist to a story that has never been written before. . . . It's brave for any parent to write about anger, an emotion so taboo it's difficult to admit these days without arousing concern. Will MacDonald be lauded for being similarly forthcoming? *Adult Onset* shows us a new Ann-Marie MacDonald, one who is willing to break away from the safe scaffolding of a historical structure and offer readers some unflinching and realistic takes on the traditional domestic novel, exploring what it's like for anyone struggling to raise kids in an age of perfection parenting. It's a lively, moving and often funny story that has the potential to help usher in a new era of honest literary depictions of families in all their permutations." Zoe Whittall, *The Walrus*

"Riveting. . . . MacDonald's strong narrative is a compelling examination of the loneliness and often-absurd helplessness of being a parent of young children." *Publishers Weekly*

"*Adult Onset*'s low simmer is a change of pace from MacDonald's previous murder-mystery spy thriller *The Way the Crow Flies*, and literary debut *Fall On Your Knees*. . . . What remains, however, is MacDonald's effortless ability to quickly spin pathos into humour, making the suffering of her characters humane and never heavy-handed." *The Georgia Straight*

Also by Ann-Marie MacDonald

Goodnight Desdemona (Good Morning Juliet)
Fall On Your Knees
The Way the Crow Flies
Belle Moral: A Natural History

ADULT

ANN-MARIE MACDONALD

ONSET

A NOVEL

VINTAGE CANADA

VINTAGE CANADA EDITION, 2015
Copyright © 2014 A.M. MacDonald Holdings Inc.

Published in Canada by Vintage Canada, a division of Random House of Canada Limited, a Penguin Random House company, in 2015. Originally published in hardcover in Canada by Alfred A. Knopf Canada, a division of Random House of Canada Limited, in 2014. Distributed in Canada by Random House of Canada Limited, Toronto.

Vintage Canada with colophon is a registered trademark.

www.penguinrandomhouse.ca

Every effort has been made to contact copyright holders; in the event of an inadvertent omission or error, please notify the publisher.

Library and Archives Canada Cataloguing in Publication

MacDonald, Ann-Marie, author
Adult onset / Ann-Marie MacDonald.

ISBN 978-0-345-80828-8
eBook ISBN 978-0-345-80829-5

I. Title.

PS8575.D38A63 2015   C813'.54   C2014-902059-7

Book design by Kelly Hill
Cover images: (balloon) © Susil, (tulip) © frescomovie, (background) © Tomas Jasinskis, all Shutterstock.com

Printed and bound in the United States of America

2 4 6 8 9 7 5 3 1

For Alisa Palmer.
And the Children.

The solitary bone cyst has not yet revealed all its secrets . . . The SBC still remains mysterious in many of its aspects. At the time of this writing, nobody can predict the occurrence modalities of this benign bone tumor. In a similar way, the reality of this tumor-like lesion cannot be precisely described. Alas, solitary bone cyst was supposed to be a lesion in children that disappeared after growth ended. Is it still true since some cases have been reported more recently in adults? This study represents a long follow-up.

"Solitary bone cyst: controversies and treatment."
H. Bensahel, P. Jehanno, Y. Desgrippes, G.F. Pennecot, Service de Chirurgie Orthopédique Hôpital Robert Debré, Paris, France

MONDAY

Dreams of an Everyday Housewife

In the midway of this, our mortal life, Mary Rose MacKinnon is at her cheerful kitchen table checking e-mail. It is Monday. Her two-year-old is busy driving a doll stroller into the baseboard, so she has a few minutes.

Your 99 friends are waiting to join you on Facebook. She deletes it, flinches at another invitation to appear at a literary festival, skims her five-year-old's school newsletter online and signs up to accompany his class to the reptile museum. She skips guiltily over unanswered messages and cute links sent by friends—including one from her brother that shows a fat woman whose naked torso looks like Homer Simpson's face—and is about to close it down when her laptop *bings* in time with the oven and the incoming e-mail catches her eye. It is highlighted in queasy cyber yellow and bears a dialogue box: *Mail thinks this is junk*. She eyes it gingerly, fearing a virus or another ad for Viagra. It is from some joker—

as her father would say—with the address ladyfromhell@sympatico.ca
and in the subject line:

> Some things really do get batter . . .

A baking newsletter from a mad housewife? She bites, and clicks.

> Hi Mister,
> Mum and I just watched the video entitled "It Gets Better" and
> I thought I'd try out the new e-mail to tell you how proud we are
> that you and Hilary are such good role models for young people
> who may be struggling against prejudice.
> Love,
> Dad
>
> PS: Hope this gets to you. Just got the e-mail installed yesterday.
> I am now officially no longer a "Cybersaur"! Off to "surf the net" now.

My goodness.
She types:

> Dear Dad,
> Congratulations and welcome to the twenty-first century!

No, that sounds sarcastic. *Delete.*

> Dear Dad,
> Welcome to the digital age! And thanks, it means a lot to me that
> you and Mum saw the video and that it means a lot to you that

She is proud that he is proud. And that he is proud that Mum is
proud; of whom Mary Rose is also proud. *Sigh.* She does not like

screens, convinced as she is they have some sort of neurologically hazing effect. She ought to write her father an actual card with an actual pen to let him know how much this means to her. She gets up and slides a tray of vine-ripened tomatoes into the oven to slow-roast—they are from Israel, is that wrong?

"Ow. Careful, Maggie."

"No," croons the child in reply.

She returns to the table, its bright non-toxic vinyl IKEA cloth obscured by bills and reminders for service calls she needs to book for the various internal organs of her house. *Bing! Your 100 friends are waiting* . . . A month or so ago she tripped on a root in cyberspace and accidentally joined Facebook; now she can't figure out how to unjoin. She has visited her page once, its silhouette of a human head empty but for a question mark at the centre, awaiting her picture, like an unetched tombstone—*we know you're coming . . . eventually.* Her unadorned wall was full of names, many of which she did not recognize, some of which bore the rank odour of the crypt of high school. What is this mania for keeping in touch? she wonders. Mary Rose MacKinnon is unused to continuity. She grew up in a family that moved every few years until she was a teenager, and each time it was as if everything and everyone vanished behind them. Or entered a different realm, a mythic one wherein time stopped, the children she had known never grew older and, as in a cartoon, people and places retained the same clothes and aspect day after day, regardless of weather, explosions or being shot by Elmer Fudd. She would not change a thing, however, each move having brought with it a sense of renewal; as though she had outrun a shameful past—starting at age three. Nowadays, she reflects, no one is allowed to outrun anything. If one kid slugs another in the park, they're packed off to therapy.

Delete.

People used to joke about Xeroxed newsletters sent by relentlessly chipper housewives at Christmas. Their effect, and perhaps their purpose, was to make everyone who received them feel bad about their own lives. Nowadays people torture one another online with pictures of their golden-retriever lifestyles and tweets about must-see plays in New York with one-word titles, new restaurants in Toronto with four tables, human rights abuses in China and the truth behind the down duvet industry. Where is the meadow of yesteryear? Whither the sound of one insect scaling a stalk of grass? The time-silvered fence post in the afternoon sun? What has become of time itself in its expansive, unparcelled state, uncorseted by language? Where have all the tiny eternities gone? Gone to urgencies, every one.

As she types this e-mail to her father, icebergs are evaporating and falling as rain on her February garden, where a water-boarded tulip has foolishly put its head up—are things getting better or worse? *Bing! Matthew is invited to Eli's Big Boy Birthday Party! Click here to view your e-vite!* A birthday party at some obscure suburban facility north of Yonge and the 401, do these parents have no compassion? She peers into the depths of *info and goodies!* trying to find a date and time amid exploding balloons and floating dinosaurs.

She used to console herself with the notion that the human species would burn itself out like a virus and Earth would recover Her bounty and diversity. But that was before she became a mother.

Nowadays? How old is she? No one says *nowadays* nowadays. She'll be making references to the Great Depression before she knows it.

It is April, today is the first—though anyone might be forgiven for getting the months muddled considering it did rain all through February. She wonders if that impacted the usual February suicide rate. *Impacted* did not used to be a verb. Sometime in the nineties it got verbed, like so many other unsuspecting nouns.

Dear Dad,

I

"It Gets Better" is an online video project aimed at supporting Lesbian Gay Bisexual Transgendered and Queer youth in response to a recent spate of suicides and assaults. Healthy adults speak into the camera and share stories of how desperate they were when, as younger people, they suffered the hatred of their peers, their parents and, worst of all, themselves. Each story ends with the assurance that "it gets better." Hilary watched it and cried. Mary Rose didn't need to watch the whole thing, she got the point and thought it was wonderful, etc. . . . It has been shown in schools, even some churches, ordinary people the world over have been watching it. There are even people in Russia and Iran watching it. But the evolutionary layers that have led Dolly and Duncan MacKinnon to watch it constitute a sedimentary journey as unlikely as the emergence of intelligent life itself. At least that is how it strikes Mary Rose for, although things have been just fine—more than fine, wonderful—between her and her parents for years now, they weren't always. So she is all the more impressed that they are, at their advanced age, making connections between the daughter they love and an actual social issue. The cursor blinks.

The sound of splashing brings her to her feet.

"Maggie, no, sweetheart, that's Daisy's water."

She bends and pulls the child gently back from the dog dish.

"No!"

"Are you thirsty?"

"Aisy."

"Is Daisy thirsty?"

"Me!"

"Are you being Daisy?"

Maggie dives for the dog bowl and gets in a slurp before Mary Rose lifts it to the counter.

"No!" cries the child with a clutch at her mother's right buttock.

Mary Rose fills a sippy cup with filtered water from the fridge dispenser and hands it to Maggie. The child launches it across the floor. The mother escalates with the offer of jam on a rice cake. The child, after a dangerous pause, accepts. Détente. Another placated potentate. The mother returns to her laptop. Ask not for whom the cursor blinks . . .

The phone rings. A long-distance ring. She feels adrenalin spurt in the pit of her stomach. A glance at the display dispels the faint hope that it might be Hilary calling from out west. It is her mother. She stares at the phone, cordless but no less umbilical for that. She can't talk to her mother right now, she is busy formulating a fitting reply to her father's e-mail. Her father, who always had time for her. *Ring-ring!* Her father, who never raised his voice; whose faith in her gifts allowed her to achieve liftoff from the slough of despond of childhood—and grow up to write books about the slough of despond of childhood. *Ring-ring!* Besides, talking on the phone works like a red flag on Maggie; Mary Rose will wind up having to cut the call short and there will go her precious scrap of time to deal with e-mail and all manner of domestic detritus before grocery shopping, then picking up Matthew and then hurrying home to purée the slow-roasted tomatoes into an "easy rustic Tuscan sauce." *Ring-ring!*

On the other hand, maybe her father is dead and this is the phone call for which she has been bracing all her life . . . His lovely e-mail will end up having been his last words to her. Maybe that's what killed him—he finally got in touch with his emotions and now he is dead. And it is her fault. Unless her mother is dead and it is her father calling, which has always seemed less likely—Dad rarely makes phone calls. Besides, in the event of an emergency, her parents would phone her older sister, Maureen, and Maureen would phone Mary Rose. She breathes. Her parents are safe and sound in their sublet condo in Victoria, where they spend the mild West Coast winters close to her big sister and her family.

No sooner has she allowed it to ring through to voice mail, however, than she experiences another spurt of fear: it might indeed be

Maureen calling . . . *from their parents' condo*. Mo visits daily and per-haps she arrived this morning to find *both* their parents dead—one from a stroke, the other from a heart attack brought on by discovering the deceased spouse. Though her neocortex deems this unlikely, Mary Rose's hand, being on closer terms with her amygdala, is already cold as she picks up the phone and, feeling like the traitor she is, presses *flash* so as to screen the call just in case someone isn't dead. Her mother's big rich voice chops through. "You're not there! I just called"—here she bursts into song—"to say, I love you!"

From the floor, Maggie cries, "Sitdy!"—this being Arabic for *grand-mother* because nothing in Mary Rose's life is simple—and reaches for the phone. Mary Rose could kick herself. She presses *end*, cutting her mother off mid-warble with a stab of guilt, but hands Maggie the phone to stave off a complete toddler meltdown and feels even guiltier since it is rather like handing the child an empty candy wrapper. Maggie pushes buttons, trying to retrieve "Sitdy!" An urgent beeping gives way to the implacable female automaton, "Please hang up and try your call again."

Maggie responds with a stream of toddler invective.

"Please hang up . . . *now*," commands the voice, cool and beyond supplication, as though the speaker has witnessed too many of one's crimes to be moved now by one's cries. "*This* is a recording."

"Maggie, give Mumma the phone, sweetheart."

"No!" Still frantically pressing buttons. She is a beautiful child, dimples and sparkly hazel eyes. She does everything fast, runs every-where, and her curls have an electromagnetic life of their own.

"Sitdy's gone, honey, she hung up." Another deception.

"Hello?" A female voice, but neither a frosty recording nor the jolly gollywoggle of Sitdy, it is—

"Mummy!" cries Maggie, phone jammed to the side of her head. "Hi, hi!"

"Give Mumma the phone, Maggie. Maggie, give it to me."

"No!" she screams. "Mummy!" She runs away down the hall.

Hilary's going to think I'm beating our child—"Hil!" she calls in pursuit, tripping over the stroller, slipping on something viscous—dog bile—"Maggie speed-dialed by accident!"

"That's okay," comes Hil's voice, tinny but merry through the phone. "How are you, Maggie Muggins?"

Maggie holes up under the piano bench in the living room. "I love you, Mummy." Hil is *Mummy* to Mary Rose's *Mumma*—the latter's claim to "ethnicity" on her Lebanese mother's side informing her designation, and Hilary's WASP heritage reflected in hers.

She retreats to the kitchen table—Hilary can always hang up if she has to—now is her chance to frame a worthy reply to her father's enlightened and loving e-mail. She takes a breath. Of course it would be Dad who would appreciate the socio-political importance of the video—he was always the rational one, the one who sat still and read books, the one who saw her intelligence shining like a beacon through the fog of her early school failures. What can she say that will encompass how grateful she is, how much she loves him? *Love.* The word is like a red bird she catches mid-flight, "Dad, look what I got you!" *Look, before I have to let it go!* He isn't just her father, he was her saviour. She has written this in cards to him in the past, but she can't have said it quite right because he never offers much indication that he has received them—he'll greet her with the usual smile and pat on the head but never say, "I got your note." She once asked him, "Did you get my note?" He nodded absently, "Mm-hm," then asked how her work was going. At these times it was as if he were coated in something pristine but impenetrable. Perhaps she had crossed the line in presuming to tell him he was a wonderful father. Are her notes too emotional? *Mushy* was the word when she was a kid. Regardless of how she words them, she always feels there is something fevered in her letters; as though she were writing from the heart of some disaster in which he is implicated—from a hospital bed or a war zone, from death row. The kind of letter haunted by an unwritten qualifier: *in spite of.*

Dear Dad,

I was touched to deceive

Delete.

I wery much appreciated your

Delete.

Thank your for you note. I love you and your message feels very healing

Delete.

"Ow!"

The child has hung up the phone on her foot. "Sowwy"—sly smile, all curls and creamy cheeks.

Mary Rose heads to the hall closet, where she takes Tickle Me Elmo down from the shelf—he sings and does the chicken dance when you press his foot, they have two of them, both gifts from childless friends—sets the fuzzy red imp on the kitchen floor. She wipes up the dog slime, fills a non-BPA plastic "snack trap" with peeled, cut-up organic grapes and thrusts it at her child. She feels like Davy Crockett at the Alamo—that oughta hold 'em for a few minutes. Maggie presses Elmo's foot and he erupts with an invitation to do the chicken dance. Mary Rose returns to her laptop, tight in the chest, annoyed that she seems suddenly to be annoyed for no reason.

Dear Dad,

There is not a single aspect of her life that is not of her own choosing. She has nothing to complain about and much to be grateful for. *For which to be grateful,* corrects her inner grammarian. She came out when homosexuality was still classed as a mental illness by the World Health Organization, otherwise known as the WHO (Me?). She helped change the world to the point where it-got-better enough for her to be here now at her own kitchen table with her own child, legally married to the woman she loves, feeling like a trapped 1950s house-wife. That was a glib thought. Unjust. Unfeminist. Her life is light years away from her own mother's. Maggie is flapping her arms along with Elmo and drowning out the music, "I can flap!" For one thing, unlike her mother, Mary Rose led a whole other life before getting married and having children; a bohemian trajectory that spanned careers as actor, TV writer and, ultimately, author of "Young Adult" fiction. MR MacKinnon is known for her "sensitive evocations" of childhood and "uncanny portrayals" of children. Her first book, *JonKitty McRae: Journey to Otherwhere*, is about an eleven-year-old girl who discovers a twin brother in a parallel universe—in her world, Kitty has no mother, but in his, Jon has no father . . . It was a surprise crossover bestseller, a hit with young and "old" adults alike. The momentum carried through to the second, *JonKitty McRae: Escape from Otherwhere*. Together they are known as the Otherwhere Trilogy—although she has yet to write the third.

"Dance, dance!"

For another thing, unlike her mother, Mary Rose has never borne a child, much less buried one.

Her partner, Hilary, being ten years younger, is closer to the start of her career trajectory and when they talked about having a family, Mary Rose welcomed the chance to be the woman behind the woman, no need for the spotlight anymore; like John Lennon, she was going to sit and watch the wheels go round and round. Except it turns out she has very little time to sit, nor is she a big "sitter" in any case. In that way she is like her mother: she has difficulty sitting and watching. And listening. All of which are what Hil does for a living, being a theatre director.

So Mary Rose gardened really hard. She cooked really hard. She cleaned like a white tornado, baby on her hip till he started toddling and Maggie came along and there were suddenly two in diapers. A writer she admires has described sex as "indescribable." The same goes for a day with two toddlers. That early period is now a blur, but Mary Rose still has the reflexes to show for it: like a war vet throwing himself over the body of a bystander at the sound of a car door slamming, she rushes in with tissues to staunch other people's spills in cafés, and has to repress the urge to cup her hand beneath the chin of a coughing stranger. She used to think she was busy when she was all about her career, but she did not know from busy till she had children. Now her life is like a Richard Scarry book, *Mom's Busy Day in Busy Town*.

She never dreamt she would be married. She never expected to become a mother. She never imagined she would be a "morning person" or drive a station wagon or be capable of following printed instructions for an array of domestic contraptions that come with some-assembly-required; until now, the only thing she had ever been able to assemble was a story.

"Dance chicken!"

They hired a part-time nanny: Candace from northern England, a real-life hard-ass Mary Poppins. Mary Rose started yoga. Wrecked her knee doing the tree. Met other moms, went to playgroups, caught all the colds, felt shame when she failed to pack snacks and had to accept the cheerful charity of the shiny mums, preened with goodwill when she was the one with the extra rice cake or unscented baby wipe. She bought stuff for the house, she renovated the kitchen, researched appliances and didn't waste time bargain hunting—another way in which she differs from her mother. She forged a new domestic infra-structure for their lives, All Clad all the time.

A mere three years before Matthew was born, she was living in boozy boho twilight with erratic Renée, three to five cats and the occa-sional panic attack. Then, in a few blinks of an eye, she was married to blue-eyed striding Hil, living in a bright semi-detached corner house, other-mother to two wonderful children. It was as though she had waved a wand and presto, she had a life.

But it was also as though she were a factory, tooled for a wartime economy. Apparently it was peacetime now, but she could not seem to find the switch to kill the turbines. Before leaving for the gig out in Winnipeg, Hilary asked if she wanted to start working again, to come out of her self-appointed retirement. Like a groundhog poking its head up out of its den, thought Mary Rose, except she'd see her shadow and dive for cover. "I can't believe you're saying this, Hil. It's like you want me to start using drugs again. I need to find out who I am without *work*. I'm tired of being a demon elf, spinning cotton into gold, I am a human being, I want a human life, I want a garden, I want peace, I want to hammer swords into ploughshares, don't make me wiggle my nose, Darren!" Hil didn't laugh. She asked if Mary Rose would consider "seeing someone."

Dear Dad,
I should have know the e-mail was from you right off the bat because of the address—I remember you telling me that's what the Germans called the Highland regiments when they came over the top in their leather kilts to the skirl of the pipes: "the ladies from hell." Was Granddaddy in both wars? He was a medic, wasn't he?

"Flap you dance chicken flap!!" A Thracian ferocity has crept into Maggie's tone. She presses Elmo's foot again—and again—and—
"Let Elmo finish his song, sweetheart."

Was Granddaddy an alcoholic? Is that why you sometimes had a hard time talking about certain

Delete.

Hil thinks that because she is in therapy it must be right for everyone, but Mary Rose is not about to risk having her creativity dismantled by a well-meaning therapist who might mistake the riches of her unconscious for hazardous waste. Even if her creativity is on hold at the moment. The cursor blinks. There is something just out of reach. Something she knows . . . witness her fingers hovering over the keyboard even as her mind draws a blank and she sits staring, as though someone has pressed *pause* . . . Her eyes skid involuntarily from side to side—is it possible to experience a seizure without knowing it? People have mini-strokes all the time and never know till they show up on a CT scan. She should google it. Something familiar is bobbing on the horizon of consciousness, something she knows but cannot name . . . she can almost see it, like a package, a crate on the sea. But when she looks directly at it, it vanishes. Slips her mind as though somewhere in her brain there is a sheer strip that interrupts the flow of neural goods and services. Like a scar.

Dear Dad,

I

Elmo has fallen silent and Maggie is climbing onto her lap. Mary Rose moves to hug her little girl, who so seldom reaches out for this kind of affection from her, and realizes too late that her lap has been scaled as a means to her laptop. Maggie thrusts out her hand and clicks *send* before Mary Rose can stop her—"No!"

She has roared it on reflex and is immediately regretful, having inherited her pipes from her mother, who definitely wore the baritone in the family. Her child sits, immobilized. "It's okay, Maggie."

It's no big deal, the letter was blank but for *Dear Dad, I.* It isn't as if Mary Rose had typed *Dear Dad, go fuck yourself*—itself an intrusive thought of the kind with which she has been plagued all her life; the flotsam and jetsam of her psyche, she knows to be part and parcel of the creativity that has served her so well she has been able to enter semi-retirement in her forties and arrive, against all odds, at this kitchen table with her child. That said, is it too much to ask not to have jam on her trackpad?

"Maggie?" But Maggie is . . . on pause. "Maggie, sweetheart."

The child suddenly looses a siren wail and Mary Rose squints against the blast—for such a rugged little hellion, Maggie can be surprisingly sensitive. Mary Rose gets to her feet and paces the floor with the howling child, back and forth past the big kitchen windows as, deep within her middle-aged ear canal, numberless cilia curl and die, drawing nigh the day when she, like her elderly dehydrating parents, will exasperate her own adult children with repeated, "What?! Did you want a pin or a pen?!" Though it would seem from her robust and sustained protest that Maggie has in turn inherited Mary Rose's pipes, the fact is this mother and child are not biologically related.

She hears a thump overhead, followed by the clickety-clack of canine nails on hardwood and the thundery thud of Daisy barrelling down the carpeted stairs. The dog, having heaved herself from her queen-sized Tempur-Pedic slumber at the sound of domestic disturbance, is now reporting for duty. *What's up? Pizza guy? Want me to kill him?*

"It's okay, Daisy," Mary Rose says in answer to the dog's RCA Victor head tilt. "Do you want to go outside?"

"Me!" cries Maggie, fully recovered, clipping her mother on the temple with the snack trap in the course of wriggling free to tackle Daisy around her thick neck.

Mary Rose unlocks the heavy oak front door and Maggie reaches up to wrestle with the handle of the exterior glass one. Daisy obligingly head-butts it open and torpedoes out and down the veranda steps, making a beeline for the gingko tree, where she drops to her side in the mulch at its base like a shot pig. The sun has come out, the earth is steaming . . . This is going to confuse the magnolia tree, dumb blonde of the horticultural world—already its buds look ready to pop, petals that ought to be pink, they'll be black with frost before the month is out, it's asking for it.

But sun is better than the unrelieved overcast of a winter that ought to have been hard and bright and blue and white. *I'll take it.* She breathes deeply the scent of soil, and surveys the dowdy shades of grey and brown and dirty green in her front garden with its skeletal trellises and spectral dogwoods. Beyond her low wooden fence and across the street, the rotted leaves that crease the curb are flecked with tissues, candy wrappers and bits of recycling that got away; all the ugly promise of spring framed by the pillars of her porch. Behind her, Maggie starts ringing the doorbell. Daisy's head jerks up, then sinks down again.

Mary Rose MacKinnon lives with her family in the Annex neighbourhood of downtown Toronto. Mature trees, cracked sidewalks, frat houses, yuppie renos and more modest, pleasantly dingy houses that cost a fortune. Theirs is somewhere between yuppie and dingy. She loves the house. It is down the street from a park where a nine-year-old girl was abducted in 1985, but Mary Rose no longer thinks about that every time she looks out the front door. She knows her neighbours and likes them—with the possible exception of Rochelle three doors up, who tried to block their renovation. There are young families—VWs and Subarus—plus a few old-school Italian hold-overs: Chevy Caprice. Among the latter is an elderly widow who has a Virgin Mary in the middle of her patch of front lawn that is otherwise distinguished in summer by the closest greenest shave in the neighbourhood—Daria pours Mary Rose a limoncello every Christmas, and dresses up as an elf. Mary Rose's children are as safe as she can make them. She uses non-chemical cleaning agents and washes all fruit, even those with inedible rinds. She volunteers for all the field trips so Matthew won't have to take the school bus. Recently she was on her front porch when two children ran past followed by their mother, who was shrieking, "Sebastian, Kayla, don't run in flip-flops!"

She isn't that bad. Nearby are good schools, a community centre and an arena, not to mention great shops a short walk away on Bloor Street. It is a shabby chic neighbourhood where the cosmos runs wild outside wooden fences in summer, sidewalk chalk and dandelions proliferate, and higgledy-piggledy hedges and trumpet vines proclaim the prevailing left-leaning sympathies of the residents. Most of all, it is the only home her children have ever known—a fact that forces her to admit that growing up on the move must have cost her something, given she has chosen to raise her own children differently.

"Maggie, no more bell ringing, please."

Bingbongbingbongbingbong.

Though she has failed to cultivate a fondness for dandelions, Mary Rose has toiled to achieve a laid-back raggedness in her own garden with old-fashioned flowering bushes and climbers, and she chides herself afresh now for having missed the boat on the roses this year—is it too late to get out there and prune above every five-leafed stem in hopes of a strong showing this summer? Or too early? She squints—what are those fluorescent orange runes spray-painted on the sidewalk in front of her gate? Is the city planning to tear up her garden to lay fresh pipes? Is this to be a season of sewage and seepage and burly butt-cracks trampling the oakleaf hydrangea? Has her house been supplied by lead pipes all this time? Has the poison already made its way into the teeth and bones of her children?

Bingbong—

"Maggie—"

The child eludes her grasp, fleeing the porch, snack trap in hand, to join Daisy in the mulch. Adorable.

For another thing, while like her mother before her Mary Rose does not tolerate dandelions, neither does she yell at them and go at them with a knife while wearing an old flowered housedress. And swearing in Arabic.

"Maggie, don't feed grapes to Daisy." Grapes are not good for dogs. Daisy's system is particularly sensitive—witness the slime on the floor. People think pit bulls are indestructible. They're not. Mary Rose descends the steps and reaches for the snack trap. "Ow, Maggie, don't hit Mumma."

She picks her up—

"No, Mumma!"

—and goes back into the house, leaving Daisy to lounge in the yard.

She returns to her laptop and remains standing while she reads an e-mail from her friend Kate. "Hey Mister, come see *Water* with me and Bridget Wednesday night." Her father coined the nickname because of her initials, and Mary Rose prefers it. She has never been comfortable with her name, it is too flowery and feminine. Exposed. On her book jackets, she is MR MacKinnon. The stark use of initials and the calculated absence of an author photo misled readers to assume at first that she was male, a fact which didn't hurt sales. To this day, many are unaware of what the letters stand for, and she likes it that way—she does not enjoy hearing strangers say her first name, does not like them having it in their mouth. She types a hasty reply—it'll be good to get out of the house and hang with friends who don't own a diaper bag. Especially on a Wednesday night.

Maggie seizes the phone anew and reprises her gleeful getaway down the hall—some things never get old when you're two. Mary Rose wavers: ought she to break down and put on a *Dora the Explorer* video? No one need know Mary Rose has resorted to TV before noon . . . But she'll pay for it: the screen, regardless of content, is brain sugar and a half-hour of peace is purchased with two hours of hell. Instead, she lures Maggie from her hiding place beneath the piano with the offer of her car key. Maggie takes it in exchange for the phone. The harmless switchblade-style key is good for a whole three minutes and it is worth the risk that Maggie might set off the car alarm.

She unplugs her laptop, jams the child safety plug back into the outlet, bangs her head on the table getting up, and dons her genuine chef's apron—the tomatoes are starting to smell good—she opens the fridge and takes out a raw chicken that she air-chilled overnight, sets it on an antimicrobial cutting board, washes her hands, slips her cooking magazine into her recipe stand and is reaching contentedly for her scissors when the phone rings. She sighs and picks up.

"Hi, Mum."

"You're there!"

"Yes, how are—"

"What's wrong?"

"Nothing, I'm—"

"How're the kids?"

"They're great, they're—"

"How's Hilary?"

"She's in Winnipeg—"

"What's she doing there?"

"She's directing *The Importance of*—"

"You're alone with the kids?"

"Well, I'm not really alone—"

"That's a lot of work for you."

"Matthew's at school all morning, it's just Maggie and—"

"You know you're not twenty-five, dear."

"That's right, Mum, I'm not resenting my children for wrecking my career, I don't want to go out dancing every night, I'm healthier than I've ever—"

"You're a wonderful mother, doll, you both are—"

"Except I'm old and decrepit—"

"That's not what I mean, Sadie, Thelma, Minnie, Maureen—"

"Mary Rose."

"I know, dear, wait now, why did you call me?"

"You called me, Mum."

"That's right, now why was that?"

"I don't know, Mum."

Silence.

"Dammit, I'll have to call you back."

Her mother is the original multi-tasker. She probably has a pot on the stove, a Jehovah's Witness at the door and a Bell telephone supervisor on hold at that very moment.

"Okay, Mum, have a good—"

Click. Her mother has hung up.

Mary Rose is used to being called by a slew of names before her mother arrives at hers. Sometimes Dolly runs through all six of her own sisters' names first, including big fat Aunt Sadie, now dead. It is not evidence of dementia, merely a vestige of having grown up somewhat chaotically as one of twelve, herself the child of a child—Mary Rose's Lebanese grandmother was, despite having been born in Canada, a bride at twelve and a mother at thirteen. Mary Rose's grandfather had come from "the old country" and brought with him certain "old country" ways. Ibrahim Mahmoud—Abe—entered Canada just before immigration from "Oriental countries" was banned. Indeed, Dolly herself was classified as non-white back in Cape Breton. When, as a young woman in the 1940s, she was poised to enter nurse's training, she overcame a daunting hurdle—according to Abe nurses were "tramps"—only to face another: the hospital in her home town of Sydney, Cape Breton, in the Canadian province of Nova Scotia, invoked the "colour bar" against her. She went nine miles down the road to New Waterford, where she was deemed white enough to be accepted into training. And met her future husband—it was Duncan's hometown. Racism is why Mary Rose is here.

Dolly's fallback has always been to call everyone—everyone female—"doll." It has occurred to Mary Rose that it is a term of endearment with the potential to double as an *aide-mémoire* should Dolly ever forget her own name. She returns the phone to its base and washes her hands again. While she has long since enumerated the ways in which she is unlike her mother, only lately has she been struck by the yawning gap between herself and her grandmother: the child bride whom she never met but who loomed large as legend. She grew up with the story: *Your grandfather was twenty and your grandmother was twelve when they fell in love and eloped* . . . It is one of several aspects of her family history that Mary Rose has begun to see afresh, as though awakening from an anaesthetic. Perhaps it is a function of having become a mother herself, this reassessment of the tropes and stock accounts of her own childhood: *My grandmother was a child*. . . Mary Rose's mother, by contrast, married at a ripe old twenty-five but still likes to say, "Mumma was good at having babies." The inference being that she herself was not.

•

December in Winnipeg, 1956.
The sky is huge and grey. The regional bus groans, its exhaust thick with carbon—no one is worried yet, air and water and trees are still in the majority, especially in Canada—and it rocks a little, blindsided by wind at the corner of Portage and Main, before labouring toward the edge of town, leaving behind a modest skyline distinguished by grain elevators at one end and the hospital smokestack at the other. It rolls past a Salvation Army Mission, a tavern with a Ladies and Escorts entrance, past an arena, a cemetery. City outskirts have yet to become franchise strips, people still save money and pay cash for homes, income is not yet disposable, but the boom that will fuel the eventual bust is well under way; factories are humming, employment is high. It doesn't take long before the big baby-faced bus is pushing between snow-streaked fields of stubble on its way north.

The view from the window is such that the bus might be standing still, so unchanging is the prairie . . . unless you were born here, in which case it is richly textured and in flux, each field unique beneath the vast overarching sky. But the young woman in the kerchief, seated alone toward the back and staring out the window, is not from here. Like so many nowadays, she is far from home.

She has opened the window a crack—a man who got on back at the arena has lit a cigarette. She has a Hudson's Bay department store bag on her lap with her purse. She's big as a house. Second pregnancies can be like that. Her husband is at work in his office on the base. Her three-year-old is with a lady from the Officers' Wives Club, but she'll be home in time to cook supper—she has taken a chicken from the freezer, it is thawing in the sink.

The doctor said, "Go home and wait. Come back when the contractions start."

"When'll that be?"

"About two weeks. If they don't start, come in anyway."

She is a nurse, she knows this.

Before catching this bus back to the air force base at Gimli, she stopped off at the Hudson's Bay department store—she doesn't get downtown that often, and it's right by the doctor's office. There was a Christmas scene in the window: Santa on a train drinking a Coke. Inside, she bought gloves. They weren't even on sale. The lady at the counter smiled and said, "Oh, when're you due?"

"The baby's dead," she said.

And the saleslady started crying.

"Don't cry," said the pregnant young woman. "I'm not crying, don't you cry."

She consoled the saleslady, and bought the gloves to make her feel better.

•

Mary Rose is reaching for her scissors when the phone rings again. She looks longingly at the raw chicken on the counter; at the scissors in their knife block niche; at the illustrated step-by-step surgical guide to dismemberment in her *Cooks Illustrated* magazine, and picks up. "Hi, Mum."

"I mailed you a package!" cries Dolly, triumphant.

She pronounces it *packeege*. Mary Rose has noticed her parents' accent coming to the fore recently, although it has been more than fifty years since they left Cape Breton Island.

"What's in it?"

"It's a surprise."

A volley of barking reaches Mary Rose from out front.

"What am I hearing?"

"It's just the dog, Mum."

"You better go."

"It's okay, the gate is closed."

Another volley. She glances down the hallway and catches sight of a movement through the glass door. "Mum, can you hang on a second?"

"Hang on nuthin', this is long distance! Call me back. Call collect!"

She hurries toward the door with the phone to her ear in time to see the mailman vaulting backward over the low fence. "Daisy!"

"Hi, Daisy!" hollers her mother all the way from Victoria, British Columbia, into her ear. "It's Sitdy!" If it were Maggie, Mary Rose would tell her to use her indoor voice, but Dolly doesn't have one.

"I have to go, Mum." She hangs up. "Daisy"—outdoor voice—"get in here!"

Daisy comes, grinning, body slung low in shame. Mary Rose waves to the Canada Post guy, but he speeds off in his van.

Uncharacteristically, and perhaps against regulations, he has dropped his delivery on the flagstone walk: a sizable package. The packeege! It has teeth marks in it—Daisy didn't actually bite the mailman, did she? Closer inspection reveals it is not from her mother. *L.L. Bean*, reads the label. Sticking the phone in her back pocket, she picks up the box, rapturous—*O sweet mystery of life at last I've found you!*—and carries it to the porch where she intercepts Maggie who is making for the four-foot drop over the side. Mary Rose grabs her by the arm and Maggie screams. One hand on her child, the other balancing the box, she struggles with the screen door and sees from the corner of her eye that the lid of the rain barrel, which stands flush against the porch, is loose and missing its bolt—she flashes on an image of Maggie floating face down in the dark water. She tightens her grip and is rewarded with a kick—she will get out there this afternoon, while Maggie naps and Matthew builds a Brio train bridge, and fix the thing. And once she has given up trying to fix it with the one tool she is capable of wielding, namely duct tape, she will call someone in to fix it . . . what's the name on the side of that van she keeps seeing in the neighbourhood? Rent-a-Husband? She will do all this right after she has called the chimney guy and got him to come at the same time as the furnace guy, filled out a "simple" form for Canada Revenue Agency, booked her mammogram and phoned her mother back. How does anyone manage to keep a child alive in this world of distractions?

In the kitchen, she lets Maggie help open the parcel for as long as she can stand it, then takes the scissors from their niche in the knife block. She loves these scissors; she bought them from a shopping channel in her room at the Fort Garry Hotel out west in Calgary on her last book tour, *the only scissors you'll ever need!* She kneels, slits open the box . . . and beholds within the ingenious foolproof Christmas tree stand she ordered. She lifts it from its foam core nest, taking a moment to admire the smooth green dome, its ergonomic clamps poised to bite into a freshly trimmed trunk. Unlike the disaster-prone stands of her childhood, it has a stable base, a patented easy-tilt mechanism and built-in water reservoir. She shakes off the pang of disloyalty that accompanies her pride in having surpassed her own father and an entire generation of family men who sweated and swore under their breath through so many festive seasons, and heads back down the hall with it. She slips through the baby gate, locks it behind her—more protests—and carries the stand lovingly all the way up to the attic, where she places it in an easily accessible spot, knowing that even though they'll use it but once a year, she'll thank herself every time she doesn't have to fight her way through a ton of junk to haul it out, cursing, hot, hurt and exhausted. Mary Rose MacKinnon has a Christmas tree stand that works and is effortlessly accessible. She has that house. She has that attic. She has that life.

She listens as the protests subside two floors below, confident there is nothing down there that can harm Maggie in the minutes she will be absent, having thoroughly childproofed their home.

·

The contractions are faint, it is taking too long, that can be dangerous, so they induce. They put the pit drip in her arm and rig a surgical curtain so she won't see and she goes into labour.

They make the delivery easier on her by compressing the infant's skull—she is not a big woman, there is no need for her to tear. She is a nurse, she knows what they do. They had wanted to do it to her first baby, born breech way down east in Cape Breton; remove it limb by limb in order to save the mother, "That's what we would do in my country," said the West Indian nurse. But the young mother said, "Save the baby." She requested a

priest, who came and administered to her the Sacrament
of Extreme Unction. But mother and daughter both
survived. "Traumatic Parturition." She saw it scribbled
on her chart.

This baby, however, has been dead for weeks. She
knew something was wrong from the start. When she first
found out she was pregnant again so soon, she felt guilty
for not being happier. She confessed to the priest, who
told her it was normal to miss her own mother at a time
like this but that God never sends us more than we can bear.
He absolved her, but she was unable to shake the bad
thoughts: *If only God had waited till I was less tired. If only
Mumma weren't so far away. If only I weren't pregnant . . .*

When she told the doctor she thought something was
wrong, he said, "Don't be silly," but since she had come all
the way into Winnipeg, he might as well examine her. He
laid the cold metal disc on her belly and listened. He moved
the disc. He moved it again. He listened, but could not
find a heartbeat. He threw down his stethoscope and walked
out without a word. She got off the table, collected her
mouton coat and told the receptionist, "I think he's really
disgusted with me."

Now she wonders, did she have bad thoughts because
the baby was dead? Or was it the other way around?

Behind the curtain, no one speaks above a whisper.
They have given her a sedative, but she is awake and
able to push. It is big, the way blue babies often are. It
does not take long. She feels a tugging. Then it is gone,
and she is empty.

A rustling sound . . . sound of fabric, the nurse is
wrapping it up. Soft-soled footsteps retreat. They take
it away.

•

Upon descending the stairs, Mary Rose meets with a remarkable sight: in the living room, Maggie, her back to the doorway, is sitting still, engaged in some kind of fine-motor activity obscured from view. She must be in the midst of a developmental surge. Nearby, Daisy is innocently nibbling her paw and avoiding Mary Rose's gaze—she is a dear old thing, if a little impulsive and, like the best dogs, endlessly shame-absorbent. Pit bulls are banned in Ontario, but Daisy is "grand-fathered": having been born before the law came in, she is permitted to live but may be summarily executed if deemed a danger. As it is, she must be muzzled in public, a law Mary Rose feels befits more the authors of the legislation than the dogs themselves.

Daisy was her name when they got her from the Toronto Humane Society—they were going to change it to Lola, but one look at her eight tired teats told them she'd been through enough. She is a tawny, brawny American Staffordshire terrier of indeterminate elderliness who snores louder than Mary Rose's late Aunt Sadie and lives in terror of having her nails clipped. Her skull is the shape of a World War II German army helmet. Her anal glands need to be expressed every few months by the vet, an effect of her having borne so many puppies. She dozes on her belly in the midst of screeching birthday parties, legs splayed like a pressed quail. She looks like Mickey Rooney when she smiles. If the vet doesn't express her anal glands, she drags her butt across the carpet till they express themselves.

She watches now as Daisy rolls onto her side and stretches out behind Maggie, providing her with a backrest. Lovely—as long as Maggie doesn't fall asleep, for there will go the morning nap. Hilary is all for letting go of said nap, arguing that Maggie will sleep better at night. Mary Rose thought, but did not say, "You mean *you'll* sleep better. What about me with a cranky toddler all day?"

Like every other room in the house, the living room is a hazard-free zone—unless one counts Maggie as a hazard. Just last week, Mary Rose fitted the coffee table with a shock-absorbent expandable table-edge bumper (which Hil is sure to remove when she returns) while on the table are harmless objects—books mostly, plus a neat stack of the *New York Review of Books* that Mary Rose is saving for when she has time or bronchitis, which amounts to the same thing. She will savour them through a haze of antibiotics once Hil is home and she can afford to get sick. On the carpet is a vectoring network of Brio train tracks where Thomas and his variously smiling and scowling friends are coupled up waiting for Matthew's return—he will know if one is out of place. But Maggie shows no sign of robbing the trains or blowing up the tracks—all quiet on the Western Front. Mary Rose takes the chance and steals back to the kitchen.

She is collapsing the Christmas tree stand box for the recycling when she spots her car key amid the packing materials—*Maggie!* She salvages the key and jams it into the pocket of her jeans. Talk about a close call . . . She folds the box and goes to open the deep drawer that houses her recycling bin, only to be momentarily stymied by the child safety lock, which she fumbles free, but not before pinching her finger on its quick-release. Washing her hands once more, she returns to the chicken, pallid and limp on the counter next to the recipe stand. *Could we take the frustration out of deboning?*

Mary Rose has mastered her squeamishness with most aspects of cooking, but one remains: when handling a raw chicken, she never holds it by the wing. There is something about the sight of the skin straining between wing and body . . . It looks like it hurts. She recalls, as a child, watching her mother prepare a chicken for the oven, slinging it by the wing from sink to counter with a thud. More of a splud, really. It didn't matter that the chicken was dead and couldn't feel it. *She* could feel it.

Still, as phobias go, it is a distant third behind the dire duo: vertigo and claustrophobia—which are really two faces of the same thing. Mary

Rose is on intimate terms with both, having been ambushed by the latter in her twenties while climbing the narrow tower of Münster Cathedral behind her sister, Maureen; and by the former upon walking out onto its gargoyle-encrusted spire three hundred feet above the Black Forest. Mo read her mind and held her gaze. "It's all right, Rosie. Walk to me." Until then she had had no fear of heights. Indeed, one of her earliest memories is of hanging placidly by the wrists from a third floor balcony. In the same country, come to think of it. And with the same person.

•

"We lost the baby," the mother tells her three-year-old.

"Where?" asks the child.

The father explains, "The baby died."

"Because you lost it?"

"No, it just happens sometimes." He didn't see it either. It was taken away.

"Where is it?"

"It's with God," she says.

"Where?"

The mother doesn't answer.

"She's in Heaven," says the father.

"Can I pray to her?"

"Sure," says the father.

"Can she give me candy?"

"Don't be silly, Maureen," says the mother.

The mother knows that the baby is not in Heaven, it is in Limbo, "the other place," reserved for those who have not received the Sacrament of Baptism and whose souls therefore retain the taint of Original Sin, rendering them unworthy of the Beatific Vision. They do not suffer, but nor do they see God.

"But where is she? Where is *she*?"

Nowhere.

"Is she in a grave?"

No grave.

"Is she going to live in Winnipeg?"

"Hush now, Maureen," says the father.

"What's her name?"

Technically, the baby had no name, not having been baptized.

The mother answers, "We were going to . . ." But she is unable to say it.

The father says, "We were going to call her Mary Rose."

·

Eyes on her recipe, she is reaching for her scissors when she hears someone's car alarm go off somewhere outside. Hand arrested mid-air, she glances up, wishing once again that she lived in a simpler time before everything beeped—say the fifties, minus polio, homophobia and wringer washers. She hooks a thumb in her jeans pocket, waiting for the sound to cease once the hapless motorist finds the right button—everyone knows car alarms are never set off by actual thieves—and it does, abruptly. She returns to *Cooks Illustrated* with its drawing of a chicken breast effortlessly yielding up its bone—only to hear the alarm start up again—is she not to be vouchsafed a single cotton-pickin' unmolested moment to unwind with a recipe? She glares out her big kitchen windows, but none of the cars parked on the street is flashing. She leans forward against the counter for a better look, but the wretched sound stops again. Returning her gaze to the magazine, she reaches for the knife block only to paw empty air. She looks up. The niche is empty. She looks around. Her scissors are gone. How is it possible? The best scissors she has ever owned. The Shopping Channel scissors. The Sloan Kettering surgical-grade never-dull kitchen scissors, capable of felling a sapling, subtly curved for ease of deboning; scissors so good she could be buried with them one day, their blades still lethal with shine. Where do things go? Who takes things? Did Hilary put them in the utility drawer? Mary Rose has, on more than one occasion and as reasonably as possible, implored Hilary to place the scissors in the special niche in the knife block—she is aware that this might not seem like a priority to someone who goes to a rehearsal room every day in fresh clothes, often in a different city, and has yet to be home for a bout of preschool head lice, but it matters to Mary Rose. She is the one who cooks and shops and takes seriously the steep domestic learning curve that is homemaking. Indeed, in military parlance, Mary Rose is at the domestic sharp end. How can Hilary call herself a feminist, much less a lesbian, if she can't even respect Mary Rose enough to put the scissors back in the right spot? But then, of course, Hilary doesn't actually call herself a lesbian, she refuses to "call" herself anything, which is so typical of bisexuals!

The rage zooms up from Mary Rose's gut and she's off. She grabs the phone from its base—impossible to "tear" a phone from its base anymore, where is a mad housewife to turn for an inanimate answer to her rage?—and is scrolling down the list of calls, on the point of speed-dialing Hilary's BlackBerry—she'll be in a meeting, but why should that take priority over Mary Rose's ability to cut up a chicken for the freezer against her homecoming next week?—when it rings in her hand. She crashes it back onto its base just as the car alarm starts up again. She would storm out in her apron in search of the bleeping car but that she mustn't leave her child unattended—like luggage containing a bomb. She pauses. Amid the beeps and br-r-rings, the only sound is that of Daisy snoring in the living room. Maggie must be asleep—would it do any harm if she nipped out? It isn't as though she is deserting her family—she remembers her own mother threatening on a regular basis, "One day I'll go out the door and never come back!" By the time she was fourteen, Mary Rose had taken to muttering, "Go ahead"—but well out of earshot.

Meep! Meep! Meep! goes the car, like the Road Runner on steroids.

She tiptoes down the hall and peeks into the living room. Daisy is flaked out on her side, eyelids twitching, her belly with its ramshackle teats heaving. Maggie is still sitting with her back to the doorway playing peacefully on her own. It takes Mary Rose a moment to process what she sees: Maggie surrounded by shreds, strips, all manner of shapes of newspaper—not torn, cleanly cut. She distinguishes another sound beneath the cadence of Daisy's snores and the jabbing of the car alarm: *rhusk-rhusk . . .*

"Maggie?" She speaks quietly.

Maggie turns, deep contentment in her eyes.

"Give Mumma the scissors, sweetheart."

Intelligence and forbearance are in Maggie's smile. She says, kindly, "No, Mumma," and resumes cutting out a column on postimperial India.

Mary Rose returns to the kitchen, takes the phone and dials her mother . . . "Hi, Mum?"

"Was it the packeege?!"

"No." She walks calmly back to the living room—no sudden moves—"I'm going to put you on speaker, Mum, Maggie wants to talk to you—"

"Hi, Maggie, it's Sitdy!"

"Sitdy!" cries Maggie, and drops the scissors.

Mary Rose gives her child the phone and picks up the scissors.

"How are ya, *fuhss*?!" shouts Dolly.

Maggie shakes the phone with both hands as though to throttle it with elation.

Mary Rose is shaking. What fresh hell was set to open, and how had she stumbled to its lip? How did Maggie manage to get the scissors from where they were safely wedged like a sword in stone, out of reach in the knife block? She has yet to register the balm of silence in the wake of the car alarm that has randomly ceased when the doorbell rings and Daisy goes crazy. Mary Rose hesitates—she is not expecting anyone. What if it is the mailman returning with Animal Control? Did Daisy actually bite him? *We have an order to seize and destroy your dog.* Feeling suddenly sick to her stomach, she peers through the eyehole. It is Rochelle from three doors up. Mary Rose opens the door.

There is nothing definably wrong with Rochelle. But she is the kid in grade six with whom you dread to be partnered on square-dancing day.

"Do you know your car alarm's been going off all morning?" Voice like a sack of cement.

Mary Rose is about to reply but experiences a linguistic derailment—this used to happen to her in elementary school, then years later at the odd book signing when she'd get overloaded. Since Maggie came along, she frequently loses nouns, occasionally verbs and whole sentences, leaving her scrabbling for purchase in a scree of prepositions.

Rochelle, perhaps misinterpreting Mary Rose's fleeting aphasia, glances at the scissors in her hand and adds with uncharacteristic geniality, "Just thought you might like to know." Her mouth stretches in a rictus of goodwill and she backs away from the door. Horse teeth.

"Thanks," says Mary Rose and, absently raising the scissors in a wan salute, realizes that, though she has always thought of Rochelle as "an old bat," the woman is probably younger than she is. She closes the door, feels in her pocket for her car key—*Meep! Meep!*—and finds the button. Silence. She sets the key on the front hall table out of range of her apparently hair-trigger hip-bone, and slips into the powder room.

She releases the new child safety lock on the toilet lid—she does not have to wonder what Hil would say, but she thinks it makes sense: Maggie could actually fall into the toilet and drown. It has happened. Somewhere. Mary Rose sits and has one of those pees of improbable duration. Through the half-open door she hears Maggie screaming with laughter and her mother's voice singing nonsense songs. She rubs her arm, the left one, it's bugging her again. She does not recall having bumped it, but it doesn't take much. Boxers are sometimes referred to as having a "glass jaw." Mary Rose has a glass arm. Graze of a car door, corner of a bookshelf, a playful squeeze—these can kick off a deep, radiating pain with never a bruise to show for it. She may have bumped it unawares in her furious search for the scissors, or perhaps Maggie kicked her there.

"One two, buckle my shoe! Three four, shut the door . . . !"

She bares her teeth in the mirror. Still good. Not unnaturally white in the bleach-crazed way that makes anyone over thirty-five look like a corpse by comparison with their teeth. But not yellowed like the soles of someone's feet in that poem. Mary Rose has naturally beautiful dentition but weak enamel. She sometimes wonders if her tendency to cavities is related to the old problem she had with her arm as a child—"Benign Pediatric Bone Cysts" put her in hospital more than once. It was unclear whether she had inherited them from her father or mother but, being an adoptive parent, Mary Rose is in no danger of passing them on to her own children. She opens her mouth and peers at the expensive new crowns toward the back.

There was a period after her second book came out when she ground her teeth in her sleep to the point where the enamel cracked and the nerves got upset, so the dentist killed them. Dark thrashing snakes of pain, he speared them, then immured them in orthodontic burial vaults that will outlast her skeleton and drop, one day, *clink*, to the floor of her casket. Or be raked from her ashes if she opts for cremation. She has a high pain threshold thanks to her adventures with her humerus—the long bone of the upper arm—long since surgically corrected. Even so, tooth pain occupies an exquisite category all its own. Mahler versus Beethoven. Mary Rose is something of a pain connoisseur—maybe even a pain snob. But it is a fact that a certain amount of it has a calming effect on her. She is at home with it.

She stopped tooth grinding thanks to a session of hypnosis in a nondescript office building in an otherwise swanky part of town called Yorkville. It was being renovated at the time and pneumatic drills were going in the hallway while she was "under." She remains uncertain whether she was ever really under, but at the time asked friends to tell her if she displayed tics such as clucking like a chicken at the snap of someone's fingers, just in case. Somehow it did the trick and she was able to throw away her chewed-up night guard. Now there is just her knee and the uterine fibroids—the recent arm pain doesn't count, being not only fickle but phantom.

She runs her fingers through her short dark hair—sprinkled with grey, but less so than many people a decade younger. She is an "older mother," one of a growing demographic who, in a previous era, would have been grandmothers by now. But she feels she brings certain advantages to the table: financial stability, patience—even if the latter is tried these days by Maggie in ways it never was by Matthew.

"One-a-penny, two-a-penny, hot cross buns!"

From her mother Mary Rose inherited, along with "the pipes," youthful skin, thanks to a Mediterranean heritage and an olive oily diet. Skin, hair, teeth: the great indicators. It is often a ball of these tissues that turns up lodged in the body of a perfectly healthy adult who is unaware, until the surgical removal of the benign lump, that they would have been a twin . . . and that by incubating the stunted tissues of their sibling, they have been in fact a living grave.

She has always taken an interest in the fringes of science—the kind of fascination that leads to great discoveries, crackpot conspiracy theories, and novels. In *JonKitty McCrae: Journey to Otherwhere*, eleven-year-old Kitty has one blue eye and one brown. She also has begun to have "spells." They transport her to another world, where she discovers the truth behind her eyes . . .

"Psychosenzoic Epilepsy Spectrum Seizure." Such is the diagnosis according to a neuropsychologist who e-mailed her after the book came out to tell her that Kitty shows signs of "seizure due to kindling"; that the child's ability to trigger a "trance state" is in fact "a manifestation of trauma." *Gimme a break,* she thought. *So is the ability to fly with the aid of an umbrella, or step through a looking glass.*

It has made her a living, this morbid fascination, but she is at a loss to explain it fully, and in answer to the most oft-asked question at literary readings, "Where do you get your ideas?" has taken to answering, "The dead people." It always produces a laugh, but it feels true even if she has never yet, at forty-eight, really lost anyone—certainly not a close family member.

She met neither of her grandmothers, both of whom died shy of sixty. She met her paternal grandfather once, at the veterans' hospital in Halifax. He'd had a stroke and could not speak, but he laughed. Her maternal grandfather lived longest, and she recalls being perplexed by his Arabic accent but not unduly perturbed since he seldom spoke to her, she being the extra daughter of an extra daughter. He did once address a full sentence to her sister, Maureen: "Close your legs."

What's more, she grew up on air force bases or in suburbs, both full of young families who reflected the sunny immortality of their early prime-time television counterparts. There were no really wrinkly people around, unless you count Granny on *The Beverly Hillbillies.* Her parents are the first old people she has ever known. And they still don't think of themselves as "old."

She never wanted to be a biological mother. Not only had she zero desire to experience the miracle of childbirth, she figured she'd have a better chance of not screwing up her children if her id couldn't claim them as flesh and blood. Hil had tried to get pregnant via sperm donated and banked by a friend—they opted not to go anonymous, intending that their child should know as much about its own story as possible. In the meantime, they registered with adoption agencies—most of the world was closed to them, but there were several Canadian provinces and a few American states where they were welcome. Still, the fact remained that, as a two-mom team, they would be at the bottom of the barrel in the eyes of most birth mothers. So, having set in motion the slow wheels of adoption, Hil diligently tracked her temperature and every time it spiked, Mary Rose accompanied her on the pre-dawn trek to the fertility clinic where, with a devotion befitting a station of the cross, they sat in the silent waiting room with the other grey-faced women over thirty-five who'd come for their intrauterine shot of washed sperm. They were put out of their monthly pee-stick misery when they got the call: a pregnant woman in Oregon had chosen them from a stack of Dear Birth Mother letters.

Anna worked as a rigger for the Cirque du Soleil and travelled the world. She hailed from West Virginia but had "knocked about some." They liked her right away. The three of them spent several weeks together before the birth, exploring the Northwest Coast. All Anna could or would say about Matthew's father was that he was Russian. Mary Rose had been aquiver with speculation: Was he an acrobat? A lost Romanov? A member of the Russian mafia? But as soon as she saw Matthew, the only thing that mattered was that he was healthy. They were present for his birth. Anna signed the papers. She pressed cabbage leaves to her breasts to staunch the leaking milk. And went away. She never held him.

They wrote to her, sent her pictures, a plane ticket. Then they lost track of her—that is, she dropped out of sight. They had been warned this was likely. Less than two years later, the sperm bank called: they were going out of business, did Hil and Mary Rose want "the material"? It was the last roll of the dice for a sibling. They got lucky. Hil got pregnant and they got Maggie.

Their donor, Ian, is that modern invention, "Uncle Dad." He remembers both kids' birthdays and drops by at Christmas. Hil went to school with him. He is a math teacher in Kitchener–Waterloo who plays guitar. It doesn't get better than that. They had toyed with asking Mary Rose's brother, but for one thing it would have killed her parents. And she had killed them once already.

Another reason Mary Rose is uncomfortable with her name is that it isn't really hers. There was supposed to have been another sister between Maureen and her: a girl, born in Winnipeg. "Other Mary Rose." Beatific. Blank. She was stillborn and, according to the Catholic Church, her soul went directly from Winnipeg to Limbo—a vast space, itself not unlike a prairie. Mary Rose has always pictured her the size and serenity of a Gerber baby, with closed eyes. Go directly to Limbo, do not pass Go, do not collect the Sacrament of Baptism.

•

"You're young," the doctor says. "You'll have another baby."

"Maybe even a boy," she thinks. *Inshallah*.

When her husband is posted again, they leave the prairie behind, along with the hospital and its smokestack visible for miles. They move east this time, east even of Cape Breton. All the way to Germany.

And she does have another baby. In the fall. Another girl. They call it Mary Rose—after the first one.

Nothing is wrong. The baby is fine but Dolly is very tired. They keep her in the hospital on the base. Move her to a quieter floor.

"Baby blues," they say. But Dolly knows, any woman lucky enough to have a healthy baby has no right to be blue. Mary Rose—the second Mary Rose—goes home without her. They say it is better that way.

"You'll be good as new in no time," says her husband, and she smiles so he will believe he has reassured her.

No time is where she is. This hospital could be anywhere. She could be anyone. Or no one. She lies still, while time goes on around her.

·

The MacKinnons were on their second posting when Mary Rose was born in what was then West Germany. They lived on a NATO air base called 4-Wing, at the edge of the Black Forest, land of big bad wolves and cobblestones; of fairy-tale scenes painted on village walls, and the smell of woodsmoke and cows. Each morning the "honey wagons" clip-clopped past; in the village, women in kerchiefs pulled braided bread fresh from the ovens and were free with *schokolade für die Kinder*. Roses grew wild and the Rhine flowed fat and peaceful. In Munich there were gaps between buildings—interior walls exposed, tattooed with absence: the outline of a picture frame, a bed-head, a crucifix. Sunlight shattered the dome of the Frauenkirche, in Cologne a street sign, Jüdengasse . . . "Don't dwell on it," said Duncan. "Think nice thoughts," said Dolly.

They drove the length and breadth of free Europe with their children, their tent, and their big Canadian sense of adventure. They were seeing the world, thanks to a world war. And they were helping to heal that world just by enjoying it, visiting castles and fountains, the Vatican and the Riviera, canals from Venice to Amsterdam. They picnicked in the Alps—Dolly panicked at the hairpin turns and Duncan laughed until the sun glinted off his gold tooth. At a lookout on a winding mountain road, they emerged from the VW Beetle to stretch their legs and survey the invisible border with "the East," while he explained to the children: The picturesque farmhouses on the other side of the valley with their thatched roofs looked the same as the ones on this side. But it was a grim mirror, a ghastly parallel world: it was *Communist*. A *hiss* in the very word.

Mary Rose knows she cannot possibly remember all this; still the scenes are vivid in her mind, part of the family lore she imbibed from her sister and from her parents' reminiscences over the years. Like Maureen's childhood version of Mary Rose's arrival home from the hospital: "I was so worried you were going to be born dead like Other Mary Rose, and Mummy didn't come home for ages because she was so tired from having you. Daddy told me you were beautiful and I pictured a princess with long blond hair. You had curly black hair like Groucho Marx and your face was red as a tomato when you cried."

"No wonder you hung me over the balcony."

"Mary Rose! I have no memory of that!"

Which has always been tantamount, according to Mary Rose, to an admission of guilt. She has yet to tire of the reliable rise it gets out of her otherwise unflappable sister.

·

By day the sky is ripped with jets and split with sirens rehearsing for a hot war that never comes. But at sunset, the air is full of birdsong. He wraps the baby in a blanket and takes her onto the balcony of the apartment. The sun is a hot, huge stain, red-streaked yellow, powerful, peaceful and slow. They are on a level with the treetops. Close to the building, a row of lindens is changing colour, but beyond the uniform lawns stands the Black Forest, dense with evergreens.

"You hear that?" he whispers. "That's the cuckoo bird."

·

Mary Rose remembers her first home in the white stucco apartment building that sparkled in the sunlight. She can see now the living room with its gleaming coffee table, and the glass door that opened onto the balcony and the beckoning blue yonder—like going from a black-and-white photo into "living colour." The balcony was a magical place, both daring and safe. They lived on the third floor but it seems in memory a majestic height. In warm weather she played out there with Maureen, who would set up two buckets of water so Mary Rose could swim from the Atlantic to the Specific—or perhaps she only thinks she remembers because Maureen regularly told her about it—more "lore." Just as she thinks she remembers being held by her father at sunset, encircled by his warmth, looking onto the vastness of the trees and sky. The balcony was where her father first gave her the world.

They were not allowed to play out there by themselves, especially if there were buckets that could be overturned and used to scale the railing. It is normal for a mother to be vigilant, and Maureen recalls being punished for leaving the buckets out there, but it does not surprise Mary Rose that their mother was especially anxious, having already lost one baby. Or was it two at that point? When exactly was Alexander born? By the time Mary Rose was big enough to swim the world's oceans on a balcony she would have been around two. In any event, there was definitely one occasion on which she and her sister Maureen found themselves on the balcony together all alone.

"The time you hung me over."

"Mary Rose, you must have dreamt that!"

•

He hires a German woman to look after the baby during the day while he is at work and his older girl is at school, but every night, he rises at the first cry. He fumbles with bottles and pricks himself on diaper pins. He walks the floor, the little wailing face damp at his neck. Though his Basic Military Training has given him stamina, nothing

in his upbringing has prepared him for the heart-gaping
loneliness of a baby in the night—or the depth of comfort
in his power to console her. He rocks her against his
chest, her toothless gums suckle his bare shoulder.

"There, there, it's all right, now. Daddy's got you."

•

The grounds around the apartment buildings where the military
"dependants" lived were immaculately tended, lindens had been
planted and mulched, sidewalks led to the operational side of the base
where her father worked and the jets took off. But a stone's throw from
their building, just beyond the new wading pool and the old bunker,
was the Black Forest. It was not a wilderness in the North American
sense, laced as it was with pathways that locals and military families
alike set out on for weekend *Wanderungen*, but it was dense. The trees,
mainly conifers, grew close together, blocking the sun, hence its name;
shade rendered the floor springy with moss, mysterious with mush-
rooms, and lively with streams that trilled down from the Alps, the
whole effect both enchanting and forbidding. If you strayed from the
paths and ventured deep enough, you might be charged by a wild boar
or lured by a talking wolf. Maureen told her that at Christmastime
elves decorated the trees at the heart of the forest but no one except
Santa Claus had ever seen them.

•

His wife is released from hospital a month or so later and
Duncan lets the German woman go. Dolly has put her foot
down: there is no longer any need for help during the day.
"I'm the mother." Nor, she makes clear, is there any need
for him to walk the floor in the night.

•

Dolly's unabashed love of getting to know people and places, her fearless brand of absurd *Kanadische Deutsch*, endeared her to the local Frauen, who looked as though they hadn't smiled since before the war. She dressed little Maureen immaculately, pulling tight her braids, meeting with approval wherever she went—"Aber schön!" Maureen flanked her as she pushed the pram with the baby in it—the second Mary Rose.

There were parties at the Officers' Mess, glittering affairs with dance bands and smorgasbords—a far cry from perogies and the occasional standing roast in Gimli. Mary Rose cherishes the recollection of her mother in an evening gown, posed next to her father in his formal mess kit—what he called his "monkey suit." Or perhaps she cherishes the stories.

Dolly got herself elected head of the Wives Club: a well-oiled machine whose pecking order mirrored the husbands' ranks, it was not without its political hazards. She unseated the CO's wife, Eileen Davies—who put a brave face on things with the offer to spearhead a commemorative recipe book—and found herself at the nerve centre of a domestic, festive whirl, from parties and welcome wagons to school concerts, bazaars and making sure every mother who needed a hand got one. Dark little Dolly from Sydney, Cape Breton, discovered she could run things. Her husband wasn't surprised. "Why d'you think I married you? It wasn't just for your looks, Doll Face." She laughed at him, because he really did think she was pretty. When she was fine, she was very very fine.

•

But she is still tired. The more so, now that she is up in the night with the baby. When it naps in the day, so does she, on the couch in the living room facing the coffee table. Beyond it is the glass door to the balcony. Above the railing is sky; below it, bars. Are they close enough together to be safe for a baby? She gets up to check.

Outside, the trees that shaded the grounds in summer are bare and look to be cowering. But the evergreens that hem the base appear to have drawn closer. She smells snow. She returns to the couch and lies back down. She hears the baby crying. She has never lived in an apartment before, high above the ground with a million-dollar view. She never dreamed she would be living in Europe, married to the nicest man in the world. She always knew she would have babies, but thought she would be more like her own mother when the time came. She is not crying, her eyes are leaking. Her breasts are leaking too, but that will stop on its own—her milk is no good. Nowadays formula is better anyway.

She hears a baby crying. What day is it? It must be a weekday, her older girl is at school, her husband at work. She gets up and goes in. The baby cries whether she picks it up or not. Whether she feeds it, changes it, rocks it, bounces, shakes—the baby looks at her as though it knows something about her.

"Mary Rose," she says. And her voice sounds flat in her ears. As though she is telling a lie.

The cuckoo clock strikes the quarter hour.

•

During the day, Duncan "flew a desk" just as he had back in Canada, but no longer mourned his lost chance at aircrew—with his blue eyes and boxer's reflexes he had been a shoo-in. He was disqualified when the Wing Commander saw that, in the box next to Marital Status, he had ticked "married." In those days, the jets were "widow makers" and the military, fresh from the Second World War, had enough of those on their hands. But the view from behind a desk was more interesting over here in Europe, to say the least. He was at the "sharp end," and not just of a pencil but of the Cold War. The Soviet Union was a thirty-second muster away. "Logistics" took on a whole new meaning in this context, and every day at sunset when he held his little one on the balcony, he understood the meaning of Peace. And that he had a role in it.

•

Is she letting it cry too long? Babies need to cry in order to strengthen their lungs.

The daylight on the balcony stays the same for a long time. She would like to go out there in the sun . . . But she feels too heavy.

She is lying on the couch facing the coffee table.

A baby is crying.

The sun has moved.

It is quiet now.

Someone is knocking at the door.

What day is it?

Someone is knocking at the door. Is it today or yesterday?

A woman's voice: "Hi there, Dolly, it's Eileen, I'm here with Mona . . ."

She closes her eyes.

Mona's voice: "Dolly, if you're home, dear, open up, we've come with a stew."

She turns to face the back of the couch.

Eileen: "Think of Duncan, dear."

At the door, she tells them she was lying down with

the baby. They look in on it. "She's beautiful, Dolly, she looks like you," says Mona.

"Reheat it in the oven at three hundred and fifty degrees," says Eileen. "And put on some lipstick."

•

Duncan knew his wife was rundown for a while after the baby was born, but she bounced back. Some men came home to women who looked as though they'd spent the day with their head in a dirty oven, but those women weren't air force wives. Even so, most women couldn't hold a candle to Dolly.

"You look right jazzy, Missus, what's for supper?"

"I made a stew."

"My favourite."

•

Babies die, it happens. Crib death. If you think a thing, it might happen . . . Think nice thoughts. But dread invades the living room, finds her on the couch, presses on her, gets inside her where it swiftly grows bigger than she is until she is inside it, looking out from a rind of shadow. Anything could happen to her baby. It could drown in the tub, it could fall from the balcony. It could be taken from the stroller while her back is turned. The hired German woman could come back and steal her. As long as her baby is here, she can be taken away. It is almost as if, as long as the baby is alive, the baby is not safe.

Is this sleep? It is not wakefulness. There is the coffee table, there is the glass door, there is the balcony. There is all this, so there must be someone seeing it. There must be an "I."

A baby is crying.

After a while, it stops.

The baby does not cry as much now. Some days, not at all. She gets up and goes in. It is not moving, but it is awake. It is a dark little thing. It stares up at her and she understands the problem. "My baby doesn't like me."

"Are you feeling better today, Mummy?"

Her older girl has turned out to be a good little helper. Home from school every day at three-thirty. "Maureen, watch the baby while I put supper on."

At five o'clock: "Maureen, set the table while I get dressed."

And when he comes in the door: "Don't you look snazzy, Missus, what's the occasion?"

One day it is as though a clock has restarted inside her. She is back. Time is the best medicine.

"Golly Moses, Mary Roses!"

The baby chuckles and the sound reminds her of a packet of Chiclets.

"Cuc-koo!" she says, popping out from behind her hands like the painted cuckoo from the clock. "Cuc-koo!" The baby mirrors her big smile.

She cannot for the life of her understand what was bothering her all winter when she could hardly get up off the couch. "What was the matter with me anyhow, Dunc?"

"Not a thing, you had a baby, you were tired."

"I was right blue, when I think about it."

"Don't think about it."

The baby pulls herself up by the coffee table. "Dunc, come look at your daughter, dear, she's standing!"

"Atta girl, Mister!"

•

Children were not permitted to play in the Black Forest by themselves, but there were other attractions to make up for the nice new playground's lack of allure. A concrete bunker was left over from the war; slits for gun barrels and pockmarks from bullets attested to its authenticity. If you had been standing in that spot twenty years ago, you would have been shot. An iron plate was welded into the ground, and Maureen told her it led to an underground bomb shelter with food and a nice table set for supper, and a playroom for the children. Then she added that Hitler had died down there. Starved and turned into a skeleton. "He's still down there, sitting at the table with a cup of tea." Mary Rose took it in. *Hitler* was a word. It had "hit" in it. Everyone knows you must not hit. One day an older boy showed up in his father's old gas mask. Blank glass eyes, obscene wrinkly snout, no ears—her first memory of fear.

•

The following spring, she gets the best news of all. She is pregnant again. She is going to have another baby, maybe even a boy. She has no right to be anything but happy.

•

The next baby lived long enough to be baptized, so his name really did belong to him. Alexander. Mary Rose saw the grave when they visited it one day in spring; remembers looking down at it, with her hands folded. She was wearing white—it matched the stone tablet, flush against the grass. Her mother's sweater was draped comfortingly over her shoulder—she recalls the gentle pressure of her mother's hand, holding it in place. Mary Rose broke the silence: "Why is he down there?" Her father replied just as gently, "Shhh." And she realized her question had been shamefully rude. She also realized she was supposed to know the answer already. But again, perhaps she merely remembers the photograph; a black-and-white snapshot in the old album that she used to pore over secretly. At the time her father took it she could not have been more than two—three?—even so, she knew the difference between a bunker and a grave. Hitter was in one. Her brother was in the other. At the edge of a forest full of Christmas trees.

With the passage of years, he became Alexander-Who-Died. His myth remained static, like his reddish hair and yellow receiving blanket—details her father never fails to include. Yellow, perhaps, for the jaundice that killed him. "There was nothing wrong with him that couldn't be fixed nowadays . . ." In Mary Rose's mind he is suspended, wrapped in his yellow blanket, like a setting sun. There is no date, no season, nor any sense that the image might belong to a sequence. A single station of the cross. Like myth, it is outside time, where it endures, as mute as the graveside photo to which she returned over and over as though hoping each time to see something new. Until one day she opened the album and it was gone.

•

The priest performs the baptism just in time, and the nurse asks the young air force officer if he would like to hold the baby. He nods and she places his son, wrapped in a yellow receiving blanket, in his arms. The corridor is

strung with tinsel. At the nurses' station a small tree
stands on the counter.

They have named him Alexander.

·

Mary Rose was shy of her fourth birthday when they were posted
back to Canada, across an ocean of time. They left him behind. Just
as they left behind the sky, the treetops, the balcony and the big hot
sun going down. Time was severed, and began again. "We're home,
kids." Snow. English. Bold seasons, big roads. Different smell. School.
"Pay attention!" Trenton air force base, with not a honey wagon in
sight, and the air full of the clumsy rumble of Hercules supply planes.
Always in view was the vastness of what in most countries would be
called a sea but in Canada was known simply as "one of the Great
Lakes." Ringed with industry, home to "the Thousand Islands" and
divided lengthwise by the US border, Lake Ontario was a burial
vault for shipwrecks and waste, or an azure immensity, depending on
the season and where you stood. They lived on a base again but
graceful lindens and glistening apartment buildings had given way
to three styles of serviceable houses, immaculate with not a garden
to be seen—gardens were long-term propositions. "One of these
days, I'll plant a tree," mused her father. Her brother was born
there—her brother-who-lived—and then they were posted again,
three hours west down the 401 to Hamilton. *See Jane run!* Different
city, same lake. New school. *See Jane fall!*

With each move the MacKinnons left something behind: broken
toys, outgrown clothes, babies. What they left they did not remember
so much as mythologize. Mary Rose left her tonsils in Hamilton.
Though less lyrical than a heart left in San Francisco, they did, according to her father, enjoy the distinction of being flushed into the Niagara
sewage system and going over the Falls. "Now you can say you've been

over the Falls without a barrel," he said with a grin. It made her feel quirky and brave, took the edge off the fiery sword in her throat.

She got older and realized her tonsils had more likely been incinerated as hospital waste and gone up the smokestack. In any case, they were somewhere. Everything was. Each night in her prayers: "God bless Mum and Dad and Maureen and Other Mary Rose and Alexander-Who-Died and Andy-Patrick and the other Others . . ." The latter were the souls of her would-have-been siblings. They accounted for Dolly's frequent, "There would have been seven of you kids, not three. Or wait now, you might have been eight." The miscarriages. Nameless "others" who became part of family lore, like Other Mary Rose and Alexander-Who-Died.

The Rh factor was responsible for all the deaths: the first pregnancy is fine, but after that if the fetus's blood is not Rh negative, the mother's antibodies attack it. Mary Rose has always thought of herself as a lucky person, a belief rooted perhaps in having been born between two dead siblings: she won the blood-type roulette. It is why she is here—that, and the fact that her older sister didn't drop her from the balcony back in Germany.

There is a cartoon she once came across in the *New Yorker*: A kangaroo stands on a busy street corner. At its feet, face down on the sidewalk lies a man in a business suit, a bullet hole in his back. The kangaroo's eyes are shifted guiltily to one side. The caption consists of its thought: *That was meant for me.*

Whenever the past started piling up behind Mary Rose, threatening to collapse, the family would move and presto, she would get another second chance. She got good at being new. They all did. The MacKinnons were always new, always almost just like everyone else. Always next door to normal. It was like growing up in the witness protection programme without changing your name.

It isn't just luck—her shiny life despite the cold draft at her back. Although she will not say it aloud, Mary Rose MacKinnon believes herself to have been the beneficiary of divine intervention. A feat for an atheist. Her grade one teacher had written "slow" on her report card back in Trenton. It was a designation that dogged her through two schools and was set to blight the third when they were posted four hours back up the shore of Lake Ontario to Kingston.

It was known as the "limestone city," with its historic forts and prisons, its universities and hospitals. Numbered among the latter was the loony bin, which was what everyone called The Ontario Hospital—itself a name that had acquired, by its very blandness, a sinister aspect. Kingston was where Sir John A. Macdonald, Canada's "Father of Confederation," had hatched the plot that would become a country, and the older buildings harboured a trillion stories, constructed as they were of the fossilized remains of plants and animals that had gone to sediment and turned to stone.

She was set to enter grade four at Our Lady of Lourdes Catholic School when Duncan made an appointment to see the principal.

Mary Rose was, by then, accustomed to being slow. Other kids would unaccountably take books from their desks and turn to page seventy-nine, or produce potatoes they'd brought from home and commence carving them into letters, dipping them in paint. She could neither draw a simple circle nor colour inside the lines. These were yardsticking offences. The blows were not severe, it being more about the humiliation factor: boys got the yardstick. To be a girl and get the yardstick meant you were outcast. Mercifully, she was already so otherwise, she was unaware of being cast out. It began in kindergarten when she failed nap, and went downhill from there.

She focused on faces, tones of voice, on the pulsations of air around the speaker, the shape and texture of sounds, colour and character of numbers and letters—*a* was red, *e* was green, 4 was brown, 5 was red, 3 was female, 7 was male, *b* was dumb, 3 was mean, 4 was kind, *m* was blue, *q* was yellow, *j* was a loner, 7 was sexy, 8 was orange, 2 was white like a stone tablet . . . She missed a great deal of what was actually said.

"Pay attention!" Letters traded places, words vaulted the page. *See Jane fall!* Did the universe cease to exist each time she blinked? Black void, yawning for one second. Or, if not, was everyone eating chocolate cake each time she blinked then hiding it the moment she opened her eyes? *See Jane run!*

The principal of Our Lady of Lourdes was Sister O'Halloran—a modern nun in boxy skirt suit, her crucifix and lipstick-free face the only clues that she was a bride of Christ. Duncan met with her and together they cooked up a plan to have Mary Rose skip grade four. A new mythology put forth its petals: her problem was not that she was slow, it was that she was smart. *"I'm not an ugly duckling. I'm a beautiful swan!"*

She had been bored, her father told her, merely in need of a challenge. "Like Einstein," he said. *No pressure.* "You're going to be accelerated." She was eight, she took it in: *I am going to be excelerated.* He framed it as an experiment in which either outcome would be honourable: If, after a trial period, she wished to fall back to grade four with her own age group, she could. No harm done. But if she thrived in grade five, then . . . "The sky's the limit."

Time opened up and swallowed grade four (which was brown). It was a change so entire that all that had come before was Chaos, and all that followed was Light. She entered grade five (red) and went from Dunce to Brain. It was a miracle on the order of Lourdes itself: Our Lady made her skip a grade. She paid attention, and got used to being the youngest.

These days she is getting used to being the oldest, hanging out in playgrounds with women a good ten or fifteen years her junior. There are worse things than having a free pass to the yummy mummy club. Not that she flirts. From her living room come strains of her mother singing *Carmen* through the phone. *"Toreado-rah don't spit on the floo-rah, use the cuspador-ah, that's-ah what it's for-ah . . . !"*

She leaves the bathroom, returns the scissors to the knife block—and remembers where she last saw them: in her own hand, opening the box with the Christmas tree stand. She must have left them on the kitchen floor amid the packing materials, and Maggie dropped the car key in exchange for them. Though it crosses her mind to blame Jesus for having invented Christmas, Mary Rose knows it was her own fault that her child was playing with scissors. Scissors that could sever a finger, sink through the soft bone of a child . . .

In the living room, Maggie is now demolishing Matthew's wooden tracks while Sitdy sings "Hello, Dolly!" indefatigably through the phone receiver face down on the floor. Mary Rose bends and picks it up.

"Hi, Mum, thanks for entertaining Maggie."

"Where's Hilary?"

Listening comprehension has never been her mother's strong suit.

"Mum, she's in Winnipeg, she's—"

"Have you heard from your brother?"

"What? Not recently, no."

She is starting to get that old familiar hazed feeling—why try to keep hold of a train of thought when it is bound to be derailed?

"What in the name o' time is goin' on, we haven't heard from him in—"

"He's fine, Mum, he's alive, he's busy."

She follows Maggie into the kitchen—the child needs a diaper change. The mid-morning sun intensifies, flooding the kitchen with light. Soon the windows will be framed with ivy and it will be like looking through an enchantment . . . maybe they should skip the morning nap and go to the park.

Dolly speaks in a stage whisper, suddenly coy. "Do you think he and Shereen will have a baby?"

"I hope not."

"Why not? He's the last of the MacKinnon line."

What are we, kings? "Mum, there's loads of MacKinnons in the world."

Her mother is a Mahmoud, an ethnic Arab—*not Arab, Lebanese!*—and yet the self-appointed keeper of the MacKinnon clan. Like the Jews in Hollywood who made *White Christmas.* Like the gays who made . . . everything else.

"He's the last of your father's line"—adamant now, a warning in Dolly's tone.

"Maybe they will, Mum." It is nothing against her brother's fiancée, there's nothing wrong with Shereen—which is actually the only thing wrong with her.

Dolly is coy again. "Maybe they'll have a boy."

It is that Andy-Patrick already has two children: grown daughters from his first marriage who, though beloved, do not count in Dolly's eyes when it comes to "your father's line," any more than Mary Rose and her sister did—although it has never seemed to bug Mo; she married a nice Pole, took his name and became safely fenced round with *z*s and *v*s. "Maybe they will, Mum." Maybe the much younger Shereen will demand fifty-fifty on the domestic front. "It could be wonderful for him."

Dolly is suddenly solemn. "I wasn't good at having babies."

Here we go . . . "Yes you were, Mum, you were great."

"How old were you when your brother was born?"

"Five."

"Were you that old in Germany?"

"What? No, I was going on four when we moved back to Canada—"

"I mean Alexander-Who-Died."

"Oh, I don't know, Mum, one or two, I guess. Three?"

"Was that before or after my mother died?"

"I wouldn't know, Mum. Maybe Dad can—"

"Do you remember what you said when I was pregnant with

Andy-Patrick and I told you we were going to call him Alexander if it was a boy—"

"Yes, Mum, I remember."

"You were just five years old and you said"—Dolly imitates Mary Rose's toddler voice—"'Don't call him Alexander, if you call him Alexander you'll have to put him in de gwound!'" Dolly laughs.

Mary Rose wonders if she really sounded that much like Tweety Bird but asks, "Mum, what's in the package?" Maybe she can get her mother off one loop by nudging her onto another.

"I've sent you a packeege."

"I know."

"You do?"

"You told me."

"Did you get it yet?"

She winces. When did her mother start using such execrable grammar? "No, I *have not yet received* it. When did you mail it?"

"Right before Christmas, wait now, right after Christmas, right before we saw you right after Christmas."

"Before your after-Christmas visit here after Christmas?"

"That's right, Sadie, Flo, Mo—"

"That's almost three months ago, mum."

"It is? Well what in the name of time is going on, dammit?"

"It's okay, Mum, it'll turn up."

"Turnip? You cooking turnip? I love turnip!"

"TURN UP. THE PACKAGE. IT WILL TURN UP."

"You don't have to shout."

"Sorry, Mum, I better go, Maggie needs her nap."

"She still has a nap in the morning?"

Sigh.

"Where's Hilary?"

"She's in—"

"What's she doing in Winnipeg?"

"*The Importance of*—"

"We're coming on the seventh."

"Oh okay, what time?" Mary Rose opens the telephone drawer in search of a pen.

"At seven."

"At seven on the seventh? Seven in the morning?" No pen. Broken pencil—

"Eleven."

"At eleven on the seventh?" That will be easy to remember.

"Did I say that?"

"I . . . don't know, Mum, did you?" Where *are* all the pens? "What day of the week is that?"

"You've got me all confused now. Where's the calendar I gave you?"

"Sorry, Mum, is Dad there, do you want to put him on and—" She excavates the calendar from the corkboard where it's been pinned since her parents' visit in January.

"Wait'll I get my purse—"

"No! Mum, don't get your purse, it's okay, call me when you know when—"

"Call someone in to help you with the kids, you've earned it, dear."

"Mum, I have Candace."

"Get her full time!"

"I don't need help."

"Live a little, Mary Rose!"

Whenever her mother does say her name right off, Mary Rose sees quotation marks around it, as if Dolly were saying a line from a play.

"Thanks, Mum."

She hangs up and looks at the calendar pinned to the cork-board—an island of clutter in her otherwise streamlined kitchen. It features a series of watercolour flowers painted by an artist who is limited to the use of his foot. There is nothing to say about the pictures except that they are foot-painted. A caption in the bottom left-hand corner thanks her for supporting the Catholic Women's League. Are her parents coming on the seventh at eleven? Or on the eleventh at seven? Mo will know.

She eyes the dead chicken on the counter, suddenly out of love with it. "The thrill is gone," she says, avoiding the wing, picking it up from underneath so it rests in her hand—disquieting in another way, resembling as it does a baby. Maybe she ought to take another stab at being vegetarian. She drops it into a zip-lock bag, and a penny drops too—the Fort Garry Hotel is in Winnipeg, not Calgary. It was in Winnipeg that she bought *the knives that will stay sharp longer than you will!* Prairies versus mountains. Vertigo versus claustrophobia . . .

She bends to the freezer drawer and tucks the chicken between a package of organic frozen peas and an ice cube tray of puréed sweet potato. She admires once again her icemaker bin full of freshly laid cubes, and congratulates herself on not having colonized it for food the way some people do. How can they live like that? There is a mysterious object toward the back; she reaches for it, then steps away—investigate one frost-bearded lump in your freezer and before you know it you're cleaning the whole fridge. She has a list of things to do today and "clean fridge" is not on it. Is her brother really thinking of starting a second family with Shereen? It isn't that she does not wish happiness for him—if he wants another baby at his stage of advanced boyhood, then good luck to him, it's just . . . it is annoying to hear her mother flaunting an old-world pride in her son's reproductive prowess. And Shereen is not good enough for her brother. *Do I contradict myself? Very well then, I contradict myself.*

She closes the freezer and registers a fresh twinge at the dents in its drawer front. The fridge was the stainless steel jewel in the crown of their kitchen renovation, and she has allowed Hilary to believe that Maggie made the dents with her doll stroller. She would spend the money to replace it if she didn't know how logistically challenging it will be to orchestrate the necessary service call.

"Maggie, no, poo stays in your diaper!" Summoning her core strength, Mary Rose grips her daughter and carries her at arms' length up the stairs like hazardous waste.

She does not usually damage things anymore, the fridge was an anomaly. At worst she might punch her own head or slam it into a wall. Back in the day, before she got together with Hil, she used to go into the kitchen, open the drawer, take hold of the biggest knife by the blade and squeeze it just shy of the point where her skin would break. But she never crossed the line into pathology—out-and-out "cutting." And there is no chance of any knife tricks for her these days, she is far more self-aware. Besides, she would not dream of keeping her good knives in a drawer.

•

She wakes up. They have kept her in. Moved her to a different floor—a quieter ward. Something is in the room and taking up space, a presence . . . it knows something about her . . . She falls back asleep.

She wakes up. Through her half-open door she sees tinsel decking the corridor . . . It was a boy. He is dead.

•

It is downright balmy as she pushes Maggie in the stroller with Daisy trotting alongside, off to pick up Matthew in time for lunch. The last crusts of brown ice are trickling into storm sewers, while overhead, trees are tight with buds; every year she promises herself she will catch the moment when they open and every year she is taken by surprise when the city is suddenly in full leaf. Sounds of traffic bulge as they near the intersection with busy Bathurst Street, but as they arrive at the lights in front of the corner store, strains of Albinoni's stately

Adagio bathe them along with the plants that the owner is placing outside on racks.

"Hello." The lady almost sings it. "How are you?"

"Hi, Winnie."

The music and plants create a buffer between the sidewalk and gritty Bathurst Street and as she waits for the lights to change, Mary Rose is held in a bubble of time, puffy and soft. No sooner has she turned her face to the sun, however, than she experiences a pang. She ought to phone her mother right now and just plain listen while the old darling loops on. Her mother has taken to talking about the lost babies, repeating stock phrases—Mary Rose noticed it last summer, and more recently when her parents visited in early January. Perhaps it is a feature of aging; tightly packed cargo from the past coming loose, sliding about below decks, making itself felt after decades—Mary Rose could understand if her mother's need to tell and retell were evidence of a grief deferred. But what is disconcerting, even eerie, is the degree of animation that has crept into Dolly's accounts. She tells them almost as if they were funny stories.

She never recollects the events in reliable order and neither does Duncan with his steel-trap mind. At the mention of Alexander's name, there ensues a customary muddled working back through time in an effort to determine whether Dolly's mother died before or after he was born, and how many days he lived, was it eight? Three? . . . As though it had all happened in wartime and, after the bombs had fallen and the sirens were stilled, fragments of events had been put back together in the wrong order, with gaps.

The light turns green and they push off—she coughs and feels a sudden kink in her throat—she mustn't get sick until Hil gets home. The stroller grinds to a halt in the middle of the intersection where cars are paused like snorting horses at the lights. Maggie has managed to kick off one of her boots, which is now lodged in the undercarriage. Mary Rose bends to retrieve it, sustains a sandpapery smooch from Daisy and rises in time to avoid being run over by some idiot in a Smart Car.

"Back off!" she bellows.

Already repenting the adrenal expenditure, she shepherds them to the other side of Bathurst.

She is uncertain how many "others" there were, but she does know, thanks to Maureen, that one of them went down the toilet in Kingston. Their house was new and therefore, she told herself, unhaunted. Although who is to say an embryo is not robust enough to haunt a house—even a suburban split-level? It had a soul, according to the Church. And yet that soul was not welcome in Heaven any more than Other Mary Rose's had been. What did God do with all those souls in Limbo? Were they recycled? Harvested like stem souls, capable of conferring immortality? Heroes often enter the Underworld in quest of a lost soul, but Mary Rose cannot think of any who have entered Limbo—"The Other Place"—for the same purpose. She ought to make a note of this. For the third novel.

She'll jot it down later, they're at the school. And there is her beautiful boy, lined up with his classmates on the other side of the glass door, waiting to be dismissed. Waiting to run to her.

•

She does not remember her husband having brought it, but it is sitting open on her bedside stand: a grey velvet jewellery box. In it is a ring. Milky blue, hint of iridescence, a moonstone. The box is open, so she must have opened it. This keeps happening. It is as though she opens her eyes on a scene from a movie, then the movie skips, sometimes backwards sometimes forwards. It is difficult to get hold of the story. In between the bits the screen goes black. This is probably due to the drugs they are

giving her. Why are they giving her drugs? She
is not sick.

This is her second time on this ward, she was here
after she had Mary Rose—the second Mary Rose, the
one who lived. She is not crazy, she knows this is
Germany not Winnipeg, she knows it is Christmas. The
ring in the box is blue. Like a stillborn baby. This baby
wasn't stillborn though, so why has he given her a stillborn ring? This baby was born alive. She heard him cry.
They did not let her hold him—"Best not to," they said.
They took him away and called a priest.

She opens her eyes. Her husband is here, sitting by
her bed behind a newspaper. He is in his uniform, he must
have come from work. The ring is now on her hand.

"It's pretty," she says.

He looks up. "So are you." He rises and leans down to
kiss her on the forehead.

Her face is wet. This keeps happening. She squeezes his
hand so he won't worry. He looks thin. "Who's feeding you?"

"Armgaard."

She lets out a dismissive puff of air through dry lips.

"And Eileen and those gals have been around," he
adds. "They brought a stew. Wasn't as good as yours,
though." He smiles. "And don't worry about the baby,
she's fine."

It takes her a moment to understand that he means
Mary Rose, who is, after all, still the "baby" of the
family—the baby at home, not the one in the morgue.
He closes his hand around hers and she feels the ring bite
against the neighbouring fingers. He is so good to her.

When she wakes up, it is dark and he is gone.

•

It is five o'clock: witching hour for children and puppies, who tend to go rangy around then, bitching hour for those returning home from work, worry-and-wander hour for old folks suffering from sundowning. It is the primal tilt between day and night that strikes low-grade dread into the heart of *Homo sapiens*, a holdover from the time when we were prey. It is why cocktail hour was invented.

Mary Rose is successfully negotiating a cocktail-free hour, blowing bubbles in the front yard for Maggie and Daisy who lunge and snap joyously while Matthew draws calmly with chalk on the flagstones. His flaxen hair falls across his serious blue eyes as he outlines a car, a dinosaur . . . His ability to focus goes with a strong, well-coordinated little body and lends his demeanour a degree of maturity beyond his five years. Before leaving to pick him up, Mary Rose attempted to restore the fractal tracks and to situate Percy, Thomas, Annabel and the others amid the possibilities, but he smelled a rat. "It's not the same," he pronounced gravely. She considered telling him the trains had come alive and rearranged things on their own. Would he buy it? Would it be wrong? "I'm afraid Maggie was playing with your train set, Matthew."

She braced herself, but he was philosophical. Even indulgent. "Oh, Maggie," he said. "She's still a baby."

So it is with a sense of her tranquility being ruffled, like a glassy lake by a finger of wind at dusk, that she watches her brother, Andy-Patrick, pull up in a shiny new BMW. He is not a frequent visitor—likely to drop by only when the interval between girlfriends becomes a drought of more than a few days or, more recently, whenever he renews his resolution to remain faithful to his fiancée, Shereen, who is often away in the course of her job as a drug pusher. Pharmaceutical sales rep. Mary Rose tends to get worked up when obliging Andy-Patrick with a sisterly lecture as to his shortcomings. Like a ringside coach, patching him up, sending him back in, "get up off the couch, listen to her without trying to fix her, change your sweatpants."

"Shereen left, eh," he says, and closes the car door with a substantial Bavarian thunk.

The kids mob him, Daisy dances him up the flagstones, administering kisses of bovine heft.

"Where's she off to this time?"

"She *left* left."

"Oh."

"It's okay," he says, beeping the car locked. "I've healed."

The scent of the Euro-male is upon him: coffee, cigarettes, cologne *pour lui*. He joins them for grilled cheese sandwiches, tomato soup, broccoli and real-fruit freezie pops. He plays hide-and-seek and horsey all over the house and even helps with bath time, reading to the children afterwards—*Here Come the Aliens!* before "tuckling" them in—his hybrid of *tucking* and *tickling*. He heads back downstairs, and Mary Rose goes about settling them in the wake of their uncle's stimulating glamour—even Matthew's hamster is up and running early in its metal wheel, while the expiring balloons from his fifth birthday party have revived to float above the floor, riding the gusts of hilarity. One nudges her as she sits on the edge of her son's bed in the darkness and she bats it away—God bless Balloon King and their money's-worth helium. He is cuddled with beloved Bun, the tattered lapinary recipient of many a grooming by Daisy. She rubs her little boy's back and he sighs contentedly. "You brushed the cloud away, Mumma."

"I brushed away the balloon, sweetheart."

"It was a cloud on my back."

"Is it gone now?"

"You brushed it away."

Surely he is too young to be burdened by a "cloud." He says spooky things sometimes, *I remember the first time I got born* . . . Maybe he is psychic. Or maybe he is just sad. He has already been dealt a blow.

Anna's heartbeat, her voice and rhythm, the scent of his birth mother. Then, gone. On his dresser is a photo of her with the big striped circus tent in the background; she is decked out in safety vest and hard hat, waving. Gone to myth. It's all for the best, but somewhere he must remember the loss, in his cells. He knows what it is to be haunted. But he also knows how to be consoled. She winds his glass unicorn and it tinkles its tune.

She goes into Maggie's room, leans over the side of the crib and tucks the duvet around her shoulders. Maggie kicks it off. "Milk," she says, ominously.

Mary Rose gives in and brings her a bottle. Just this once. She tries to cuddle her, but Maggie does not wish to be held. At least not by Mumma. She claims the bottle and rolls onto her side.

From the outset Mary Rose was less able to console her daughter than her son. To a degree this was natural—Hil was Maggie's biological mother and was breastfeeding. Mary Rose understood this was what fathers often felt: second fiddle not only in the mother's but the baby's affections, despite long nights of walking the floor with the infant. Her own father walked the floor with her in the wee hours for the first several weeks—months?—while her mother was kept in hospital. Despite his gender and generation, he mothered her during the crucial early time, with the result that, for her, his body was the soft one, his voice, his gaze, safe in his arms on the balcony at sunset, *Good night, sweetie pie. See you in the morning* . . . Mary Rose herself has been the very model of a modern Other Mother: supportive at the birth, game for night feedings, endlessly patient while she waited for the honeymoon to resume with Hil. And waited.

She hears Andy-Pat downstairs playing the theme from *A Charlie Brown Christmas* on the piano—it's almost Easter, maybe he could use a foot calendar. Her arm feels too warm. She dekes into the bathroom and pops an Advil—although, considering the pain in her arm is all in her head, she ought to be popping a placebo.

At the kitchen table she pours them each a Scotch. He says, "Want to see the birthday present I got for Shereen?"

"Why are you buying her a present if you've broken up, what are you hoping to achieve?" She kicks herself for lapsing into lecture mode again—the guy is forty-three years old even if he is her baby brother.

"Just ask me to show you her present."

"Okay, show me her present."

He holds out his wrist and flashes his chunky new TAG Heuer watch.

"What about the BMW?"

"Oh that's not retail therapy, that's a necessity." He leans forward, conspiratorial. "It's a cheap lease, okay? This mechanic, I may have mentioned him, Slavko, who was looking after the Hyundai?" A warm smile breaks across his boyish face. "He's this great huge bear of a man, eh, totally foul-mouthed, could snap you in half, but the type of guy'd give you the shirt off his back, you know? So he puts me in touch with this dealership that's essentially virtual, okay?" His tone becomes brisk, manly. "They don't keep any actual cars on any one lot, they move them around as needed, so zero overhead, which is good news for me." He sits back, nonchalant, and rests his gaze on a corner of the ceiling.

Mary Rose knows that look, it is her father's look, she used to cultivate it herself to advantage—the old still-waters-run-deep look. As far as she can tell, it masks chronic low-grade dissociation and self-deceit, but her brother gets away with it because he's a guy—it even helps him get laid. He does look great, though. Both he and Mary Rose have an advantage in the conventional good looks department; their mother has a schnozz, their father sports a beak, their older sister boasts a Roman profile, but the two youngest, by some stroke of recessive luck, have cute little noses. Maybe it goes with the lucky blood type.

While Andy-Patrick has his share of good looks, however, it is the glint in his eye that makes him attractive, and it is back. Gone are the saggy chinos, the faded fleece of Christmas Past, along with five or six pounds. He is wearing a hip new T-shirt with a silk-screened vintage coffee ad, Diesel jeans and a groovy cowboy belt. He's had a total heartbreak-over.

He narrows his eyes—*Bond, James Bond*—"I'm getting my hair done Wednesday, just some discreet highlights, want to come?"

He is a liaison officer with the Royal Canadian Mounted Police, which seems to mean he can show up for work when he wants but has to be ready to don his scarlets and head for a podium at a moment's notice. People don't think cops go in for retail therapy of the sumptuary kind. A new snowmobile or flat-screen TV, sure, but hair? Great-ass jeans? "Look, I'm not going to sit here and drop the C-bomb like some guys I know, but Shereen is . . . you know, she's young, she's got stuff to do, she's a . . . she's not a bitch just because she left me."

"The C-bomb?"

He grins. "I'm watching *The Sopranos* again, eh, it's my therapy."

"I know, it's so comforting."

"I know, weird, eh? So I'm not going to sit here and call her a—" He gives an apologetic wince that reminds her of their father, then mouths the word, *cunt*. Which does not.

She sips. "What did you mean, you've 'healed'?"

He flashes a roguish smile in answer.

She deadpans, "Do the words 'Gerald McBoing-Boing' mean anything to you?"

"I'm not on the rebound, Mister, this one's strictly . . . recreational."

"Is that why Shereen left?"

"No. No, no, no way, this postdates that."

She waits for the "tell." He scratches his cheek. Vindicated, she inquires, "Do we bother with names?"

"Naw, she's nice, but . . ."

"How old is she?"

"She's a big fan of yours."

"Please tell me she's at the twenty-five-year-old end of the YA readership spectrum." She has spoken with asperity but suppresses a vicarious macho buzz—as if she were chalking up a sexual conquest of her own.

"She'll be twenty-three in two weeks. I stopped her for an illegal left turn."

"You don't do traffic."

"I'm always on duty."

She feels her face heating up. "Andy-Pat, you have to stay away from young ones, they're a waste of time, even women in their thirties, the thirties are when people let themselves go 'cause they don't realize they're getting older, plus their divorce is too fresh and they're dealing with custody. Find a nice teacher in her forties, her kids are older, she's intelligent, well-rounded, plus she's looking after herself now, she's a frost-free tower of perimenopausal sex with no waxy buildup. *You* don't have to look great to get a great woman, Andy-Pat, you just have to be an employed straight white male with a pulse." She freshens their glasses. "Up yer kilt."

"We're not actually, technically, *white*, Mary Rose. Mum is a visible minority."

He's had sensitivity training through the Force.

"She's not not-white, Andy-Pat, she's just Lebanese, she's Canadian—"

"She's of Arab extraction. I think we both know what that means nowadays, Mister Sister." He swirls his Scotch a tad ruefully.

"It means everyone wants to eat our food even though they made fun of us for it when we were kids."

"Try entering the US with the name Mahmoud stamped on your passport instead of MacKinnon," he says with police-forcely *gravitas*.

Try growing up as a lesbian in our family. But she doesn't say it.

"What happened to your fridge?" he asks.

She tells him: she threw Maggie's doll stroller across the kitchen. The doll wasn't in it at the time. She'd been ransacking the house, looking for something—lost objects are her *bêtes noires*—her gaze fell on the stroller and she allowed herself the outlet.

"Do you remember the time Dad broke his hand on the doorstep?" she says with a grin. Her question is rhetorical: the Time Dad Broke His Hand is canonical, a stock "remember-when." Or, as Andy-Patrick used to say when he was little, "me-member."

Their mother was the one with the short wick, but their father used to assault inanimate objects, always with an expression of outraged innocence followed by red-faced Highland triumph. "There! That'll teach that godforsaken lawn mower a thing or two. Probably designed by a Frenchman!" Garden hoses, bicycle spokes, boot racks, all manner of *things* tasted his wrath—except for the time he throttled Mo over the missing tent pegs, but that became a funny story almost immediately.

The doorstep thing happened way back when they lived in Kingston; the screen door caught Dad on the heel and he yelped—dangerously funny to Mary Rose and Andy-Patrick, who must have laughed, perhaps triggering the face-saving assault on the doorstep, for their father turned, genuflected and brought down his fist like a gavel, breaking one of the myriad tiny fishbones that make up the human hand. It required a cast, of which they were perversely proud, and their father told the story better than anyone, insisting, with a twinkle, that the door frame had been dealt "just retribution." Was that before or after her first surgery when she wound up in a cast of her own? Was it before or after her mother's last miscarriage? Time measured out in dead babies, broken bones and postings. You had to be there to know it was actually loads of fun a lot of the time.

She expects Andy-Patrick to laugh about her dented fridge—she is laughing. But he says, "We were raised with a lot of rage."

She nods. If he wants to go there, she can go there with the best of them. "Exactly," she says. "Which is how I know the difference between a dented fridge and a battered child."

"What? I, I didn't mean that."

"I know how we were raised, Andy-Pat, I was there long before you came along."

"I'm sorry, I know you're not like that."

"Like what?"

"Like Mum."

"Are you saying Mum battered us?" she retorts casually.

"No! No, no."

"Some people would call it that."

". . . Would you call it that?"

"I'd call it . . ." —she pauses—". . . colourful."

"Me too."

She bellows suddenly, "'C'mere till I annihilate the both o' ya!'"

"'C'mere till I beat the daylights outta ya!'" He captures the quivering vulnerability at the white core of anger.

"'C'mere, demon!'"

"'C'mere, hateful!'"

They laugh.

Sip.

"Mum was from a different time and place," he says, relaxing, stretching out his legs.

"Mum was incredible, it's incredible what she accomplished, she was the only one in her family to go past high school."

"Apart from the priest and nun," he points out.

"Exactly. Mum was amazing. Remember the time she conducted the church choir and got them to sing 'Hava Nagila'?"

"Remember when you opened the back door on my birthday cake and she iced it anyway and called it a 'hurricane cake'?"

They get giddy again. They sip.

"People did all kinds of things to their kids back then without batting an eye."

"I got the strap at school," he says.

"I got the yardstick."

"Did you get the belt?"

She looks up. "No. Did you?"

"Once or twice."

"Mum never gave me the belt."

"Not Mum. Dad."

"Dad gave you the belt?"

She hesitates. Does this change anything? Mum-on-the-rampage is one thing, but Dad . . . discerning, even-tempered Dad—the mere fact he might think you deserving of such humiliation, never mind mete it out . . .

"When?"

"Aunt Sadie was visiting, I think I was five."

"Why?" she asks.

"I don't know, I was a brat—"

"He must have been under some kind of pressure. Well, can you imagine living with Mum?"

"We don't have to imagine it," he says with a grin.

Does the belt mean her brother suffered more? Surely she is the winner of the family suffering sweepstakes. The thought has landed like a stray ball over the fence . . . She will examine it more closely later, but for now Andy-Pat needs the benefit of her clarity.

"Okay, that's my point, A&P." She knows he has never minded being nicknamed after a grocery store chain—it beats being named after a dead sibling. "I've got Hilary and the kids now and I don't dwell on what I went through with Mum and Dad, but you need to take a good hard look at some unresolved issues—"

"I want to meet someone like Hilary. Someone beautiful and nice and funny who's a bit smarter than me."

"She's not smarter than me."

"In the Dad way, yes she is, you know, someone with a tidy mind."

"I mean, Hilary's smart, but . . ."

"I wish I was a lesbian."

"Mum was . . . rough with us—okay?—by today's standards, but . . ." The Scotch feels to be dissolving her stomach lining—it's okay to drink booze with Advil, it's Tylenol that's the problem. "Whether it's physical or verbal, it's all . . . it's the shame factor, right? I mean, it didn't wreck us or anything, we had a lot of great times . . ."

"We had tons of great times."

"But we're kind of wrecked," she says.

"We're a bit wrecked."

"We're great, too. Mum and Dad were great."

"They were great."

"But it makes you hate yourself," she says.

"And that makes you dangerous."

". . . Say that again?"

"It makes you dangerous," he says. "A person who hates themself is dangerous."

"Andy-Patrick, that is really smart."

"I got it from Amber."

"Who's Amber?"

"The marriage counsellor—Mary Lou and I saw her together, then I kept going for my own, you know, issues."

"Wow, Andy-Pat. Good. Really good."

Her brother has actually had psychotherapy. The RCMP will have paid for it, of course, courtesy of the Government of Canada . . . which bugs her a bit, her commitment to social democracy notwithstanding, because if she needed psychotherapy, she would have to pay for it herself. It wouldn't even be tax-deductible. She cannot deduct so much as a Pilates class from her income, even though her core strength is keeping her off the public tit to the tune of a future double hip replacement. She has literally outrun the family curse of high cholesterol at the expense of her knee, for which she is on an arthroscopic waiting list behind a bunch of fat slobs who never get up off the couch, and should she seek therapy so as not to beat her children or chase them screaming through the house with a wooden spoon, the cost-saving ripple effect of her sparing society two more screwed-up people will merit not a penny's deduction come tax time.

"Right, so based on all that," she says, "why do you think you go from conquest to conquest, seeking your reflection in the adoring eyes of younger and younger women whom you do not allow to stick around long enough to find out what a worthless person you are so they can't shame you for it all over again?"

He furrows his brow.

She continues, "You have a deep sense of inadequacy that was engendered by Mum's rage and reinforced by Dad's blind eye—except for when he gave you the belt, of course—but the point is: it cost you two marriages, an engagement, it's put your relationship with your daughters at risk, and it's preventing you from being happy in your own skin."

"As opposed to someone else's," he says with rakish good cheer.

"Ideally both."

"I know you're right, Mary Rose? And I totally appreciate it, but . . ." The gleam re-enters his eye. "I'm actually having a pretty good time at the moment."

"I'm just a jealous housewife, you look great."

"No, you're right, I'm a shit—"

"I didn't say that."

"Dad always said that, I mean, he's the gold standard, right? Dad's a gentleman."

"You're a gentleman." She wishes she sounded more convincing.

"Not like Dad."

How to support him while not enabling his sexism? "You're a nice uncle," she says feebly. On the other hand, why rain on his parade? If it doesn't matter to him, why should it matter to her that

Andy-Patrick has baggage? Steamer trunks and duffle bags and fanny packs . . .

"And now he has a stolen car," says Hil on the phone later that night.

"No he hasn't. He's a cop, he would know."

"I'm sure he does." Hil has a light touch and it goes for her voice too; satiny, a slight breathy quality. Mary Rose found it sexy at first—still does, of course, but after several years of marriage she has become attuned as well to the undertone of steely authority. Which is also, of course, sexy.

"Oh my God, are you saying he knows?" Mary Rose is leaning against the kitchen counter in front of the big black windows.

"Maybe he doesn't want to know that he knows, which is why he's telling you in such loving detail about Boris . . ."

"Slavko."

"Slavko, whom he talks about with the same warm . . . zeal that people who've just met your mother talk about her."

"You're comparing my mother to a car mechanic with ties to the Russian mob?"

Silence.

"Hil, that was a joke." Hil is adept at using silence—tweezery bits of it—to advantage. Another skill that eludes Mary Rose. "Why do you have to cut through everything with your brain-diamond, why can't you just laugh along with the absurdity of things?"

"Why would I laugh? Your brother's in crisis." Steel creeping in . . .

"He's not, he's just—he's an overly entitled, overly charming, middle-aged, middle-class white guy, he's right in the demographic sweet spot."

"You're in one too."

"Oh, you mean the middle-aged lesbian single-mother housewife sweet spot?"

Mary Rose is uncertain whether she has pitched it with jam or vinegar until Hilary laughs. "That's the one!" Jam. Phone-fight averted.

She tells her about Rochelle and the car alarm—but not the scissors—and Hil laughs again. She moves from counter to table and relaxes, stroking Daisy's broad head as the old girl lumbers past, en route from her basement bed to her upstairs bed. "Then my mother called back just as Maggie started changing her own diaper."

"I think she may be ready to start toilet training," says Hil.

Mary Rose suppresses a sigh. The prospect of the painstaking attention required, the random trips to the potty for long unproductive stints followed immediately by accidents, strikes Sisyphean ennui into her heart. Surely it can wait until Hil gets home next week.

"I don't want to rush her into anything. How's it going?" she asks, steering into safer waters. "Have you done a run-through yet?"

"We had our first dress rehearsal today. Maury had to do the second act without a wig."

"Oh my God."

Maury's playing Lady Bracknell.

"Yeah."

"How many previews does Alberta Theatre Projects give you?"

"Eight."

Eight chances to get it right in front of a paying audience before opening night. "Excellent." Hil normally pulls rabbits out of her hat with far less.

Hil brings Mary Rose up to date on the crew guys and the flies—the ones that haul sets through the air, not the ones you swat—relishing technical challenges as much as aesthetic ones, loving how they are linked. "He keeps them lubricated, but no one has actually used them in years."

"Who does?"

"The Tech Director. Paul."

"Great. It'll be amazing if you can just fly in the hedge maze."

"I know, plus funny."

The Importance of Being Earnest features one of Mary Rose's all-time favourite lines, and she speaks it now for Hil in Lady Bracknell's craggy voice: "'To lose one child may be regarded as a misfortune. To lose two looks like carelessness.'"

She tells Hil about the lost "packeege!" and her father's lovely e-mail. "Some things really do get *batter*." She tells her about Daisy almost biting the mailman, about the Christmas tree stand—

"I thought we already had one."

"Not one like this."

"Are we getting rid of the old one?"

"We'll keep it as a backup."

"Why do we need a backup if the new one's perfect?"

"Okay, we'll get rid of it, I don't care."

"What are you going to do tomorrow when Candace comes?"

The question rankles Mary Rose. *What does she think I'm going to do with my nanny time? Get together with "the girls" for lunch? Buy a new hat?* "I have a doctor's appointment," she replies grimly. Long-sufferingly.

"Is it your arm?"

"My arm? No."

"It was bothering you."

"Yeah, and I dealt with it, it's basically demon."

"Demon?"

"Phantom, it's nothing, I'll google it."

"Don't google it! Go to the doctor."

"I went to the doctor, it's nothing." She coughs.

"Are you coming down with something?"

"No, I just did too much laundry tonight and now I'm a bit tired."

"Don't let yourself get rundown."

"I can be tired, Hil, I'm single-handed here—"

"You're doing a wonderful job."

"They're alive, anyway."

"I love you. I've been thinking about you."

"Oh yeah?"

"You're beautiful," says Hil. "I hope you don't mind . . . I've been using you."

"Be my guest."

Warm silence.

From upstairs comes a sleepy cry.

"Maggie's up, I should go before she wakes Matthew."

"She's still waking up at night?"

"Yeah." *Martyred sigh.*

"Even without the morning nap?"

"I better go."

"I love you."

"Love you too."

"Wait, when're your parents coming?"

"I don't know, soon."

"Let me know."

"Why? It's like early next week sometime. Or late this week."

"I know, but . . . I know it's not nothing when you see them."

They've had some of their worst fights on the heels of visits with her parents, no matter how nice a time it has been—why does Hil have to dredge that up now?

"Don't worry, Hil, you won't even be here."

"That's not what I mean, love."

She has braced herself for archness, but Hil's tone is . . . kind. She stiffens. "I better go." Upstairs, Maggie has started singing. "It'll be fine, really, my mum's so jovial now, it's bizarre, it's almost worth it that she's losing her marbles."

"You think she's got some dementia?"

"No, I don't know, not like that, it's just, she's starting to come loose like an old sweater."

". . . She doesn't seem that different to me."

"Well, she's not your mother. I can tell, she's looping."

"She's loopy?"

"Looping, you know, round and round, the package, the babies, the package."

"What babies?"

"The dead ones, plus she asked me twenty times today where you were, I kept saying, Winnipeg, Winnipeg, Winnie-the-Pooh Peg!"

Silence.

"Hil?"

". . . I'm in Calgary."

Upstairs, Maggie is quiet again—perhaps she was singing in her sleep, Hil sometimes laughs in her sleep. Mary Rose swallows. Does she have early onset?

Hil is saying, "Sweetheart, you've got a lot going on—"

"You're in Calgary. Jesus Murphy."

"It doesn't matter where I am, the point is, I'm not home and—"

"I knew that, I know you're at ATP." Alberta Theatre Projects. Mary Rose lives in Toronto, smack in the middle of the country if not the universe, but she does know the difference between the provinces of Alberta and Manitoba. "God."

"They're both west," says Hilary kindly.

"God." Mountains versus Prairies.

"You're focused on the kids and that's all you need to—"

"I better go, I can hear Maggie." *Lie.*

"I love you."

"Love you too."

Her arm was not bothering her when Hil asked, but it is now. Her large bag is hanging over the railing post at the top of the back steps. She digs out the tube of Advil she has taken to carrying and swallows one. That makes three today, but it's best to get the jump on pain because once it starts it creates its own momentum. There is nothing actually wrong with her arm—she consulted an orthopaedic surgeon last fall; the pain is apparently merely a nuisance. He called it something . . . not "phantom" per se, something else . . . she can't remember. She ought to go to bed now, but the imp of the perverse lives in her laptop—how else to explain why a tired adult who needs to get up early with children lifts the lid on that glowing box of ills?

She refrains from googling "Adult Onset Pediatric Bone Cysts," less due to the absurdity of the search words than to the certainty that she will diagnose herself with bone cancer in minutes. Over Christmas she innocently researched home remedies for a sinus infection and wound up with a rare paranasal tumour.

There is an e-mail from Kate confirming the movie Wednesday night—it'll be good to get out for the evening—out of her own head before she goes out of her mind. Bridget and Kate are rich and really fun—in the intervals when they're not on the rocks. They donate a lot of money to women's health causes, and renovate a great deal. There is an e-mail from her old buddy Hank, who is somewhere in Mexico—he's sent a photo, "Does this Harley-Davidson chopper make my prostate look big?" Best friends from back in their twenties, Hank is the last of the very few guys she ever more or less slept with, Mary Rose having approached heterosexuality rather like math: she worked at it until she achieved a C then felt justified in dropping it. While she might prefer to forget the awkward episode, the fact of their once, long ago, having "kissed with tongues" has injected a companionable wry note into their friendship. Hank cooked his way to the top of the Toronto food chain during the culinary explosion of the nineties and now has his face on bottles of sauce, but claims, "If I could write like you, Mister, I'd trade it in a heartbeat." He has also advised her that she could make a fortune writing lesbian porn. "But tastefully, you know," he added. *"Fifty Shades of Gay."* He got some iffy results on his last checkup, and went out and bought the bike.

Bing!

Duncan MacKinnon, we have found 454 3rd degree relatives!

It is from Origin-eology.com in Texas. She ordered her father a DNA kit online for his eightieth birthday and is now the regular recipient of special offers to do with the Y chromosome. Duncan has been working on a family tree for years now, tracing the first of their forbears to board a plague ship from Scotland for the New World. Why are people so pumped about nth degree relatives they've never met, when they can barely cope with the ones they know? *Bing!*

RE: Some things really do get batter
Dear Mister,
Well that was a heck of a cliffhanger! You ought to try your hand at writing ;-)   (I just learned how to do that winking face!) What were you going to say? You've got me in suspense now.
Love,
Dad

She glances down the thread.

Dear Dad,
I

And hits *reply*.

Dear Dad,
Sorry, Maggie hit "send" then the doorbell rang at the same time as the phone, and Daisy just about ate the mailman! Do you think Mum may be experiencing the early stages of

Delete.

Mum tells me you'll be leaving Victoria and heading east again in the next few days. I'm really looking forward to seeing you both at the station for the usual "stopover." I'll alert the Tim Hortons! Would you mind dropping me a line to let me know when your train will be arriving? By the way, did Mum mail a package for me?—speaking of "cliffhangers" ☺ (hey, can you do that?!)

What kind of "reply" is that? She has written two books and she can't even write one lousy e-mail to her father. She is evading his touching e-mail of this morning. No she isn't, she is tired—her eyes skitter side to side again as though to prove the point. She is not a retired management consultant, she does not have time to compose touching e-mails. She will call him on the phone tomorrow and have an actual conversation.

Delete.

. . . unless there is something wrong with her visual cortex. She googles "involuntary rapid sideways eye movement, symptom of stroke?" It takes less than thirty seconds to confirm that she has experienced a series of Transient Ischemic Strokes. It is unlikely they will kill her. They mimic the effects of déjà vu and "a sense of unreality" that is symptomatic of depersonalization, depression and psychosis. Otherwise they are asymptomatic. "Autopsy can confirm the presence of neural scar tissue." If only she could be present at her own autopsy to exclaim, "I knew it!" She decides to keep it to herself: why worry Hil?

For some reason, Mary Rose told Hil she had done laundry tonight, which was untrue but only according to the rules of this universe wherein we recall the past but not the future; she had no reason to lie about laundry. Is there a tear in the amniotic sac between worlds? Memories leaking, mingling . . . she'll make a note of this just as soon as she's put in a load.

She heads upstairs, picks up the children's overflowing hamper and, on the way back down, steps on the hem of her housecoat and nearly pitches headfirst to the bottom. She needs to be more mindful or she'll wind up painting calendars with her mouth. In the basement rec room, she switches on the baby monitor, puts in a load of teensy T-shirts and tiny Y-fronts, and tunes into a rerun of *Law and Order*. Jerry Orbach and Chris Noth barge into a Manhattan boardroom and collar some fat cat—her favourite type of episode. She reclines on the shameless La-Z-Boy couch and relaxes, kind of wishing Hil were here with her, kind of glad she isn't. On the walls, framed show posters and book jackets have been upstaged by laminated crayon renderings of murky flora and fauna and various wheeled objects, along with family photos—including an Olde Tyme portrait of the four of them dressed as outlaws with Daisy in a bonnet.

Chris and Jerry have just stopped at a hot dog stand in midtown Manhattan when the monitor emits the first tinny snufflings that Mary Rose knows will shortly become a full-blown—"Mumma-a-a!" She runs up the stairs. After she has changed Maggie, brought Matthew a glass of water, rewound his unicorn and settled Maggie with yet another bottle, she goes to her bathroom, takes another Advil—four in a day is hardly an overdose—and hauls up her sleeve.

Down the front of her left arm, from pit level to a few inches above her elbow run the scars, one superimposed upon the other, layered—sedimentary scars. Like limestone, they tell a story. The longer scar is the older one, having grown with her from the time she was ten. Her father told her she would be getting bone from the bone bank, and she pictured a metal safety deposit box with a bit of bone in it. "Probably a piece of someone's kneecap," he added with a grin, making it sound quirky and mischievous. She thought of her Halloween skeleton costume and grinned back. The base of the shorter scar widens into a slight depression: site of a post-op infection that she understood to be serious when her mother calmly said, "Tsk-tsk," as she dabbed at the ooze with a sterile Q-tip. This shorter scar dates from the second bone surgery, when she was fourteen. She was her own donor that time.

Mary Rose is O negative, which means she is a universal donor. As such she can donate tissue to any human on the planet, but only someone with her blood type can donate to her. So the second time round, the surgeon harvested bone from her iliac crest—which sounds more important than "hip bone"—thus there is a third scar down there at her "bikini line" that tends to mind its own business unless clipped by the corner of a countertop, at which it kicks up a scintillating sort of pain like a vampire awakened at noon.

The bone grafts were done to repair bone cysts. Unlike other kinds of cysts, which are the presence of unhealthy tissue, bone cysts are an absence: cavities in the bone that fill with a yellowish fluid. Sometimes they contain bone fragments—bits that flake and fall from within, so-called "fallen leaf fractures." If the cysts go untreated, they can invade the growth plate and you end up with one limb shorter than the other—a limb that will just go on breaking. Mary Rose was lucky and she has the scars to prove it.

•

The funeral director speaks good English. He asks the young air force officer if he would like to hold the casket. Duncan reaches out and takes the small white coffin. His commanding officer is present along with the air force nurse. His wife is still in hospital, and in any case, there is no need to put her through this. Afterwards, he drives to the cemetery with the casket on the front passenger seat beside him.

•

Mary Rose does not dwell on her time in hospital—it seldom comes up unless she is required to enter one. The memory, while vivid, is stored in a separate file, such that were she to have a near-death experience, the repeated injuries and surgeries would not be included in the movie of her life that would flash before her eyes—though they might play as a blooper reel. The whole experience exists outside her personal timeline, because it is an anomaly: bone cysts are ahistorical. "Idiopathic, likely a congenital flaw," said the surgeon. "That means you're born with them," said Dad. "It doesn't mean you're an idiot." Bone cysts are a singularity, like a meteor strike: a good story on their own but unlinked to the main narrative. She was past thirty before an old slow penny dropped: the bone from the bone bank hadn't come from some plucky donor's kneecap, as cheerfully shared as a pint of blood. It had been cadaver bone. That may be why the tissue failed to grow with her.

She cannot remember a time before the age of ten when she did not have a "sore arm." It was normal for her, she thought everyone had one. It was an artifact among her and her siblings: "Mary Rose's sore arm." Even Andy-Patrick respected her *sorearm* and would punch the other one. Hot and searing, or cold grey thudding; one kind of pain had more blood and bruise in it, the other more bone. It came and went.

Her first memory of the searing dates from the summer she was four. They had moved from Germany to Canada, and were "down home" on Cape Breton Island in the broad bosom of Dolly's family on the beautiful Bras d'Or lakes. Cabins called bungalows dotted the clearing on a hill above the shore. A brook ran pure and cold through the trees, spanned by a tiny footbridge and lined with moss-cushioned rocks, the ground itself springy with life. It wasn't the Black Forest— you were more apt to meet a fairy than a talking wolf—but it was enchanted in its own way. Down on the shore, dozens of cousins sprinted and leapt from the rickety wharf, the older ones drove the boat, and there was always pop. At night, she counted her mosquito bites and wondered where to sleep. Her sister was housed with the older kids, her mother with her own sisters, and her father had yet to arrive—he would join them when his leave started.

Dolly was beloved in her family but, being both junior and female, reverted in their company to the status more of a younger sister than a mother, with the consequence that, while food was celebrated, luscious and Lebanese—spits turning on the fire, picnic tables groaning, coolers overflowing—Mary Rose at times went to bed hungry. At four, she felt it would be rude to ask for food, it would be like saying, "You haven't fed me," and that would be rude. The men and boys were served first—*sah t'ein!*—and by the time Mary Rose understood that it was suppertime, somehow it was over. It would be all right when Dad arrived. She would sit on his lap and eat from his plate, and at night he would tuck her in, somewhere. In the meantime, she was free to roam, the salt water healed all scrapes and the green world of the woods beckoned.

One afternoon, he arrived. "Dad!" Like a prince, strolling down the winding dirt drive beneath the canopy of pines and birches. Like a movie star, a god. He gave all the kids airplane swings, grasping them by ankle and wrist, all the cousins lining up, "Unca Dunc!" His was the only blond head in a sea of ebony, his the only blue eyes amid lustrous brown, "Swing me, swing me!" Tirelessly he swung them. He swung her round and round and it was tummy-thrilling, until fire broke out inside her arm. Snapped into flame like a twig, it leapt and spread. When he set her down, she held her arm by the elbow. She did not throw up.

"What's wrong, sweetie?"

"Nothing."

"Is it your arm? Let's see. Is it okay?"

She didn't want to hurt his feelings by making him think he had hurt her. "Yes."

"Can you bend it?"

She did not want him to go away and stop playing. She bent it. And asked for another airplane swing because he looked worried. She offered her right wrist this time and, too late, realized her mistake, for while the right arm was fine, the left one swung out; round and round it flew, unable to make its own way back to her side. She waited for the swing to end.

She did not cry.

"Want another one, sweetie?"

"No thanks, that was fun."

Then they went swimming. The cold felt good. Like an injured dog, she hid the pain as though it were to do with shame. But by nightfall she could not conceal her need to support the arm by holding it against her body with the good one and her mother asked what she had been up to. "Nothing."

The Bras d'Or lakes are not lakes at all, but an inland sea where fresh and salt water merge. The name means Arm of Gold.

The next day, her mother fashioned Mary Rose's first sling from a colourful nylon scarf. It stopped hurting after a while and they forgot about it. Until the next sling.

The bone cysts were diagnosed in the nick of time thanks to another miracle. On the frozen waters of Our Lady of Lourdes Catholic School, ten-year-old Mary Rose MacKinnon slipped and fell the first time. It was a fall that would eventually lead to a doctor, a diagnosis and cure. Our Lady made her break her arm.

It was during recess. She was in grade six, a good student, excelling at History, her ostracism now to do with high marks—no one could have suspected she used to be slow. She had one friend in class, a somewhat sinister bookish girl named Jocelyn Fish, but when it came to recess, it was more fun to play with the younger kids. She was among a group taking running slides on a strip of ice beside the yellow brick wall of the school, and was on her third turn when she fell and the burning broke out. It went swiftly from red to black, became V-shaped and loud. It grew bigger than she was, like a monster in a dream, until she was within a kind of enclosure looking out at the throbbing air; with something hard lodged in her arm, something that did not love her, something that did not know who she was or that she was anyone. She leaned against the wall and waited for it to stop. She held it by the wrist. The bell rang.

The arm was heavy, and after recess could not take itself out of her jacket on its own. She looked down at her hand, limp and yoked to the pain farther up. The hand looked worried. It looked rather ashamed too, for feeling fine—like a friend who is with you when you get run over. She sat at her desk but could not concentrate on the Boston Tea Party. When the hand moved, it made the pain wake up and scream, so it kept its head down. The pain would not go away. It made her have to go to the bathroom, pressed against her like a scary mentally retarded kid, getting heavier like a wet coat, getting darker, it gave her no choice but to go to the teacher and say, "I hurt my arm."

The teacher knew her mother was away in Cape Breton visiting family, and she remarked to the new principal that Mary Rose was "just looking for some TLC." Mary Rose did not know what the initials stood for, but smiled and nodded in order to make up for the bad manners of her arm, and the principal sent her home. "Tell your father you pulled a muscle."

Sister O'Halloran might have called the doctor, but she had been transferred to Africa where they needed her more. The muscle refused to heal, despite the massages administered by her father, and by her older sister, Maureen, when he called her in to help, "Maureen, I need you." There was a bit of a lump where the muscle was swollen, he gave it special attention. She stayed very still. This was what a pulled muscle felt like. She did not cry, sissies cry, crying feels like throwing up through your eyes.

"Thanks, Dad, that feels better now."

He did not know how to tie a sling, so he used a length of duct tape to secure her arm to her side. "How's that?"

"Way better." And it was.

When her mother came home, she fashioned one from a nylon scarf—paisley this time—which made it feel even better because Mum, being a nurse, was an expert and Mary Rose got her second sling.

It was still tender a few weeks later when she fell again. It was now Christmas holidays. She tripped on the picks of her new skates—they had appeared under the tree, her first pair of "girl's skates." White, high-heeled and treacherous, figure skates nonetheless spared one the shame of being seen in "boy's skates." They were brand new and she had smiled hard to ward off the pathos occasioned by the thought of how sad her parents would be to see her disappointment. Andy-Patrick got a set of Hot Wheels complete with carrying case.

The "Waltz of the Blue Danube" was playing when she hit the ice face down at Kingston Memorial Arena. She was with a friend of sorts—a nice girl whose parents knew hers via the air force. She nearly threw up when she smacked to her stomach, but as long as you don't cry, nothing will be wrong. Still, the darkness flared in her arm and she knew she had pulled the muscle again. She took the arm out of the sleeve, tucked it inside her fuzzy jacket and went to the friend's home as planned. It was a two-storey house with a family room, in a subdivision on the other side of Kingston. They had a colour TV set.

By bedtime, the pain was cold and metallic like an aircraft wing, but quiet as long as she lay still. She felt very rude the next morning when she failed to eat the Lucky Charms and asked the friend's mother if she could go home. It was inconvenient—the dad had not planned on driving her till after lunch. Mary Rose said, "I forgot, I'm supposed to go home for lunch." She felt the disapproval of the mum and the annoyance of the dad. She could tell they thought she was lying—she was, but she was also at a loss to explain that she was not a liar. It did not occur to her to tell them her arm hurt.

She was not invited back. But she had known she had to go home at all costs. The friend's kitchen was too bright. There were too many echoes, the ceiling was crooked. And the shape in her arm was a black triangle. Her mother was home this time.

But her father resumed first aid duties.

"I think I pulled the muscle again."

She did not move during the massages. *Get mad at it.* Still, it seemed unfair that it should hurt more this time. After a while she said, "It's okay, you can stop massaging now if you're tired."

"I'm not tired, sweetie."

"You can stop now, Dad. It feels better."

Another scarf, another sling. Her third. It did not get better.

"I guess I'll call Dr. Ferry," said her mother.

He came to the house. Mary Rose liked him, he always treated her as if she was a cool kid and it didn't matter if she was a girl or a boy. Dr. Ferry examined her arm and said, "I thought I told you to quit jumping off the roof." She grinned and felt better.

He took her mother aside in the front hall—they often joked together, both being medical types, but this time Mary Rose felt giddy as she heard his tone and caught some of the words, ". . . you telling me she's . . . and you didn't . . . till now? . . . what can happen? . . . what it could be?!" He was scolding her mother. No one did that—except, occasionally, her father, with a smack of his hand on the kitchen table, "That's enough, now, Missus."

An X-ray was ordered and it turned out she had bone cysts; her arm had been special all along, but too modest to boast. Her mother liked to tell the story. "Dr. Ferry really gave me what-for. It turned out her arm was broken all along! But how could we know? She never cried, she never complained!" Mary Rose basked in the account of her own heroism, humbled before the majesty of her "high pain threshold," so chose not to remind her mother that even Andy-Patrick knew about *sorearm.*

"Good news," said Dad. "You're going to have an operation." The miracle was accomplished. *Rise and go forth!*

•

This section of the Canadian military cemetery is reserved for dependants—wives and children—a tranquil corner, closer to the forest, dotted with stones and crosses, none older than the Peace itself. There is no snow, though it's less than a week til Christmas, but the ground is hard and dull; he carries the casket across the welted grass, staring straight ahead—the mass of firs less green than grey, a dense blur.

He stands looking into the small grave. He can see roots, severed white, the earth still a living network for the trees that have been cleared in recent years to make this section of the cemetery. He hands over the casket, and they bury his son.

•

The mirror tells her there is indeed no bruise, just the faint green vein that snakes at right angles beneath the scars and disappears round the back of her arm. Mary Rose has come to see her scars as a guarantee that, should she get amnesia and wander off without her tweezers one distant demented day, she nonetheless, like Odysseus, will be recognized if she makes it back home—unibrow notwithstanding.

She lies in the dark, thinking about Hil thinking about her . . . but her mind keeps wandering. Has her libido fallen temporary victim to motherhood, or is this perimenopausal decline?—the descent into "even more meaningful intimacy," to quote the earnest book that her sister Maureen sent her. *I don't want meaningful intimacy, I want sex.* Or is her inability to concentrate an effect of the cobwebby plaques that even now are colonizing her cortex? Hil reassured her, and it is true: what does it matter precisely where out west she is? Mary Rose's world is a circumscribed domestic one at the moment, a multitasky maelstrom wherein Hil is a mere binary function: here/not here. Still . . . it was an odd mistake. She should google it. No. That really would be demented. To google "early onset Alzheimer's" in the middle of the night with two sleeping children and an asthmatic pit bull. She switches on the light, reaching for a book from the stack on her bedside table—she is a slow reader but always has four or five on the go—is that a sign too? She tries to focus on *Drama of the Gifted Child*, but her eyes rove the page. She ought to call her family doctor in the morning and see about booking a memory test—the kind where they ask you what the date is and who's the prime minister . . . although the latter is something she'd prefer to forget. She trades childhood anguish for *Guide to Healthy Lesbian Relationships* and dozes off.

•

She was discharged from the base hospital this morning.
Her husband opens the door to their apartment and
extends his hand for her to precede him. He is carrying
her bag. She is wearing the moonstone ring to please him.
Her big girl is sitting on the couch in a velvet party dress,
her hair in awkward braids parted crookedly down the
middle. "You look lovely, Maureen."
    "We kept the tree up for you, Mummy."
    She opens her arms and her daughter comes to her.
She tries not to let the child see she is crying.
    "Mummy, are you sad because the baby boy died?"
    "Don't think about that, now," says Duncan.
    "I'm crying because I'm so happy to see you, Mo-Mo."
    She releases the child and stumbles, her husband
steadies her.

"I've been lying down too much." She smiles. She
is thinner, but she's done her hair, and has her lipstick on.
A record is playing on the hi-fi, Nat King Cole. On the
coffee table are the silver tea service and a plate of store-
bought ginger cookies. "Isn't this nice," she says. *She's not
old, she'll have another baby. Maybe even another boy.*

In the corner of the living room by the glass door to
the balcony stands the tree decked with paper chains and,
atop it, a homemade star. On the floor, a scattering of dry
needles encircles the stand. She looks at her husband. He
is pale. No one has been feeding him. "Mumma could
feed an army on one chicken," she says.

He looks at a loss for a moment, then says, "Do you
want to see the baby?"

What is he telling her? She feels sick. It is her badness
coming out in her if she is crazy now, and it serves her
right. Is she awake? *The baby died.*

He is staring at her. *He is going to send me away.* He
turns toward the hallway and calls, "Armgaard."

And with that, she understands what he means by
"baby". She watches as the same German woman, with
her neat bun and capable arms, emerges from the hallway
and sets down a child whose hair, at two, is not long
enough to braid. It is black and thick like Dolly's own.
The child looks at Dolly and smiles. Dolly sees something
in that smile . . . something bad is looking out from those
big dark eyes . . . mocking her. Dolly frowns, already
asking God to remove the thought from her mind—no
wonder she is so bad at having babies, she does not even
deserve the one she has. The child hides its face in the
German woman's apron.

"Geh zu Mutty," says the woman with a little push.

"Nein!" yells the child.

Her husband laughs and swings the baby up into his arms. "Go ahead, Mister, give Mummy a kiss." She clings to him, screaming, as he tilts her toward her mother. "She missed you," he says.

But Dolly knows the truth. Her baby still doesn't like her.

•

She wakes an hour or so later with an old clammy feeling: guilt—as though she had killed someone or molested a child and it slipped her mind. A brew of shame and pathos, it feels like a car crash in her stomach . . . dead father at the wheel, head flung back, mother's face obscured, pregnant belly buckled against the dash, innocent family belongings pitifully strewn, exposed. The feeling used to greet her regularly upon waking, her own brand of morning sickness. She gets out of bed to pee—and a good thing too, because she is bleeding again. She rifles the drawer for a super jumbo tampon—so stout is it, one hardly knows whether to insert it or strap it on. She is suddenly roasting hot. Downstairs, she makes her way across the darkened living room, gouges her bare foot on a piece of Lego, knocks over Tickle Me Elmo who busts out singing, and turns the furnace off. It ceases with a sigh. In the kitchen, she gets out a box of ancient grains that failed to prevent the extinction of an entire people, and opens her *Cooks Illustrated* . . . "Rethinking Macaroni and Cheese" . . .

Andy-Pat gave her a fridge magnet of a dead clown with *X*s for eyes that says, "Can't sleep, clowns will eat me." She gave him one of a haggard cartoon train slouched over a beer at a bar, "The little engine that didn't give a rat's ass." Just because there are no dents in Andy-Patrick's fridge does not mean he is less dysfunctional than she is—and just because he once got the belt does not mean Dad was worse than Mum.

True, Mum was often funny. She tumbled backward off reclining chairs, did bellyflops from the wharf when the rest of the womenfolk were beached in stretch pants on the shore; committed whopping faux pas and was always the first to laugh at herself. But her rage was not funny. Unvariegated with humour. Unmarbled with the fat of mirth. "C'mere till I smash you!"

Besides, Mary Rose was merely following orders: her father always said, "Get mad at it." Whether a math problem, hurt feelings or parallel parking. It worked for a long time.

Her mother always said, "Do your best. Then do better than your best." The immigrant credo.

She threw the stroller at the fridge because she couldn't find her yoga mat. Then she phoned Hil in the middle of rehearsal to ask where it was. Hil said, "It's probably right in front of you." And it was. It's their joke now. Whenever she can't find something, that is usually where it is.

Journey To Otherwhere

Kitty McRae had always played well alone. Not that she was disruptive or unpleasant to play *with*, it was just that since her mother's death, when Kitty was still a baby, she had had to learn to amuse herself. She had never been much for toys, especially dolls—there had been one long ago, but she grew out of it and never missed it. Kitty McRae did not need toys because she had something infinitely better. She had her father.

And he had a very important job that required him to be on the move at a moment's notice. Kitty had grown up travelling with him to the ends of the earth. There were many wonderful things about Dean McRae, but one of them was something people might not notice from the out-side: he always made his daughter feel as though she were absolutely necessary.

Eleven is a powerful age. Kitty had mastered the log-arithms that allowed her father to track winds and weather patterns; alerted him to shifts in the earth's crust and the formation of tsunamis long before they swept ashore with obliterating force; enabled him to predict the path of fires and floods. She had seen many futures on his laptop, sce-narios that played out over a millennium, merely by adjust-ing one of a multitude of factors—the level of plankton in the St. Lawrence River, a drop in the population of midges in the Great Rift Valley—watching as deserts swept conti-nents, and jungles squeezed whole cities in their coils. But there was nothing "virtual" about the helicopters in which she had flown, palms pressed to the glass, grazing houses submerged to their rooftops or rendered skeletal with flames; over land-slid highways, buckled bridges. And each time, the fires subsided, the waters retreated and, step by step, life went back to normal. Her father had even credited her as a research assistant on his latest submission to the *Journal of Geo-Engineering*. "Do it your way, Kit-Kat"—whether it was a math problem or an ice cream sundae. Dean McRae was a Disaster Relief Expert, and Kitty couldn't think of anything she would rather be when she grew up.

Now that she was almost grown up, Kitty could see the situation clearly: her father, being the kindest of people, had always made her feel necessary even when she must so often have been in the way. This gave her a mighty, not entirely comfortable feeling in her chest, as though her heart were hot and outsized. She identified this as a surplus of love, a form of energy that could be harnessed. She was eleven. She was in her prime, ready now to be really useful.

"Kitty," he had said, "would you mind coming with me into the study, I'd like to have a word."

The study was her favourite room in the world. In contrast to the hi-tech tools of her father's trade, this room contained objects that were powered entirely by history. There were gyroscopes and sextants that dated back to Columbus, and lethal-looking mathematical instruments that had belonged to her grandfather. On the wall over the desk hung an antique map. According to the cartographer of the time, the world consisted of a thin strip of Europe, a dollop of Africa, a blob of Asia and a sinister rind of *Terra Incognita*. At opposite corners, puff-cheeked Zephyrs blew the winds across the globe, while a tentacled sea monster bobbed amid the waves and fire-breathing dragons lurked at the uncharted edges. Presiding over it all was a big roll-top desk complete with pigeonholes that resembled a nesting wall for ocean birds, each harbouring a treasure: the tooth of an ichthyosaurus, a two-thousand-year-old lotus seed that her father meant to plant one of these days, a sixty-five-million-year-old whorl in stone called an ammonite, a vial of volcanic ash from the latest eruption in Iceland . . . The desk top was perpetually awash in papers, for her father said he still thought best with a pen in his hand.

On the one clear corner of her father's desk stood a photograph in an oval frame. It was the only picture they had of Kitty's mother, and for Kitty it was the sole image, for she had no memory of her mother's face. Asha Singh. So pretty, so lively looking; if it were a yearbook photo, the caption would be, *Least likely to die young*. There was something wistful in her mother's smile. It almost seemed to say, *I'm sorry*.

Kitty was good at math but, try as she might, could not keep straight just how old she had been when her mother died. She did not like to ask her father because it caused him pain . . . he seemed to shrink and Kitty could almost see the energy departing from him. She feared that every time she brought up the subject of her mother, he lost a little more of whatever it is that keeps a person alive. And she could not shake an uncomfortable feeling that it was up to her to keep him alive. Why had she not simply written the information down when she had the chance? Worse than embarrassing, it was weird, for who in their right mind forgets when their own mother died? She had asked Ravi, but he too seemed uncertain. He said, "That is a question for your father, Kitty."

Ravi had spoken only Hindi and was barely more than a child himself when Dean McRae hired him off the street in Lucknow and sponsored him. Ravi was now more

Canadian than Sir John A. Macdonald, a fan of the deep Montreal winters, alchemist of spices with which he seared away Kitty's coughs and colds. In the early days he would oil her hair and braid it, and while she put a stop to that when she turned nine, to this day it was thanks to him that, while Kitty refused to be seen in a dress, she did consent to wear a sari at Christmas. His strong, lined hands, the colour of smooth wood, were synonymous with safety, and next to her father, Kitty loved Ravi most in the world.

Over the fireplace hung a gilt-framed round mirror like a big eye, which reflected the whole room as though through the wrong end of a telescope. It had been salvaged from the wreck of her great-great-grandfather's ship and was speckled with age where the mercury had begun to eat through. Kitty did not like to look in it because it made her eyes go funny, as though flakes of silver were drifting down the glass like snow in a paperweight. It was a symptom of the "atypical idiopathic migraines" the doctor said were behind her "spells." They didn't hurt, which was why they were not "typical." And "idiopathic" did not mean she was an idiot, "It just means you were born with them," said her father. Kitty did not think much of the diagnosis—it was a grown-up-sounding name for something grown-ups did not understand. She stole a look at herself now, however, small and distant where she stood on the carpet, ready to receive her "marching orders."

This room and everything in it would be hers one day, but the carpet already was. It had been woven for her by a Bedouin elder in gratitude to her father for putting out a fire that had raged for months, fed by a sea of oil beneath the desert. Every handwoven carpet is special, but this one had a band of scarlet snaking through in the shape of her initial: *K*.

Their adventures always started in the same way, with Kitty standing at attention on the carpet and her father relaxed in the leather armchair. So it was with a pleasant tingle of anticipation that she saw him settle into it. And a modicum of surprise when he said, "Have a seat, Kitty."

She hesitated, then sat down cross-legged on the carpet, brushing a thatch of hair from her eyes. Her hair might be described as the physical manifestation of her brain's energy field: growing in all directions, fractal and increasing in complexity every day—why bother brushing it? "That's your story and you're sticking to it," Ravi always said. He had given up trying to make her brush her hair, but he did insist upon teeth and she could see his point. Ravi had looked after her as long as she could remember, and it was thanks to him that she could speak a little and understand a lot of her mother's first language. She enjoyed the response she got when she introduced him as "my manny"; and of late there had been plenty of opportunity, for a parade of girls her age had been produced as though via some marketing magic by her "Aunt" Fiona. A partner at the public relations firm Tullimore-Spinx, Fiona Tullimore wasn't really Kitty's aunt but her father's girlfriend, and it was in both capacities that the wonderful woman brimmed with plans to "improve" Kitty's life. But Kitty's life was already perfect. She had her father, she had Ravi, and she had her secret.

"What's up, Dad?"

"How are you feeling today, Kit-Kat?"

"Great."

He hesitated, as if he didn't know whether to believe her, before saying, "Good."

"Don't worry, Dad," she reassured him.

He had taken her to a specialist for her spells, though Kitty had tried to tell him there was nothing to worry about. She liked Dr. Quinn, he gave her tests but not like the ones in school. The only thing that frightened Kitty was the hospital smell. It made her stomach chilly and put her skin on alert, as though at any moment someone might stick a needle into her or worse. But it was worth the smell and even the wasted worry on her father's part just to have slid bodily into the big clanking tube that took pictures of her brain, layer after layer. She got to see them afterwards, on the doctor's computer, blue maps and shadowy shapes . . .

"Where are we going this time?" she asked her father.

"Kitty, there is a trip in the offing, but I'm afraid I can't accompany you on it."

For one queasy moment, Kitty feared he was about to tell her that she was going to have to return to the Hospital for Sick Children for an operation . . . what if there really was something wrong with her brain? What if they had to cut open her head? The next instant, he interrupted what she thought was her worst nightmare, only to surpass it with one that involved no scalpels but nonetheless entailed a severing that she feared she could not survive.

He was sending her away.

TUESDAY

If a Leaf Falls in a Fracture, Does Anyone Hear?

S he has just returned with Maggie from a harrowing parents-and-
tots swim class in the tepid pool at the community centre. The
pallid dads and moms all bobbed about, clutching their eighteen-to-
twenty-four-month-olds in controlled chaos under the eye of a teen-
aged instructor wearing nose plugs. Those parents with a hint of
colour in their heritage looked especially unhealthy, any pigment-
imparted gloss dulled by chlourescence—the Libyan dad got the
worst of it. They all sang "Wheels on the Bus" and swam the gaunt-
let of "London Bridge," chest hair streaming, arm flab jiggling and,
in Mary Rose's case, middle-aged sinews straining, while the tiny
future-adults screamed or rejoiced according to their allotment of
nature-nurture. Finally, the red plastic slide was produced that really
separated the stamp collectors from the venture capitalists. Maggie

dutifully waited her turn then clambered up the two steps—itself a risk-barnacled undertaking for any toddler—as Mary Rose slipped back into the water, poised to catch her. "Okay, Maggie!" And instead of going down on her bottom, Maggie dove straight at Mary Rose's head. They went to the bottom butt-first, Mary Rose hanging on to Maggie and scrabbling for purchase on the slippery tiles. They finally shot to the surface with a sputtering laugh from Maggie, a heart-barfing gasp from Mary Rose and the stunned looks of the other parents.

"Maggie, you must go down on your bum next time."

"Okay."

She climbed the slide and did it again.

It is now 9:30 a.m. on that most innocuous of weekdays, Tuesday, and Mary Rose is safe in her kitchen. Her skin smells like chlorine and she has a bad case of hat-hair, but she is basking in *gemütlichkeit*—that untranslatable but universally recognized sense of well-being. The one that arises when you've cleared your inbox or survived a plane crash. Maggie is on the floor rearranging the Tupperware cupboard—it isn't really Tupperware and Mary Rose will have to replace it all with BPA-free stuff anyhow. Perhaps she oughtn't to allow Maggie to play with it, but she isn't putting it in her mouth, so . . . Daisy appears and goes to her bowl where she hoovers a late breakfast with a series of grunts—the pooch is keeping dowager hours these days.

Mary Rose leans against her soapstone counter in front of her big kitchen windows and reads the *Toronto Star*—in the food section is an article about an ordinary woman who makes her own ricotta . . . and runs a corporation. Tuesday is Candace's morning, she'll be here soon—Mary Rose ought to get down on the floor and play with Maggie before she arrives. She closes the newspaper and in glancing up her eye is caught by a woman standing on the corner. She has a toddler by the hand and a baby in a stroller weighed down with grocery bags. She is trying to cross the street, but her toddler refuses.

He sits. He cries. The mother waits—she is doing the right thing. The hard thing. Mary Rose has been there.

Recently she read in the paper about a woman who killed herself and her husband, and tried to kill their three young children. This happened a ten-minute walk away, on Harmony Street. The article mentioned a dog "found wandering at the scene."

She looks at Daisy, out cold now in front of the sliding door to the deck, legs twitching—chasing a dream squirrel.

The article quoted a neighbour saying she saw the woman, "a nice, quiet young woman, they were a nice couple," walking down the street from the Loblaws store, pushing her baby in the stroller, laden with grocery bags, her toddler and six-year-old in tow. "She had a blank look on her face." Mary Rose recalls something her friend Andrea said— Andrea is a midwife, the one who "caught" Maggie. In the flush of that first hour when bliss had kicked in full force and they were still hugging and weeping and laughing, Andrea turned to Hilary. "I'm going to say to you what I say to every mother post-partum: three months from now when you want to throw that baby out the window, call me."

What if someone had come up to the nice young woman from Harmony Street and said, "Can I help you with those bags?" Or was she already too far gone?

The children survived. The dog probably had something to do with that.

The mother tried to cut their throats.

It occurs to Mary Rose to go out there and help that woman; maybe she isn't patient, maybe she is depressed. Maybe she is going to go home and murder those children, and it will be Mary Rose's fault— she hears a rattling behind her. Maggie is shaking something in a plastic container . . . a penny! Hil was sorting pocket change before she left and dropped some on the kitchen floor. She swore she had picked it all up and now Maggie has it in her hand, halfway to her mouth, poised to choke on it.

"Here, luvvie, give the penny to Mumma."

"No." She closes her fist over it. "Mine."

Mary Rose pries open the little hand and Maggie bops her in the face with the container.

Mary Rose rips the container from Maggie's hand and hurls it down the hall, regretting the action even before the thing bounces harmlessly off the front door. The child screams as though she has just witnessed the evisceration of a pet rabbit.

"It's okay, sweetheart, Mumma didn't break it."

She retrieves the container and returns it to Maggie, who promptly hurls it back down the hall. So much for the teachable moment. Hil is a worse mother for leaving pennies on the floor. Mary Rose lies down suddenly, pretending to be asleep, and lets Maggie wake her up over and over again. Soon the big brown eyes are wet with laughter and Mary Rose catches the child as she flings herself repeatedly at Mumma—the closest thing to a hug Maggie will consent to from her.

The back door opens, Daisy *mwuffs* and Candace walks up the four steps to the kitchen, already pushing up the sleeves of her skin-tight, long-sleeved T and exuding the air of cheerful authority that owes less perhaps to her training as a professional nanny than to her years as a Manchester barmaid. Daisy's back-end fishtails in greeting, Maggie deserts her and runs to hug "Candies!" She watches as Maggie buries herself in Candace's ample embrace and reflects that if she spent only hours a week with her child, perhaps Maggie would love her too—then catches herself; after all, she *wants* Maggie to love Candace. Mary Rose is just jealous—though whether of Candace or of Maggie, it is hard to say.

Candace addresses her charge in forthright full sentences. "Hello, Maggie, how are you today?"

Maggie responds in kind. "I fine, Candies, I will go to the park with you."

Mary Rose follows suit. "Maggie, what would you like to do at the park?"

"No."

Mary Rose laughs in order to show Candace how easygoing she is, then takes charge. "By the way, Candace, we're going to try phasing out Maggie's morning nap."

"Oh, I thought we'd already done with that, I've been keeping her up my mornings, sorry, did you want me to put her down now?"

"No, no, yeah, we've done with it, I just didn't know if I'd mentioned it. Great, thanks."

Maggie sobs hysterically when her mother goes out the door. Mary Rose tells herself it is a sign of healthy attachment.

Behind her, she hears Candace say, "Here now, Maggie Muggins, what's got your knickers in a twist?"

•

After Christmas, her mother dies. She does not go home
to Canada for the funeral. She has no baby but she still has
a little one. She hears it crying. Is it big enough to climb
from its crib? She lies down on the couch. The light on the
balcony stays the same for a long time. She hears her
two-year-old crying. Feels it clawing her hair.

•

Twelve minutes later, Mary Rose is locking her bike out front of Mount Sinai Hospital downtown on University Avenue, a six-laned wind tunnel lined with medical centres and insurance towers, when her brother phones and says, "I need you to come look at my butt." He is at the Roots store in the Eaton Centre a couple of blocks away on Yonge Street.

"I'd love to, but I'm about to get a sonohystogram." He doesn't ask what that is.

By 10:45 a.m. she is on the table in the examination room, feet in the stirrups. The gynecologist, Dr. Goldfinger—he can't help it, he was born with the name—removes the "wand" and hands it to the nurse. It has a camera at the tip and is wearing a condom. Mary Rose was assured she would be getting a female gynecologist but has wound up not caring because Dr. Goldfinger is over sixty and very good at his job. And it isn't as if female Dr. Irons—another birth defect—had the lightest touch with the speculum when she diagnosed the "benign fibroids" that have been shredding the lining of Mary Rose's uterus.

She was given a choice: tough it out till after menopause, when the estrogen-guzzling fibroids will waste away on their own; or have a new procedure wherein the surgeon will cut off the blood supply to her uterus, thereby inducing an infarction, then implant her with a morphine pump for a few days—in other words, her uterus will have a heart attack and die and it will hurt like hell. Or she can have a hysterectomy. Her mother had a hysterectomy back when they lived in Kingston. It was after her second miscarriage—third?—and the doctor pretty much ordered it, but Dolly asked the priest for permission first. Afterwards, she started taking what she called her "nice mother pills." Sometimes she would forget.

Mary Rose's uterus is one organ she has always preferred to forget she has, and this she managed pretty well, its monthly Calvarys notwithstanding, but she cannot bring herself to mount an all-out assault on it. "A poor thing, Sir, but mine own." Her journey through the gynecological-industrial complex has taught her that the "perimenopausal" uterus is seen the way the appendix used to be: as a disease magnet that ought to be removed at the first peep. But who really knows? While it is too late for her tonsils, Mary Rose does still have her appendix, that vestigial organ of digestion, and thus is among those who stand to survive should the species be reduced to eating bark for survival post–climate change. It is like the section found at the end of some books: *Appendix*. Stuff which isn't necessary now but might be vital later. It is difficult, however, to imagine the other organ doubling as a literary term: *Uterus.*

Mo said, "They'll try to tell you it's useless, but it isn't. It's doing something, hang on to it." So she toughed it out until six months ago when she overheard a conversation through the fug of the change room at the pool: "Try soy milk, it's loaded with phytoestrogens and it's better than taking pregnant horse piss, which is what Premarin is." It took a moment for the meaning to congeal, but when it did, she froze. In an attempt to be virtuously vegetarian, Mary Rose had, for the previous year, been replacing everything with soy. Soy milk, soy burgers, soy bacon—there is nothing that cannot be textured into soy, the great shape-shifter. Like syphilis, it disguises itself, the Zelig of the food world. She had always suspected there was something spooky about soy. Now she realized she had been feeding the fibroids all along. She went straight home from the pool and flushed her entire soy stash like a drug dealer a step ahead of the cops.

She turns her head to watch Dr. Goldfinger as he peers at the pulsating field of grey on his computer screen that is a window unto her womb. She strains to spot them amid the murk—they are only fibroids, but are they getting better or worse? A nurse swishes in, whisks the condom off the camera and swishes out again. It is probably safe to take her feet from the stirrups now—bare steel, unlike the ones in her family physician's office, thoughtfully covered with oven mitts. She searches Dr. Goldfinger's face for a sign of the verdict. In a previous era he would be wearing a waistcoat and cravat and treating her for "hysterical pregnancy"—it's what got Charlotte Brontë. A second nurse swishes in for no apparent reason, and swishes back out. Mary Rose knows how lucky she is: not only does she not live next to a graveyard in Yorkshire, she has merely had to endure month-long periods with their attendant child-birth-calibre contractions, referred to as "cramps" by the uninitiated, along with "heavy days" wherein she has been delivered of miscarriage-sized clots of uterine tissue. They dropped from her body into the toilet with the *plop* of a hearty soup—evidence of a transitioning female reproductive system that will not go down without a gorey fight. It all flies in the face of the lithe androgyny she has cultivated her entire life.

She didn't tell Hil what her doctor's appointment was about, no need to get all menopausy with your girlfriend. Partner. Wife. Whatever. Why isn't there a better word? Apart from the flagrant *lover*, sexless *partner*, and dowdy *spouse* . . . She dislikes most of the words associated with femaleness. She can barely say the word *period* unless referring to a BBC miniseries. They are icky words, embarrassing to say. Or else inadequate: *Vagina*—as if that told the whole story. *Lesbian*: lizardy. *Menopause*: a bilious woman sitting next to you on the bus to Brockville. Oddly, *uterus* is okay, resembling, as it does, an order of nuns.

"They're shrinking," says Dr. Goldfinger. He smiles briefly, and leaves the room.

Yes! She could fist-pump for joy, but that would be too American.

Nurse number one swishes in again and passes her a massive sterile wipe for the lubricant, and as she is mopping up, the second nurse returns and the two of them, smiling shyly, produce copies of *JonKitty McRae: Journey to Otherwhere* and *JonKitty McRae: Escape from Otherwhere* along with a pen.

She writes:

*Best wishes,
M (Lister) R MacKinnon
Room UL 230B, Medical Imaging Wing
Mt Sinai Hospital
"Smile, you're on Candid Camera!"*

Then she puts on her pants.

"When's the third one coming out?"

•

She thinks it may still be winter, but it is difficult to tell because even if she were to sit up, from her vantage point on the couch, the balcony door affords a view only of treetops and sky—the Black Forest is thick with ever-greens so, unless there is snow, she cannot be sure. It occurs to her to pin a calendar to the wall so that she will be reminded, without getting up, what season it is. She is lying on her side on the couch, one hand beneath her cheek, the other extended, palm up. The moonstone is on this hand, and her baby is dead. She wants to phone her mother long distance and tell her, "Mumma, I lost the boy." Then she remembers, her mother is dead.

She has let the German go. There is no need for help, she just has the one child at home during the day.

It is standing on the other side of the coffee table, in diaper and undershirt, howling. Rigid. On its cheeks, taut drops look to have burst straight from its face. Dolly closes her eyes. As long as she stays lying down, nothing bad will happen.

•

Mary Rose leaves Room UL230B and is immediately lost. Did she come up the orange elevators or were they yellow? She peers down a corridor, at the end of which stands a set of double doors, marked PROCEDURE ROOM. She sets out in the opposite direction, wishing she had thought to bring a sack of breadcrumbs, trying not to breathe too deeply. Perfectly clean words become queasy when used in a medical context: *proce-dure* . . . the euphemism taking on a quality it was calculated to conceal. She is not a fan of hospitals, but is grateful for the absence in this wing of the smell of disinfectant and rubbing alcohol; surgical smells that reawaken dread, make her shiver, and bring ghost-story tears to her eyes. The smell of piercing . . . She reminds herself that in fact the worst smell is that of hospital food; truly the bread—and applesauce and mushy peas—of sorrow. She has never understood why anyone would wish to make a career in a hospital. Her own mother was a Registered Nurse; an O.R. nurse to boot, having had no fear of blood.

She passes Mammography—at least she is to be spared the panini press today. She turns the corner, BONE DENSITY CLINIC. Is that what is behind the capricious pain in her arm? Is it perhaps not phantom at all, but a symptom of osteoporosis? More of "the riches of menopause"? Nothing showed up on the X-ray. Still, that was six months ago . . .

She feels like Detective Columbo from the old seventies TV series. Rumpled, blind in one eye and with a shambling gait, he was master of the false exit: just when the suspect thought the bumbling detective was leaving empty-handed, Columbo would pause in the doorway, then turn and say, "You know, somethin's been botherin' me at the back of my mind . . ." And nail the perpetrator.

She spots an emergency exit with a stairway symbol and a warning, ALARM WILL SOUND IF OPENED. She opens it.

•

A different sound now. Ragged, moaning protest. No longer crying. Hot breath against her face. Smell of wet cotton, urine. The word, a dry entreaty, "Mummy." Repeated. Gathering fresh urgency—rooted in a new source, a scorched place. She feels the small hand alight on her face, hot. There is the word again, accelerating, metal on metal, the word is going to catch fire, *Mummy!* Fingers probe her eyelid, push it open. The hand travels to her scalp and a fistful of her hair is pulled taut, her head yanked, the child is shaking her. She keeps her eyes closed. It takes all her strength, but she manages finally to roll over and face the back of the couch. After a while the blows to her back and shoulders cease. The child is incapable of actually hurting her, it is only two years old.

•

In all the years since her last bone surgery at fourteen, apart from the odd histrionic bump, Mary Rose has never felt a peep out of her arm until recently. It soldiered on through a summer in the militia, through the rigours of theatre school, through countless drunken escapades and bouts of contact-improv, through two babies. Until last summer.

It was the first summer without Hil's mum. Patricia had died of complications following minor surgery the previous fall. She was a beautiful woman with crystal blue eyes and a gracious manner—a woman who referred playfully to her husband as "the Doctor" but spoke reverently of their respective "realms"—hers having been at home with the children. Hil was grief-stricken, naturally . . . although at the funeral reception, Mary Rose had been shocked to hear her state bitterly to a childhood friend, "My mother died of a bad back."

They had come to the end of their exhausting summer holiday on the East Coast. Maggie was about to turn two and Matthew had suddenly gone into reverse, demanding diapers of his own. The shore was gentle, but a child can drown in an inch of water and the woods were full of bears and Lyme disease—

"No they're not, Mister, not 'full.'"

"*Ixodes scapularis* has been migrating north, it just takes one tick."

Moreover, the children might wander into the forest and die of exposure. "How?" asked Hilary, who had somehow managed to read an entire novel over the course of two harrowing weeks. They closed up the old hunting cabin and loaded the car while supervising their toddlers—perhaps her mother was right, Mary Rose was just too old for this game. Finally they were ready to head into Halifax for a last overnight with Hil's dad and younger sister. Mary Rose went upstairs to lie down on the couch in her father-in-law's den before supper and could not get up again for sixteen hours.

Everyone thought she was tired, but Mary Rose knew she was gone. She had dropped below some line. It was like the diagram in her high school science textbook of the earth's crust in cross-section. Some distance down was the "water table." She had slipped below the water table. Immobilized. Unable to blink, to sleep, she saw herself laid out and suspended in the ground. At some point she heard the family singing "Happy Birthday" downstairs, and remembered: today was Maggie's second birthday.

Where was the switch? She had not known it was possible one day to lie down and never get up. Was this "hysterical paralysis"? Even if she did get up this time, it would remain possible in the future to be struck still. She had gone there now, there was an event trail carved out. A pathway.

Where was the switch? Daisy came in and face-butted her, mushy wet. Hilary plied her with juice. Hil's father looked in on her. White-haired and tall, he was both the image of a 1960s television doctor, and a real one—"realish," he liked to say. A psychiatrist. He pulled up a chair and gently inquired if she was "on something." She almost answered, "The couch." "No," she said, "I'm just tired." He nodded, then asked if she wanted "something." Would he have slipped her a Valium on the spot? Hil's mother had indeed had a bad back. There is a glass of wine, then there is a glass of wine with Percocet . . .

"That's so kind, Alisdair," replied Mary Rose, "but I feel better now."

She loved her father-in-law, but was grateful not to have been the beneficiary of his modern methods back in the day. She wondered if he had ever administered shock therapy. At least he and Hil's mother had never waged a campaign to turn their daughter "straight." She packed up her hysterical parenthesis and put it behind her.

They got on with the trek west, stopping over in Ottawa as usual, where her parents lived in easy-listening air-conditioned comfort in a condo development called Corrigan's Keep for reasons as obscure as those behind the various Vales, Heights, Castle Views and Downs that surround every North American city. The pain ambushed her on the second night in the basement guest suite. She woke up, surprised. The numbers on the clock glowed red: 2:00. She rose carefully so as not to disturb Hil—the mattress was like Gyproc on springs. Hil said it merely needed a layer of memory foam. Didn't we all? She crept between Maggie in the Pack 'n Play and Matthew on the folding IKEA chair-bed.

She slipped into the bathroom and switched on the light. The mirror leapt into surgical view and there she was, crazy hair, sheet-wrinkled cheek. On her arm, the scars, the vein, no bruise.

Mary Rose was accustomed to the thousand cuts that maternal flesh is heir to. She had nicks on her fingers that took months to heal because she was always rinsing something at the sink; discovered bumps on her head while washing her hair, bruises on her legs while shaving, all in a day's work—who has time to feel the bite of a coffee table on the shin when they're breaking a toddler's fall? It was unsatisfying, however, to endure pain without a mark to show for it.

The pain dogged her all the way home to Toronto and persisted into the fall. She was about to google it when Hil caught her and laid down the law, "Call Dr. Judy." So Mary Rose dutifully made an appointment with the family physician. Then, as though the very act of seeking bona fide medical attention had dislodged a suspicion, something began "bothering her at the back of her mind . . ."

Old memories took on fresh meaning. She recalled Dr. Ferry scolding her mother out in the front hall when she was ten and on her third sling, "*. . . you know what can happen?. . . what it could be?!*" She heard again her mother telling and retelling it as though it were a funny story—"*He really gave me what-for!*"—a sure sign, even then, that something was amiss. She saw once more her father's sealed profile as he walked her down the halls of Radiology, replayed his jaunty tone, "They're going to snap pictures of your entire skeleton just to make sure there's no holes anywhere else," and it dawned on her now: he had been terrified.

Four years after the first operation, she stood with her parents in the surgeon's consulting room, and saw something else in her mother's face when the doctor said, "They've come back."

They were living in Ottawa by then, but had driven the two hours to Kingston General Hospital for her twice-yearly checkup—they always went for pizza afterwards and it was nice having her parents to herself. Big Dr. Sorokin stood before the X-ray that was mounted in the light box and tapped with his pencil at the fresh shadows in her humerus. "Here, here and here."

Her father nodded and compressed his lips. Mary Rose and her mother, in rare emotional unison, turned to face the window—across the way stood the hospital smokestack, drab bricks against the November sky. She saw tears in her mother's eyes and was shocked to find herself on the verge too, explaining it away inwardly with fourteen-year-old detachment, "I'm not crying, but my body is because it remembers the pain."

She could not recall ever having seen her mother cry. This was sobering in itself, but there was something else in her mother's face as she stared out the window. Something grave. Something dignified. Grief.

There was a silver lining to the surgeries: they were the best times with her mother. Dolly was in her element on a hospital ward, the only person who made Mary Rose feel safe—her face, her voice, made even the pain fresh and sane. Especially the last time when, at fourteen, Mary Rose knew enough to worry the surgeon might make a mistake.

"It's the left arm, the one with the scar already," she told them as they shifted her from the gurney to the operating table. They appeared not to have heard. They were wearing masks. A big light was suspended over her. Everything was clattery and steel, the doctor's forearms were hairy but his hands were chalky white. She could not move, but she could talk. They had given her a needle out in the hallway where she'd been parked among the other gurneys like aircraft lined up on the tarmac. A nurse had come along and jabbed it into her thigh without warning. The drug splintered painfully into her bloodstream. Mary Rose asked, "What is that?" "It'll calm you down," answered the nurse. She had already been calm, but now she became anxious as her limbs filled up with wet concrete. Time blinked and blanked and jumped, then it was her turn to take off. They wheeled her into the O.R. under the interrogation lights and slipped the point of a finer needle into the back of her hand—its syringe-body rested against her skin like a patient insect. Before the anaesthetic doused her with black, she said, "Don't cut it off." She may have heard a laugh.

She had also known enough to realize she might not wake up. "That's a virtual impossibility," her father had reassured her with his incredulous chuckle. At fourteen, however, Mary Rose did not like the "virtual."

As she lay recovering, Dolly would breeze in, all Broadway in her leopard print tam and matching coat. Everyone else, even her father, made Mary Rose very tired. She would smile and make it okay, but Mum would sweep in, call the nurses by name and get fresh sheets under her. Dolly found the bedsores forming on Mary Rose's heels and elbows and got her to sit up. "That's it, now rotate your feet around your ankles, open and close your fists, that's right, keep moving." It was possible to get gangrene from lying still. Dolly got her to breathe deeply so she wouldn't get pneumonia. "That's it, take a big drink of air. Now let it all out again." It was possible to die of lying down.

The nurses loved Dolly, she was one of them, and they were nicer to Mary Rose as a result. Except for the night nurse, who hadn't met her mother.

Last fall when the pain in her arm failed to go away, the thing that was bothering her at the back of her mind came to the fore: she began to wonder if her parents had known something about her arm that they had never told her. What if they had not been *benign* pediatric bone cysts? What if she had actually had pediatric bone cancer and her parents kept it from her because everything had turned out fine? She needed to know, because what if it recurred? She needed to know, because . . . it was her story, and if it was being held hostage by her parents, she had to get it back. So no sooner had she made the appointment with Dr. Judy, than she redialled and asked the receptionist to requisition her medical records from Kingston General Hospital, where she had undergone both bone grafts.

It was a Tuesday morning, just like today, a child-care morning early last fall, when she sat in Dr. Judy Farber's examination room, averting her gaze from anything too clinical such as swabs and hypodermics, focusing on the cheery oven mitts bedecking the stirrups. Still, her stomach went cold as she watched Judy open the large brown envelope and scan the few photocopied pages before reading aloud, "'Benign pediatric bone cysts.'"

"That's all?"

"What were you expecting?"

"Cancer?"

Hypochondriac. Think of all the people with actual cancer, meanwhile here she was sniffing about for tumours like a toxic truffle pig.

"Definitely not."

This was, of course, good news and she tucked her tail neatly between her legs and rose to depart Judy's office, conscious of her debt to that mythical beast, "the taxpayer," who had funded her flight of fancy, chastening herself for overdramatizing like the flaky artist-type she was. Wanting her special arm to be that much more special.

"Wait, what about the pain?"

"Oh yeah, I forgot," said Mary Rose.

"That's why you're here."

Judy had her remove her top, and palpated the arm, the bone . . . a creepy feeling but not exactly painful.

"Can they come back?"

"Of course not."

"Good." Nothing is more reassuring than having your fears scoffed at by a physician.

But Judy added, "Why am I saying that? I actually don't know for sure. If you're worried I can refer you to an orthopaedic surgeon."

"Are *you* worried?"

"No. But I err on the side of caution."

Dr. Judy referred her to a specialist, and one balmy October morning a few Tuesdays later, she left Maggie with Candace and headed off on her bike. This time she cycled down through rapidly gentrifying Kensington Market to Toronto Western Hospital on Bathurst Street across from Balloon King, where jaunty skeletons cavorted with witches and pumpkins in the window. She locked her bike outside Emergency and removed her jacket. "Unseasonably warm." When would we dispense with denial? As though Earth were merely having a bad hair day.

She waited in Radiology, but she had brought a book, *The Brain That Changes Itself*, and naturally her arm felt perfectly fine.

She lay on the slab for the X-ray. The technician asked, "Is there any possibility that you are pregnant?"

You've got to be kidding. But she said, politely, "No."

She had to admit she was pleased, in the way a thirty-year-old is pleased to be carded at a bar. He entered the glassed-in nuke-booth in the corner, then re-emerged instantly. All done. There was no *cashunk* sound as in the olden days.

The technician, a lugubrious former East Bloc citizen—no doubt a brain surgeon barred from practising in Canada due to bureaucracy—seemed to have forgotten she was there. She felt sheepish; there was nothing wrong with her. *Paging Dr. Freud!*

She waited for the *komrad* to hand her the X-ray so she could schlep it over to the specialist's office, but when at length he looked up, as though surprised to find her still there, he merely muttered, "Digital."

Not only was she a hypochondriac, she was a dinosaur . . . No one toted around actual X-rays anymore. She nodded at his instructions on how to get to the Orthopaedic Clinic, "western wing, northeast elevators" . . . *second star on the left, straight on till morning* . . .

She wandered off past a supply cupboard stacked with Phisohex, past doors that afforded unlooked-for glimpses of lumpy bedspreads, trying not to breathe too deeply of hospital smells, past the nursing station where no one so much as glanced at her. *What if I were a maniac, here to murder helpless patients?* Past the Emergency Eyewash Station, past a laminated chart illustrating the degrees of "Hazardous Waste," until she found the elevator. She emerged into a sky-lit nexus on the fifth floor where a plump volunteer with a name badge told her to follow the white footsteps. "White for bones!" she chirped.

She found a seat in the waiting room—it was still warm from the previous occupant and she shuddered at the vinyl exhalation as she sank into the roomy ass-print. Her eye was drawn, like a moth to a flame, by the muted television mounted in a corner of the ceiling, its "live eye" tracking traffic on the Don Valley Parkway while across the bottom of the screen, a band of news text unspooled like a postmodern novel, its content neither sequential nor linked to the words a female commentator was mouthing, which appeared as closed captions in a band across the top and which could not possibly be accurate, ". . . WHAT IT MEANS TO BE A HUMAN BEAN IN THIS DANE AGE . . ." She tore her gaze away, opened her book and read about a girl who'd been born with half a brain.

"Mrs. MacKinnon," announced the brusque West Indian receptionist.

Mary Rose looked up—*Mrs. MacKinnon's my mother, dude!*—and stood meekly.

Dr. Ostroph turned the computer screen on his desk to face Mary Rose—gone were the days of the shadowy X-ray in the light box. Just as shadowy, but on a computer screen now, was the long bone of her upper left arm in all its forensic glory. Her humerus.

He pointed with a pencil—some things don't change—at the various, to her indiscernible, old fracture sites. ". . . you can see where the bone healed here, here, here and . . ." She noted that Dr. Ostroph was pale but had excellent bone structure. She determined to be the best patient he had seen that day, the most informed, the least needy. He had golf clubs on his tie. He talked fast, she talked faster, out-brisking the specialist, "So an injury that wouldn't harm a normal bone causes a bone cyst bone to break," she said, helpfully paraphrasing in case he had not understood himself.

"It's called pathological fracture."

"Right," she said.

Like the frozen puddle.

"Bone cysts go undiagnosed a lot of the time because they're asymptomatic unless there's a fracture."

Like the skating rink.

"Sorry, what?"

He spoke slowly—did he think she was stupid? "You don't feel the cysts unless the bone is broken."

Like the airplane swing.

And because she still must have been presenting with all the facial cues of a carp, he added, "It hurts. That's your first clue."

Like . . . every time it was sore.

He was saying something. She wondered if he knew who she was—perhaps his kids or his wife had her books and he'd twig to it when he got home this evening, *Hey, you'll never guess who walked into my clinic today . . .* He stopped talking. She blinked. "I beg your pardon?"

"I said, where are you on the pain scale?"

"What's the pain scale?"

"One to ten, one being low."

She came clean. "At the moment I'm not on it."

"You had pain, though, recently."

"It comes and goes." Like the Looney Tunes frog in top hat and tails that would sing and dance so long as no one was watching. She chuckled.

"From one to ten?"

He was getting impatient with her. What was the right answer—what was the question? "Uh, three. Eight?"

His eyebrow flickered.

"I have a high pain threshold," she said.

"Pain is subjective."

"Have they come back?"

"No."

"Could they?"

"I know of no research to support that."

"Is it, are they, is it from adhesions?" she asked. "Like old scar tissue?"

"Is what?"

"The . . . soreness."

"All that would have resolved long ago."

"Okay. So there's nothing I should or shouldn't be doing."

"Don't jump in front of an oncoming car."

"Ha-ha." He wasn't annoyed with her after all. "It's hard to know, with kids, though, if they have a broken bone, right?"

"In very young children it's called a green-stick fracture and no, you might not know."

He was typing something into his computer. Probably billing the government at that very moment. Was this her cue to leave?

"Especially if you weren't aware of anything actually having happened to them, unless they cried or complained."

He looked up. "Why wouldn't they complain? My kid complains about everything."

"Do I have cancer?"

He did not crack a smile. "I see no indication of that."

"Thanks, I only ask because I'm here at the urging of my partner and my family physician, so they'll be glad to know . . ."

He was already turning the screen away and she was halfway to the door when he said, "What about the pain?"

"Well obviously it's in my head." She smiled. She wasn't going to let him be the one to say it.

"Well, yeah, that's what pain is, information."

"Absolutely." Brain plasticity. She brandished her book. "I've just been reading about—"

"Messages."

"Exactly, neurological—"

"You get an old pathway kicks up in the brain, it's literally 'remembered pain.'"

She flashed on an illustration from her childhood *Treasury of Fairy Tales*, of a prince hacking his way through brambles on an overgrown path beyond which could be glimpsed the castle of Sleeping Beauty. She mirrored Dr. Ostroph's clipped tones, "So you shut down the pain pathway with what, like with what, surgery?"

"Doesn't usually work."

"So . . . ?"

"Antidepressants."

"Really?" Had she missed something?

"I can't prescribe those."

"No, that's fine, I don't want them, although that is quite fascinating—"

"Here." He scrawled something on his prescription pad and handed it to her.

Tylenol 4s.

"Oh."

"You want fives?"

"No, no, this'll do, I'm sure."

"We're talking bone pain, right?"

"Yup, I just don't like to take a lot of drugs, you know?"

He bent over his pad once more, tore a sheet off and handed it to her, saying, "This one's right in the building."

She thought he was talking about the pharmacy, and figured the second script was for a lower dose of Tylenol.

"Thanks." She retraced the bone-white footsteps to the elevator, crossed the echoey food court toward the pharmacy—might as well have something on hand in case the pain came back—her own "nice mother" pills. It had given her pause to learn that her arm had been in a state of chronic friability throughout her childhood—was, in fact, broken sometimes. Several times. Often. But what did it change? It was in the nature of bone cysts to fracture without fanfare—witness the airplane swing at four, which would account for one of the *here*s at the end of Dr. Ostroph's pencil . . . how many *here*s were there? The swing was the first to result in a sling but may not have been the first fracture. Still, if her arm was injured enough to merit a sling, why did it not merit an X-ray? Because no one thought it could possibly be broken because bone cysts cause bones to break and no one knew she had bone cysts—which came first, the chicken or the egg? Her mother provided her with a sling because it seemed

Mary Rose had pulled a muscle. Seen from this perspective, Dolly was very attentive indeed—all that fuss for a mere muscle. If Mary Rose had made it clear her arm really hurt—if she had cried—she might have got an X-ray and been spared the ensuing saga. It was her own fault.

She handed over the second prescription and the pharmacist was already turning toward his dispensary shelves when he stopped and handed it back.

"This not a prescription," he said in his Chinese accent.

"Yes it is, I just got it from Dr.—"

"Dr. Ostroph, yes, no, not for drugs, miss, look."

She looked. It was a referral to a psychiatrist.

"Thanks," she said, and left empty-handed.

That night, Hil brought a tray of nachos, salsa and two glasses of wine down to the basement rec room. She was wearing her fuzzy mauve dressing gown that sounds dowdy but is sexy—Hil has a way of turning a tea towel into a seventh veil. She bent and her shingle of dark hair fell forward to graze Mary Rose's cheek as she administered the very married kiss that said, *I love you and I know we're both too tired, so let's just watch TV,* and said aloud, "So what did the doctor say?"

"He said there's nothing physically wrong."

Mary Rose was kneeling in front of the DVD player. "Which disc were we on?"

"What about the pain?"

"There's no pain unless it's broken."

"But if it only hurts when it's broken—"

"Yeah, no, it's not broken now, the pain I've got now is called 'remembered pain,' it's like a neurological thing, are we going to watch?"

"What?"

"*Sopranos.*" Mary Rose put in disc five.

"No, if it only hurts when it's broken, then—"

"It isn't hurting, I thought it away." *Throb*.

"Then that means when you were a kid, it was broken every time it hurt."

"You can't know without an X-ray. What episode were we on?"

"I think we were halfway through three."

Mary Rose pressed *play*.

Hil said, "Why didn't they get you an X-ray?"

"They did, eventually."

"Why didn't they before?"

Mary Rose pressed *pause*, somewhat irked—this was their one chance to re-watch a whole episode before they fell asleep from exhaustion or Maggie woke up. "Because no one thought my arm could be broken, that's the point."

She fast-forwarded, chuckling as the familiar frames jerked past.

"But it hurt," said Hil.

"Yes, but I was stoic, so they couldn't know."

"Even your brother knew it hurt."

Mary Rose pressed *pause* again.

"Okay, my darling, my mother was busy, bereaved, okay? Angry, pregnant, whatever, I don't know, she had a hard childhood, I must've looked perfectly fine by comparison."

"She was a nurse."

"Exactly, the children of health professionals rarely get a Band-Aid, look at you with your dad. He didn't even give you an Aspirin the time he sewed up your finger on that fishing trip when you were eight."

"He's a psychiatrist."

"All the more reason."

Play. Tony Soprano settled himself into an upholstered chair—

"How many times did your mother make a sling for you out of an old scarf? She must have known something was wrong."

Mary Rose sighed. "Three times, and it was usually a new scarf, are we going to watch?"

Hil's bathrobe had fallen open slightly—seductive, in a 1950s housewife kind of way. Mary Rose pictured her bending over to clean the oven . . . in G-string and garters. *"What's a nice girl like you doing in a place like this?"* Enter, woman with tool belt, here to lay tiles. *"Hey, can I give you a hand? . . ."* Hank is right, she should be writing erotica—which is what women say when they don't want to say "porn."

"Sorry, Hil, what did you just say?"

"I didn't say anything."

Hilary was a human authenticity-detector. The little lies that allow so many marriages to float, if not merrily, then at least gently down the stream were provocations to Hil. Not that Mary Rose was lying. In Hil's gaze now was the mixture of curiosity and concern that Mary Rose recognized as the signal that she was starting to listen "behind the words." This was good news and bad. It meant that Mary Rose was about to be understood whether she liked it or not.

"Look, Hil, what you have to understand is, that was a different era."

"The era of what, stupid people?"

"Please!"

"I'm sorry—"

"It's okay, just—I don't have cancer, okay? I don't have bone cysts, I'm not beating my child." She chuckled.

"What's that got to do with it?" Hil's lovely blue eyes narrowed unattractively along with her mouth. "Are you telling me you've hit the children?"

"Of course not."

On screen, Tony Soprano was frozen, lids half closed, finger raised as though poised to order a hit or a pizza. *Play.*

"It *is* new," said Hil.

Pause.

"What is?"

"Every time it hurt, it was broken. That is new information."

There was no winning an argument with Hilary Creaghan once she had you in her Socratic sights—she had missed her calling as a Crown attorney. Maybe it wasn't too late for her to go to law school and get a job with a benefits package so Mary Rose need never write the third in the trilogy.

"Fine, you're right. But it doesn't change anything, which is my point—"

"It means you grew up normalizing pain."

"I already knew that."

"No, you knew you had a high pain threshold, but you didn't know why. I don't think a pain threshold is something you're born with, like bone cysts, it's something you learn. If Maggie had a sore arm—"

"Well, she doesn't."

"How do you know?"

"I'm her mother."

"You just answered your own question."

"Hil, why are you cross-examining me, I'm just telling you what he said."

"Why are you so angry at me?"

"I hate arguing, you enjoy it, I hate debating, I was forced into the debating club in high school and it scarred me for life, Dwight Dumphy was president, he had a damp little beard. I'm not angry, I'm making a joke, you're the one who's angry, you sound hostile."

"I'm really not, Mister. And it hurts me when you talk to me like that."

Sigh. "Like what?"

"Like I'm your enemy."

"I'm sorry, it's cultural, okay? I'm half Mediterranean, I'm not a WASP, you're the one who sounds scary, all calm and rational—where are you going?"

"I think I'll go to bed."

"Don't walk away! It makes me crazy when you—"

Mary Rose balled her fists and jammed them against her forehead.

Hilary sat down again. "What do you want me to do, Mary Rose?"

Mary Rose bored her knuckles into her scalp, rigid with anger, furious at herself for being furious. The only way to get unfurious would be to have a huge fight with Hilary, during which Hil would unleash her victimy wrath before becoming rehumanized in Mary Rose's eyes by crying, after which she would reassuringly resume her pedestal by being coldly critical of Mary Rose who would silently batter her own head and wind up rocking in the fetal position on the guest room bed so as not to wake the children while she waited for the corrosive tide of neurochemicals to retreat, repenting of everything, most fervently of the fact that she had ever been born. Unless Hil was going to slap her. She stole an upward glance from between clenched fists.

But Hil wasn't crying. Nor did she look poised to strike. She was looking at Mary Rose in a way that made her feel . . . disoriented. Which was a change from furious.

"Watch *The Sopranos* with me," Mary Rose answered meekly.

"Okay."

Play. Tony was mad at Dr. Melfi for dissing his mother who had just put out a contract on his life. Mary Rose laughed. Hilary was silent.

Mary Rose said, "I just remembered something my mum used to say when I would tell her about my arm being sore, she'd say, 'If it's sore, that's your badness coming out in you.'"

"I thought you said she didn't know it was sore."

She decided to let Hil have the last word. She was a woman after all. So was Mary Rose, of course, but . . . Hil was more traditionally feminine . . . even if she was a lot like Mary Rose's father. What does it mean when you marry your father and she's a woman who favours heels and handbags?

Later that night they were in bed and Mary Rose was slipping deliciously down the slope when she zoomed awake for no reason. She listened. Hil was asleep. "Hil? Are you awake?"

"Hmm?"

She felt Hilary's hand find its way around her waist—even through sleep, Hil's touch was elegant. She laced her fingers through Hil's and turned toward her. Maybe they could just have sleepy sex—like the good old days, when Hil could get right into it without the aid of a twenty-minute back rub. But as though she had heard Mary Rose's thought, Hil suddenly got out of bed.

"Sorry," said Mary Rose.

"What for?"

"Waking you up."

"You didn't wake me up, I'm hungry."

"Oh, I thought you were—I thought you thought I was trying to—never mind."

"I'm sorry, sweetie," said Hil, "I woke you up."

"Actually, I woke you."

"Oh, did you want to have sex?"

"No, no, I was just, um . . ."

"I'm going to get some cereal."

"Do you want a back rub?"

"No, I'm just hungry."

"Do you mind if I come down with you?"

"You make me sound like the common cold, of course I don't mind, Mister."

She could not shake an abject feeling—perhaps it was the disorientation of not having had a huge fight with Hil—it was as though she were back in grade three with a shameful crush on Lisa Snodgrass. Rising, she felt the familiar capsule break in the pit of her stomach and the dark elixir seep into her bloodstream. *Guilt.* But why? Her Catholic upbringing had left her prone to attacks of it like recurring bouts of malaria in old soldiers. Maybe she'd been born with a low guilt threshold, the way people are born with green eyes or black hair. Or bone cysts.

She followed Hilary down the stairs, Daisy barged past, a four-legged emergency vehicle, and it came to her: she was guilty of having wasted the taxpayers' money with her trip to the bone doctor today, *bingo*. The dark elixir gave way to a malodorous shame cloud, as though she had been caught masturbating in Dr. Ostroph's waiting room—another unbidden thought, not to mention absurd, *humerus clitoris!*

She would take guilt over shame any day—the dark elixir over the smelly cloud. *Dark elixir* . . . like the Black Tears with which the Ebony Elf replenishes her enchanted pool. In the second book, Kitty is aided in her quest to save Jon by a girl with pretty but painful feet who is really a unicorn under a spell of disenchantment. The girl can lead Kitty to the Land With No Name where the Black Tears flow, but only if Kitty brings her the magical instrument whose song will restore her true nature: a flute fashioned from the bone of a Bird of Pray . . . But what, Mary Rose now wondered, were the Black Tears actually made of? And how might Dr. Quinn use them to further his evil plan? These were questions for the third in the trilogy: *Return to Otherwhere*.

She reached for the magnetic pen next to the phone and jotted on the grocery list, *Black Tears = grief/guilt? Cure/cause cancer?*

Hil was at the pantry cupboard, pouring cereal into a bowl. "Do you need me to pick something up tomorrow? I can do the shopping."

"No, I just thought of something."

"For the third?"

"Maybe."

She felt Hil kiss the back of her neck, but she slipped the embrace, went to the fridge, pulled open the freezer and promptly forgot what she was looking for.

"Do you want to go back to work?" asked Hil.

"Why? Am I doing such a lousy job here?" She tried to make it sound like a joke.

"What are you doing?"

"I'm cleaning the vinyl stripping on the freezer drawer," said Mary Rose. "You should see it, it's ready to sprout."

"Look at these Halloween cookie cutters," she said the next day, hauling jute bags up the back steps into the kitchen. "I got them two for a loonie."

"You didn't have to do the shopping, babe, I was going to," said Hil.

"You can help unpack."

Hil held up a blue package. "We already have Q-tips."

"We have them in our bathroom. These are for the kitchen."

". . . Why?"

"How do you think I got the vinyl stripping on the freezer so clean? And look at the buttons on the Bose, you can see the edges now, they were gummed over. And see? Everyone thinks a dishwasher is clean by definition, right?" She opened it and pointed with relish. "Well, all along the inside edge here . . . gross, eh? . . ." She tore the plastic from the fresh box of Q-tips.

"Can't you just go upstairs and get Q-tips whenever you want?" asked Hil.

Mary Rose straightened and sighed, unaware, until she spoke, of the depth of her outrage. "Why should I have to? Why, in my own house, can I not have a box of kitchen-specific Q-tips? You never have to see them, you never have to use them—why *would* you, since I'm the one who does the shopping and the deep cleaning anyway"—she could hear herself over-articulating, like her father, a caricature of expository calm, but she could not stop—"I fail to understand why, at forty-eight, I have not earned, along with a decent amount of money, the right to have kitchen Q-tips."

She saw Hilary's expression harden, and quailed. She had gone too far. She laughed. "Hilary, I'm just making fun of myself."

Maggie climbed onto the stepstool, turned the water on and started "doing the dishes." Matthew drove his train into the kitchen. Mary Rose knew she didn't have a chance, Hilary would zero in for the kill, knowing Mary Rose would not risk escalating in front of the children and therefore would take anything Hil dished out.

But Hil said, "You're right. I just wonder if you really need to clean that hard."

"Cleaning is important to me. It's part of my job."

"We have a cleaning lady."

"She does the broad strokes."

"We could ask her to Q-tip the kitchen." Hil looked amused.

Mary Rose realized she had been yearning to see that look, to have the forgiving Hilary back, the easygoing one who could laugh at Mary Rose's faults and turn them into foibles. And here she was, beautiful, smiling, surpassing even her sympathetic forbearance of the night before when Mary Rose had been channelling Tony Soprano. *I love you, Hil.*

But she said, "Well, you may consider it beneath contempt, but I don't think it's a waste of my time, there are Zen masters who do this."

Hil straight out laughed, but Mary Rose maintained her stony composure.

"As long as you're happy," said Hil.

"I'm happy," she hissed through clenched teeth. And watched the amusement die in Hilary's eyes.

•

The child is standing with its hands pressed against the glass door to the balcony.

"Come away from there." says Dolly.

Bang. Bang, bang.

It is a warm sunny day. April, now. But she has closed and locked the door—her husband says the bars are too close to allow the child to slip through, but Dolly can't be sure.

Bang, bang!

"Cut it out, now."

Bang. Bang. Bang.

She turns her face to the back of the couch. She can stay lying down, nothing bad will happen.

•

The alarm does not sound—not that she can hear—but she runs down the six or seven flights of stairs anyway. At the very bottom she exits through another fire door, expecting to emerge onto Mount Sinai Hospital's retail concourse and food court, only to find herself in a quiet corridor, its walls of cinder block painted a grief-green. A wheeled yellow bin is parked directly in front of her, its side stamped in black letters, INCINERATE. She bangs back into the stairwell and does not breathe until she has crossed the busy concourse and emerged onto University Avenue where she takes a big gulp of healthy Tuesday traffic. It is 11:10 a.m., she has fifty minutes all to herself before she has to be home to relieve Candace.

She hops on her bike and, conscious of a not altogether unpleasant squishiness left over from the lube, rides up the urban canyon. To her left, Princess Margaret, the hospital that cancer built; to her right, the Hospital for Sick Children, its main entrance adorned with a neon train to mitigate terror—most of it the parents'. She stands on the pedals, ascending the slope of an ancient lakebed, rolling over millennial mysteries, over bones and battles up to Queen's Park, the noble neo-Gothic pile where the provincial government sits and her brother liaises with it. She sails around the Legislature and coasts into the park proper, where a copper-cast King Edward VII presides astride his fiery steed. Despite municipal efforts, the horse's penis is perpetually painted red, owing perhaps to the proximity of the University of Toronto and its scheming spires. She looks up as she glides along—overhead the threnody of bare branches hums with new life set to burst into song. This year she will catch the moment when the world turns green.

She exits the park at the war memorial, to her left the Royal Ontario Museum—the ROM—rite of passage for schoolchildren province-wide with its dinosaur skeletons and mummies, its totem poles and tomb treasure—all that separates a memorial from a museum is time. And power. To the victor the stories . . . She reaches Bloor Street and turns left, heading west.

The Museum was recently the subject of lively controversy owing to a glass addition that some hailed as a "world-class" architectural landmark and others reviled as a barnacle. Toronto is like that. Its truly beautiful buildings do their job without drawing a lot of attention, neither soaring nor splitting light. Some, like City Hall, testify to the optimism of the sixties when space was there for the curving, and as for the rest, it is a preponderance of Victorian utility that in some quarters has lent itself to gentrification, in others hipsterfication, while vast tracts retain the spartan rectitude that earned the city its nickname, "Toronto the Good." A combination of corruption and consensus has often stymied visionaries such that the city has not gelled in the popular imagination around any one icon. The CN Tower is tall. So are a lot of things. What Toronto boasts is life, bulges with it, a metropolis of non-joiners, a collection of communities from all parts of the planet that swell and spill into one another. At the corner of Spadina Avenue, she stops at the lights—maybe she ought to nip across and rejoin the Jewish Community Centre, start getting back into serious shape—"You don't have to be Jewish to join!" But as she navigates the crush of pedestrians she spots her ex, Renée, sitting in the window of the adjacent Second Cup, and presses on, pausing to give a loonie to the woman who, for the past ten years, has stood at the northwest corner of Spadina and Bloor chanting, "Can you spare a loonie for my son and I?" Mary Rose again resists correcting her, "For my son and *me*," as she drops the dollar coin into the chewed-looking Tim Hortons coffee cup. She has never seen any sign of a son—clearly the woman has worse problems than faulty grammar. She continues west along Bloor, past the Shoppers Drug Mart where she and Hil spent a fortune on pee sticks, and wonders what to do with her extra forty minutes.

She has lived here long enough to have seen the street change clothes if not character, and behind every new facade she can still see earlier ones layered like old movie posters. She passes the Bloor Superfresh that everyone still calls the Bloor Super Save—it was the first twenty-four-hour store on the strip and in the days before Sunday shopping, certain aisles were cordoned off, it being for some reason legal to buy milk but not Q-tips on the Lord's Day. She sees one of the dads from Matthew's school.

"Hi, Mary Rose."

He is a political cartoonist—or is he the physicist? She slows.

"Hi . . . Keith."

"When's the book coming out?"

It's a funny turn of phrase, as though the book were cowering in the closet. "When Maggie's in university!" she replies. Past the natural food store with its medicinal whiff of buckwheat. Vegetarians used to be cadaverous killjoys with no use for food other than to push the food that was already in them out, but now the woods are full of friendly vegans—some things really do get better.

Past the corner of Brunswick Avenue where academic loafers huddle over cappuccinos on the crumbling patio of By the Way Café that used to be Lickin' Chicken; a woman at a rickety table raises a hand in greeting. Mary Rose waves back, "Hi . . . (*Blank*)." The woman used to run the box office at the Poor Alex Theatre—she looks old. Perhaps she just looks her age. Note to self: when past fifty, avoid Bolivian shawls unless you are Bolivian. Past the candy store that used to be a Hungarian restaurant, past the hip clothing store that used to be a Hungarian restaurant, past the Wiener's Hardware that has always been Wiener's Hardware—outside Indra Crafts a knot of schoolgirls sample sticks of incense and examine tiny carved elephants on a table crammed with wares; amid a thickening braid of pedestrians from every sidewalk of life she spots the Native guy striding with his German shepherd off-leash at his side. She rides on, past the old Bloor Cinema on one side and Lee's Palace on the other, temple of indie rock where she did performance art back in the day and got drunk and met Renée—its exterior is still graffitied, but professionally so now; past a Lebanese restaurant that used to be a Hungarian restaurant, past a Hungarian restaurant, past the bookstore that is still a bookstore, and the Starbucks that used to be everything else.

She thinks Renée may have put on a few pounds, but she looked good just now, she has grown her hair, she looks a bit like Carole King if Carole King wore a blue boiled-wool caftan and jewellery made of river rocks and computer parts. Mary Rose and Renée have been on cordial terms for years. Even Hilary has overcome her allergy to Mary Rose's ex. Renée is someone who can make art out of anything, but when they were together she was also someone who couldn't make anything into a job. Mary Rose was racked with guilt when she finally left, convinced Renée would fall apart, drink herself to death and wind up homeless. *Spare a loonie?* Renée got a full-time job at a community college and bought a condo. She kept the cats, one of which is still alive at eighteen.

Mary Rose brakes at the lights and considers heading across to Honest Ed's, the flashing neon emporium where "only the floors are crooked!" But she would need more time for that, not to mention a GPS to find her way out again. She crosses the street and hesitates before Secrets from Your Sister. Professional bra fitters with nary a gnarly old lady in sight to bully you into the right brassiere—the word itself a burpy bugle-bleat, herald of humiliation and Aunt Sadie palpating Mary Rose's eleven-year-old chest, "She's gettin' bumps, Dolly!" Mary Rose locks her bike—she is a middle-aged, very married mother, there is nothing remotely suggestive in a spontaneous bra fitting mid-week mid-morning. She could use a sturdy new *bustenhalter*, as they say in Germany.

She enters the store with its savvy range of lingerie and everyday "intimate wear"—she brought her own mother here in January. An efficient young woman in heels and a topknot secured by chopsticks greets her with a smile of recognition and Mary Rose prepares to receive serenely the forthcoming gush of admiration along with the inevitable query, "When's the third one coming out?" But the young woman says, "You're Dolly's daughter."

"That's right."

"How *is* she?"

When she has finished bringing the young woman up to date on her mother, she is told, "I'll need more than five minutes to do a proper fitting on you." She turns an appraising eye on Mary Rose's chest as though seeing right through to the faded, ill-fitting sports bra. "I'll book you in." As though for a *procedure*.

"That's okay, I'll pop by later." *Pop.* Her mother's word.

She tries to flee but is snagged by a lacy confection as ornate as it is insubstantial. Hil would look over-the-top in this. Worth its weightlessness in back rubs . . .

"That cut would be great on you," says the girl, "you're on the small side and super fit."

"Not for me. My partner."

The young woman does not bat an eye. "Your wife will love it."

Mary Rose looks at her sharply, but clearly no irony has been intended in the young woman's use of the W-word. Mary Rose is suddenly aware of having missed a beat, finding herself once again scrambling to keep up with a world she helped to change.

"Doesn't my . . . wife have to be here to get fitted?"

"No, it's for you."

It all happens so fast. Suddenly Mary Rose is back on the street with a tissue-wrapped girly sex costume. She stuffs it into her fleece-lined L.L. Bean three-season jacket, hops on her bike and rides with renewed energy up Howland Avenue against the flow of one-way cars.

Aunt Sadie had an arranged marriage that blossomed into love twenty-five years in when she threw a knife at Uncle Leo. He ducked. The relationship with Renée lasted well beyond the best-before date and likely would have ended sooner had Dolly and Duncan not been so opposed to it and all that it represented. Renée saw her through the worst of it; they weathered the storm together, tenderly at first in their apartment, then in their own house, neither of which Dolly and Duncan ever visited. As a card-carrying feminist, Mary Rose ought to have clued in after the first time Renée smacked her. But there were extenuating circumstances . . . alcohol, professional recognition (Mary Rose's), depression (Renée's) . . . as well as Mary Rose's maddening capacity to find fault with someone just when she had managed to get all their attention. *Smack.* And to be fair, Hil had smacked her too, once or twice in the early days. Mary Rose could get anyone to hit her. She could probably have got Mother Teresa to hit her.

She lets go of the handlebars and relaxes, surfing the speed bumps through the Annex with its big old Victorian houses. Someone in a Volvo drives by, it looks like Margaret Atwood. It is Margaret Atwood.

She puts her bike in the shed, enters her house and tiptoes up the back steps to see Candace and Maggie at the small wooden craft table in the corner of the dining room. Candace hands Maggie the cap from a marker and waits while she snaps it into place. It takes ages. Then she hands her another and waits. Maggie is completely focused. Candace, completely calm.

Upstairs in her walk-in closet, she takes the ridiculous bit of fluff from Secrets from Your Sister and hides it behind a pair of brogues in her hanging shoe shelf. It will be safe there until she finds time to return it, first making sure chopstick girl is not on duty.

Downstairs, the message light on the phone is blinking.

"It's Mum, you're not there." *Click*.

"You're still not there? Did you get the packeege?" *Click*.

An automaton. "To claim your prize, press two—"

And one from her old pal, Gigi, in her spicy tones. "Hi, Mister, I'm making a pot of spaghetti, should I bring it to you or do you want to grab the kids and come here?" Gigi must be on hiatus between episodes of the cop show she's running as production manager—not that wrangling a fictional SWAT team has ever stopped her making a batch of meatballs. It might be fun to get together—then again it might be too demanding to be around someone with a fully functional social life.

She reaches into her pocket to pay her nanny.

"Thanks, Candace, see you next Tuesday."

"Don't you need me tomorrow night?"

"Oh yeah, the movie, see you."

Candace leaves by the back door and Mary Rose goes out the front to check the mailbox. There is no package. There is a letter from Canada Post. She opens it: NOTICE OF SUSPENSION OF HOME DEVILRY. She blinks. DELIVERY. There follows a menu of reasons with corresponding boxes for ticking. DOG ATTACK *Tick*. She feels her tongue thicken, her esophagus go to glue. Daisy will be seized and destroyed. It is the law. It doesn't matter that she's half blind and great with kids, it doesn't matter that she is old, she's a pit bull.

What will they tell Matthew? Hil will be devastated, Maggie will grow up grieving and not know why. She wills herself to read on.

Her heart pounds back to life. She has merely to sign the form promising to keep Daisy out of the front yard during delivery hours in order to avoid triggering an inspection by Animal Control. The DOG BITE box is unticked. Thank God.

Pit bulls were once known as "the nanny dog" because they were so good with children. In the seventies, there was a rash of St. Bernards biting kids' faces off, but no one ever banned them. She signs the form and puts it on a corner of the kitchen table. She and Maggie can drop it at the post office on their way to pick up Matthew from school this afternoon—there's one at the back of the Shoppers Drug Mart on Bloor. No doubt the packeege is being held there. She'll be able to phone her mother and break the latest loop before having to endure it in person when she meets her parents' train next week. This week? When, precisely, are they coming?

Ring-ring!

•

Her daughter arrives home from school.

"Are you feeling better, Mummy?"

"Look after your sister."

At her age she was already helping to raise the younger ones. Her own mother was a married woman at twelve.

Before her husband gets home from work, she dresses, puts on her lipstick and steps into a pair of pumps. "Come help me with supper, Maureen." Then she takes a rag and cleans the tiny handprints and mucousy smears from the glass door to the balcony.

He comes in and kisses her. "Boy, something sure smells good, Missus!" He tosses his uniform hat to the hall tree hook and catches the little one up in his arms— "Hey Mister, how's my little scallywag?"

"Maureen," says Dolly. "Set the table."

•

"Maggie, it's time to go, please put the marker down and come to Mumma."

Maggie does. Wow. Then she goes, without being asked, to the top of the four steps that lead from the kitchen down to the back door and sits smiling at Mary Rose. There is something a little disconcerting in that smile almost . . . mocking. If it were Matthew, Mary Rose would describe it as mischievous. Thus armed with awareness of her own double standard, she smiles back and stations herself on a lower step. Daisy pushes past them both and sits expectantly, tail sweeping the doormat in anticipation of a walk. Mary Rose takes one small foot in one hand and one winter boot in the other—they will pick up Matthew and stop at the post office on the way home and submit the form, which reminds her, she'll need to grab it from the kitchen table before they go out the door—and goes to slip it on, but Maggie wriggles free and seizes a ladybug boot from the rack. Mary Rose decides not to insist. It is warm enough for rubber boots, indeed it's balmy out.

"Okay, Maggie, but wear these boots instead." Durable, tasteful L.L. Bean boots with reflectors.

"Not these boots, Mumma."

"Yes, these are your rain boots, Maggie."

"I will wear Sitdy boots."

Another full sentence. Very good.

"No, sweetheart."

She takes hold again of Maggie's foot and is rewarded with a sharp kick.

"NO!"

Breathe.

When Matthew was this age, Mary Rose was like Daisy: he could poke her in the eye, pull her tail, nothing riled her. Maggie is a different story. And Mary Rose is a different dog. "Maggie, you may not kick Mumma."

"Me may!"

Kick.

The trick is not to mind it. She has seized the little foot once more and manages now to get the Bean boot onto it, but as she reaches for the other boot, Maggie kicks off the first and looks at her with frank and infuriating glee. It is a look of entitlement that makes Mary Rose see red—how dare this child assume anything about the safety of this world or her right to the good things of it? Maggie laughs and grabs the ladybug boot. Mary Rose grabs it back. Maggie kicks her—

"STOP IT!" Mary Rose whacks the boot against the step, grazing the little legs. Maggie freezes. Daisy barks, her tail still going.

Breathe.

"I will let go of your foot now, Maggie, but you must not kick."

She lets go.

Maggie does not kick.

"Good, Maggie."

"Sitdy boots."

Mary Rose sighs. If she gives in now, she will have taught her child to get her way by kicking. On the other hand, maybe she ought to reward the child for not kicking just now. She should have dispatched the "Sitdy" boots to the Goodwill the moment her parents left in January. Shiny red with big black eyes and antennae, *ladybug, ladybug, fly away home!*

"Okay." She holds the ladybugs just out of reach. "What do you say?"

"Peace?"

She hands them over.

"Sank you, Mumma."

"You're welcome."

She resists helping, aware that Maggie's determination to dress herself is developmentally appropriate. She waits. And reflects that child rearing resembles war: long stretches of boredom punctuated by all hell breaking loose. At last the boot is on.

"Good, Maggie. Let Mumma do the other one."

"No sank you."

A *War and Peace* later, the boot is on.

"Wake up, Daisy, we're going now."

Maggie stands and smiles up at her proudly. How could Mary Rose have seen anything but variations on a theme of joy in her child's smile? A block of sunlight has barged through the back-door window and it softens upon contact with the child, making of staticky stray hairs a halo for her toddler-plump face, shiny red mouth, green lights in her eyes. She has a dimple. The boots are on the wrong feet.

Why can't Mary Rose enjoy the moment? This is the sweet time. She knows it. Can see it from the outside. Mother and child on the steps. *Look, Mumma, I did it, Me-self.* The mother is healthy, youthful. It is a nice house. It is a nice day. A nice dog. Just add feelings.

The boots will get bigger. The little shoes in the rack will give way to ever-larger shoes. Increments of time marching away to adulthood and beyond, then gone. Know it now. Feel it.

Dead. Flat and grey, like sheet metal pressing against her chest where spongy feelings ought to be. Are other people just pretending to have feelings, she wonders? Or do they really feel them? Everything is fine—shiny ladybug, silky head, mother on the steps. But the mother has a blank look on her face. Smile: *Tick.* Now get behind it. It is only a moment. And the next, and the next, and the next, passing, frame by frame by . . . Can you catch one of those moments, catch it like the window of a passing train, catch one and get into Time?

But the train disappears, the prairie is empty but for the tracks, silent now, though still hot to the touch. Vibrating.

•

As long as she stays lying down, nothing bad will happen.
Bang. Bang, bang.

•

They were halfway to the school when Maggie insisted on walking, which was, of course, another good sign, but anyone who has ever walked from A to B with a toddler knows how non-linear it can be, not to mention hard on the back. Now Mary Rose buckles her safely back into the stroller as they wait to cross the speedway that is Spadina Avenue.

She joins the lively scene outside the old rectory that houses Matthew's Montessori school, and chats with the other parents and nannies milling about. Several, like her, are on foot with dogs and younger siblings, some are on bicycles, others in vans and environmentally sensitive SUVs. There's Keith—Kevin?—again. He is approaching her, smiling. Mary Rose quickly turns to the mom next to her and asks out of the side of her mouth, "Is it Keith or Kevin?"

"Philip," says Saleema.

"Mary Rose, sorry I accosted you like that, you must get sick of people asking when the third one's coming out."

She smiles back. "Not at all, Philip, it's . . . nice to be asked."

He is a cell biologist.

"Why did I think you were a cartoonist?" she says.

He looks at her oddly. "I wanted to be a cartoonist."

Philip rides his bike year-round, and Mary Rose is familiar with his nose in every season, sunburnt in summer, frost-nipped and drippy in winter as he hauls his twin girls in a covered kid cart. Maybe he is on sabbatical. Or maybe he is a stay-at-home dad . . . making snacks, taking whacks, wondering if he'll ever get any me-time, wishing his wife would pay just a little more attention to him and just a little less to the children when she gets home in the evening . . . Which of them requires the back rub?

"I can't wait to read it," he says. "My whole book club is ready to pounce."

Mary Rose is speaking with a heterosexual man who is in a book club. *O brave new world that has such people in it!*

The glass door to the lower level of the school opens and the pre-elementary "Casa" children begin making their exit, each pausing to shake hands with the teacher before being dismissed. Mary Rose spots Matthew waiting his turn, in animated conversation with Saleema's son.

"Saleema, can we borrow Youssef this afternoon?"

"That would be awesome," replies Saleema in her usual tone of urgency—as though she operates at a constant level of orange alert. "But can it be tomorrow? I have to shop with my mother then." Her mother is seated inside a Toyota Matrix at the curb with its lights flashing. Her chador is black to the ankles, unlike Saleema's fuchsia head scarf.

"Your mum can come play at our house too."

Saleema laughs. She is an engineer. She can use the laughs.

The steps are suddenly full of small children clutching artwork and being claimed by caregivers. Several of the little ones surround Daisy, jamming the sidewalk, Mary Rose untangles the leash from the stroller and the children. Maggie cries out for inclusion and control, "You can pat my dog!"—desperation is the mother of syntax. She will be joining her brother here next fall and Mary Rose's life will change again. Another shoe size.

The teacher looks up between handshakes. "Hi, Mary Rose, how are you?"

Keira is a young woman with a huge smile and she is in full, pregnant bloom with her first child.

"I'm terrific, Keira, you look great!"

Mary Rose sees what Keira sees, hears what she hears: a happy, energetic mother with two beautiful, healthy children. Keira is sweet, smart and decent like the rest of the faculty and staff—Mary Rose has often wished she could enrol herself here and start school all over again, peeling carrots, tracing letters, learning grace and courtesy and big bang theory in a sane environment.

"Mumma!"

He still runs to her every day. That will change in a couple of years too. He thrusts his construction paper at her.

"Oh my goodness."

"It's a whale."

"It is beautiful, sweetheart."

"Maffew!" Maggie has leaned forward and bellowed at ten decibels. A few adults turn and laugh, so does Mary Rose.

Saleema says, "She is so much like you, Mary Rose," as she hustles her son over to the Matrix.

"Thanks, Saleema. I think." She turns back to Matthew, catches sight of Keira again and sees a knife slide into her pregnant belly—she blinks reflexively with a sudden intake of breath and turns away. "Matthew, don't tease your sister, sweetheart."

He is bobbing and weaving in front of the stroller just out of reach, Mary Rose can hear the scream taking shape inside Maggie's laughter. He dances in close and Maggie gets a clump of his hair. Now he is screaming. "Maggie, no!" hollers Mary Rose. Eleven decibels—she glances round to see if any of the other parents is looking at her. Does she sound too angry? Sue catches her eye and waves. Did she hear? Mary Rose smiles and ducks on the pretext of untangling Daisy—she has to be feeling really good about herself to feel okay around Sue. With her high blond ponytail, tall Hunter rain boots, down vest and all-round air of private school confidence, Sue is the type of woman Mary Rose would never know if it weren't for their children. She is like Hilary minus theatre plus student council. Indeed, they both have startling blue eyes and project an aura of command. It would stand to reason that Mary Rose ought to feel at home around Sue, but she feels plungingly inadequate. Worse: shamefully homosexual. Something in Sue's demeanour triggers the old self-loathing . . . the Lisa Snodgrass effect. *Remembered shame.* She has confessed a sanitized version of this to Gigi, "I'm still afraid of WASPs even though I'm married to one." Daisy barks her high-pitched play bark two inches from Mary Rose's head—the aural effect of a garden spade to the ear—and she straightens with a wince. Matthew has his hands clapped to the sides of his head.

"Daisy, gentle-speak, you hurt Matthew's ears."

"No, you did," he says.

She chuckles in case anyone is listening.

"Mary Rose MacKinnon, what's your time like tomorrow afternoon?" Forthright five-foot-ten tones.

"Oh, hi Sue, how are you?"

"I'm taking the boys to Jungle Wall."

Mary Rose smiles back. "What a brilliant concept, eh? Your kids drive you up the wall so you might as well climb one with them."

Sue laughs. "The best part is Steve's making supper afterwards."

"Oh Sue, I'd love that, but . . . I promised Saleema I'd take care of Youssef."

"Bring him."

"Oh, you know what? I just—I can't believe I forgot, tomorrow's Wednesday, I'm going to see *Water* with my friends Kate and Bridget—" Too much information, she sounds as though she is lying. "After the Youssef play date that is." Is this her cue to invite Sue's son Ryan to join Matthew and Youssef?

"*Water*'s amazing," says Sue. "Let's try for the weekend, Hil's still away, right?"

"She's home next week."

"How're you doing on your own?" Sue's socially appropriate solicitude, her perfectly calibrated degree of sympathetic brow-furrowing are nerve-wracking to Mary Rose.

"Doing great." Plastic smile. "It's great sometimes to just, you know, do things your own way without having to check in with your partner?"

Sue smiles back—Calvin Klein laugh lines.

Gigi, in her self-appointed capacity as professional lesbian, has said, "You've just got the hots for her." *That is so not true*—in fact, at this moment Mary Rose feels her smile starting to melt like a tire fire, convinced her face is emitting a bad odour. *Some things really do get batter.*

"Mumma," announces Maggie. "I will walk now."

"Cool boots, Maggie," says Sue, with a wink to Mary Rose in acknowledgement perhaps that they're on the wrong feet. "I'm going to hold you to the weekend, MacKinnon."

Sue jogs off, pushing the all-terrain stroller with baby Ben buckled in, five-year-old Ryan riding shotgun on the rumble step and seven-year-old Colin powering his two-wheeler on the sidewalk ahead. Super woman with a tennis diamond. Mary Rose watches and wonders, is Sue making a "special project" out of her? Does Mary Rose seem like that much of a mess? Maybe the wrong-footed boots are a sign. *How're you doing on your own?* Sue is the last person to whom Mary Rose would admit the slightest maternal misgiving—the type of woman who has no clue what it's like to go down the rabbit hole.

Around her now, the tide of parents is turning over, older children are being dismissed. Keira has headed back inside the school with a wave. Mary Rose unhooks Daisy's leash from the wrought iron fence post and takes Matthew's hand as cars come and go from the curb, pulling in and out of the four lanes of rush hour. The knife thing was a fleeting unpleasantness, another unbidden thought.

"Mumma," says Matthew, "You're hurting my hand."

Though the catastrophic thoughts intruded once or twice when Hil was pregnant, Mary Rose came to believe the magnificent world-blast of Hilary getting down on the floor and giving birth to Maggie had banished them for good, along with so many other demons that fled like rats in the wake of her new life. Now she sees herself take hold of the stroller with Maggie in it and tip it into the traffic. She banishes the image by unclipping Maggie's seat belt and swinging her up into her arms. If anyone is watching, they will see that she loves her child.

•

As long as she stays lying down, nothing bad will happen.
She gets up.

•

They are under way, Matthew pushing Daisy in the stroller, Mary Rose piggybacking Maggie, who rattles with laughter like a packet of Chiclets. They stop at the park, Daisy bolts from the stroller, and Mary Rose catches the leash just in time, nearly dislocating her shoulder in the process—dogs are forbidden in the playground enclosure, and Daisy loves to hang by her jaws from the swing, a simple pleasure that makes her look all too pit-bully. Matthew runs for the swings, Maggie gives chase, falling in that weightless way of toddlers, scrambling to her feet, running, falling again like a ball of wool, getting up, running. Mary Rose hooks Daisy to the gate, leaving her to bark protectively, yearningly, and realizes the vagueness between her ears is hunger. Luckily, she has packed snacks for the children. She upends two boxes of mini-raisins into her mouth and chases them with a handful of spelt animal cookies. Matthew is already swinging, but Maggie has flipped over twice in her effort to mount a big-kid swing. Mary Rose picks her up and stuffs her into a baby swing—her protest turns to glee when she feels the pressure of Mary Rose's hand at her back. She pushes them in tandem, one on each hand. Maggie kicks off her boots, the left one sailing right, the right one left. Matthew throws his head back, his hat falls off and his hair flies. She delivers tickles at unpredictable intervals, a squeeze at the knee, snap at the heel; they laugh and their breath bubbles up and out into the air, bits of them, their cosmic signature, the particular way in which a piece of the universe has passed through them and been changed forever just now, indelibly with every breath, propelling the message, *we're here, we're here, we're here!*

Mary Rose pushes her sweet so-young children on the swings . . . A woman pushes her children on the swings while her dog dances and barks. *That woman is happy.*

•

She gets up.

•

Matthew's whale is pinned to the corkboard next to the foot calendar—April's watercolour is a tulip. Mary Rose makes supper while he makes construction sounds amid a rising tower of oversized Lego on the kitchen floor—he is more than ready to manipulate smaller shapes, but with his sister not yet three, the household is some months away from stocking toys suitable for choking. Maggie, rather than pursuing her career in demolition, is in the dining room, bent quietly over something at the craft table—Mary Rose's gaze flicks to the knife block, but the scissors are safely stowed.

She joins her, and looks over her shoulder. "What are you doing, Maggie?"

"Witing."

Swirls and hieroglyphs . . . the child is using a real pen—from Mary Rose's datebook. A mosaic is taking shape beneath her little fist, coiling graphemes embedded in squares and spirals reminiscent of Hundertwasser, if Hundertwasser had decorated Egyptian tombs.

Mary Rose feels her lips part as though to read aloud what is written there, but its meaning remains beneath the surface. She watches, somewhat awed, determining to be more like Hil, who allows the children to go through her purse and play with her phone and lipstick. Mary Rose does not have a "purse." She has a bag with a different zippered pocket for everything—large enough to accommodate a manuscript should that ever become necessary again. Along with an array of pragmatica, she carries a fountain pen that she keeps meaning to fill. She ought probably to carry a Bic pen, having read it is possible to perform an emergency tracheotomy with one. Hil would scoff, but Mary Rose knows that most serious accidents happen in the home.

"Good work, Maggie." She is so focused. Candace is here only five or six hours a week these days but it's paying off. Mary Rose wishes she could hire Candace to look after her too—is there such a thing as nannies for grown-ups?

Of course there are, they're called therapists.

"Sank you, Mumma."

She returns to the kitchen, wondering if she would be capable now of *witing* a book with a pen. How did the Victorians do it? They went blind and died young.

She pours a Scotch and turns on CBC radio. *This is . . . As It Happens . . .* She dances a little, nerdily, to the familiar theme music as she tips the plate of tamari-marinated tofu cubes into the frying pan . . . *for Tuesday, April second . . .* and picks up the phone to call her sister in Victoria . . . but there is no dial tone.

"Hello?"

"Rosie?"

"Mo? I just picked up the phone to call you."

"I just dialed you."

"That's so weird."

It isn't that weird, it happens a lot.

"How are you, Rosie Posie?"

"I'm great, I'm cooking tofu."

"Oo, yuck."

"I know, it's for the kids."

Maureen counsels inmates, parolees and burnt-out corrections officials. *But who will counsel the counsellors?* Duncan posed the question way back when Maureen switched her major from cartography to criminology. She did not start working outside the home, however, until her youngest was in high school. Now Maureen is the unassuming white lady at the back of the sweat lodge, the lone woman at the weekly halfway house potluck; she sings in her church choir, gardens, quilts, belongs to two book clubs and goes to Vegas twice a year with her husband. She sees the occasional ghost and sometimes continues conversations with Mary Rose that have begun telepathically.

Mo bucked the trend of her generation by marrying young and having five children. Now she is a grandmother with a boomeranging son in the basement.

"How's Rory?"

"Oh, he's doing pretty well, he's working on his websites, he's been great with Mum and Dad."

As if Rory were a therapy dog, thinks Mary Rose. But didn't families used to make room for that kind of thing? The homebodies who made themselves indispensable. Is Rory a homebody or a shut-in? Contented or depressed? Maybe he will fool them all and make a fortune inventing a computer game.

"Mo, do you know when Mum and Dad are going to be leaving Victoria? I'm supposed to meet their train when it stops over here."

"I'm not sure, Mum's misplaced the tickets."

"You're kidding, not again."

"I'm actually a little concerned about them, Rosie."

"I know, do you think Mum's starting to lose it?" Mary Rose tops up her finger of Scotch.

"Poor Mummy, she's been quite vague all winter."

Maureen has always called their parents Mummy and Daddy, unlike her and Andy-Patrick, for whom they have always been Mum and Dad—if either ever sported a *y*, it was shed like a tail and never grew back.

"I know. She couldn't remember the difference between Winnipeg and Calgary." She sips guiltily.

"A lot of people are in the same boat and we're not asking them to go for a cognitive assessment."

Mary Rose registers the rebuke and wonders why it is that, even when she is agreeing with her older sister, she so often feels she has given offence. Yet Mo spends half her waking life with offenders. She shakes the pan and the tofu sputters. "They're probably just in her purse."

Mo chuckles. "I'm scared to look in there."

Mary Rose chuckles back. "I know, God knows what might be coiled at the bottom!"

"Oh, I don't mean that, Rosie, I just mean it would be like an archaeological dig, we'd need to get out stick pins and little labels and call in the British Museum."

"We might find the Elgin Marbles or a piece of the True Cross."

"We might find Jimmy Hoffa," says Mo.

Mary Rose laughs out loud and wishes she'd said that. But then Mo might not have found it funny. She opts to push her luck. "Maybe Mum should have an MRI."

"Why?"

"I was just thinking, do you think it's possible she might actually be experiencing changes in her . . . you know that part of the brain, what's it called, the um, the memory lobe—you know, it sounds like an endangered species?"

"No."

She has heard a crimp in her sister's voice. It is important not to upset Mo. She shoulders everything and it has begun to tell. She is in remission from an autoimmune disorder that the doctors finally labelled "polymyalgia" because everything hurt and they had no idea what else to call it. Stick "poly" in front of something and you know you've got an imposter on your hands—why not call it "everything-hurtsia"? Whatever it was, the disease grew tired of waiting for someone to guess its name and slunk away. But who knows what might awaken it?

"Good, I was hoping you'd say that, Mo. I was beginning to get worried, especially after their last visit here, Mum was so *nice*! Ha."

"Mummy has always been nice."

Is Maureen on drugs? Or is she just . . . nicer than Mary Rose?

"Don't worry, Rosie, I don't have dementia. It's just that Mummy is mellowing, and that used to be considered a normal part of aging . . ." Is Mo choking up? Oh no.

"Mo, I'm sorry, I didn't—"

"It's okay, it's just that I remember a different Mummy than you do, Mary Rose," *sniff*, "and I'm sorry that you didn't have . . . what I had."

Until I came along and wrecked it. "I know, Mo, she was, she's still, they're still, they're really sweet."

"Don't be worried."

"I'm not, I'm just . . ." *irked.* "She can't seem to remember when Alexander was born or exactly when he died. Neither can Dad, but Mum keeps on—" *don't say "looping"*—"returning to it. As though she gets caught in a thought-snare, and the harder she struggles to remember, the tighter the . . . loop gets."

"What a lovely way of putting it, Rosie, you really have a way with words."

"Thanks, Mo." She sips. "Maybe if we can nail down the dates, it'll help her let it go."

"There's a great deal of unprocessed guilt there," says Maureen.

"And guilt is toxic."

"I said grief."

"No, you said guilt."

"Rosie, I know what I said."

"How's Zoltan?"

"He's driving me crazy."

She chuckles. "Good."

"I've given him an ultimatum: either he cleans out the garage or I'm dialing one-eight-hundred-got-junk. I stepped on a rake and nearly concussed myself reaching for a case of juice boxes." Mo's nest will never be quite empty, she still buys bulk. "How are you doing on your own with the kids, Rosie? You're really in the trenches."

"It's okay, it's great, it's a learning curve."

"I wish I were next door and could help you."

Mo visited the winter after Matthew was born. She cooked and cleaned and picked up six months of frozen dog poo from the back-yard. They drank Ovaltine spiked with cognac and watched *Pride and Prejudice*; she changed diapers, organized the spice drawer and replaced the flapper thing in the downstairs toilet tank; she laughed every time Mary Rose did her impression of Melanie singing "Ruby Tuesday." Then Maggie was born and she did the same thing, plus helped Hil with the breast pump and mended Matthew's beloved Bun, cross-stitching into the night. But for all that, Mary Rose wound up on antibiotics both times—perhaps she too is being stalked by a Rumpelstiltskinny disease, weakening her, one dry hacking cough at a time.

"You do help, Mo, Mum and Dad spend every winter out there practically next door to you and I don't have to worry about a thing." *Cough.*

"Mummy and Daddy are going to need some form of assisted living soon. I wish they'd darn well move out here for good."

"Have you talked to Dad?"

"He changes the subject."

Dolly and Dunc spent a good deal of their married life moving their family from one posting to the next. So long as another move remains on the horizon, they don't have to think of the place they are currently living in as the last place. Or admit that the next move will be the last one. And neither does Mary Rose. But what if her parents do move out to the West Coast? So much for the regular visits. Her children will miss out on whatever brief time remains with their grandparents—they've already lost Hil's mother. It'll be all packeeges and phone calls and e-mails, *Dear Dad, I . . .* She says, "I wish they'd move here." Will she go to hell for this lie? Is it a lie?

Silence. Then, "Rosie, you don't mean that."

"I guess I don't really."

"You've got your hands full already."

"I know. I wish the country wasn't so big."

"I know, me too."

I'm going to lose my parents again . . . my sister is taking them away.

"I wish Zoltan were here to de-Facebook my computer." Now that is a lie. Her brother-in-law is a highly qualified IT systems and security engineer. She doesn't want him anywhere near her computer.

"I can put him on the phone, he's just driving up—"

"No, that's okay—"

Calling, "Zolty!" Then, to Mary Rose, "Oh no . . . oh, what's he doing? Oh for Pete's sake, he's taking a big Home Depot box out of the back of the Jeep—"

"I better let you go."

Mary Rose loves Zoltan. He taught her to play Risk when she was eleven—doubtless more out of an excuse to spend twelve hours at a stretch in the MacKinnon house than even his considerable enthusiasm for the game. Mary Rose wonders if Andy-Patrick would be better adjusted if he had a big brother. Alexander would have been three years older than A&P. Two?

And as though reading her mind, Maureen says, "The dates would be in the photograph Daddy took at the grave."

"Oh. Wow, you're right. Mo, you're amazing."

"Look for the album next time you're in Ottawa."

"It's not in the album."

"Did you take it out?"

"No, Mum must've, it's been gone for ages."

"I never liked looking at that picture."

"Neither did I." *Lie.* "Do you think she tore it up?"

"Well, can you blame her?"

Of course. Mum may have got rid of the photo because it was painful. Mary Rose, with the egoism of a child, had blamed herself for its disappearance. But now it makes sense. Adult sense.

"He was born in December," says Mo slowly, "but they placed the stone in spring. I can almost make out the numbers . . ."

"Is that around the time you hung me over the balcony?" She grins.

"Rosie, why on earth would I have done that?"

"Because you had to look after me and I was a terrible-two."

She hears Maureen sigh. "Okay, smarty-pants, where was Mum while this was supposedly going on?"

". . . Wow, Mo, I just realized something. I've always thought of the balcony as this kind of funny, bizarre thing? But . . . if it really happened, then it means Mum must have been really . . . out of it."

"Rosie. She was depressed."

"Of course. I know that, I guess . . . I just never really connected those dots before."

Mo sighs again. "I see what you mean. Mummy could hardly get up off the couch. Of course it could have happened. Cripes. I'm sorry."

Mary Rose says, "I forgive you," and chuckles. But Mo is silent. "Mo? It's actually one of my favourite memories." Her triumph in getting her older sister to admit to the "balcony scene" is short lived. Now she feels guilty for making Maureen feel guilty.

"Mo, what time is their train, I can't get a straight answer out of Mum."

"Don't worry about any of that, Rosie, I'll let you know as soon as I know."

That's more like it. Efficient Mo. The-boss-of-me-Mo.

"Thanks."

"Now, try to be early. I'm afraid Mummy may wander and Daddy will carry the bags himself and run into difficulty." *Die of a heart attack in public, leaving Mum lost and keening. Or making loads of new friends. "I'm not crying, don't you cry!"*

She glimpses Matthew heading into the powder room and resolves to bite the bullet and start potty training Maggie first thing tomorrow—Hil is right, it isn't fair to hold her back.

"I'll be there. Wait, when?"

"Sometime this weekend—I'll let you know for sure. Have a good evening, Rosie Posie." Mo has to go, she is at work after all, it's three hours earlier out in Victoria.

"Oh, Daisy almost bit the mailman."

"I hate our mailman," says Mo with sudden bitterness.

She is on Lipitor—so are Dad and Andy-Patrick, while Mum is on something for her adult onset diabetes. Mary Rose is the only one not on meds. She pours another fingernail.

"Why?"

"He kicked Molly Doodle."

Molly Doodle is a cairn terrier, every bit as territorial as Daisy, but at nine pounds, while her transgressions might cost a new pair of pants, Daisy's will cost her her life. "That's horrible." A howl arises from the bathroom—"I gotta go."

She rushes in. Matthew is standing with his pants down, crying. He has peed all over the floor, having been unable to get the child-locked toilet lid open.

"I'm sorry, sweetheart, that wasn't your fault, come let's get you changed."

She rescues the tofu and steams some green beans. After supper, the marathon that is bedtime is achieved with the usual gnashing of teeth and rending of towels, splashing, laughing, screaming; toothpaste is ingested, hair is combed, a flood averted, jim-jammies are snuggled into, stories read, songs sung, glasses of water fetched and mopped up. In due course, they are in bed.

She kisses Matthew on the forehead. "Good night, sweetie pie."

"G'night, Mumma." His words are muffled by his thumb as he slips it into his mouth. He is only five. There will be time enough to worry about orthodontics and oral fixations later. He has every right to self-soothe.

She winds his glass unicorn and it tinkles his favourite tune. It was her first gift to him, and he keeps it on his windowsill where it prisms the light each morning.

She slips into Maggie's room and sees she is asleep, baby brows furrowed, sucking intently on a soother. She reaches down to stroke her back, but the child pulls away.

She sighs.

Is it that Maggie is a girl? That isn't supposed to be a problem for card-carrying feminists. From the start, Mary Rose was aware of a gap between her and her daughter; lapses on her own part that no one ever saw and which would never be termed "neglect." Her gaze for Matthew was glued, unbroken, she fed on the sight of her child and he was securely tethered, brave in that beam. Then there was Maggie. Crying inconsolably in her arms. Angrily. She cried whether Mary Rose picked her up or not. Whether she stroked her, fed her, changed her, rocked her, bounced . . . Everyone talks about that magic "baby smell." Matthew had it and so, supposedly, did Maggie, but not for Mary Rose. Sometimes—and this is chilling—she even forgot Maggie was there. Perhaps deep down she really is jealous of Hil for having borne a child—even so, Mary Rose is convinced that what was a soul-shifting miracle for Hil would have been, for her, annihilation. *Mind the gap.*

She waited for it to close, come together and heal like an incision. But with time, absence took on substance. A layer formed like a soapy film, then hardened into Plexiglas: *My baby doesn't like me.*

Maggie would look at her as though she knew something about her—something Mary Rose thought she had outrun long ago. She knew this was crazy, and over and over she reached for the love she was supposed to feel, the love she could see. It was like the illustration in her childhood book of fairy tales: Snow White unconscious within her glass coffin, beautiful, unreachable, a bite of poisoned apple lodged between her lips. Time and again Mary Rose reached, and time and again her hand struck glass.

She leaves Maggie's room and bats away the balloon that has drifted from Matthew's. It makes its wan way down the hall like an aimless ghost, yellow head at a vacant tilt, the tinkly tune of the unicorn trailing behind, plaintive and sweet, "Where Have All the Flowers Gone?" She rubs her arm—dull patch of soreness, seems worse at night.

She goes to the living room, intending to find a nice cozy murder mystery on the bookshelf, but bends to remove the expandable bumper from the coffee table. It is ugly and it is overkill and it did not prevent her child from playing with scissors. Mary Rose, like the entire baby boom generation, grew up with unpadded coffee tables and survived; no one "childproofed" in those days. She recalls the gleaming coffee table in the living room of the apartment in Germany—her first home. She can see it plainly, in black-and-white, as though in an old photograph. Like the one her father took at Alexander's grave. In it she stands next to her sister and in front of her mother. Her hair is in a little bun, her mother's hand rests on her shoulder, protective, reassuring, holding in place her sweater as though Dolly had just now removed it from her own shoulders and placed it warm around her child.

And perhaps this is why Mary Rose returned to the picture over and over again—not merely for the morbid frisson that spawned an entire literary career, but because it was evidence that her mother could be gentle. Attentive. *Are you cold, Mary Rose?* Even though the photo was a stock image from her childhood, it is only now that she tries to imagine standing as an adult at her baby's grave with Hilary.

And taking a picture, because they know that soon they will be moving far away and will not be able to visit that grave again for many years . . . Maureen is right, the dates would be in the photo.

What will become of all the old black-and-white and Kodacolor snapshots when her parents have died and she too is gone along with her siblings and their children's children? They will be sold in bulk at an estate auction and turned into ironic greeting cards. Or merely incinerated.

Her mother's difficulty with before-and-after, cause-and-effect—a species of temporal dyslexia that blighted Mary Rose's own early school career—perhaps it runs in the family, like bone cysts. *See Jane run!* For that matter, when exactly was Other Mary Rose born? And what did they do with her body? It was certainly not put in the ground beneath a stone.

Mary Rose bends back down and re-fits the hideous padded bumper. Coffee tables can be lethal.

•

She gets up.
She gets up.
She gets up.

•

Mary Rose is changing the biodegradable bag in the recycling bin when Hil calls and asks, "How's your arm feeling?"

"My arm? It's fine, why?"

"You went to the doctor."

"That was last fall I saw the orthopaedic guy."

"Oh, what was today's appointment?"

"It was just . . . routine."

"What kind of routine?"

"Fibroids, okay?" She hates even saying the word, sodden as it is with *female troubles*. "They're shrinking, I've killed them, it's done."

"Okay."

"How're rehearsals going?"

"Well, we're previewing in two nights."

"Oh wow, great." Mary Rose finds a pen in the telephone drawer and makes ready to jot it in the Thursday box on the foot calendar. "So the fifth."

"That's Friday."

"Oh, okay, Friday."

"Yup."

Mary Rose jots it in the Friday, April 6 calendar square: *Hil 1st public preview.* Hil is getting ahead of herself as she always does when stressed, thinking she'll be previewing two nights from now on Thursday when in reality it's in three nights. "Previews don't usually start on a Friday."

"No, they don't. Are you okay?" asks Hil.

"Yes, do I sound not-okay?"

"I just wonder if you're in pain."

"I'm fine, can we not talk about my uterus?"

Hil doesn't laugh. Oh no. Is she going to start crying? Does she want another baby? Is she having an affair?

"Hil? Are you okay?"

"I'm fine, I'm lonely."

"Maggie dived right at my head in swim class today, it was hilarious . . ." She tells her about the swimming lesson. About Daisy's postal parole and Maggie kicking off her boots in the park—but not about the altercation on the stairs. About Matthew's flying whale.

"The kids are so lucky to have you, so is Daisy. I miss you."

She hears in the silence that Hil is indeed crying. Mary Rose envies it somewhat, this ability to turn on the waterworks and get some relief and sympathy. She could use some time at the Emergency Eyewash Station herself—maybe she would sleep better.

"I wish I could see your show, love. I know it's going to be amazing." She speaks in Lady Bracknell's voice. "'To lose one child may be regarded as a misfortune. To lose two looks like carelessness.'"

"That's not the line."

"Yes it is, it's my favourite line."

"Yes, but that's not the line. It's 'parent,' not 'child'—'to lose one *parent*.'"

"Are you sure?"

"Mary Rose. I'm doing the play."

•

Mary Rose is dangling by her wrists over the balcony. It is a sunny day. She can feel the bars of the railing at her back. Three storeys below, on the lawn of the apartment building, their father is playing catch with another man. Both are in white dress shirts open at the neck, their sleeves rolled up. She watches the ball arcing back and forth between them. She knows if her father looks up and sees her, she will fall. Where is Mummy?

•

She ought to go to bed now. But first: she removes the child lock from the toilet lid—it really is unlikely that Maggie will dive in there. And if she does, she would haul herself out again. In the kitchen, she unlatches the bin drawer and drops the ingenious bit of landfill into the garbage—Hil need never know it was in the house. Mind-buggeringly long ago, when Earth was in its infancy, chemical changes were afoot that would result in the human ability to fashion the plastic toilet-lid lock from the complex bounty of this, our planet. How long will the return journey take?

Last summer, in her parents' Ottawa home, she watched Dolly search frantically for her train tickets so that she would be able to tell Mary Rose exactly when she and Duncan would be stopping off in Toronto on their way out west. It was many months before their departure, but they are seniors and plan everything well in advance. She watched Dolly rifle her purse. She watched Dolly disappear into her bedroom. Heard drawers opening and closing, accompanied by the occasional, "So that's where that is." Finally Dolly returned to the kitchen, brandishing a green folder, "I found them."

She handed the folder to Mary Rose, who opened it and stared. "This isn't a ticket, Mum. It's a receipt for your cemetery plot." Dolly grabbed it back—"So that's where that is!"

Duncan looked up from his newspaper and observed dryly, "It's a ticket, all right. It's a one-way ticket." He caught Mary Rose's eye, his face tightened to a grin, turned red, and he laughed till she saw his gold tooth. Dolly doubled over in her chair and almost peed her pants.

The train tickets turned up soon after, just as the currently lost tickets will. Besides, replacements are easily downloadable from the VIA Rail website. Unlike the elusive packeege, which is an actual object in space, travelling at the speed of matter.

She turns off the kitchen lights but for the one in the range hood over the stove. Now she can plainly see the school across the way and the quiet street itself, lined with parked cars, and, at the end of the block, the blinking red light at the school crossing. A young man rides past on a bike. A neighbour is out walking his aging greyhound—he rescues them, retired racers. She watches him wait patiently as the dog sniffs and ponders whether to leave a "message," and reflects that she has lived in this house for three greyhounds.

Upstairs, she takes an Advil before climbing into bed—she wouldn't really call it pain but knows that any discomfort intensifies the moment one tries to sleep—and resolves to phone her mother tomorrow and be nice. She is too hard on her mother—her funny little mother with her big brown eyes and snowy old-lady hairdo. And now Mum has sent her something—a gift, however kooky or mis-conceived . . . Maybe something Dolly has made herself, another quillow—pillow-quilt combo that folds into itself like an airbag. She brushes her teeth and avoids her reflection—she does not like look-ing in mirrors at night. Especially when Hil is away.

It is three hours earlier out in Victoria, she could phone her funny little mother right now, lately so much like the child she must once have been . . . lost amid siblings in the apartment over the barbershop in Sydney, Cape Breton. Child of a child. Little Dolly, singing for her supper . . . Pathos takes up residence in Mary Rose's chest and makes room for Guilt beneath Her dark cloak. They merge. A hump on the highway at night you hit with your car, only to stop in horror and find . . . nothing. You drive off convinced that, contrary to all evidence, you have killed someone. A child.

She stands in her tank top and silk boxers with lavender lipstick prints and braves the mirror—Dolly always said if you stared too long in one, the devil would appear behind you, his horns framing your head. Avoiding her own gaze, she steals a look at her arm—still no bruise.

When she went under the knife the second time, her parents told her that when she recovered she could have plastic surgery to hide the scars, including the new one on her hip, so she could wear a bikini and not feel bad. But she had soldiered on with her arm like a wounded comrade by her side since before she could remember. It had suffered. How could she strip it of its badge of courage? She had earned her stripes. Perhaps that is why she has never been tempted to get a tattoo—apart from the prospect of sagging geriatric body art—she has her scars. Carved into her skin, through muscle down to bone, sewn, sealed.

The third scar, the one on her hip, is bravest of all, because it is the donor scar. *I was a teenage bone donor.* Like a B movie. Perhaps, too, the surgeries explain her failure to experiment with hallucinogenic drugs despite her status as a "boomer": having tripped elaborately in hospital, she associates the magic carpet with pain and the frequent vomiting that racked the edges of the incision, set it to seeping, and quaked the jaundiced expanse of her chest. Not that she dwells on it.

She opens the mirrored cabinet to put away her toothbrush and catches a movement behind her in the gloom of the walk-in closet. She freezes. The children are in the house. If there is an intruder, she has to find out. She forces herself to turn around. She switches on the light.

Nothing.

Ridiculous. If there were someone, Daisy would have heard them and made a meal of them by now. Still . . . she enters the walk-in closet and her heart leaps painfully even as her peripheral vision identifies the shrunken head of the yellow balloon. She seizes it by the ribbon as though to throttle it and drags it downstairs. Daisy's tail thumps as she passes.

She is reluctant to pierce it, so she stuffs it into the garbage. Shrivelled though it is, it takes up a lot of space, bulging with the pressure of her hand as though fighting for breath, squeaking. She feels suddenly appalled, as though she were committing some sort of bizarre infanticide. Finally, she takes a knife and puts the thing out of its misery with a *pop*.

The message light on the phone is blinking in the darkness. With each pulse she experiences a spurt of adrenalin. She ought to dig out the Canada Post form right now and put it where she can't miss it tomorrow morning when they leave to take Matthew to school. The mail devilry will resume, the freaking packeege will arrive and her mother can stop calling her about it.

But the form is not on the kitchen table where she put it—did Candace take it? Did Maggie "clean it up"? There is no number she can phone for a new form—unless you count the call centre in New Delhi. It's got to be somewhere—everything is—and not just in the cosmos, in this house. She hunts. Behind the piano, under the couch, in the freezer . . . She prowls, turning her ankle on perpetually disgruntled Percy, and lopes upstairs. Under the crib, behind the curtain, in the toilet . . .

She should not be looking for the form at night. She should never look for anything at night. Sit and breathe, stop walking—like a shark, she is feeding on movement, escalating alone in the quiet house. Part of her agony is that she cannot blame Hil for the lost form. She forces herself down to the basement because she has to hit something, "Mother-fucking Jesus Christ on the cross where is that fucking piece of paper, you fucking postal fuckheads!" She assaults the metal pole in the basement with a bright orange couch cushion, but that is unsatisfactory. She grabs an empty Rubbermaid laundry basket and swings it against the pole, breaking its ergonomic handle. She needs to hurt something without breaking anything valuable like the TV, so she gives in and punches her own head as hard as she can until she sinks to the couch in relief and catches her breath.

She toyed with the idea of getting anger management counselling when Matthew was a baby. It was around Christmas. She was pulling out of the parking lot of a government building in suburbia where she had gone ballistic on a civil servant who informed her, after a long wait with her baby, that she would have to return with his adoption papers in order to show that she was eligible to apply for a health card on his behalf. She had taken her portable infant car seat with her infant in it and stormed out, registering split-second interruptions in her consciousness as she rode the elevator down. She got in her car and, as she pulled up to the parking booth, glanced out of habit in the rear-view mirror, only to see that there was no infant car seat snapped into the infant car seat base, and no infant. She had left him, securely buckled, on the ground, next to her parking spot. On the yellow line. She had driven all of thirty feet away. It had been all of fifteen seconds. More than enough time for hell to have opened up and swallowed him. But he was safe. She vowed to get help. Then Maggie came along and she just got too busy again.

She never knows when it might strike. The rage. And when it does, she loses her grip on herself—literally. At times, she could swear she sees another self—shiny black phantom, faceless, as though clad in a bodysuit—leaping out of her, pulling the rest of her in its wake. Over the edge.

If someone had injected her with a potion labelled *Mr. Hyde*, it would make sense, for the rage always feels like it comes out of nowhere. It is only afterwards that she recognizes that whole sections of her brain have been shut down, whole circuit boards. For example, she loses language. Gone. It is akin to what used to happen to her in the bad old days when a strip of world would cease to exist in her visual field, just as though it had never been. Or, equally disconcerting, when a giant yellow orb would appear right in front of her, blocking her view—it was like trying to see around a big yellow sun. "Incomplete classic migraine," said the ophthalmologist. "Panic attack," said Dr. Judy, and asked if she would like to "see someone." But Mary Rose knew they were really evil spells—she needed a sorcerer, not a shrink.

Those times are like dreams or the pain of surgery however—they get filed separately. She has undone many evil spells since becoming a mother—even so, there is still a spinning wheel somewhere in the kingdom and she never knows when she might prick her finger . . .

There is nothing wrong with her life. She has a loving partner and two healthy, beautiful children. She has put money into education funds, she has put photos into albums. She can make pancakes without a recipe, she knows where the IKEA Allen key is, and has memorized the international laundry symbols—she has not Polaroided her shoes, she has her inner Martha Stewart in check. That is a slippery slope: you start making your own ricotta, next thing you know you're in jail.

•

That spring they place a stone on his grave. They bring
the children. He says to his little one, "Stand close to
Mummy, Mister. That's right."

Then he takes a photograph of his wife, and children.

•

She wakes at three a.m., curled cold on the La-Z-Boy couch, and goes
calmly up to bed.

•

Other Mary Rose never became Mary-Rose-Who-Died,
because she was born dead. This blurred the notion that
she had ever been alive and potentially someone. Not
baptized. Therefore not fully named. As if her name had
been laid over her like a sheet that kept slipping off.
Nothing sticks to a dead baby.

Journey to Otherwhere

Her father was showing her a brochure, *St. Gilda's Academy for Girls is among the top private schools in the country. Set amidst the beautiful Laurentian Mountains* . . .

When she found her voice, she said, "It makes absolutely no sense, why would you send me to a Catholic school, we're supposed to be atheists."

"You won't be required to attend church—"

"If I'm anything, I'm Hindu. What if I decide to become devout?"

She saw him almost laugh and felt a glimmer of hope, but he continued. "Kitty, it's my fault, I've deprived you of a normal life—"

"I don't want a normal life."

He shook his head. "Aunt Fiona's right—"

"She's not my aunt." Next thing she knew, Dad would be telling her to call that woman Mom.

He looked sad now. "It's not fair to you, Kitty, I've tried to turn you into a little version of myself—"

"What's wrong with that?"

"Nothing, if that's what you choose later on, but so far, whether you realize it or not, you haven't had any choice—"

"Then let me choose! I choose you, I don't choose that school!"

He regarded her sadly. "Kitty, have you ever heard the expression, 'I must be cruel to be kind'?"

"It sounds like something grown-ups say when they want to get their way and have their kid feel sorry for them at the same time."

He shook his head. "I'm not going to win an argument with you." His smile was wistful. "You're like your mother."

She could not explain why this made her so angry that for a split second all she saw was a flash of black.

He continued. "You can either pack your things yourself or Ravi will send them along later."

At the mention of Ravi, something terrible happened. Kitty started to cry. Kitty McRae *never* cried. It broke over her with the inexorability of one of the floods she had witnessed.

He winced and rose from the leather armchair. "I'm sorry, sweetie pie. I'm not much good to you sometimes."

She balled her fists against her eyes until the pain doused her tears, then called after his retreating back, "You wouldn't send me away if I were a boy!"

Her father paused but did not turn. His shoulders sagged and she saw a shred of silver, no larger than a hanky, flee his side as he went out the door, leaving her in the room that had always been the safest place in the whole wide world. Until ten minutes ago.

WEDNESDAY

I'm a Baby. I Can Drive Your Car. (And Maybe You'll Love Me.)

It is sleeting. The kitchen windows are streaky grey. On the craft table, she checks out Maggie's masterpiece. The page is now covered with her "witing." Is it possible, she wonders, that Maggie can actually wead what she has witten? Is it a form of infantile literacy that she will unlearn as she grows older? Perhaps the child is an amanuensis, channelling a chronicle from another world, secrets of the universe from the nibs of babes, if only we had the means to translate . . . a cosmic Rosetta stone. She ought to jot that idea down for the third in the trilogy. But she remains motionless before the page, her gaze semi-focused . . . and it comes true: there is a secret message. It shimmers beneath the veil of colour, surfaces, and Mary Rose is able to read it: NOTICE OF SUSPENSION OF HOME DELIVERY.

Maggie is in her high chair, redistributing her oatmeal around her Bunnykins bowl.

"Maggie, this is beautiful work, but you took Mumma's piece of paper from the table."

Maggie replies, "Bunny is packing the car."

"Maggie—"

I'm not angry. She is a baby, and she has made something beautiful. "Is it for Mummy, for when she gets home?" Maggie shakes her head with a sly smile. Mary Rose smiles back because she knows her patience with the boots and the walking to school yesterday and her phenomenal forbearance with the form just now are about to be rewarded. Maggie's masterpiece has been lovingly rendered for her: *Mumma*.

"Candies," says Maggie.

Mary Rose feels the smile curdle on her lips. "That's so nice, Maggie, Candace will be so happy."

Maggie picks up her bowl and displays it, sufficiently empty now to reveal the Bunnykin family loading a picnic into the back of their VW Beetle—the manufacturers were apparently unaware that the trunk in a Bug is up front, a flaw that Mary Rose suspects will make it a collectors' item. She takes it from Maggie before she can drop it—meanwhile, Matthew's porridge is growing cold. She goes to the foot of the stairs and calls him. No answer. She goes up to his room.

He is sitting on the edge of his bed, having struggled into his undershirt and pants, one sock on—he has begun dressing himself, and Mary Rose has learned to let inside-out shirts and odd socks lie.

"Do you need help, sweetheart?"

He starts crying.

"Matthew, love, what's the matter?"

His distress always exerts a mortal pressure on her heart, as if the spot reserved for him were pre-tenderized from some previous injury. He does not answer, his head is down.

"What is it, honeybun, is it Tico?" She peers into the plastic network of tunnels and cubbies, but the hamster is curled and breathing in its pod. Thank God.

She joins him on the side of his bed. His little hand is closed over something.

"What are you holding?"

He moans.

She makes to pry open his hand gently, but he pulls away—not before she glimpses what is in it. Glass.

"Are you cut?"

He shakes his head but will not meet her eye.

She glances toward his windowsill. The glass unicorn is standing there, headless.

No! "What happened?"

He shakes his head.

She keeps her voice level. "Did Maggie come in your room and drop your unicorn?"

No answer.

She gets up. Before she is out the door, it is out of her, *"Maggie!"*

"No!" screams Matthew—he sounds hysterical—"No, No!" and with each word he strikes his head with his fist.

She rushes to his side and catches his arm. "It's okay, sweetheart, it was an accident, here, give it to Mumma please, I don't want you to cut yourself."

She puts her arm around him and he opens his hand. She takes the glass head with its tiny horn. Nothing a little Krazy Glue won't fix. She slips it into her pocket.

"Mumma can fix that."

"I don't want you to fix it."

"Matthew, why not?"

He clamps his lips together.

She kisses the top of his head.

He stiffens. "I don't like it when you yell."

———

She drives her son to school, then heads for Whole Foods. Halfway through tony Yorkville, she slows as she passes the hypnotism building. Remarkably, there is a parking spot available right out front. It is a sign. She is about to back in when she sees her accountant coming out—she puts it in forward and drives off.

He was likely visiting another office—there is a payroll company in there—but she takes it as another sign: if a hypnotist can trick her into forgetting the pain in her arm, what else might they pick from her psychic pocket? Or maybe it's a sign she shouldn't be spending so much money at Whole Foods. She pulls a U-turn and heads back toward her own neighbourhood. It starts to rain.

She glances in the rear-view mirror at Maggie strapped into her car seat and playing with stacking cups—she has been talking non-stop back there. There's to be no nap this morning, perhaps after grocery shopping they'll go to the Early Years Drop-In so Maggie can run around and build up her immune system with the germy toys. It's in the community centre at their local park. She was last there in February, seated on a miniature chair in the stuffy gym as toddlers staggered and gnawed on things while it sleeted outside. An attractive younger—they were all younger—mum sat next to her. Her name was Anya. She was pretty but tired, her hair in a fly-away ponytail and her Lululemon yoga wear had gone through the dryer once too often. She looked as though she had probably been in peak shape two years ago. Anya started talking and Mary Rose soon realized she couldn't stop. Her smile was lovely, chapped lips notwithstanding and she spoke rapidly, one eye on her two toddlers as she told Mary Rose all about the miscarriage she had had. Last week.

She drives past Honest Ed's on one side, Secrets from Your Sister on the other, and is into the strip of Korean restaurants. She turns right and the great basin that is Christie Pits Park spreads out on her left. A green gouge in the city that started out as a gravel pit, it encompasses an outdoor rink, a pool, a playground and has become the tobogganing destination of choice for new Canadians in winter, while in summer it draws shirtless self-styled soccer stars from every non-hockey-playing nation on earth. On hot nights a giant light standard reigns over the diamond where serious games are called from the booth and cheered from the hill. In the early thirties Christie Pits was the scene of a riot sparked by swastikas at a baseball game, but Toronto, like much of Canada, has cultivated a selective memory, such that few of the dog walkers down there today have any clue of its checkered past. She pulls into the big lot at Fiesta Farms supermarket—unlovely depot on the outside, garden of Eden on the inside.

She lifts Maggie into the shopping cart seat and hands her a snack trap of organic Cheddar Bunnies. Mary Rose loves Fiesta Farms. The CBC National News anchorman shops here—he looks strange without a tie. Her elderly Italian neighbour with the Virgin Mary in her front yard shops here—

"Hi hawney, how are you, kids okay?"

"Hi, Daria, they're great, say hi, Maggie."

Funny how you think of someone and then you run into them—

"Hi, Dawia."

"Ma bellissima!" She gives Maggie a Hershey's chocolate Kiss without asking Mary Rose—Daria is old school. "You take one for Matthew too, okay, hawney?"

She heads up the dairy aisle and encounters a heavily tattooed musician she used to see at parties. He is sporting his signature porkpie hat but has a baby strapped to his chest. She tells him about the recyclable disposable diapers she and Hil discovered, he says it's all about papaya these days. He is glazed in that four a.m. feeding way, they speak rapidly then move on, veterans who know enough to spare each other the niceties.

In the pasta aisle, she sees Anya—is there something special about today? If she thinks about Renée, will she appear? Anya has her two toddlers and is looking quite attractive, not so tired, her hair is shiny. Mary Rose feels a rush of warmth. "Hi, Anya"—slowing her cart in benevolent anticipation of a chat tsunami. But Anya smiles and moves on without a flicker of recognition—Mary Rose loses sight of her behind a pyramid of Paris Toasts.

She tries to imagine pouring her heart out about a dead baby to a strange woman, only to forget all about it. Perhaps she has done so and can't remember. That's what forgetting is . . . She stops, momentarily caught in an Escher print of her own psyche, pondering, not for the first time, the degree to which a set of agreed-upon facts, combined with functional memory, determines reality. What is it that holds her, meshed, in this moment? Why is she not falling through time in a vertigo of identity displacement? Does Anya know she is missing a piece? Has her psyche grafted a patch of donor memory over the blank spot? Or did she rip the memory out herself and suture the flaps together? Does she have a scar? Yes, but she would be at a loss to explain it. That's what "invisible scars" are.

"Mumma," says Maggie pleasantly. "Peace?"

"Sure," she says, and lets Maggie choose the pasta.

"Sank you, Mumma."

Whatever Mary Rose might share incontinently with a stranger, it would not involve a dead baby—that's her mother's shtick. While it may seem heartless to refer to it, even inwardly, as "shtick," it does capture the odd Borscht Belt timing and tone with which her mother has taken to repeating the tales. Like so much trauma chatter.

She hunts for her reading glasses while scrutinizing the ingredients list on a can of tomato soup. The contents are organic, but the lining of the can contains toxins. The soup in the glass bottle, however, is not organic . . . She jumps when she hears her name bleated, as though speared by a gull. She turns. A beaming younger—of course—

woman is towering over her, in her cart a baby, at her feet a toddler who has already begun emptying the lower shelves. She speaks in an English accent. "Maggie looks more like you all the time, Mary Rose!" She makes it sound like *Mewwy Wose*. "Don't you, Miss Maggie!" The woman has large square teeth. Who is she?

She launches into an account of her upcoming move, as though continuing an earlier conversation: her husband has been transferred to Columbus, Ohio, and has gone ahead while she stays behind with the children to sell the house and organize the move. Now is not the time for Mary Rose to practise her politically correct, "Actually, I'm not Maggie's biological mother, I am her Other Mother." Besides, she can't get a word in edgewise—the woman is rabbiting along about having nearly lit her baby's sock on fire while stirring spaghetti sauce—she hoots with laughter—she has parked on the street in front of the store and is worried she'll get a ticket. "Back in two ticks, Mewwy Wose!" and she flits off down the aisle, rounds a pillar of kosher salt and disappears. Mary Rose looks at the children. "Hi, guys."

Maggie starts climbing out of the cart. Mary Rose goes to stop her but thinks better of it and heaves her out onto the floor, where she distracts the baby and plays with the toddler. Mary Rose plays peekaboo with all three. After ten minutes she wonders if she ought to alert someone, have the woman paged. Was she cheerful or hysterical? Was she crying out for help with a smile on her face? She confessed to having almost incinerated her child—some say there are no accidents. What will become of these children if it turns out their mother has abandoned them in the pasta aisle? Will their fates be inextricably bound up with Mary Rose's? Will what began as parallel lines become an intersection? Does it matter that it is pasta and not condiments? Just when she is set to call the manager, the woman comes flurrying back, still smiling and talking. She continues talking as Mary Rose melts away toward the hummus.

Where did she go? Perhaps she drove away then changed her mind; or considered mounting the curb and going over the side of Christie Pits, accelerating straight down in her minivan, crashing to a stop at the base of the concrete light standard, crushed hood smoking, car horn jammed on one note. Who is helping these women? All the logorrheic ladies, gushing taps of chatter with their funny stories about pain and loss, betrayal and bewilderment—*I'm not crying, don't you cry.*

She chooses three lemons and reflects that women have their trauma chatter—like reverse Cassandras laughing at the gates, *This happened this happened this happened!* But what about Porkpie Hat? Does he have it better? With men it can take a different form. She thinks of her father with his family tree endlessly branching—"Look, you see here? In 1794 you have an Angus MacKinnon who is listed as possessing thirty-nine sheep, now you have to understand that in those days . . ." rendered in ultra-expository tones, the verbal equivalent of walking with prosthetic legs, one syllable placed laboriously after the other. With age, their lectures become islands of coherence disconnected from the mainland: "It took a government commission on systems analysis to systematically analyze . . ." "I'm going to wheel you into the sunroom now, Mr _____." Although they sound saner than the women, the men may be compelled to spread rich and creamy information over something that is howling just as hard. She stops dead in the produce section as it strikes her that the *Mewwy Wose* woman may indeed have been continuing an earlier conversation with her: one of which Mary Rose has no memory. What might she have poured out from the crude oil of her heart to the tall woman with the air-raid smile? She frisks her *memowy* but cannot come up with a single *miscawwiage.* And though she seeks irreverently thus to dismiss it, her hands are cold as she squeezes an avocado.

"How are you, Fluffy?"

Why did I let myself think of Renée?

"Hi, Renée," *whom I would not dream of addressing as "Frisky."*

"Hi, Maggie, it's great to see you, kiddo, do you still like cats?"

Maggie loves Renée. Mary Rose reflects that Renée's narcissism plays well with children—not unlike Dolly's. Within moments she has Maggie enthralled by her necklace—an eclection of electrical cable sheathing, seashells and a handful of fox bones that Mary Rose found on their last camping trip together. Maggie carefully examines the necklace. Renée leans forward and her wavy mass of auburn hair frames the face that is fuller with age, but brighter too. Surely, however, it is too early in the day for cleavage. Mary Rose fights the twin urges to flee and to fling herself into a big smothery hug. Somewhere in a parallel universe the past is playing like a movie rerun wherein she loves and desires a slim, supple Renée; the one whose kiss tastes like Camels and tequila, the dyke with the purple crewcut and three silver earrings whom she has just met at a Pride Day brunch. Flash forward through cherishing, perishing codependence, the dearth then death of sex, drunken scenes and slaps, to Mary Rose driving away in her VW Rabbit through a grinding of gears with Renée in tears, unemployed and bellicose on the front porch. To Fiesta Farms grocery store here on a Wednesday morning.

"Bring the kids over sometime."

"I will."

"I'll put down plastic and we'll do action painting with vegetable dye."

"Excellent."

She is at the checkout. Maggie is handing her the groceries to put on the conveyor belt—she breathes patience. She has no reason to hurry, merely a hurry-habit, a metabolic hair-trigger. It has got her where she is today, but it will also strike her down with an autoimmune disorder that has twenty-five different names but that used to have just one—"hysteria"—if she doesn't smarten up and smell the roses.

"You're doing a good job, Maggie."

The man behind them in line gives her the evil eye. She feels her scalp prickle. He sighs. She stares, prepared to go postal. *Go ahead, make my fucking day.* He looks away. Maggie hands her the apples, one by one.

Maggie does look like her. A lot of children do, she has generic good looks. All babies look like Winston Churchill and all children look like her. And all white guys look like her brother.

In the parking lot, she is buckling Maggie into her car seat when suddenly the child hugs her fiercely and emits a roar of happiness. It was worth the whole painstaking apple by carton by tube process. Her cellphone rings in her pocket. She straightens to dig for it and bangs her head on the door frame—"Shit!" Maggie laughs. The call display says *Harlots*.

"Hello?"

Andy-Patrick is calling from a Queen Street salon. "You gotta get down here, Mister, I look like Billy Idol without the track marks." He puts the hairdresser on the phone and she and Mary Rose joke like old friends. The girl asks if "Andrew" is an actor because she can't believe such a cool guy is a cop.

"Hey, Maggie, want to go see Uncle Andy-Pat?"

She drives down to Queen Street and in another fell swoop of parking karma finds a spot steps from the salon. She unbuckles Maggie and hauls her out. She lets her walk. It has stopped raining.

It is turning out to be a good day, the chill grey notwithstanding. Maggie is being really good . . . a real "little buddy." Mary Rose decides not to confront her with the broken unicorn. Of course she covets her brother's special things, she may even have broken it on purpose. She is two: capable of anything, guilty of nothing. Still, it hurts her heart when she thinks of Matthew this morning, shielding his sister, pretending he is the one who broke the unicorn.

They amble past a small art gallery and a knot of grizzled homeless men out front of St. Christopher House, to the lights—"What colour is the light, Maggie?"

"Geen."

"Good!"

They enter the salon, athrob with an unfamiliar song that has mugged a familiar one . . . a folk song in whips and chains. She surveys the line of severely hip stylists, scissors nibbling at customers' napes, blow-dryers trained on glossy heads—he is not in sight, he must be in the bathroom.

The Goth receptionist listens to Mary Rose with an empty expression. Is she stoned? Perhaps she recognizes her—she is young enough to be a fan. Her neck piercing is oddly alluring. She swivels her raven head and announces, "This lady's looking for her brother."

Mary Rose used to live over the Legion in an actual loft—not a "loft conversion"—on this strip before it was cool, she did radical street mime and wore a biker jacket through the winter in the days when winter was cold, she is not anyone's "this lady"—*you suburban twit, you'll live to regret that tattoo.*

The girl turns back to Mary Rose. "You just missed him, ma'am."

What did she expect? She kicked the football again and wound up flat on her back—her brother has probably already gone home with the stylist. He may have dropped Mary Rose's name and scored. It would not be the first time.

"Here we go home again, jiggedy jig!" she sings as she buckles Maggie back into the car seat.

"No!"

Maggie does not want to go home, she wants to see Uncle Andy-Pat. Mary Rose pulls out into traffic—she ought to call someone for an impromptu play date. Like Sue—but then she'd have to listen to her talk about her trek over the West Coast Trail with her husband, Steve, and, somehow, their two kids and the baby. The windshield is suddenly rattling with hail. Maggie stops screaming. "Maggie, look, the sky is falling." *No.* "Not really, love, it is hailing."

"Helling!" *Exactly.*

They could drop by Early Years—the weather is foul enough— but she might run into the happy English child-deserter. Maybe they really should drop in on Renée, she doesn't smoke in the house any-more and the vagina sculptures have almost all sold—she tried to get Mary Rose to "sit" for one shortly before they broke up, but something told her to decline; proof there really is such a thing as a guardian angel. She dials her cell while driving but puts it on speaker.

"Hi, still feel like doing some action painting?"

"What's that? Oh. Gee, Fluff, I'm just so tired suddenly, I could barely pick up the phone, I thought you were the cleaning lady calling back. I had to cancel, I can't handle the stimulation."

"Are you okay? Do you want me to drop something by?"

"Nooo." The resigned upper register of the mild invalid. "I just need some downtime to recharge creatively." She's in bed with the cats, the new Alice Munro and a box of Timbits. Fair enough.

A glance in the rear-view mirror reveals Maggie asleep. "Maggie, wake up! Wake up, sweetheart!" If she naps now, she won't nap this afternoon. "Maggie, where's Daisy?!"

She watches as Maggie opens her eyes and registers in one bleak existential blink that there is no Dog. Her face—and perhaps, too, her faith—crumples, and she cries. It was a dirty trick, but it worked. "Daisy's at home, sweetheart, waiting for us."

A piteous wail rises to a howl when they make the turn onto Bathurst Street and head north.

She turns up the defogger and remembers the mulch. She'll have to get out there and spread it over the garden before the frost hits. Then she remembers it is April. Can she blame climate change? Perhaps it is a sign that something is cooking in the back of her mind. The third in the trilogy, gestating . . . shifting through Time . . . She has the sudden conviction that it will have something to do with time travel . . . It makes perfect sense: from Other*wheres* to Other*whens* . . .

She feels around in the glove compartment for a pen. In the rear-view mirror she sees Maggie, tear-stained but calm, with a crayon in her fist.

"Maggie, give Mumma the crayon."

"No."

She reaches into the back, her hand like the head of an anaconda looking for prey. Her phone rings: *Captain A.P. MacKinnon.* It is no longer legal to use a cellphone while driving in Ontario, but she answers—after all, it's a cop calling.

"Where the heck are you? I went all the way down to the hair salon."

He does not answer. She hears the *whoosh* of ambient reality at his end.

"A&P? Hello? What's that sound, are you there?"

He is gulping air.

"Are you crying?" Oh my God, it's Mum, it's Dad, this is the phone call—she always thought it would be Maureen breaking the news. "What's happened?"

"Nothing." He gasps. "I don't . . . I can't . . ."

"Andy-Patrick, breathe." No one has died. He is having a panic attack. "Where are you?"

"My car."

"You shouldn't be talking while driving." She swerves to avoid a cyclist and turns onto her street. Maggie renews her protest. "I'm not talking to you till you pull over."

"Okay. I've stopped."

"Are you in park?"

"Yeah."

"Okay. Now what's wrong?"

He has been triggered—by what, he does not know—and cannot find the off switch. Maureen has her comfy autoimmune disorder, while the two younger MacKinnons are united in pointless panic: the garden-variety plunge into an "I"-free zone of bowel-searing fear. For no reason. Occasionally accompanied by visual phenomena, elevated heart rate and esophageal spasm, *some restrictions may apply, see website for details.* "Where are you?" she says. "I'm coming."

"I'm on the 401 at Cobourg."

He must have flown! "I can't come there. I have to pick up Matthew at noon."

She turns into her driveway and puts the car in park, jams the phone between her face and shoulder, leans into the back seat to undo the five-point restraint buckle, and Maggie knuckle-punches her in the ear. She carries her brother and her child to the back door, both of them crying.

"I don't know what's the matter with me, Mary Rose, I'm going to get out of my car and walk into the road, I can't—I can't—I can't—"

"Stay in the car." Six lanes of superhighway. "Do you hear me? Answer me."

"Okay."

"Now breathe through your nose, it's going to be okay."

She listens to his convulsive breathing as she makes it inside and up the four steps to the kitchen. Maggie allows herself to be consoled by Daisy, who goes to work on the salty toddler cheeks, while Mary Rose goes to the fridge for her daughter's drug of choice, mango juice—it's organic, but the mangoes come from China, so . . .? "Andy-Pat, are you still in counselling? Are you still seeing that therapist? What was her name?"

"Amber."

"Is she a real therapist? She sounds like a stripper."

He chuckles. That's better.

"She's real," he says.

"Are you still seeing her?"

"No. Yeah, but . . ."

He has slept with her—oh for God's sake—Mary Rose does not want to know, she wants to hunt Amber down and get her tax money back. Pin it to the corkboard next to the dead clown magnet: *Amber, five thousand dollars.*

"Mary Rose? How come I'm such a fuck-up?"

"You're not. Well, you are somewhat, but I think you're within the normal range. For a straight white male cop."

"You know what?" She hears him clear his throat, staving off more tears. "I love you and Maureen more than anyone in the world, I'd be dead without you guys."

"No you wouldn't, but you might be less screwed-up."

"That's what Dad always said."

"He was afraid it would turn you gay, having sisters and no brother."

"How ironic. I wish I was gay."

"No you don't."

"Mary Rose? How come—" He breaks off, crying in the choked way of a boy fighting the humiliation of tears.

"It's okay, Andy-Pat. Andy-Pat? I love you. Maggie's here. You want to say hi?"

"What's the matter with me, Mister?"

"Shereen left."

Perhaps all their panic attacks are this simple, a choreography of chaos designed to avoid the quiet thing behind the curtain: loss.

He whimpers. She starts singing "Boom Boom, Ain't It Great to Be Crazy?" They used to sing it on family car trips—in between her bouts of carsickness. She sings it softly now, as though it were a lullaby, wondering dispassionately as she does so, How did this get to be my life? But he says, "No. The other one."

She sings the whole thing. Somewhere around the verse about the soldiers who have all gone missing, she hears him blow his nose. His voice is ragged but steady. "Mister, how come you always help me, but I can never help you? I never help anyone. Dad was right, I'm a 'useless shit.'"

"That's not true. He was probably jealous of you."

"What? Why?"

"Because you had a father."

". . . Wow."

"That'll be a hundred and twenty-five dollars plus HST."

"See?" he moans.

"You've helped me."

"When?"

But she can't think of an example. Maggie spills her juice and starts fingerpainting with it. Daisy starts licking it up—she will have diarrhea later, her system is that sensitive. "You help just by being my brother." She has spoken like a Hallmark card but suddenly it hurts, like a splinter in her throat, the word: *brother*. She mustn't cry too. Through her kitchen window she sees a stolid middle-aged man jog by. He is in the here and now.

"I better go," he says. He is back. "I look like I've been crying."

"You probably just look hungover like all the other cops."

"I'm a man."

"Yes you am."

He is off to Kingston to stand next to the premier at the dedication of a new monument to "the fallen" in Afghanistan—as if they'd tripped on something. *See Jane fall*. He asks if they can meet for coffee tomorrow morning at nine. "Sure, I'll come right after I drop Matthew at 8:45." She feels a pang of remorse over how ticked off at A&P she was for standing her up at the salon. Hil was right, he was actually in crisis. His binge of shopping and primping on the heels of a breakup ought to have tipped her off that he was heading for a crash. He was on the rebound, falling for himself all over again, getting infatuated only to find there was no one on the other end of the embrace—existential *horreur*! Why can't she and her brother just be sad when it is sad? Sad = Cry = Feel Better. Even Maureen cries. Why do she and A&P need to go through so many hoops? Krazy Klowns.

They hang up. It will be good to see him tomorrow, they will have an unfraught coffee. She tears off a wad of paper towels and swipes through the mangoey mess on the floor, having broken a rule from *The Parents' Guide to Survival:* never pour more than you plan to wipe up.

"No!" shrieks Maggie.

Mary Rose forgot it was art. Maggie laments bitterly, sticky hands clawing the floor in Trojan Women–sized despair. Mary Rose leans down to pick her up from behind, just as the child jacks to her feet and Mary Rose sustains the toddler head-snap to the bridge of her nose. "Oh my God." No blood, just pain.

These are the wages of cold turkey—there is forty-five minutes before she has to go get Matthew, time enough for Maggie to have a mini-nap—a methadone nap. Mary Rose herself could do with a twenty-minute "sizz." What would Hil do?

She turns on the faucet, puts it to "spray" and pulls it from its retractable base. "Here you go, Maggs . . . Aim into the sink, that's right. The sink!" Mary Rose moves out of range to the small utility sink where she unpacks the produce and starts the wash along the rind.

She buys organic but avoids the subject with her mother, who scorns the term—"I don't buy anything organeek!" Her father is fond of inquiring with MBA-ular skepticism, "How do you know it's organeek? Where's the proof?" She has explained to her parents that organic is not new, it is what they grew up with. It is one reason why their generation will probably wind up having been at the apex of human longevity. "Just think of it as food. It's all the other stuff that should be hyphenated. Why do you think cancer rates are soaring, along with allergies and obesity?"

"'By your children be ye taught!'" declaimed Dolly, and pretended to slap her.

Mary Rose tries not to rant, but her parents must enjoy baiting her. Why else would her mother see a rejection of her own values in Mary Rose's healthy choices when Dolly herself paved the way with

Lebanese cuisine and a refusal to waste money on processed "fog"? Why would her father persist in making right-wing remarks when he is in fact well left of many people far younger?

He likes to wait till the end of a visit. "I see where there's a new auto mechanic shop opened up downtown and their claim to fame is that all the mechanics are female. Why are they making such a big deal of their gender, it just begs the question, if you're so great, where've you been for the past two thousand years?" *Mechaneek.*

He knows the answer, he taught her the answer, coached and rooted for her till she breached every last barrier—*Do it your way, Mister*—to the point of coming out of the closet long before anyone thought "it gets better," at which point he stopped cheering. Still, it is nothing new, it goes all the way back to Germany and one of her earliest memories.

She is sitting on his lap, steering the car—before the days of seat belts and child safety laws. It does not get better than this: you may not be fully toilet trained, but you can steer the car. "That's it, Mister, nice and easy, turn the wheel." His hands halo hers as the wheel spools beneath her fingers. There is the smell of diesel and leather. I AM STEERING THE CAR. Over the red dashboard is the horizon of windshield, the clown nose at the centre of the wheel is the horn. "You're a good driver, Mister." I AM A GOOD DRIVER. "Now let's shift gears." She feels his leg tighten beneath her as he steps on the clutch. She cups her palm over the ball of the gear stick with its strange carved symbols, and feels the force of his hand bearing down on hers as he thrusts them through the thunking. DON'T BE SCARED OF THAT. "Good stuff, now we're in second." The shaft of the stick is impaled in a soft leather pouch, like the wrinkly snout of an animal that is getting wrenched about the nose, but it doesn't hurt it—it is just a thing—and you're not supposed to look at that part of the car anyway, KEEP YOUR EYES ON THE ROAD. It was a cream-coloured VW Beetle with red leather interior. At some point he took to teasing her. "When the boy is born, you'll have to sit in the back seat and he'll steer the car."

"No, I steer."

"Boys sit in the front, girls sit in the back."

"No, me do that."

"Nope. You'll be in the back seat with your sister."

"No!"

"The boy will be up front with me."

"NO!"

He laughed until she saw his gold tooth. The rage tore up her throat like grit—gone was the horizon over the dash in the blur of an eye, she was turning into a tangle, as if she were scribbling over herself with black crayon, until finally, "I HATE THE BOY!"

Clotted words, flung like ink, she was black but she was back.

His voice was suddenly sad. "Don't say that, Mister, he's just a baby. He's going to be your little brother."

He looked sad and bewildered. She had hurt him. And she had hurt a poor dear baby. Her own brother. Shame engulfed her, rising from within like the warm, wet odour of pee. "Sorry, Daddy." Tears.

Back then it was not possible to know the sex of a fetus, so while her father's certainty must have been wishful thinking, he was right. The baby she cursed was a boy.

Mary Rose does not need to pay a psychotherapist to know that deep down she is convinced she killed Alexander, robbed him of his birthright and deserves to be punished for her place in the driver's seat. It is right there in the pages of her own book: Kitty and Jon McRae are twins who, in their respective worlds, absorbed one another in utero and were born as singles. Each has one blue eye and one brown, a vestige of their missing sibling. And each, merely by having been born, has robbed the other of that which could heal their respective worlds . . . Even if she failed to see it until she had written the second book.

Perhaps that is why she used to pore over the graveside photo in secret. She was returning to the scene of a crime, stealing away with the album to the bathroom or the crawl space—almost as if it were a dirty picture; limiting her viewings so it would retain its "power." Closing her eyes, she would turn to the correct page, count to three then open them . . . as though to catch the photo in the act. Of what? She once enlisted Andy-Patrick in a furtive viewing, but cut it short. "You're too young," she said, closing the album. Then she scuttled from the crawl space and held the door closed on him in the darkness until he stopped crying.

Is it her fault Andy-Patrick is a mess?

She was five when she heard her mother make the call to Cape Breton, a catch in her voice as she cradled the phone receiver in both hands and told her own father, "Pa? Pa, I've had a son! I've had a son, Pa!" She was nine when her father took to sitting her and Maureen down and regretfully laying at their feet their brother's inability to stay out of trouble at school or get along at home—not to mention his taste for playing dress-up: "You have to remember he's a boy in a family of girls. He doesn't have a *brother*. He is outnumbered by *sisters*." He spoke in the ultra-expository tones he reserved for math problems and travel directions. But with a plaintive note. "You can't expect him to act like a little *girl*. He's a *boy*."

There would be a pause. She would feel shame seeping warm and sickly. "Mary Rose, you're closest to him in age, you have the biggest influence." Whenever he used her actual name, she felt pinned. This is what is behind the tomboy nickname and the carefree wink from Dad: a girl's name. You can hurt yourself on it if you forget it's there. "You've got to let him be a boy."

Few things were more shaming than knowing you were preventing your brother from being a boy—like barging into a bathroom lined with urinals, who do you think you are? Molesting his masculinity, that sacred, powerful, delicate thing that was none of her business yet her business to protect. This seemed to mean that Andy-Patrick was to be supported in wreaking havoc, lest he grow up weak and effeminate. Mary Rose robbed her dead sister too, of course, but only of a name.

She opens her dented freezer to put away a container of cut-up bananas for smoothies, but it is a tight fit. She reaches into the back, extracts an opaque brick and sets it on the counter. Wrapped in layers of what looks to be surgical dressing, stained with something dark . . . her mother's Christmas cake.

It has to be eaten before next Christmas. It must not be discovered intact next January when her mother brings another Christmas cake . . . unless her mother has died by then and this Christmas cake turns out to have been the last one. Her throat thickens painfully at the thought of her mother's busy brown hands stirring the batter in the white vat set atop the banged-up freezer out in the garage, "C'mere kids and give the Christmas cake a stir for luck!"

Who is going to look after her parents if the emergency comes while Dolly and Dunc are at their home in Ottawa? Mary Rose is four and a half hours away by car, and even if Andy-Patrick gets posted to RCMP headquarters there, how will he cope if—when—something happens? He will shatter. He will swallow his tongue and pee his pants. She and Maureen need to find him a solid, capable woman they can rely on to find their parents dead one day. Otherwise it will be a nice neighbour. "We noticed the mail piling up, dear, and your parents hadn't mentioned they were going out of town, so I used the key they gave me, and . . ."

As it is, the best she can hope for is that her parents drop dead in Victoria, where people are used to scraping seniors off the sidewalk and defibrillating them in malls. Her father, a poster-senior for successful bypass surgery, is still a candidate for heart attack. What if he infarcts behind the wheel, mounts the curb and kills a pedestrian pushing a stroller?

Dolly had wanted to call the new baby Alexander, but Mary Rose said, "If you call him Alexander, you'll have to put him in the ground." She thinks she remembers this, but it is so much a stock part of family lore that perhaps she merely remembers having been told the story. No wonder she clung to the old graveside photo; it was a moment captured in time, unlike the unstable atoms of memory. Considering the intensity with which she examined the photo, every detail ought to be burnt into her brain, including the dates on the stone. But memory plays tricks, recording the flotsam of a flowered sweater and erasing the lifespan of a lost baby boy. In any event, thanks to Mary Rose Andrew-Patrick got a fresh name.

He would have been around a year old, and she would have been six, back on the air force base at Trenton. He was sitting in a heap of baby fat at the bottom of the stairs, dressed in a plaid jumpsuit, crying. Clear baby drool mixed with tears. Mary Rose was consoling him when her father came and crouched next to them. She expected him to pick Andy-Patrick up and comfort him—Dad was patient and loving. But Duncan looked straight at fat little Andy-Pat and said, "What're you crying for like a sissy girl?"

Mary Rose went hot. She felt dreadful for her father for having said this in front of her. For a moment it was as though the air were made of sheet metal, searing like the sun on the wing of a fighter jet. How could she stand up for herself while allowing room for him to have meant something different?

"Dad? All girls aren't sissies."

"Oh, I didn't mean that," he said in his harmless voice. "It's perfectly normal for girls to cry, but what you have to understand is, we don't want anyone giving your brother a hard time when he's older."

"I'm a girl and I don't cry."

"I know, little buddy."

She never cried, whether she fell off her bike or was facing shots in net in exchange for playing road hockey with the boys. She thought, but would not say, "I didn't even cry when you gave me the airplane swing," because that would be like saying, "You hurt me, Dad."

"Not all girls are sissies," she said. "Most of them are, but I'm not."

"I know, Mister, you're tough."

And having been offered a sliver of space, she squeezed under the umbrella.

Brother and sister did, however, maintain a bond. When he started toddling, their mother would tie him around the waist with two diapers knotted end to end and fastened to a bar of his crib, "so he won't climb out and hurt himself." Sometimes at night Mary Rose would steal into his room, kneel at his crib-side and, closing her hands round the bars, whisper consolation. He would respond with pleading hazel eyes and downy brows—she cried too, because they were pretending he was in jail. She once made the mistake of untying him, which meant it was her own fault when he got out and pulled her hair. Mum hauled her away by the arm, which hurt but only because it was her sore arm anyhow.

By then they were living in Hamilton, "the Steel City," beneath its yellow cloud that was visible for miles—you could not see the cloud when you were under it, but often you could smell it: rotten eggs. "That's the smell of prosperity," said Duncan. The smelters worked day and night, eternal flames shot from smokestacks into the sky, effluent ran from pipes into Lake Ontario, and framing it all like a dirty rainbow was the mighty Skyway bridge. Up there, wind buffeted cars and rocked the trucks, and anyone foolhardy enough to get out of their car with a camera might be blown over the rail.

It was winter. Aunt Sadie had come to stay while Uncle Leo was "sorting things out back home" again. They were outside playing, Andy-Pat was Michelined into his snowsuit, teetering on tiny galoshes. Mary Rose does not recall what precipitated it, but recalls vividly her aunt's advice. "Dolly, don't hit him in the face. Hit his little hands, like this." Mary Rose watched as Aunt Sadie demonstrated the proper way to hit a child, taking Andy-Pat's hand in one of her own and smacking it sharply with her other. "See? Don't hit him anywhere on the head." *Smack.* Andy-Pat's face turned red and he cried.

They lived in Hamilton for nine months while Duncan did his MBA at McMaster University. Maureen started high school at Cathedral Catholic Secondary and played guitar in the groovy new folk masses, Andy-Patrick discovered that blobs of tar on the sidewalk could be chewed like gum, and Dolly had another miscarriage. Mary Rose entered grade three at St. Anne's Catholic Elementary School and fell in love.

The sight of Lisa Snodgrass in the next row was like lemonade on a scorching day, like vanilla ice cream on a sore throat, like—*Pay attention!* Mary Rose looked up. Mrs. Peters resembled a pterodactyl with lipstick. She had a visible mole on her scalp and a frightening habit of smiling when displeased.

"Show me that note," she said, beaming.

Mary Rose had not intended to pass the note, having written it only in order to see the words on paper. Mrs. Peters read it silently then looked at her strangely before saying, "That makes no sense at all," and tearing it up.

Mary Rose waited until she was home to rewrite the note in pencil on a scrap of paper by the phone. She looked at the words for a long while, then for some reason she tore up that note too.

I love Lisa Snodgrass

They moved to Kingston, where, for the first time, her parents purchased a house. Her father planted a flowering crab in the front lawn, its endearing sparseness reminiscent of Charlie Brown's Christmas tree. "This tree will be flowering long after we've moved away again," he said in the mournful tones of Scottish contentment.

They lived in a new subdivision. These were the days when children "went out and played"; there were woods and creeks that had yet to be tamed into suburban lots, and for endless summer days Mary Rose could "light out" like Huck and not return till supper, socks burred, runners soaked.

To get to the Royal Military College where her father worked you had to drive past the Dairy Queen, the Kmart, three prisons, the loony bin, Sir John A. Macdonald's house—with his small bed and undersized boots that showed what life had been like before vitamins—Queen's University, Kingston General Hospital and across the lift bridge to the stone archway that led to the ivy-bearded walls wherein her father taught economics, "the dismal science." Eventually Maureen would get a weekend job lifeguarding at the pool there and meet Zoltan Zivcovic, an officer cadet whose pillbox hat and sticking-out ears made him look like a tall, serious monkey. Andy-Patrick moved from a crib into a room of his own equipped with everything Mary Rose could desire in the way of vehicles and weaponry, not to mention clothing—she felt like an imposter in girls' clothes. But she continued to love her brother when he was sad, sick or asleep—he got mononucleosis shortly after they moved in and he was adorable.

Her father sent her off on the first day of school with a firm pat on the head, "Do it your way, Rosie." She lined up outside Our Lady of Lourdes with the grade fives, awaiting the bell, conscious of the butterflies in her stomach aflutter with the secret of the miracle, *You have skipped a grade!* She looked up and down the line, assessing which girl would be the object of her crush, a worthy successor to Lisa Snodgrass . . . and stopped herself, suddenly aware that it was wrong. *And they knew they were naked.* Having crushes on girls was something to be left behind along with her place in the slow readers' group. It belonged to a benighted past that need never cast its shadow so long as she did her best, then better than her best. She looked up and down the line again. And chose Danny Pinder. Another miracle. Our Lady made her become normal.

She was unable, however, to leave behind the soreness in her arm. It smelled of the grave.

"Maureen! Come, I need you!" cried Dolly.

It was the middle of the day, but her mother was taking a bath. They were not at school so perhaps it was the weekend. Mary Rose followed her sister up the stairs but Mo hurried in and closed the bathroom door behind her. She pressed her ear to it, then opened it a crack. Her mother was in the tub, the water was red. Maureen turned, saw Mary Rose and slammed the door in her face, shouting at the same time, "It's okay, Rosie!" That night her mother was quiet and they got to order pizza.

It was the last "other."

One summer day, Mary Rose ransacked the steamer trunk in the basement for Aunt Sadie's sateen dressing gown from the forties, a flowing affair in gold and scarlet paisley, and other mothbally sundries—her mother's nursing cape, a plastic sword from a giant bag of puffed rice—and she and Andy-Pat along with a couple of neighbourhood kids devised and put on a play. They wrestled the lawn mower and snow shovels out of the aluminum garden shed, using it and its dented sliding doors as a proscenium stage, thus linking forever the magic of theatre to the smell of grass cuttings and motor oil. *The Curse of Roderigo.* Mary Rose had cast five-year-old Andy-Pat in the title role, furnishing him with a hunchback courtesy of a couch cushion, but he insisted on playing the damsel in distress, "Lady Jenniah," with lipstick, fan and Aunt Sadie's sateen.

She summoned the family and neighbours to the driveway, where they watched from the comfort of lawn chairs. The sun set, swords were drawn, Lady Jenniah wept and danced, Roderigo fought and swore to avenge her death. Andy-Pat was brilliant. Everyone clapped. Afterwards her father took her aside, "Don't be getting your brother to dress up like a girl, Mister."

She did not question him this time. She was old enough to identify the scent of shame. Andy-Pat retired from the stage and went back to pulling out clumps of her hair and she went back to hating *that little brat.* The end of their mother's rope was frayed. "C'mere till I annihilate the both of you!"

No matter how many clumps of hair he pulled from her head, or how often she told their father on him—"Dad is going to kill you!"—she and Andy-Patrick returned to one another, compelled by a *folie à deux*, or merely their job description that mirrored that of the sheep-dog and coyote in the old cartoon, each punching the clock at the dawn of the workday—"Mornin' Ralph," "Mornin' Fred"—then proceeding to do battle.

She took to terrorizing them both with an entity called Zygote from the Planet Zytox. They'd be in the basement rec room that their father had finished with wood panelling and scalloped plaster on the ceiling—this was the room where the whole family had watched the moon landing. The room with the crawl space. Heralded by an inter-galactic beeping that she produced by sucking in air backward through her larynx, the alien who had inhabited Mary Rose's body would croak in a metallic voice, "I am Zygote from the Planet Zytox. Your sister, Mary Rose, is being held prisoner there."

She had bangs and a pixie cut. A&P had a brush cut—his eye-lashes were extra curly, having been recently singed when he leaned over the manhole where Travis Orr had emptied go-kart fuel and fol-lowed it with a lit match.

"If you do not follow my instructions, she will be killed immediately," rasped Zygote. Andy-Pat's lip quivered and he swore to do whatever he was told to save his sister—he even attempted to assault Zygote, who nipped it in the bud: "Your feeble attempts to harm me only make it worse for your sister, who at this very instant is being tortured on Zytox."

Andy-Pat would cease, meek once more, and might be rewarded with a breathless "visit" from the real Mary Rose, who was able to break through intermittently—

"Andy-Pat, you have to do whatever Zygote says, don't tell him I've been here, and remember, even when you think it's me, it's really him doing a perfect imitation of me, but I have a plan, I've found an ally on Zytox, just pretend—"

A screed of static would intervene and reptilian Zygote would be back:

"Andrew-Patrick, who was here in my absence?"

A&P would tremble. "No one."

The ante was upped when Zygote's mother, Zygrette, broke in and, in kinder elderly metallic tones, said, "My son is evil, dear Andy-Patrick, you must be brave, I am trying to save your sister—" But Zygote ousted her and, with larynx-shredding cold-bloodedness, delivered the *coup de grâce*, "In a moment, the woman who calls herself your mother will call you for supper. Go upstairs and act normal. She is an imposter from the Planet Zytox. So is the man who calls himself your father. Your real parents are both being held prisoner on the Planet Zytox. If you don't act normal, they will be killed."

And from upstairs would issue their mother's summons, "Kids, come for supper!"

She walked her brother to school on the days when he was neither sick nor suspended, and they never knew when, in an eerily neutral voice, she might inquire, "Who do you think that is, putting the sprinkler out on his front lawn?"

"Mr. Chown."

"No," she would say serenely, "it looks like Mr. Chown, it sounds like him, but it's not him. It's a man called Mr. Mannington. What street are we on?"

"Our street."

"It looks like our street. The houses look the same and have families that are identical to the families on our street, but this is not our street. It is actually a street called Prince Duke Avenue on the Planet Mearth. You think we are speaking English, but we are not. We are speaking Mearthingian."

One fall day, Maureen bundled her and Andy-Patrick into the

family Buick to get them out of the house because Mum was hurling herself into the walls. Mary Rose had seen Maureen's room and thought that was why Mum was angry—it was even messier than usual, drawers yanked out and overturned, closet looted of clothes that lay strewn across the floor, some still on hangers, looking like people who'd been mowed down by gunfire. But it turned out Mum had done it.

It was after lunch and Mum was still in her shortie nightgown and nylon slippers that Aunt Sadie had knitted. Her powerful pony legs were bare, her varicose veins, "from carrying you kids," stood out against the frills of her nightgown. She was staggering and bellowing, but Mary Rose caught only a glimpse because Maureen seized her head, jammed it face-first against her chest and marched her backward out to the front porch where she had already put Andy-Patrick. "Get in the car." Maureen had turned fifteen. Old enough to flee the advance of the Red Army with a family in tow, older than her grandmother by the time she had had three children. But not old enough to drive. Mary Rose and Andy-Patrick sat at attention in the back seat grinning while Maureen muttered something and lurched into reverse.

She drove out to the locks at Kingston Mills. It rained. They looked at the canal. There were places where you could drive a car right in if you weren't careful. Andy-Patrick and Mary Rose listened respectfully as Maureen explained the feat of nineteenth-century engineering. "Wow, Mo, that's really neat." Their sister was good, and they clung to her and her clean knowledge fiercely like the demons they were, grateful to those who mistook them for human children.

Their father was back in Hamilton, finishing up his MBA, paralyzed with concentration over a stats book. For them.

It was just before or after her first operation, for her arm was in a sling, when Mary Rose succumbed to temptation yet again. Taking the photo album along with a flashlight, she ducked, careful not to bump her arm, through the small door in the rec room wall and into the crawl space. She sat cross-legged, hunched beneath the joists, with the album in her lap and closed her eyes. She felt for the particular series of three notches along the edge of the velvety old page, opened the album, and then her eyes. To see a blank spot. The photo was gone. All that remained was a darker black square where it had been, and the caption, written in white pencil in her mother's hand, "Cemetery." The flush of shame was immediate, she felt her face turn red in the dark. Her mother must have seen the way she looked at the picture over and over again . . . And taken it away.

That winter, Dolly took a ceramics class and fired no fewer than thirty miniature Christmas trees.

·

Mary Rose was standing next to her father before the Hudson's Bay department store window in downtown Kingston, watching teddy bears skate on a silver pond as a train wove through glittering hills. Santa was in the caboose, drinking a Coke. Her arm was in a sling made from her mother's scarf. It was dark out. The pit of her stomach felt hot and wet. She was keenly aware of the privilege of being on her own with her father, no Andy-Patrick there to share the limelight, no Mum to hurry them along, and yet something was not right. She was conscious of an unbidden sexual excitement as she watched Santa tipping the bottle to his lips. She knew something the teddy bears did not know. She was not worthy to be watching them along with her father and the other innocent children. She had a secret simmering within her. A bad one. It was connected to the pain in her arm. Pain like extra information she carried around. Pain that was no more than she deserved.

Being with her father sometimes made the pain worse; perhaps because he lived in such a sunny place—a place that was at times too bright, like the glassy pond. When the pain went away, so did the sense of being exiled to a narrow vantage point, a crack in the rocks. It was a pain that dwelt in darkness. The pain that dared not speak its name.

•

It is snowing. Outside her kitchen windows, the sky has turned opaque and produced a razzle of crazy flakes. Mary Rose is barely able to make out the fence much less the hopeful crocuses on the ground—it is as if February had snuck up on April, whacked it on the head and taken its place. She turns on the radio, *Hi there, and happy Wednesday . . .* The mummified Christmas cake sits on the counter looking like something from the Royal Ontario Museum.

She wonders if it is freezer-dead or if it can be resurrected. She should learn to make these things. Andy-Patrick makes their mother's Lebanese Easter bread, she should get him to come over and show her how. Her kids are not growing up with the same smells as she did, they don't have a mother who covers her hair with a cloth diaper and flips dough in the air while singing made-up words to *Carmen*. A mother who uses Arabic endearments. And calls them "demon." And chases them through the house with a wooden spoon. And threatens to "annihilate" them, and swears to "massacre" them. And promises to "smash" them. And wears Chanel No. 5 and moonstones.

She belongs in the loony bin is what she heard Maureen mutter that day when they escaped in the car. It made Mary Rose feel something beyond sad or scared or even ashamed—those are clean words that can be read and said—it made her feel like there was tar melting inside her.

From then on it seemed the days when their mother yelled and failed to change out of her nightgown or do her hair were coming up more frequently in the revolving bingo ball of life. The Dolly who canvassed for the Heart Fund and the Liberal Party, ran the Catholic Women's League, conducted the choir, made her own wine with a catheter tube and two vats, balanced the bank book, sewed matching outfits and regularly fed an army of guests was less in evidence. "C'mere till I smash you." When hollered, it was no more than turbulence, but when spoken with level tone and lowering gaze it was terrifying. Mary Rose was nine and standing in the kitchen. Slaps and pinches, yanks and shoves, were merely sticks and stones, but words hurt. On this day the words issuing from her mother were dark and heavy, and she was immobilized under the weight of them, able neither to put up an arm against them nor outrun them, laughing. She saw herself from behind and slightly above, as though she were hovering near the ceiling. Then she witnessed a kind of miracle—it did not cross her mind to attribute it to Our Lady, so perhaps it was more of a scientific phenomenon: she watched as a transparent but impermeable shield like a force field took shape around her, and suddenly she was back in her body, behind her own eyes, within a hard transparent dome. She saw the dark shapes of her mother's incoming words stop short upon contact with it, and fall to the floor, and she understood, "They are just sounds."

Behind her, on the floor, Maggie is "swimming" in a laundry basket full of plastic balls—an idea Mary Rose got from a McDonald's they stopped at in desperation on the 401 last summer.

Now is Mary Rose's chance to slip into the living room, lie down on the couch and close her eyes—ten minutes is all she needs. Churchill napped, naps won the war. As long as she's lying down, she can't lose her scissors, her yoga mat or her temper, as long as she is lying down nothing bad can happen. But she returns the cake to the stainless steel drawer, so like a morgue, and closes her dented freezer. "Let's go pick up your brother and Youssef from school now."

At the back door steps she gets Maggie into her snowsuit no problem, but the child balks at the boots.

"Sitdy boots."

The phone rings. A long-distance ring.

"Maggie, it's snowing, you need your winter boots this time."

Ring ring.

Maggie kicks her. Mary Rose sighs and takes her firmly but gently by the shoulders, focusing the child's attention just as the books advise. She does not feel angry. "Maggie, you may not kick Mumma."

Maggie hits her in the face.

"NO!"

She seizes the little arms, "STOP IT!" resisting the impulse to lift her child and slam her back down onto the steps. "DON'T DO THAT!" Resisting the impulse to yank her up, up from the steps and haul her across the kitchen floor by the elbow—instead she rages into the child's face, "DON'T YOU EVER HIT ME!" She is not doing it, but she can see herself doing it. Up by the elbow like a chicken by the wing, and the more she does not do this, the harder she squeezes, as though to keep herself from merging with the phantom self that is giving in to lust, sobbing for release, the desire to—her hands spring open, "I DIDN'T HURT YOU!" The crazy words hang in the air, black and straining, leashed. Maggie is screaming. Mary Rose hears Daisy clicketing across the kitchen floor. The dog arrives on the top step, riding-crop tail going a mile a minute.

Mary Rose is faint with anger. Her breath is shallow. Her hands drop to her sides—nothing bad is going to happen, she knows how to make parts of her body go dead. Daisy *mwuffs* and mashes her wet muzzle against Mary Rose's throat.

"It's okay, Daisy." She breathes and stares up at a corner of the ceiling. She hears Maggie rustling. Hears her say, "Do it *Me*-self."

She risks moving her hands, but only to thrust them safely into her pockets, withdrawing her left one suddenly with a yelp. She is bleeding. She has pricked her finger . . . She reaches back in and fishes out the broken unicorn. She mounts the stairs calmly, leaving Maggie to her boots. She puts the unicorn and its head on the kitchen counter and runs cold water over her finger.

How do you tell yourself what you already know? If you have successfully avoided something, how do you know you have avoided it? Land mines of anger left over from a forgotten war, you step on one by chance. Sudden sinkholes of depression, you crawl back out. A weave of weeds obscures a mind-shaft but cannot break a fall, you get hurt this time. A booby-trapped terrain, it says, "Something happened here." Trenches overgrown but still visible from space, green welts, scars that tell a story. You press on.

Years pass and you become aware of a blind spot. A blank. White as bone. A strip of mind where fear has scorched consciousness clean, obliterated fingerprints, freckles, follicles. Smooth as a stone slab.

As an old scar.

.

When she woke up in the recovery room, her throat was sore and she thought she was back in Hamilton with her tonsils out. She was very thirsty. She was lying on a hard, narrow bed on wheels called a gurney, which sounded like a type of cow. Right next to her was another gurney with a bulging sheet on it. The sheet was going up and down. A noise was coming from it. A farmyard sound. Like a cow. She managed to turn her head enough to see that it was a person. A fat old man with something like a gas mask over his face except it was see-through. A plastic snout. His eyes were closed and a tube was coming out of his mouth. It was the same kind of tube that her mother siphoned homemade wine with . . . there was a foamy streak in it. She turned her face to the ceiling. She tried to ask for water, but no sound came out. After a while a nurse came with a tiny paper cup like the kind you get at the dentist's. She tried to swallow but could not and the water trickled out the side of her mouth. She wanted more, but the nurse said no, it was not safe. She saw yellow paint on her chest, and a blood patch on the white bandage, and remembered it was her arm not her tonsils.

.

"A lesbian gave me this mug," said Dolly in 1982, so Mary Rose thought it might be safe to come out.

They were in Dolly's kitchen in Ottawa—she had a nice part-time job as staff nurse in a government building, and the lesbian had confided in her, asking for advice on how to talk to her own mother. Dolly must have helped, hence the mug: *World's Best Nurse.*

It wasn't safe.

"Everything you do is a reflection of me. You're saying to the world, 'I had a terrible mother, I had a terrible father.'"

She refused to set foot in the home Mary Rose shared with Renée.

"Would you visit Hell?"

Refused to allow Renée or any other "friend like that" to set foot in her home. She issued it like an edict—a fatwa.

"Would you let the devil in?"

They were sitting at the kitchen table.

"I didn't give you shit to eat, why are you living in it now?"

Her father was staring up at a corner of the ceiling.

"I'd rather you were a murderer," said Dolly.

Mary Rose saw the words float toward her, hot foul shapes that glanced off an invisible shield.

Duncan spoke. "If you had a broken leg, we'd have taken you to the doctor. In this case it is your *mind* that is broken, and how were we to *know*? You *kept* it from us. You didn't give us the *chance* to help you."

"I'd rather you were burnt at the stake."

Friends assured her they were bound to "come round."

"If you want to be close to that part of a woman, I'll come live with you when I'm old and senile and you can change my shitty diaper."

Friends urged her to cut them off.

"I'd rather you had cancer."

It was always at the kitchen table. In Dolly's eye would be the glint Mary Rose recognized from when her mother read tea leaves;

an indication that she was seeing through something to something else. But in this case, someone else. Who?

Her father would turn away, eyes on the ceiling. Smooth, impenetrable. Glass.

Down below, Mary Rose sat immobilized as the air changed around them, thickened like a welt.

"I'd rather you'd never been born."

She sat watching herself watching, and waited for it to be over.

She thought she was calm.

"I'd rather you'd been born dead."

Then they would play Scrabble.

The very hyperbole of her mother's curses had a prophylactic effect, sealing them in shrink wrap, allowing Mary Rose to swallow them like drugs she thought would pass through her harmlessly.

She was twenty-three.

Around this time, she experienced the first of the episodes that would persist for over a decade. They struck in clusters. Panic attack. What's in a name? Not enough. Beyond, "I was terrified." For whole hours, there was no "I." At times, preceded by a visual sense of the world constricting and retreating as though seen through the wrong end of a telescope—so-called tunnelling; at others by a dread that mushroomed into disorientation. Vertigo, with both feet on the ground. Lost on an ordinary day, in an ordinary place. A parking lot. Wedged at an odd angle behind her own eyes, she would make her way home and lie down in the most dangerous place in the world, her body. To misplace car keys in those days might be to drop into the void, to misread the clock or forget someone's name set off adrenal terror fuelled by an outsized guilt that made no sense; as though, along with the "synesthesia" of numbers and colours, her emotions were cross-wired. Nothing stayed where she put it, including herself.

She hit bottom in a hotel room on a book tour in her mother's hometown, retreating alone to the Cape Bretoner Motor Inn, knowing it was the least unsafe place—it is worse to be among those who are living in the normal world when one has lost hold of it. The carpet was orange, the bedspread was orange, the sunset painting above the bed was orange. There was no one she could call, the sound of a familiar voice would serve only to confirm the gulf between herself and the normal world and push her out of it for good. After a while, her hand turned on the television. A documentary about the last days of the Third Reich was playing. Himmler's children lay dead in their night-gowns, as though sleeping, on the floor of the bunker, killed by their parents with strychnine-laced cocoa. She prayed. Our Lady spoke to her and told her the only thing that mattered was Love. She remained abject with fear all night, but survived. Maybe none of it happened. Maybe it was happening all the time.

•

When she could sit up, she gazed at it. It was compelling. The left side of her chest as well as her shoulder above the surgical dressing was painted yellow—probably some sort of disinfectant. The snowy white dressing was wound round her upper arm as if she were an Egyptian mummy, at its centre a bright red stain dulled to burgundy at the slow-spreading edges. Below, the fingers of her left hand were pain-free and bewildered, like survivors of a car crash who have walked away without a scratch. It hurt to touch anywhere on the yellow paint, so perhaps it was a bruise.

•

Mary Rose did not harbour hope of her parents' coming round, nor did she cut them off for it came to her that sanity would not survive the severing. That part of the brain known as "executive function," in its crisp white shirt and narrow tie, picked up and deciphered a dark, thrashing message from several neural floors below, the racket and shit-flung panic of which she remained consciously unaware, and coolly articulated it: *Your parents lived to adulthood before you came along and are thus equipped to recognize themselves in a world without you. But you have never known a world without them.* They were the sky. Her mother was a thunderhead, but living without a sky was not an option.

So she continued to visit their home, alone. She got on with her life—which was what she called her career. She drank and raged and laughed, saw dots and big yellow orbs, forgot how to blink and breathe, all while cleaving to a notion of wholeness and the wisdom of embattled contradictions. Yet she could not bring herself to say "we" in their presence when referring to Renée. *Renée* was a word that went to glue on the roof of her mouth and sucked her down to the undertow place of no-language. She experienced an interruption of reality when she spoke the name—as though in the real world, the one her parents inhabited, there was no such word, and she was crazy for having made the sound. Nothing is lonelier than crazy. She was "out" to the whole world, but her parents could obliterate her with their refusal to acknowledge a name.

Maureen went to visit Dolly and Dunc with Zoltan and their young family shortly after Mary Rose came out. Mo phoned from their parents' home to say that, while she still loved her as her sister, Mary Rose was not welcome to bring Renée, or any other "friend with that lifestyle," into contact with her children. It lasted a few months, at which point Mo phoned again, this time from her own home, and apologized with the dazed remorse of an ex–cult member. Soon after, she adopted a policy of refusing to discuss the subject with their mother, hoping thereby to starve the fire of oxygen.

Mary Rose's father sent a letter by registered mail. It must have taken him quite a while to hunt and peck it out on the old Remington typewriter. She read it once and tore it up. She recalls nothing beyond the first sentence but knows it was as different from "Some things really do get batter" as possible.

> Dear Mary Rose, You have chosen to go down
> a path that we, as your parents, cannot
> follow . . .

"I'd rather you had cancer." But Dolly never wrote it down.

Her anger turned out to be more frightening in its power to endure than it had been in its power to erupt. "Who touched you?" she took to asking Mary Rose. "Did someone touch you? Did your father touch you?"

The air was shocked.

Her father's gaze remained pinned to the corner of the ceiling— what was it in his own story that enabled him to leave the room without leaving his chair?

Who touched you?

It was as though Dolly were telling a story over and over again— or rather, a story was working its way through her.

Did your father touch you?

With Herculean effort, as though hauling herself up from an afternoon death sleep, and with a disorienting sense of betrayal of what up to that point had been the agreed-upon reality at the kitchen table, she finally said to her mother in the midst of one of these performances, "No, Mum, my father never touched me. Did your father touch you?"

The moment she spoke the words, she felt a coolness against her face like cool water as she understood that reality was what she was in now, and that a moment ago she had been inhabiting a state akin to the drug-induced numbness preparatory to a surgical procedure.

The light changed in her mother's eye again. She looked like a mischievous child as she replied, "Why would you ask that?" And giggled.

Dolly never posed the question again.

The lesser liturgy remained:

... *shit.*

... *cancer.*

... *dead.*

It lasted ten years.

The curse lifted without fanfare. It was just after her first book came out. She and Renée were visiting Andy-Patrick, who was living in Ottawa at the time—this was before his first divorce. He had not been around when she came out; he was busy getting tied naked to a tree somewhere in New Brunswick and force-fed alcohol in the course of basic military training before switching to the RCMP in search of a kinder, gentler way to serve his country. He never bothered forbidding her to "influence" his children with her "lifestyle." Mary Rose has never doubted that he relied on long-suffering Mary Lou as a moral compass, the way some men do—as their father did—downloading their emotional lives along with the attendant thank-you-note writing and telephone chit-chat onto their wives, not to mention the task of disowning their children ... As for Mary Lou, Mary Rose pegged her as one of those straight women who romanticize lesbianism as an orgy of empathy—one long back rub.

They were hanging out in his kitchen while he cooked supper and Mary Lou fed the baby, Renée regaling her with tales from the empathic crypt over a third glass of wine, when Dolly phoned and asked him to come for supper with his family.

"I can't, Mum. Mary Rose and Renée are here. We're having supper together."

Mary Rose gestured for him to shut up. He was either stupid or evincing the blissful ignorance of the entitled male, casually tossing that incendiary name around.

He passed her the phone. "Mum wants to talk to you."

She cringed. "Hi, Mum."

"Come home."

"I can't. I'm . . . not alone." She still could not say the name.

"Bring Renée," said her mother. "I've lost enough babies."

She didn't go. She figured, so this is how it ends: Andy-Pat declines the summons and Dolly lifts the curse; not because she does not wish to lose her daughter, but because she fears losing her son.

·

The nurse changed the dressing a couple of days after the surgery. She supported Mary Rose's elbow with one hand while with the other she deftly unwound the bandage. It hurt, but they had given her a needle for the pain, so it wasn't too bad. Also, this nurse was nice, she was pretty and knew how to do everything just right. Mary Rose watched the cool fingers as the stain grew darker and the bandage stiffer until there it was. Puckered, withered. Stitched.

"That's a beautiful incision," said her mother in unusually measured tones. She was a nurse; such things were beautiful.

"Isn't it?" said the young nurse. "Gorgeous." And she smiled.

Mary Rose stared at it. The arm looked like a badly laced sneaker. Black threads poked out at intervals along either side of the raw seam, like insect legs encrusted with blood . . . she went to touch it—

"Don't touch," said her mother quickly.

The nurse said calmly, "Go ahead and touch the skin but not the incision."

Mary Rose did, and it was with wonderment that she felt the shrivelled skin of her arm respond with a sensitivity so acute, she thought, "This must be what it's like for babies."

The nurse gently sponged her chest and shoulder. The yellow had begun to recede, leaving in its wake a streaky violet, as though the sun were setting on her chest. The nurse had nice breath, cool and light. She wrapped the arm in a fresh dressing and it looked clean and sane.

Mary Rose knew, however, what was under the dressing. It was there when she closed her eyes, imprinted on her lids: something bad, through no fault of its own. Like a demon that could not help having been born.

•

Mary Rose broke up with Renée and got together with Hil. Duncan declared Hilary to be the spitting image of his revered Aunt Chrissie— unmarried nurse-veteran of the Great War. Dolly stood on tiptoe and gave Hilary three kisses on alternating cheeks, "that's what the Lebanese do!" And just like that, Hilary was part of the family.

Soon after, Dolly paid them a solo visit to Toronto in time for International Women's Day. She wore a sequined caftan, a red turban, a gold rope with a Blessed Virgin Mary medallion, and dangly earrings. They took her to the Five Minute Feminist Cabaret. Afterwards, she read tea leaves in the backroom of a College Street bar till three a.m.

She told an astonished dub poet, "You're going to fly. Just you in mid-air, I don't know how, but you are."

To which the poet replied, "I just booked a skydive for myself, oh my God, am I going to be okay?"

"Yes, dear, I see only good."

In the cup of Cherry Pitts, of the punk band Cuntry, Dolly saw "someone who loves you and wants to be close to you but they're afraid to show it," and went on to provide initials, at the mention of which punk-pallid Cherry was seen to blush.

She saw a new house in the cup of a flamenco dancer, a cooking class for a stand-up comedian and a trip to Niagara Falls in the cup of a taciturn piano virtuoso who had eschewed melody on political grounds and had recently survived a suicide attempt, though Dolly could not have known that.

"Do I come back from the Falls?" asked the pianist.

"Oh yes, and you've brought . . . not exactly a souvenir, a . . . well, it's a dog, dear. You're going to get a dog there, whether you mean to or not . . . it's an ugly dog . . . you don't seem to mind that."

At which Li Meileen was seen to smile.

In Hil's cup she saw "birds, lots of birds, I forget now, are birds happiness or babies? Well, what's the difference, they're the same thing! Oh, Hilary, there's so much love in this cup . . ."

Hilary smiled, her hair fell forward and caressed her cheek, and Mary Rose swelled with the pleasure of feeling . . . normal. My girlfriend likes my mother. My mother likes my girlfriend. We're going to have a family. An entire missile base vanished from the landscape . . . Never mind the resulting crater, it will grow over in time, a slight depression filled with dandelions.

"Do you want babies, Hilary?" asked Dolly.

Hil blushed and nodded, wept and smiled. Dolly stroked her cheek, brown on white.

In Mary Rose's cup she saw, "Money."

She plucked off her sparkly earrings and gave them to a bleach-blond leather-dyke who admired them. "Your mum's amazing."

"I love your mum," said Phat Klown, who earlier in the evening had performed a trick onstage involving a nipple ring and a string of pearls.

"You know, Mary Rose," said Dolly at dawn over corned beef hash in Mars diner, "God loves you and your friends specially, because you are making the most of the gifts He gave you."

They turned the page.

Mary Rose wrote another book. She got serious money for the first time, mortgage-torpedoing money. She and Hil married as soon as the law came in—they eloped, it was simpler—so while Dolly didn't sing "My Best to You" at their wedding, when Matthew was born, along with the cheque from her and Dunc, Dolly sent them a card. On the cover was the Blessed Virgin Mary. Inside, it said,

Prayer for a Wonderful Mother. Dolly had crossed out the *a* and added an *s* to *Mother.*

Maybe the crack in the Berlin Wall had been Dolly's fear of losing her son, but she wasted no time tearing it down and driving west in a Lada. Or east in a VW . . . It was a miracle on the order of Our Lady of Lourdes. And Duncan followed. Or perhaps he was along for the ride in the back seat.

•

The hardest part of being in the hospital was having her father visit on his own on his way home from work.

"How're you feelin', sweetie pie?" He tossed his air force hat onto a hook near the door of the room she shared with Tracy-the-snowmobile-girl. "Have you had a bite to eat yet?"

She wished he would just go straight home. Now she would have to worry about him driving in the dark. It was February, five o'clock. "Not yet."

The worry was an ache that echoed—spooned around—the physical pain: Dad's new green Buick overturned on Days Road between the Kmart and the penitentiary. Just because there was a Dairy Queen on the corner didn't mean you couldn't die there.

"It's a ten-minute drive, old buddy, I'll be home before you know it."

You could drown in a cup of water, five seconds was all you'd need in a car.

"I'm worried, Dad."

"What are you worried about?" He gave her his incredulous grin. She saw his gold tooth.

She tried not to say it, but couldn't help it this time. "What if you have an accident?"

"Are you kiddin'?" he said with a chuckle.

"No. I'm scared you're going to have a car accident."

She had never gone this far before, she felt like she was breaking a pact. Or revealing her true identity to both of them in a way that wasn't very nice. But it felt involuntary, *I have only a moment for this transmission, I am the real Mary Rose, and I am being held prisoner on the Planet—*

"I won't have an accident, Mister."

"But what if you did?" And it slipped from her like something dark and dense, a lump of driftwood charred from a long-ago campfire, "What if you died?"

He lowered his chin and regarded her from beneath hawk-like brows, mock stern. "There's an old saying: 'Don't shake hands with the devil before you meet him.'"

She smiled, so he would believe he had reassured her.

Her supper came.

"Eat it all up now, it'll put hair on your chest."

Slice of turkey under sheen of gravy, ice cream scoop of mashed potato, triangle of mushy peas, individually sealed portion of applesauce, pebbled plastic cup of apple juice with a paper lid like a crinoline and bendy paper straw, some kind of cake thing. It all smelt like baby food. She glanced across at Tracy's milkshake, sitting on her tray, beading condensation—she was asleep. Tracy could eat only milkshakes because she'd been on the back of her dad's Ski-Doo when they went through a pasture fence at night.

Dad sat and read the paper while she ate, then she had to throw up right away.

She pushed aside the wheeled tray and began carefully to lift her sheet and the openwork white blanket, all of it very clean and cardboardy.

"Where you goin'?"

"I have to throw up."

He was hesitant. "Should I call the nurse?"

She walked slightly bent over, cradling the darkness on her left side.

Mum wasn't here, she could rest when Mum was here—she was "in like Flynn" with the staff, Dad liked to say, indestructible. Her father was here on his own. Pale, fragile in his lovely uniform. Like a unicorn, too beloved to be durable. Breakable. She wished he would go home so she could know he was safe. "No, it's okay," she said.

It took a long time to walk across the room to the toilet, it was dizzying. There was a smell—Phisohex and rubbing alcohol, needles and fluorescent lights, white sheets. The smell of metal wheels and getting sliced open, so cold so cold so cold. She knelt at the porcelain—white dignity of the Virgin Mary.

Dad followed and stood behind her—she wanted to close the door but hadn't managed it. She vomited, which was hard because it yanked the surgery, spasmed the streaky yellow, with each heave it seemed impossible to continue but less possible to stop—she'd had no idea how many muscles it took to throw up.

"Y'okay, sweetie?"

"Yup."

The after-trembles were friendly, they shook her gently like a leaf, shook the slime from her lip, said, *It's over now.* She brushed her teeth.

She felt him shadow her back to bed, a hovering presence in the shape of help, like a Guardian Angel, huge and beautiful but powerless. They loved you, but they couldn't stop anything from happening to you. They worked for God.

She had forgotten about the gaping back of the hospital gown. She climbed onto the bed and it was sweet to lie back in the Javex sheets.

She said, "You can go home now."

"I don't have to go just yet."

His light optimism was powerless here. Mum had power here—this labyrinth was her domain. Mary Rose felt bad about not showing him how reassured she was. She slept.

When she woke up, it was dark and he was gone.

•

Everything has been fine with her parents for over a decade now, but something is bothering her at the back of her mind . . . like one-eyed Detective Columbo, hesitating at the exit, she is aware of a blank spot. The bad time ended abruptly and everyone carried on as though nothing had happened—they turned the page. But lately she wonders if in fact they burned the book.

•

A few times, she had supper in the sunroom at the end of the hall with the other children on the ward. The big windows shone black with the February night. Here were no visitors and no grown-ups. Warm light was cast by reading lamps that squatted on mismatched end tables, a world away from fluorescent corridors and sterile hospital rooms. There were shabby easy chairs and worn toys; blocks with faded letters, a basket of old Lego, games of Chinese checkers and Monopoly—the money frayed with use. The smell was less clinical too, more a fug of flannel and crayons than Phisohex and isopropyl.

On each occasion, an inner circle of children had gathered as if the hospital were their home, and this was the playroom, where they could relax and toys might come alive at midnight. Some of the children had been admitted months before, while others were in and out on such a frequent basis they all knew one another. They were not a mean clique, however, they were more like a family with no parents. Stranded. Stoic. They were kind to one another, and they opened their circle to Mary Rose.

The leader was a girl who, though a year older, was smaller than Mary Rose and seemed like a grown-up. A nice one. She was round like a robust doll, with blue eyes and a mass of corn-coloured curls she wore in a frizzy ponytail like a pompom. Her blue sateen robe was belted snugly round her middle, she was cheerful, and she looked after the other children—one, named Norman, had "a nervous condition." He was prone to seizures and walked leaning sideways, unblinking. Another was so lively it was hard to believe there was anything wrong with him—he wore hard shoes with his pyjamas and slid on the freshly waxed floor.

It was like being in an orphanage. It was alluring, and Mary Rose was dimly aware that she oughtn't to allow the others to believe she was truly one of them. She needed to remember that she would be going home to her real life . . . she would not remain here in their dear dilapidated child's realm. They were like a community of damaged toys. Friendly, fun, but take care lest they lull you into forgetting your life as a real child, hard as that life may be sometimes, tempting as it may be to stay in the land of lost toys . . .

They ate at a long low table, seated on child-size wooden chairs. On the first night, the leader girl in the blue robe suddenly peed, right at the table. Then she rose and cleaned it up efficiently, without the slightest embarrassment. None of the other children took much notice. She explained genially to Mary Rose, "I was born with syphilis."

Mary Rose politely ignored the pee the next night. She could have got used to it, but she was discharged soon after.

She had a checkup a month later, and an X-ray twice a year after that, in case the cysts came back. There was a chance they would if the bone from the donor didn't grow with her.

•

Youssef and Matthew have built a jungle-farm-airport in the living room which is being threatened by a snake that eats airplanes while Maggie is down for her blessed afternoon nap. Mary Rose has had time to reflect on the debacle with the boots this morning; clearly, she displaced her old anger at her mother onto her child, the ladybug boots having acted as a trigger owing to their association with Dolly—

not to mention the ringing of the goddam phone. Armed thus with self-analysis, she speaks the words aloud, "Never touch your child in anger," as she applies a fresh bandage to her pierced finger and wonders how people who are less aware and educated than she is manage to avoid murdering their offspring. She frightened Maggie, but didn't actually hurt her—not to the point of physical harm. If the bar for child abuse were that low, nine out of ten parents would be behind actual bars. She gets the Krazy Glue out of the "it" drawer and glues her thumb to her index finger. Then she glues the unicorn head to her thumb. Then she glues the head to the body.

She calls Kate and cancels tonight's movie date—*Water* is supposed to be amazing, but she is simply too tired for child brides and adult conversation. She unglues her hand from the phone. The doorbell rings, Daisy goes crazy, and Mary Rose lets Saleema in. Today's hijab is a dazzling emerald, and she says in her hurried, worried way, "I have to pray, where can I go?"

Mary Rose shows her upstairs to the small sitting room off her bedroom. "Use the Pilates mat if you like."

Downstairs, she puts the kettle on in anticipation of Saleema's grateful acceptance of a cup of tea for which she has no time, and reflects that her Muslim friend is praying to Allah a few feet from the bedroom of a lawfully married lesbian couple, and for a moment Mary Rose cannot think of a single way in which life could possibly get better.

"I'm done, thanks," says Saleema, hurrying back down the hall, hijab billowing about her like a nun's habit of old—if nuns' habits had been electric green—and takes the steaming mug, "I'll just sit for a second." She talks happily of her parents and sisters in the UAE, of a life on the move from Somalia to Vancouver, Saskatoon then Toronto. She is pretty and bespectacled and dark brown, her hands never still, her brow slightly furrowed even when she laughs, which is often. There is an ease between them and it strikes Mary Rose that she never imagined she would have a friend who was an engineer.

A battle cry from upstairs—Maggie is awake and ready to vault from her crib. Saleema is leaving with Youssef and she says something in Arabic that sounds familiar.

"What did you say?" asks Mary Rose.

"Ysallem ideyki, it means—"

"Bless your hands."

"That's right."

"My mum used to say that. Why did you say it just now?"

Saleema laughs. "Because I know you've got them full!"

Mary Rose watches them leave down the flagstone path and registers a sadness. Perhaps even envy . . . Although why does she assume that Saleema's mother never needed to hate her? She remembers to call Candace and cancel tonight's child-care. Thirty bucks kill-fee down the drain.

That night on the phone, Hil says, "I thought you were going to a movie with Kate and Bridget."

"I'm too tired to go out. How did you even know about the movie plan?"

"Didn't you mention it?"

Hil put them up to it.

"I'm just going to have a quiet evening and watch *Transporter 2*."

"Why don't you call Sue and get her to come over with her boys for supper tomorrow."

"It's too much of a production."

"Get her to bring food."

"I don't mind cooking."

"Order a pizza."

"It means the kids'll go to bed late."

"Get Candace over while you and Sue go to a movie."

"Why Sue? Why always Sue? Sue is just so J. Crew, I can't stand it, okay?"

"What about Hank—?"

"He's in Mexico."

"Andrea—"

"She's started chemo."

"Oh my God, that's right. How is she?"

"She's fine, I mean she feels terrible, but it's going to be, they think it's fine."

"Tell Gigi to bring over a pot of spaghetti—"

"You don't have to solve my life, Hil, please just understand I need some quiet time."

"Pay Candace to do bedtime so you can watch a movie at home on your own."

Why didn't she think of that for tonight? Instead, she is paying Candace to stay away when she could have used the break.

"You could use the break."

"I don't need 'a break,' this is what I do, I look after the children and the house and I complain about it sometimes, can't I even complain without you dialing 911? I'm sorry, I'm not serene Susie Homemaker, okay?"

"Okay."

"Don't be mad."

"I'm not, Mister, you're the one who's . . ." *Sigh.* "I have to go."

"Don't go to bed angry."

"I'm not going to bed, I'm on a supper break."

"You're rehearsing tonight?"

"Mister, it's our third dress."

Mary Rose hears a voice in the background. Male? "Is that the stage manager?"

"No, it's Paul. Wait—" Hil covers the phone, says something, laughs, then, "Have a good night, love."

"What? Wait."

"What is it?"

"I love you, sleep well. I mean—"

"Good night."

She takes an Advil.

Jason Statham successfully delivers the package in his black BMW, vanquishes a horde of martial arts villains in a warehouse with an oil-slicked floor and returns to his Mediterranean villa with its modest shoebox of memories and sleek Tuscan tiles. He obviously has a great cleaning lady. She switches it off, already craving *Transporter 3*.

Journey to Otherwhere

Kitty's bags were packed, she had pretended to eat enough breakfast to stop Ravi fussing, and she had stolen upstairs for one last look at the study. The next time she entered this room, she would be a different girl. A St. Gilda's girl. If that Other Kitty thought of This Kitty at all, it would be with a sigh of relief that she had left that weird kid behind. "Let the brainwashing begin," she whispered. Bitter tears stung her eyes. She heard her father calling from downstairs. "Kitty, are you ready?"

She looked at her mother in the silver frame—as though she could intervene and stop the execution. But her mother remained static, her smile captured long ago and put behind glass.

Would her father be sending her away now if her mother were alive? Or would she already have been saddled with a "normal" life, staying home with her mom and waving good-bye to her dad all those years? She stared hard at the picture, hoping to make *it* shimmer for a change, willing a vision, a movement of her mother's face.

From downstairs came the *whoompf* of the front door opening, followed by the dulcet tones of Aunt Fiona—she wasn't a monster, she was far worse: she was nice. Kitty had a sinking feeling that Aunt Fiona would succeed this time in convincing her to join the so-called real world. "It's not such a bad place, Kitty."

"Kitty . . ." called Aunt Fiona. "Shall I come up, love?"

Kitty went to rise but found, somewhat to her perturbation, that she could not. She had been sitting cross-legged so long, perhaps it was a case of pins and needles. But there was no tingling in her toes and when she pinched her legs she felt it. She tried again to get up, tried reaching for the corner of the desk, but it was as if she could see her own phantom arms lifting and her phantom legs standing up, only to collapse back into her inert body still seated on the carpet. Paralyzed.

She was frightened now. What if she opened her mouth to scream, and nothing came out? She did not dare try, knowing that to confirm her fear would be to unlock a terror that she suddenly recognized like a long-lost enemy, and which she could smell like electricity. She looked down at the carpet. Her secret. It had never failed to soothe her and she turned to it now, perhaps for the last time, knowing that once St. Gilda's got hold of her, she wouldn't need magic carpets anymore, there would be neither visions nor nightmares, and if she could have, she would have run downstairs there and then and begged her father to drive her straight to the school, pausing only to grab a hairbrush from Ravi's astonished hand.

But she could not move. And sure enough, the scarlet threads that formed the stealthy K began to shimmer and she relaxed her gaze, allowing the colours to bleed and blur. It was working . . . the buzz arose behind her eyes and dripped like honey down her back, the carpet pulsed and rippled, and she experienced a soothing sense of being held by something infinitely more restful than sleep.

She called it magic but knew it to be purely scientific— something to do with her "visual cortex, likely the occipital lobe." That is what the doctor had said. It wasn't a secret that she saw the carpet move—the secret was that she did it on purpose. There was no point trying to explain why, even to her father, because it was indescribable. Besides, she didn't want him to feel there was something missing in her life with him, should she succeed in explaining how wonderful it was in there. Sometimes she thought Ravi had an inkling.

When she had drunk her fill of solace, buoyed by colour and motion, she breathed, waiting for the waves to subside, for the blur to resolve back to pattern and for the whole to resume the solidity of an ordinary rug . . .

"Kitty? There you are, it's time to go, love."

Aunt Fiona's voice was closer now; time to come back . . .

But the final pulsation resulted not in the usual contraction of the carpet, but a sudden expansion in which every thread became visible and proceeded gracefully to untwine from its mate in a slow pinwheel. The whole dissolved into specks of light like stars until all that remained were two bare threads. Coiled but no longer touching, they hovered poised like serpents, then began slowly to reverse their motion. Likewise, the stardust around them set to revolving counter-clockwise as the two threads grew closer and closer to one another . . .

"Kitty, are you all right?"

Then Ravi's voice, "It's all right, Miss Fiona, don't touch her."

Kitty reached into the slow swirl and saw her own hand, silvery and trailing at the edges, shot through with motion like the northern lights . . .

"Dean, come quickly!" cried Aunt Fiona. "She's having another seizure!"

. . . and clasped the threads. At that instant, they flew together with a jolt of rare earth magnitude and she felt herself pulled into a vortex of dust and light and frantic blackitude. Along with speed, the pinwheel picked up colour and texture, a colliding scope of threads as the carpet wove itself back together again and accelerated to a tremendous stop.

She was back in the study. Aunt Fiona needn't worry. Dad needn't wait. She looked up from the carpet—and straight into her own astonished eyes.

The face was oval like Kitty's, the nose straight to the point, the lips spare and sure, and the hair a dark mass like hers. And there was no mistaking her own eyes: one blue, the other brown. It was like looking into a mirror, except her— the other "her"—left eye was brown while the right one was blue. These were indeed her own eyes, but . . . reversed.

"I'll be right up," came the female voice from beyond the door. It had to be Aunt Fiona, but she sounded different.

"Where did you come from?" asked Kitty, her voice barely above a whisper.

"I didn't," said the other Kitty in a husky tone, more adamant than hers. "*You* did."

Impossible, she hadn't left the room. There was the carpet between her palms, there was the—but no . . . the scarlet threads that formed her initial were gone. That is, they were still there, but . . . Was it possible the carpet really had unravelled, then re-ravelled itself back the wrong way? Because in place of a *K*, there was a definite—

"Jon! There you are, we're waiting, honey, it's time to go."

Kitty looked back at her doppelgänger, freshly astonished to realize that she was a he; a fact that seemed downright banal the next instant when, turning to follow the boy's gaze, she saw, standing in the doorway, large as life, her mother.

THURSDAY

Cooks Irritated

She leaves Daisy leashed outside the Starbucks, in her pink fun-fur coat. The snow has melted and it is too warm for the coat, but it makes her look less like a pit bull. Somewhere online Mary Rose could probably buy a pink fun-fur muzzle. A fuzzle.

She manoevers the stroller through the door and looks around for a table. The place is packed. The bag lady with the elephant ankles heaves herself out of a chair and makes for the door. Mary Rose makes their way over to the newly vacated spot, digs a baby wipe out of the diaper bag and runs it over the tabletop and chair before sitting.

She waits. She commits to a latte. "Can I have your name for the cup?"

"No, thank you."

The young man in the green apron regards her with equal parts surprise and pity. "No problem." He smiles. Smirks? "You can be smiley face." And he draws one on her cup. Why is she here? There is a better café across the street—Starbucks' pro–gay marriage stance notwithstanding.

"Hi!"

She turns warily. Another nice young man in a green apron. "You're Dolly's daughter! How *is* she?"

"She's great, thanks." Brittle smile.

His name is Daniel. For some reason, Mary Rose remembers this but has trouble recalling which city her own wife is in—what is this thing called "brain"?

"Smiley face?" chirps the barista.

She slinks over and claims her cup.

Maggie dissects a muffin. Mary Rose takes out her antique flip-phone and calls her brother's BlackBerry. "You've reached Captain MacKinnon, liaison officer for the federal government and special envoy to the provincial legislature . . ."

"Hi, A&P, it's Mister Sister, just making sure we're on the same page re the Starbucks at Bloor and Howland, see you soon."

His phone is probably being monitored by CSIS which will pass on the info to the CIA which will hand it to the NSA which will alert the RCMP and he will be disciplined for using it for personal calls. Then renditioned to Syria once they discover he is half Mahmoud. And it will be her fault. Maybe he has left a message on her home voice mail. But why would he do that when he obviously has her cell number?

Maggie is through with her muffin and bored with the sugar packets, her best-before fast approaching. Nearby, a fashionably ill-shaven metrosexual in tapered brogues is fussing with his iPhone and preparing to pounce on her table the moment she stirs. She avoids his eye and calls the home voice mail on the off chance . . . there is indeed a message from Andy-Pat. He sounds busy. Preoccupied with manly concerns. Keeping-the-world-safe-for-women-and-children concerns. His ceremony in Kingston went "later than originally scheduled" and he "had to crash with a colleague" and drive straight back to Queen's Park this morning for an "important" meeting. "Hope you get this in time, Mister, I don't have your cell number with me."

She sweeps crumbs, crystals and stir sticks into a paper napkin—as the mist leaves no scar, so I with my toddler—but Mr. Metrosexual descends, blocking her cumbersome exit. *Does he want me to leave or not?!*

"Excuse me," he says in the arrogant tones of the freshly minted thirty-something.

In a previous era, a guy like this would have had to be gay or Italian, but because of the sacrifices Mary Rose and her generation made, he is free to be straight. He flaunts his phone—the type of guy who, if he ever bothered to open a book, would tap the page.

"Are you MR MacKinnon?" he asks.

"Yes."

"Oh my God, I *love* your books, they saved me, wow I can't believe I'm meeting you, I just texted my girlfriend and she freaked."

"Thank you."

"Can I—I'm sorry, this is so rude, but can I get a picture with you?"

"Sure."

She puts her arm around him and smiles. He holds the phone in his outstretched hand and flashes.

"When's the next one coming out?"

Such an intelligent, sensitive young man. Some things do get better.

"I'm not sure," she says. "I'm hoping I'm writing it right now in a parallel universe."

He smiles politely, but remains in earnest. "I know I shouldn't ask. But will Kitty get to see her mother's face in the third one?"

Mary Rose hesitates. It is as though they are discussing family members she hasn't seen in a long time. "But she did see her mother. In book one."

The young man is respectful yet firm. "No. She saw Jon's mother. But that's not really her mother. Not her mother from her own world. Not the mother who can see her back."

With his large brown eyes, he looks like a supplicant. What does that make her?

"Oh." She nods—sagely, she hopes, then feels a grin stretch across her face. "By your readers be ye taught!" Is she a crazy lady and doesn't know it? At least she doesn't pretend to slap him.

But his gaze is steady, and he speaks again. "I love you. I can't believe I just said that."

"Thank you." She flees, an imposter in her own life; husk of whoever it was that, once upon a time, created a world that others could claim, a world in which readers could immerse themselves . . . and feel they belonged. It is a world from which she blithely exiled herself, confident she could return any time. Perhaps Hilary is right, she needs to start working again. But what if she attempts a return only to find the portal barred? Like Narnia. She fears she may have committed herself to a life in which a closet is just a closet.

Daisy trots to keep up as Mary Rose pushes the stroller along Bloor Street to the Shoppers Drug Mart that has the post office at the back. She re-musters the troops for another assault on the great indoors, but when she gets to the counter there is no package waiting. There is no mail, period. It turns out her mail is being held across town at Postal Station E, which is also where she needs to submit the signed form. No, they do not have any forms here, but she can download one from the Canada Post website.

"Thanks."

"You're welcome."

She buys Advil, swallows one red pill dry and rubs her arm. Maybe her grafty old bone is becoming arthritic . . . reacting to the damp April day and the thousand natural shocks that climate change is heir to.

"Candy, Mumma?"

"No, sweetheart, medicine."

Is Postal Station E too far to walk? Cabs are smelly, the drivers are homophobic immigrants—or is that internalized racism rearing its head? Her own grandfather was a homophobic immigrant, a marrier of child brides, a mumbler of "close your legs." Yes, it is her own internalized racism. Feeling better already for having shed a character flaw, she nonetheless forbears to hail a cab for the psychology-free reason that she cannot have Maggie ride with no car seat. Not to mention Daisy—few drivers, regardless of their origins, would welcome a tank of a pit bull into their cab.

"Maggie, no."

The child has kicked off her winter boots and is attempting to climb out of the stroller—impossible but annoying. Mary Rose jams the boots back onto the little feet.

"We'll go to the other post office then we'll play in the park."

"Buckle my shoe!" rails Maggie.

Mary Rose does not turn in the direction of Postal Station E, however, rather she power-pushes the stroller east up Bloor Street, toward downtown. Daisy canters alongside, teats swinging, through the crowded intersection at Spadina—

". . . Can you spare a loonie for my son and I . . . ?"

Of course, that is what Kitty would see if she were to time travel: her real mother. What else do the readers know that she does not know she knows? An old saying floats to mind, "Physician, heal thyself."

Maggie points at a parkette, but Mary Rose is on a mission now, the purpose of which will become clear as she marches. In the display window of Williams-Sonoma she sees a splendid hanging pot rack; romantically lit, dripping with copper cast cookware—her feet slow and her heart beats a little faster, but she presses on. She is suddenly surging with energy. Her phone rings, it is Gigi but she doesn't answer, and she doesn't stop till they get to Baby Gap.

•

She was fourteen with the second surgery, so they put her on the children's ward again. Her room was at the end of the hall with a view of the smokestack. "That's where they put the body parts and crap," said the girl in the next bed. She was Mary Rose's age, and had just had some kind of "abdominal surgery," which put Mary Rose in mind of the Abominable Snowman in the animated Rudolph movie. The girl was pale and in pain and showing it. She was from a reform school. She clutched her belly and told of the staff "doing stuff" to her and of some of the girls also "doing stuff" with each other. "The matron's a pervert, eh." Mary Rose pretended to be asleep. She saw the girl's words turn to black crayon squiggles so they couldn't go in her ears. The girl said she'd had "a D&C. Which is proof I'm not a perv, eh."

She did not ask what the letters stood for intuiting a queasy female connection. "They scrape it out of you, eh," said the girl. She wanted to keep in touch with Mary Rose after they got out of hospital. The girl had no visitors. She was gone when Mary Rose returned from surgery, so she had the room to herself. There were two other teenagers on the ward, but the girl cried constantly and the boy, while nice, had leukemia. It did not occur to Mary Rose to visit the sunroom at suppertime, she was too old.

•

Home again—no time for the park, she has to make a pit stop before doubling back to pick up Matthew; it won't do to show up at his school laden with shopping bags, she doesn't want to look like one of those women. She leaves Maggie in the backyard, resisting but safely restrained by the stroller with Daisy to guard her, and slips into the house, down the stairs to the laundry room, where she stuffs all the new Baby Gap clothes straight into the wash; partly to get the factory chemicals out of them, partly so they won't look screamingly new when Hil gets home. Hil doesn't criticize Mary Rose's spending, and it's hers to spend, it's just . . .

She runs back up the basement steps and out the door to find Maggie asleep in the stroller. "Maggie, wake up! No nap, no nap, sweetheart!"

Maggie wakes with a moan. Mary Rose rummages in the diaper bag for a juice box. "Let's go, guys."

Daisy doesn't budge. Mary Rose pulls at the leash, but the dog is sitting with a force of gravity akin to a collapsed star. "Daisy, come." Daisy looks up from beneath an obstinate brow. Her chin has started to go grey recently. Is it greyer today than yesterday?

Mary Rose goes into the house and returns with the water dish, then stands back while Daisy laps up a tidal wave.

"Do you want to go in the house?"

Daisy wags her tail and hauls herself to standing. The morning's excursion actually must have tired her out—good to know it's possible. She opens the door and watches Daisy haltingly ascend the four steps to the kitchen and disappear round the corner. She turns. "Let's go, Maggie."

The boots are off. How did the child manage it? Maggie stares up at her—a hint of triumph in her face. Mary Rose withdraws into the house without a word and returns with a roll of duct tape. She has the advantage, Maggie is a prisoner of the stroller. She puts up her hood so the child can't claw her hair, and withstands the rain of blows while she calmly duct-tapes each winter boot back onto each little foot.

•

Somewhere down the hall was a baby that cried all night. Dark, etching cries that woke her, full of diesel and desperation, like a car spinning its tires in a snowbank. She would forget him during the day when his distress was either lost amid hospital clatter or soothed by visitors. She saw him once.

She'd been making her way down the hall for the first time since the surgery—her mother said she had to because one day you might lie down and never get up again. Her arm bound and slung, hip bandaged—the incisions this time were sutured with a wire that rippled beneath her skin—she inched along the wall. She heard him wailing. She got closer and realized the cries were issuing from her old room. It took her several minutes to pass the open doorway, so she could not help but see.

He was lying on his back in her old bed, eyes squeezed shut, profile blue with strain. Tears stood stiff on his cheeks, as though they'd erupted straight from his face. He appeared to be no more than a year old, but his anger was fully grown, as though, too young for words, he nonetheless KNEW, and would not be soothed. His legs were elevated in stirrups rigged to a metal frame, he had no feet.

·

When she gets to the corner near the school, she pauses and considers whether to remove the duct tape before arriving. If she does, will that be like saying she was wrong to have applied it in the first place? It isn't as though she has taped the child's legs to the stroller. She presses on toward the school, ready to make a joke at her own expense should anyone comment or give a look.

Time plays tricks. It feels to Mary Rose as if it has taken hours to cover the final block. The grey of morning has turned to glare. A stillness is forming within her like a bulge, slowing her down. Heavy, unmoving. She arrives at the school door.

The cheerful cacophony of parents and children becomes a cardboardy jumble all around her like empty boxes filling the air. She is part of it, chatting with Philip and Saleema. She feels a smile manipulating her face in socially appropriate ways. Hears her mouth making socially appropriate noises. She is not quite behind her eyes—she is set back a ways. Probably hungry.

She reflects that this is the retail counterpart to a sugar crash; she shopped voraciously and now she is as spent as her money. "Hi, sweetheart!"

Matthew is running up the steps, proudly thrusting something at her.

"It's for you."

"Matthew, it's beautiful."

"I made it."

A macaroni necklace. She puts it on.

Sue nabs her before she can escape. "MacKinnon," she says with jockish good cheer. Mary Rose turns to her and smiles but keeps the stroller pointing away—don't let Sue, of all people, see the duct tape.

"Come for supper tonight," she commands, straddling her bike with the kid cart hitched to the back.

"I'd love to, Sue, thanks so much, I can't, I thought I could, but . . ."

"Chicken pot pie."

"Wow, that sounds amazing, it's just, I promised my friend Gigi . . ."

"Let's make it happen."

"Absolutely."

Mac 'n' cheese 'n' peas.

The message light . . .

"It's Mum, you're not there. You know we're coming on the seventh at . . ." Mary Rose digs her cinder block of a datebook out of the diaper bag, is poised with a pen— "Dammit, where's my—did you get the packeege yet? It's something you wanted. Did I give it to you last time? I can't remember now what it was. Check and see if I already gave it to you." *Click.*

Hi there, and happy Thursday . . . She turns off the radio, closes her datebook, and stands staring out the window, on momentary neurological overload, while Matthew clears his lunch plate, and Maggie follows suit, loading her bowl, spoon, cup and everything in sight into the dishwasher, including the placemats, the ketchup . . .

"Good job, Maggie," she says absently.

The last time she saw her parents was in January when they stopped off in Toronto for three days on the way from Ottawa to Victoria on the West Coast.

She bundled Maggie up and went to meet their train.

She had left in plenty of time but wound up late with the effort to find parking—the station was being "renovated to serve you better!" By the time she got there with the stroller, her parents were nowhere to be seen. She waited at Arrivals next to the deserted Traveller's Aid counter, but that was no guarantee; at Union Station nothing guided the traveller toward Arrivals, itself an undefined limbo, whereas an imposing granite ramp drew them up into the heroic main hall where two sets of brass doors opened, she knew, onto a perilous moat of perpetual construction where the sidewalk used to be. Who knew how many elderly people had already pitched into that polyurethane tangle never to be seen again? Maybe her parents were out there now, drifting toward a beeping backhoe—was her father wearing his hearing aids? Worse, she dreaded lest they had ventured down an escalator and into the PATH: a twenty-seven-kilometre maze of weather-indifferent retail. She pictured them: two little old babes in the wood, jostled mercilessly . . . Nonsense, they had travelled the world, Dolly had fended off muggers in Red Square with the centrifugal power of her purse, wielding it like a mace—Duncan still told the story. But that was back in Dolly's glory days of rage and roses. Now she would simply fall, break a hip and die of pneumonia, and it would be Mary Rose's fault for having been late to the station.

She checked to make sure her cellphone was on, though she knew her parents would not call it, regarding it with equal parts reverence and mistrust. They too had a cellphone but never turned it on. It was for "emergencies." She risked venturing up the ramp, and emerged into the hall where a throng eddied about the base of the soaring digital display. If she called Andy-Patrick, perhaps he could have her parents' cellphone located by the RCMP. Maggie cried out, "Sitdy!"

She hung up to see her mother cannoning from the crowd, all four-foot-eleven-and-a-half of her, jaunty in her beret, her bling, her snow-blindingly new running shoes, hurrying toward them with a funny splay-foot walk that reminded Mary Rose of Maggie. Was that new?

"Hi, doll!"

Duncan came into view behind her, walking stolidly as though over rugged terrain, his mouth set in the Highland perseverance that peopled the globe and its boards of directors, dapper in his peaked cap, yellow windbreaker and rubber-soled brogues.

"Hi, Mum."

Dolly's brows arched above her big dark eyes, her mouth formed an *O!* of astonishment, she raised both hands, framing her face with delight, and swooped down on Maggie, assaulting her with "Sitdy kisses"—this used to make Matthew cry, but Maggie screamed with laughter. Duncan looked on, amused, then after the first flurry he crouched, took Maggie's hand and said softly, "Hi there, Maggie, how are you, sweetie pie?"

"Jitdy," said Maggie, just as softly, and reached for his cap. He gave it to her.

Jitdy was Arabic for "grandfather," a name that, for Mary Rose's blue-eyed father, was a source of pride and amusement.

Dolly cupped Mary Rose's face in her warm hands and looked up into her eyes. Mary Rose looked down into the familiar overheated expression of affection; the old eye-laden look that staked mute claim to martyrdom.

She formed a smile and received the slightly too-long hug, registering a guilty yet inexplicable annoyance with her adorable little mother.

Duncan rose with an attempt at spryness. "How are you, Mister, you're lookin' great." He bonked her on the head with the flat of his hand like a shingle—the Scottish equivalent of a hug. She was almost feverishly glad to see her father. It was always this way, as if an engine revved inside her, stoked with an urgent message. *Dear Dad, I!*

"How was your trip, Dad?"

"Like the fella says, 'uneventful,'" he replied heartily if a mite hoarsely, she thought.

No sooner had she lost the battle with him over who would carry their overnight bag—it was on wheels, but he insisted on carrying it by the handle—than she turned to see the stroller standing empty.

"Where's Maggie?"

"I let her out," confessed Dolly with a mischievous glint.

"Jesus Christ, Mum!" Mary Rose swung to face the crowd—a blur, a black inland lake. "Maggie!"

"Relax." Her father's voice behind her, the one he used on her mother. "There's no panic, Rosie." *Paneek.*

She looked down. Maggie was sitting on the stone floor, going through Dolly's purse, grown-up legs scissoring past her.

Dolly said, "Golly Moses, Mary Roses, I didn't mean to upset you."

"I'm not upset."

Maggie made to scoot off into the human thresher, but Mary Rose reached out and caught her by the arm.

"Gently!" yelped Duncan.

It snagged her attention, she turned. "Dad, it's okay." Maggie exploited the distraction and swung out. "Ow!"

"She's got a great left hook." He laughed.

She plunked her daughter back into the stroller, asserting her authority over her child, her parents and the entire spoiled Depression-era generation with its full employment and exceeded expectations, its freakish longevity and insatiable demand for filial gratitude from its stressed out, greying, autoimmuning offspring by swiftly engaging five points of restraint with one click.

"Noooo!"

"You tell 'em, Maggie!" he said with a grin.

Dolly giggled. "I've finally got my revenge, Mary Rose. She's just like you!" And she laughed. That is, she did an impression of a saucy stage laugh in which Matthew would have recognized a very creditable *na-na-na-na-boo-boo!*

Mary Rose blinked, dry and humourless as an iguana.

"Aren't you, *fuhss*?!" continued Dolly, kneeling on the floor, covering Maggie with kisses, turning toddler tears to laughter.

Arabic is a beautiful language. Thanks to her mother, Mary Rose knows terms of endearment and a lot of food words, otherwise her vocabulary is limited to *shit* (feminine and masculine forms), *shut up, slap on the ear, money, enjoy your meal! God-willing* and *fart*—which was what Dolly had just called Maggie.

An incomprehensible announcement echoed over the PA system in French and English.

Duncan commandeered the stroller and was on the move. Working swiftly, Mary Rose deployed the telescoping handle on the overnight bag with one hand and took her mother's in the other—it was surprisingly soft. They set out against a tide of commuters a hundred thousand strong and together entered the PATH.

"How's Hilary?" asked her mother. "How's Mark, I mean Matthew?"

"They're fine, Hilary's heading out west soon to direct *The*—"

"'Same day heel replacement,'" said Dolly, reading a sign. "'We deliver.' Did I tell you, we ran into Catherine—Catherine?—Dunc, is it Catherine or Eileen we ran into on the train who wanted Mary Rose to sign a book?"

"Darned if I know," he replied.

She turned back to Mary Rose. "She was so thrilled when she saw me, she said, 'You're Mary Rose MacKinnon's mother!'"

Mary Rose braced herself and Dolly continued, "I used to be Abe Mahmoud's daughter, then I was Duncan MacKinnon's wife, now I'm Mary Rose MacKinnon's mother!"

You could almost beat time to it.

"Sure, I'll sign her book, Mum."

"'Big and tall, we have them all!'"

"Where the heck did you park?" asked Duncan.

"Sorry, it's the construction—"

"Just like Ottawa." He nodded ruefully. "We have two seasons: winter and construction."

"Phyllis Boutillier's grandson," said Dolly.

Mary Rose looked around; was this too written on a sign? "Where?"

"He was married to her, but they got divorced," said Dolly.

"He . . . What? Married his grandmother?"

"Don't be saucy." Dolly pretended to slap her.

Mary Rose winced reflexively. "Mum, please don't—"

"How's the book coming?" asked Duncan.

"It's on hold."

"Take your time. Do it your way, Mister."

"Hurry up and write it so I can buy all three in a box set, you know you'll sell more that way, Mary Rose."

Duncan laughed. "Your mother's going to save the publishing industry."

"Catherine!" exclaimed Dolly. "The gal with the book—Eileen, I mean—dammit, I've got it written down." Dolly slowed and made to open her purse.

"Don't open your purse!" cried Duncan. He winked at Mary Rose. "We'll be here all day."

Dolly laughed and hugged her purse to her little pot-belly as though to resist the temptation to open it. "Dunc, you know exactly who I'm talking about."

"Her name is Catherine not Eileen," said Duncan in a tone of beleaguered management consultancy. "I don't know who Eileen is, I've never heard of an Ei-leen since Germany. *Cath-er-ine* was married to Phyllis and Mike Boutillier's *son*."

They pressed on through the white-collar lunch rush, Duncan pushing the stroller with the inexorability of an icebreaker.

"You know he died," said Dolly.

"Who?" asked Mary Rose.

"Mark, Mick, Mike."

A laugh escaped Mary Rose, dry and humourless no more, she felt suddenly like herself. But her father's tone was reverent. "Mike Boutillier. Heart attack, just like that." He snapped his fingers—no mean feat, considering he'd lost the tip of his middle one during a stint in the coal mine more than sixty years ago. "He's the one got the condo association to sue for new magnolias to compensate us after I discovered the cracks in the foundation."

Sobered, she nodded; a man's dignity was at stake.

"A great bear of a man. You wouldn't want to run into him in a dark alley, boy, but you couldn't ask to meet a nicer fella, give you the shirt off his back." He cleared his throat.

"Druggers Shop Mart," said Dolly.

Duncan and Mary Rose turned and stared at her as she continued, "Druggers . . . Shoppers Drug Mart!" she exclaimed.

Duncan grinned from ear to ear, his gold tooth flashed. Dolly went silent, overcome with mirth, her face a carnival freeze-frame.

"Breathe, Mum."

Dolly bent and grasped her knees with her hands.

"Dad?" There had to be a defibrillator in the vicinity, they were under three bank towers.

Finally they laughed out loud—they were breathing. They wiped their eyes and walked on.

Dolly described how she stood in the train aisle and sang "My Best to You" for the newlyweds and everyone clapped, including the head porter, "a lovely French-Canadian gal, she remembered us from last year, so I said, 'Then you probably remember we had the stateroom west of Toronto,' and she upgraded us on the spot."

"I should have bought stock in Via Rail when I had the chance," said Duncan. "Your mother's got customer service whipped into shape and, if you'll notice, our train arrived on time."

"Yeah." Mary Rose smiled. "Only Hitler and Mussolini were able to do that."

He laughed.

"'Puddle Duddle Rain Wear,'" said Dolly. "Look, Mary Rose, will I buy you a pair of rubber boots?"

In the shop window were boots with dots, boots with stripes, boots with triangles and zigzags that looked like the scintillations she used to see prior to panic attacks. She looked away. "That's okay, Mum, I'm pretty much fixed for boots."

"Not for you, for the kids, oh, look at the ladybugs!" Dolly stopped in her tracks.

"Maggie already has rubber boots," said killjoy Mary Rose.

"Boots!" cried Maggie, reaching toward the ladybugs in the window.

Dolly leaned down, eyes wide, clapping and chanting, *"Ladybug ladybug fly away home! Your house is on fire, your children at home!'"*

"Adybug adybug!" Maggie drummed her heels wildly.

Duncan steered the stroller into the store, Dolly followed, still chanting.

Mary Rose stayed outside and watched them hunt for the right size. Watched Maggie patiently submit to the trying-on process.

Maggie had her legs extended when they came back out, engaged in a staring contest with the big black ladybug eyes.

"We haven't got anything for Matthew!" cried Dolly.

"It's okay, Mum, we can shop later."

"I'll buy you an outfit, Mary Rose."

They headed for the sign marked *P* and an arrow pointing down.

Duncan asked, "How's big Matt doing, you got him up on skates yet?"

"He's getting there."

"No rush. Gordie Howe didn't own a pair of skates till he was twelve."

"Although Maggie might play hockey—"

"'Wokking on Wheels,'" said Dolly.

"Mum, do you need a snack before we get in the car?"

Duncan said, "Women's hockey is better than some of the nonsense you see in the NHL nowadays. I remember Gordie Howe's last game at the Montreal Forum . . ."

Mary Rose knew this story like the back of her hand, but she also knew her father didn't talk hockey with her sister, and even A&P wasn't much of a hockey fan—which, according to some, made him virtually gay. She savoured her position as honorary straight son. "Wow, he went the whole length of the ice like that?" she enthused.

Dolly bobbed between them. "Have you heard from your brother?"

"Not recently," said Mary Rose.

"Is he still seeing that nice little gal, what's her name?" asked Duncan.

"Shereen," said Mary Rose.

"He lives here now," said Dolly with an air of sudden realization.

Was it just a blood sugar thing? Even Mary Rose had trouble remembering he lived in the same city as she did—not to mention the name of his latest squeeze—did she have early onset? Her mother had always done ten things at once, got hilariously confused, interrupted herself and everyone else. Apart from how much her mother had mellowed—which was a good thing—what was the difference?

Within moments of their arrival home, Mary Rose's kitchen counter was littered with itty-bitty items that Dolly had deposited like the incoming tide. Packets of jam from the train, half a Tim Hortons doughnut, dollar-store gifts for the kids—lead paints, made in China—a pop-up lint brush/comb, "That's for you, Mary Rose!"

A baby food jar of stewed prunes resembling stool samples, another of candied chickpeas that pass for treats in Lebanon; a bag of Skittles . . . the visual equivalent of white noise. And amid the debris, some good stuff: Dolly's homemade baba ghanouj.

"My favourite!" exclaimed Hil, leaning down to hug Dolly.

Along with the Christmas cake.

"I didn't bake that, my cousin Lena did. She died."

Hil laughed but stopped short when she realized it wasn't a joke. "Really, Mum?"

"Wait now, when did Lena die?" Shouting toward the living room, "Snuggles, when did Lena die?!"

The answer came, adamant if reedy, "Nineteen seventy-four."

Dolly turned back to them. "Oh, I guess I baked it after all."

All three of them laughed.

"Your father wants a cup of tea."

Duncan was in the living room, reading the paper with his eyes closed. Mary Rose dutifully put the kettle on—she'd laid in enough Red Rose to sink an American Revolution—while Dolly opened her purse and came out with a paperback copy of *JonKitty McRae: Escape from Otherwhere.*

"Did I tell you, we ran into Catherine on the train—was it Catherine or Eileen?" Shouting, "Dunc, was it—"

"It was Catherine," said Mary Rose.

"She was thrilled when she saw me, she said, 'You're Mary Rose MacKinnon's mother!' I used to be Abe Mahmoud's daughter, then I was—"

"Sure, I'll sign it, Mum."

She looked in the telephone drawer for a pen, but there was none to be had. How do pens migrate? "Mum, have you got a pen?"

"A pin or a pen?"

"A *pen.*"

"You don't have to shout, doll."

Dolly plunged back into her purse and Mary Rose watched as a bingo ball of objects churned into view; a folded tartan tote bag, plastic pill container stamped with the days of the week, a rosary, a small grey velvet box, half a stick of Wrigley's Spearmint gum, a brooch—"There's my CWL pin!"—a one-inch square of plastic that opened to a full-size raincoat, a pair of rolled-up nylon slippers knitted by dead Aunt Sadie, a church pamphlet called *Living with Christ*, which sounded like *Living with Cancer*, a pussy-cat change purse . . . Mary Rose looked away, starting to feel hazy.

"Eureka!" Dolly held up a Best Western pen.

"Is it Catherine with a *C*?" she asked, preparing to sign.

"No, this one's for Phyllis's granddaughter."

"What's her name?"

"Phyllis."

"The granddaughter's."

"That's right, it's for her granddaughter."

"What is Phyllis's granddaughter's name?!"

"Linda Kook," said Dolly.

"Really?"

"Yes. What?"

Hil and Mary Rose were laughing.

"Mary Rose, you've heard me talk about the Kooks, I'm in the choir with her mother-in-law, Dorothy Kook, Dotty Kook."

"Mum, stop."

"Phyllis has lupus," added Dolly. "What's so funny about that?"

"Nothing, I'm sorry, Mum."

Mary Rose wiped away tears, and signed the book.

"Every time I turn around," said Dolly. "Last week at choir practice this new little girl"—Mary Rose knew this meant a woman under fifty—"came up to me and said, 'Are you Mary Rose MacKinnon's mother?'" She raised her hand and began to slice the air. "I used to be Abe Mahmoud's daughter—"

"Mum, why do you have Skittles?"

"For my diabetes."

It was not worth going there again. Dolly had type-2 diabetes, Dolly was a nurse. Dolly knew better, but she also knew best.

She went there. "Mum, fruit is what you need, not candy, candy is—"

"'By your children be ye taught!'" Dolly pretended to slap her face.

"I wish you wouldn't do that, Mum."

"Do what, I've always done that."

"No, it's recent, it makes me feel like you want to hit me."

"Well, if I did, it would be a love slap."

"That's a contradiction in terms."

"You kids are so sensitive, you're all MacKinnons!"

Thus the jocular banishment. Mary Rose and her siblings were each subject to it from time to time, stripped of any claim to the Mahmoud side, shorn from their mother. "If your hand offends you, cut it off," said God. He also said, "Psst, Abraham, take Isaac for a picnic and bring along a knife . . . Never mind, I was just testing you." God did go through with killing *his* son, however. People are always harder on their own kids.

"You know, in the old country, a woman didn't believe her husband loved her if he didn't beat her."

"What old country was that, Mum? Cape Breton?"

"Don't be saucy."

"Was your mother born in Lebanon, Dolly?" asked Hil. "I would love to go there sometime, I know it's a beautiful country."

And you have beautiful manners, Hil. WASP avoidance strategy.

"It *is* a beautiful country, Hilary," said Dolly, sounding quite WASP herself now.

"Have you ever visited, Dolly?"

"Yes, once."

"She went during a ceasefire in the seventies," said Mary Rose.

"Oh my goodness."

"Hilary, it was amazing. I walked down the street and everyone looked like *me*!"

Hilary rested her chin on her hand, and looked at Dolly with genuine affection. "I can imagine what that must have meant to you."

"But your mother was born in Canada, right, Mum?"

"That's right, but Puppa wasn't, he was from the old country, and you know in the old country a woman didn't believe her husband loved her if—"

"I guess that's why you married Dad."

Dolly looked comically nonplussed. "Your father didn't beat me."

"That's what I mean. But somehow you could tell he loved you."

She was suddenly coquettish. "Oh, I could tell, I had six babies. Five. Wait now, how many are you?"

"Mum, are you saying your father beat your mother?"

"Sometimes a woman needs a good slap."

"There's no such thing."

"No one can tell me Mumma didn't love Puppa. When're we going to play Scrabble?"

The kettle shrieked.

Hil made tea. "I thought you were going shopping," she said, no doubt desperate for some peace.

Dolly turned to Mary Rose. "I was going to buy you an outfit."

"Oh, um, I'm pretty well fixed for outfits, Mum, but is there anything you—"

"I need a new bra."

"Okay, I know the perfect place, it's right on Bloor, let's go—"

"Don't go just for my sake, Mary Rose."

"I'm not, that's where I buy my bras."

"Do you need a bra?" Dolly pronounced it *bra-a* as in *brand*.

"No, Mum, but they can help you find one, they're professional bra fitters."

"What do I need another bra for, I've enough bras, I got bras coming out the yingyang. And you know, Mary Rose, it'll be you kids having to go through all that stuff when I'm dead, I'm not buying any more *stuff*!"

"Okay, let's just go for a walk, then."

"No, let's go to the bra store." Hollering to the living room, "Dunc, we're going to the bra store on Bloor! I'll buy you a bra, Mary Rose," she said, and burped.

Hil was preparing a tray for Duncan.

"Don't forget the sultanas," said Mary Rose. She turned toward the cupboard and walked into a kerfuffle, her mother was tossing something at her—did Dolly's purse harbour a false bottom? She caught it before it could put out her eye.

"You forgot that in the summer."

"Oh. Thanks, Mum."

The foot calendar. Mary Rose had "forgotten" it in Ottawa. She pinned it to the corkboard next to the dead clown.

Dolly was ready at the back door, bundled in her coat, hat and . . . nylon slippers.

"We're off, Dunc!" she called, and started singing, "Please Don't Talk About Me When I'm Gone."

"Mum, you're going to need your boots, it's chilly out."

Hilary appeared at the top of the four steps with Dolly's boots.

"Are ya ever nice!" said Dolly. "You're almost as nice as Dunc!"

"How're you fixed for cash?" called Duncan from the living room. "Need any mad money?"

Dolly winked. "Your father's so good to me." Then she called in reply, "I've got my credit card, dear!"

"Look out!"

Mary Rose waited while Dolly bent to pull off her slippers and almost fell over.

"Can I help you, Mum?"

"What for?" She sat—*kerplunk*—on the step and struggled to pull on her boots. She would soon overheat in her puffy coat.

"Mum, you might want to take your coat off while you—"

"I can't be bothered with all that rigmarole."

She managed to jam one foot into one boot with a grunt. She reached for the other.

"Mum, let me help you."

"I can do it myself, Mary Rose." *Do it Me-self!*

Mary Rose backed off and waited.

At last, Dolly stood up, wobbled, staggered theatrically and steadied herself.

"What's going on with these boots? Have I grown out of them at my age?"

Mary Rose looked down. "They're on the wrong feet, Mum."

"Get out, they're not." Dolly looked down and laughed. "I must be going senile, look what I've done. Dunc! Come look at your wife, dear, I've got my boots on the wrong feet!"

"What's that?" came the sleepy voice from the living room.

Could the brain take only so much lurching between chemical states before it lost elasticity and plaqued over? Had Dolly mood-swung herself into atrophy? It used to be called "second childhood." If so, it says a good deal about the founding personalities of those so afflicted. Judging by these criteria, Dolly Mahmoud had been a cutie-pie. A handful. But a honeybun.

She kicked off the boots, steadied herself with the railing, sat back down on the step and renewed her efforts, saying *sotto voce*, "I'm not really senile, Mary Rose. Just preoccupied."

It hadn't snowed much for January, all was damp and grey. It was as though Earth had forgotten how to do winter, or else was mixed up as to which season came after which—the planet itself in the grips of dementia. They reached the corner of zooming Bathurst Street. Dolly was wearing the tam Mary Rose had given her for Christmas—leopard print like the one she'd had back in Kingston.

"'Archie's Variety,'" she read aloud. "Are they from Cape Breton?"

"Korea."

Mary Rose waved to the lady through the window.

"Who's that?"

"The lady who runs the store."

"Will we go in and say hello?"

"What for?"

But before she knew it, her mother was in the store. She followed, already hearing the greeting sung from behind the counter, "Hello, how are you?"

Ten minutes later, they were back on the street, Dolly having acquired Kinder Eggs for the children along with the lady's life story. Her name was Winnie, she had been a university professor back in Seoul. "And her with a math degree, imagine!"

They walked south.

"'Grapefruit Moon Restaurant,'" said Dolly.

Mary Rose saw Rochelle disappearing into the restaurant and looked down in order to spare them both the necessity of a greeting. But bloody Rochelle stopped and said an unprecedented, "Hi." Mary Rose introduced her mother, then feigned interest in the dry cleaner's next door till her mother rejoined her. "Now that little gal has a back problem—"

"What 'little gal'?"

"Your neighbour, Rachel."

"Rochelle."

"'Freeman Real Estate,'" said Dolly.

"Let's cross at the lights, Mum."

They crossed Bathurst and proceeded down quiet, signless Howland Avenue beneath the bony-fingered trees, and to her surprise Mary Rose was able to keep up with her mother. At four foot eleven and a half, Dolly nonetheless had a stride—rather, she had had one—and on every back-to-school shopping excursion, "Walk tall, Mary Rose, walk as if you own the place." "Mum, it's the Kmart." "I don't care if it's the Taj Mahal!" Now Mary Rose realized her mother might need to rest. When they got to the corner of Bloor, she said, "Would you like a cup of tea, Mum?"

"Oh, that'd be lovely!" she groaned, and they stepped into the Starbucks.

They found a table by the steamy window that was stencilled with non-denominational snowflakes. A sleek young man in signature green apron approached their table with a tray. "Would you like to sample a mini-cup of our festive chocolate peppermint candy cane holiday whip?"

"Golly Moses!" said Dolly, and knocked one back.

The young man offered her another.

"You're bad!" she giggled.

"Sister, you got that right!"

She downed the second one—her blood sugar had to be going through the roof—then ordered the real thing.

"Can I get your name for the cup?"

"It's Dolly."

"Well hello, Dolly," he said.

On cue, they belted out the first few bars together. Customers nearby applauded. He told Dolly what he was studying, where his parents were from, he told her about his bee sting allergy, and before Mary Rose knew it, he was calling her Sitdy and hugging her. Another lucky winner in the instant intimacy sweepstakes. Mary Rose sat on the sidelines with her tall, humourless no-foam latte.

Though she often felt like a killjoy in her presence—spectre at the feast, ghost of murdered Banquo—Mary Rose was nonetheless proud of her mother's ability to connect with people. Stewardesses sent her photos of their babies. Cops smiled at her, she got a few dollars off everything.

"You're not eighty!" the young man exclaimed.

"I'm eighty-one," declared Dolly with mock solemnity.

He told her how close he had been to his grandmother who had come here from the Philippines and raised five children from behind the cash register of a corner store. Dolly told him the story of how her father had sold dry goods from a donkey in the back country of Cape Breton Island, of how he had eloped with her mother. The young man had tears in his eyes. Mary Rose thought, but did not say, "I'll give you something to cry about, buddy, my grandmother was twelve."

The young man slipped away but soon returned with a *grande* version of the mini-cup—that was another thing: Dolly got table service at Starbucks. Mary Rose took one look at the candy-striped confection and wondered if she would recognize the signs of diabetic shock. What if her mother went into a coma? Collapsed? Died at Starbucks? *Can I get your name for the gravestone?*

The young man said, "My name is Daniel? So just let me know if there's anything else you need, okay?" He withdrew, and Dolly leaned confidingly over her minaret of whipped cream. "Now that young fella is gay, is that right?"

"That's right, Mum, in all likelihood."

"I love you, doll."

Mary Rose felt guilty for not feeling warm and happy. Instead of melting into a smile, she felt her face go positively Soviet in a pre-glasnost kind of way. She knew she looked like Brezhnev and there was nothing she could do about it. If she rummaged in her basement, she could probably find the box marked WARM AND HAPPY. But who knew what else might be down there, she didn't have time to go through it all. *Nyet.* She hesitated. Was it worth it to disturb the peace? On the other hand, her mother had raised the subject . . . maybe she wanted to talk about it. Fill in the missing bit. In movies, this was the poignant conversation that led to "closure."

"It was hard before you . . . arrived at that." She sounded like a robot in her own ears.

Dolly looked at her quizzically. "It was?" Head cocked, like Daisy.

Dolly's expressions were often like caricatures of real expressions; as if she was in constant clown mode. Larger than life. But, Mary Rose wondered now, what's wrong with life-sized? What remains when the trumpets and bells fall silent and the ringmaster sets down his megaphone? When the dancer pulls the red shoes from her bloodied feet?

"Yes," said Mary Rose.

"Why? What did I do?"

This café table was a world away from the kitchen table of yore, and yet she was still . . . anaesthetized. There must be considerable emotion collecting within her somewhere—as with fluids in a corpse. "You wouldn't set foot in my home. Remember?" She felt like she was lying. It wasn't that the words she was saying were untrue; it was the fact of her speaking them at all. "And you wouldn't have Renée in your home, remember?"

Dolly looked perplexed.

Coffee table, kitchen table, operating table . . . like a *Sesame Street* song, *one of these tables is not like the others* . . .

"You said some bad things," said Mary Rose. Her hands were cold. She had stumbled into a chilly gap in time.

"I did? What did I say?"

I would rather you had cancer.

There was no point speaking the words, they were only sounds and might wound her mother unnecessarily.

I didn't give you shit to eat . . .

"Mum?"

"Yes, doll?" Dolly leaned forward and placed her hand in the centre of the table. Brown and still smooth, it was an old hand now, exquisitely veined; hard-working but fine. Mary Rose loved this hand. It was somehow like a whole other mother. As if her mother had two faces, and this hand was one. The real one. What would it say? Did it remember? Mary Rose was suddenly alive again, no longer a puppet under a spell, she had a lump in her flesh-and-blood throat. She wanted to lay her face on that hand, feel it turn and cup her cheek in its palm, and take the weight of her head. Tears welled up and, rather than trickling down, they stood, liquid lenses whose function seemed to be to impart acuteness to her vision, for it was then that she noticed: "Mum? Where's your moonstone?"

Dolly looked at her hand, alarmed. "Golly Moses!" And lurched to look beneath the table—a thousand calories leapt from her cup and she nearly tumbled from the chair.

"Mum!"

"I must've dropped it."

"It's okay, I'll look."

Mary Rose got up, already scanning the floor.

The server was on them. "Did you lose something?"

"It's okay," she said.

"It's not okay!" cried Dolly, and the cry pierced Mary Rose's heart.

She was shocked to find herself in danger of sobbing at the pathos: the moonstone ring that her father had given her mother way back in Germany during the sweet years, the years of Rhine and roses . . . kicking around now on the floor of the Starbucks. Or lodged in a sidewalk crack between here and home, on its way back, back, back . . . She bit the inside of her cheek and blinked away the blur.

"What did you lose?" asked lovely gay Daniel.

"My ring!" moaned Dolly. "My husband gave it to me when our son was born."

"That sounds really special."

"It is really special, he *died*."

Dolly sounded like a first-grader pleading for help in sorting out what and how much she felt: *Is this too much? What if it spills on the way home?*

"I'm so sorry, why don't you leave me your number and if anyone finds it, I promise—"

Dolly was already emptying her purse onto the table. Mary Rose looked away, grey in the soul, and headed for the door, eyes on the floor, unable to bear her mother's frank distress, desperate to recover it—stone marker for a dead baby gone to grass long ago in another land across the sea, now it was lost and the genie was out. Memory was zooming around Starbucks like a bird trying to escape, *bang* against the glass . . . *Bang bang!*

"I found it!"

She turned. Her mother was smiling broadly, holding the small grey velvet box.

"It was in my purse!"

Daniel embraced Dolly and she held him and patted his back like a baby.

Mary Rose returned to the table, oddly drained, revisited by the sense that half of her had shut down. The humorous half. *Humerus.* She should be the one embracing her vibrant mother, mirroring the ups and downs; after all, a diva is just an extroverted martyr. But Mary Rose was brittle. Bag of bones. She sat back down at the table. *Shclink* went the bones.

Dolly swept her belongings from the table back into her purse in one motion, causing the *Living with Christ* pamphlet to flap to the floor. Mary Rose bent to retrieve it along with a small "Sunday Offering" envelope that she tucked back into it. She wondered how much was in the envelope and how her mother squared supporting the church with her love for "you and your friends specially."

Daniel wiped up the spill and retreated. Mary Rose watched as Dolly slipped the ring back onto her finger. *Home.* She put her warm hand over Mary Rose's cold one, saying, "I guess it really was a hard time, now that I think of it."

"Yes, it was."

"And it couldn't have been easy on you, you were so young."

"That's right."

"I was so afraid."

Mary Rose was amazed. She was in reality after all. Her mother was making it real. Her mother, in her leopard print tam, sweeping into Mary Rose's hospital room, making everything okay . . . She tried not to move a muscle.

Together, she and her mother had crossed over into a world where people call things by their name and love their children and are sorry for having injured them and say *I see you*. She hunted frantically about inside herself for an appropriate feeling state, but all she found were lumps, frost-bearded comestibles. She grabbed one at random and set it on the counter to thaw. She would find out later what she felt; for now, it was important simply to witness . . .

"I understand, Mum. Fear of the unknown." And she returned the pressure of her mother's hand.

"'Unknown' nothing! I knew what I was afraid of, I was afraid I was going to hurt you."

"You . . . did hurt me."

"I did?"

Mary Rose nodded.

Dolly's brow furrowed. "Is that what happened to your arm?"

"What? No, Mum. I mean hurt me emotionally."

"Oh." This appeared to strike Dolly as a novel idea. "You'd've been too young to remember any of that."

"I wasn't too young."

"You remember that far back?"

"Yes."

Dolly's manner was mildly perturbed, as one who recollects trials in tranquility. "I didn't know what to do or where to turn, and some days I couldn't even get up off the couch and you'd be crying so hard—"

"When did I cry?"

"You cried all the time! Oh, it made me so mad sometimes and I'd get up and go in to you and then I'd really scare myself so I'd lie back down, and you'd *stop* crying and that got me really scared—"

"Mum, I didn't cry, I'm not a crier, I don't know what you mean."

"Don't you tell me you didn't cry, I was the one who was alone with you day in day out, you *cried*. And you ran everywhere, I was afraid you were going to run right into the glass—"

"Mum, I wasn't even living at home."

Her mother had lost it. It was Mary Rose's fault, dredging up bad stuff, torturing Dolly over a transgression for which she had already amply atoned with love and gifts and garrulity, *God loves you and your friends specially* . . . She was going to bring her mother back to her father this afternoon in a state of geriatric distress.

"It's okay, Mum, would you like another candy cane whip?"

"Dammit all, Mary Rose, you've got me all confused, I'm talking about when I came out of hospital after Alexander was born! What in the name of time are you talking about?!"

". . . Oh. *That* hard time."

"Yes, 'that hard time,' what 'hard time' did you mean?" It was the old Dolly. Straight from the lip.

"Never mind."

"Don't you 'never mind' me, tell me." A flash of the old ferocity.

"I was talking about . . . when I came out to you and Dad."

"Came out of where?"

"Came out as a lesbian." There was the word in all its scaly ignominy.

"Oh, that!" Dolly laughed.

"You said you would rather I had cancer."

Dolly paused. "Did I object that strongly, Mary Rose?"

Mary Rose nodded.

Dolly's forehead creased. She shook her head slowly, regretfully, and said, "I don't remember."

She looked past Mary Rose toward the window, as though the memory, recently released, might still be playing about on the other side of the glass before darting up and away. Then she turned her liquid eyes full on her daughter, seeming to enclose the two of them in a grotto, a kind of sacred darkness that was as close to an embrace as Mary Rose could bear from her mother, and said with a note of sincere bewilderment, "I'm sorry, Mary Rose."

Daniel caught them on their way out the door. He gave Dolly a gift certificate for "a beverage of your choice at any of our stores."

"Aren't ya nice!"

"I'm sorry about your husband, Dolly."

"My husband? What about my husband?"

For the first time, Daniel looked at a loss. He turned to Mary Rose, but she stone-faced him. *Go back to your own mother who loves you just because you're you, you wimp, and quit sucking up to mine. She'd've had your balls for bookends.*

He turned back to Dolly. "I thought you said he died."

"That wasn't my husband, that was my son!"

Dolly delivered it with the force of a punchline and supplied her own laugh track.

Out on the street, Mary Rose offered her left arm and Dolly took it. "What were you afraid of, Mum?"

"When was I afraid?"

"When I was a baby."

"I went to a psychiatrist."

Mary Rose stopped in her tracks. This was more surprising than her mother's embrace of Queer Nation. "You did?"

"I told the doctor I was scared and he told me I should see a psychiatrist, so I did. In Munich."

She was conscious of keeping her tone neutral so as not to startle her mother off whatever track she had stumbled upon. Was this how it worked? Some neural pathways got gummed over while others became unmasked? A *psychiatrist*? Her mother might as well have said Mary Rose's father had been moonlighting as a trapeze artist. Her parents were from Cape Breton. They didn't go in for "head-shrinkers."

"Did Dad know?"

"Daddy drove me."

The phrase gave Mary Rose slight pause—a bird alighting on a twig in her mind, but off it flew before she could identify it. "Did it help?"

"Oh, I think it must have."

"Why?"

"Well, here we are." They were outside Wiener's Home Hardware.

"Did Dad want us to pick something up?" He had announced his intention to replace the weatherstripping on her deck door—*"You're heating the outdoors!"* Should she buy caulking? And a caulking gun? She could caulk it herself, how hard could it be?

"I don't think so," said Dolly. "Do you need something in there?"

"No, I thought you did. You said 'here we are.'"

In the display window, next to sacks of road salt and sand, the holiday scene was still up, teddy bear conductor on a choo-choo train winding through a snowy olde tyme towne.

"That's right," said Dolly.

Santa was drinking a Coke.

"But we're not here."

"We are so."

"Mum, this is the hardware store, we're going to the bra shop."

"I didn't mean we were *there*, I meant we're *here*."

Was dementia contagious? *Who's on first?*

"Where's 'here,' Mum?"

"Here!"

Dolly flung Mary Rose's arm loose and waved her hands in a gesture of general *here*ness. Mary Rose's arm twanged briefly, her brain clanked and shifted like a funhouse floor. Dolly said, "I wasn't good at having babies."

Her mother seemed to have switched tracks again, but at least Mary Rose was familiar with this one. She took a deep breath and felt it catch, as though something were lodged in her chest—maybe they had a tool in the store that could remove it, a crowbar. "Let's go, Mum."

Unless she was having a heart attack—heart disease often went undiagnosed in women. What were the symptoms? She would google it when they got home. She got them moving again down the crowded sidewalk. Pigeons poked along in front of them, incense wafted sweet and cloying from Indra Crafts, the Native guy with the bandana bounced past them looking free but purposeful, his dog loose at his side. Across the busy street, the neon swirls of Honest Ed's were still bolstered by blinking wreaths and angels. Outside, a line had formed, women in saris and parkas, people from the four corners, the darker faces among them diminished by drab winter clothes, all waiting to cash in on the special. It might be chickpeas, it might be towels, turkeys or toothpaste, all for a dollar ninety-nine.

"'Come in and get lost!'" cried Dolly. She stepped abruptly from the curb and onto busy Bathurst Street—

"Mum!"

"You don't have to grab me, Mary Rose!"

"You have to wait for the lights."

"'By your children be ye taught!'"

Mary Rose ignored the pretend slap, the lights changed and they crossed.

"'Secrets from Your Sister,'" said Dolly.

Mary Rose stopped her mother at the door, gently this time, with a hand on her forearm. "Mum? What were you afraid of?"

"I was afraid I was going to hurt you," said Dolly, as if this were self-evident, as if they had been over it a thousand times.

"Hurt me how?"

Dolly's brow contracted with effort, she gestured with her right hand, as though urging something on, attempting to rouse memory and dress it in words . . .

"I was afraid . . ."

"What were you afraid of?"

"I was afraid of my hands."

She said it with an air of bemusement, as though she had just come across something at the bottom of a drawer, something she had forgotten she'd lost.

She disappeared into Secrets from Your Sister. Mary Rose followed.

A young woman whisked Dolly away—she had chopsticks in her hair. Mary Rose heard giggles and chit-chat coming from the change room as two young women went in and out with various sizes and styles. Laughter gave way to murmurs and Mary Rose made out the words, "Well, she started crying, so I said, 'I'm not crying, don't you cry . . .'"

Half an hour and a bra fitting later:

"Your mum's amazing."

"I love your mum."

Home.

Supper.

Tea.

Dolly went out for a walk without telling anyone, got lost and was escorted home by another "nice young fella."

Scrabble.

Dolly placed two letters for thirty-seven points—the origami of Scrabble. Mary Rose placed VIOLINS and got the bonus fifty. Dolly won.

She ensured her parents were settled comfortably in the guest room, then headed upstairs.

Her mother's ramblings were the most unreliable form of evidence: eyewitness testimony. And what did it change? Her parents were old, they had reached cruising altitude. What right had she to roughen their ride with questions belched from the past?

She got into bed and reached for The Origins of Totalitarianism.

But she did not grow drowsy, she was . . . vibrating. It wasn't Hannah Arendt. *The tea.* Her parents drank it like water and slept like babies.

"Do you think they're warm enough down there?"

"I put the heater in their room," said Hil.

"I don't want them to catch cold."

There was a missing piece of the puzzle that plagued her: why had her father sat by while her mother savaged her over that ten-year period? His glassy silence, his averted gaze.

I was afraid of my hands.

"So it wasn't the first time she tried to kill you."

Hilary was sitting up in bed moisturizing her feet.

"She didn't try to kill me, that's the point." She knew she shouldn't have told Hil. "She was afraid of her thoughts."

"She pictured harming you."

"She . . . I don't know what she pictured."

"That's a sign of depression."

"I'm not depressed."

"I mean your mum. She probably had postpartum depression. How could she not have?"

Depression was a word Mary Rose had never known her parents to speak unless prefaced by the words *the Great*.

"Well yeah, of course, that . . . makes complete, perfect sense."

"I think that's what happened to me after Matthew was born," said Hil.

"But . . . we adopted him." This was the danger of downtime: true confessions. Intimacy. *When can we all just go back to work?*

"That doesn't matter," said Hil.

"Did you . . . picture harming him?"

"I pictured harming myself."

"Jesus. I thought you went into therapy because I was driving you crazy."

"I actually don't think it had anything to do with you."

"Oh. I guess now you're going to tell me climate change and the Middle East aren't my fault either. I don't know if I can handle this much mental health, it's killing my ego."

Hil leaned forward, gave her a peck on the lips and put the jar of ultra-rich foot therapy into the drawer of her nightstand. Mary Rose glimpsed the fuchsia dolphin-shaped vibrator and said, "Do you want a back rub?"

"Sure," said Hil, surprised.

And fell asleep five minutes in. When it came to sex lately, Mary Rose had begun to wonder how much less she could take. She lay, conscious of her own mature largesse in not resenting Hilary for falling asleep. Hil worked hard. She needed her rest. "Hil? Are you asleep?"

"Mm? Sorry."

"That's okay."

"I just—can you not sleep? I'm sorry, babe, I'm just not in the mood while we have guests."

"You mean having my parents in the guest room doesn't function as an aphrodisiac?"

Hil chuckled.

Mary Rose continued, "Oddly, somehow it does for me. Maybe my parents were right, I *am* sick."

"Stop it."

"What? It's funny, I was . . . being funny."

"It's not funny. Come here."

"What? No, not if you're not into it."

"I'm into it."

"You don't have to just to please me."

"Why shouldn't I want to please you?"

"Because . . ."

"I love you, I want to please you."

She pulled Mary Rose on top of her and bit her neck, took hold of her hips, started to move beneath her.

"I'd rather you were into it," said Mary Rose.

"I am."

". . . I'm not."

"I guess you're not 'sick' after all." Hil rolled over.

"Don't be mad. Are you mad?"

"No, Mister, I'm not mad, I'm . . . I feel for you."

After a few moments, Mary Rose became aware of the peaceful cadence of sleep on Hilary's side of the bed. "Hil? What did you mean, 'it wasn't the first time'?"

Hilary sniffed awake, then said, "When you came out she tried to kill you."

"No she didn't."

"You said she wished you had cancer. She wished you were dead, choking on shit—"

"Not 'choking'—"

"She cursed you."

"Exactly, she didn't try to 'kill' me."

"I'm happy for you."

Tug at the duvet, reprised roll-over.

"Why are you being mean now?"

"I'm sorry, that *was* mean, I just . . ." Hilary turned to her and propped her head on her hand. "They were cruel to you. Young people commit suicide over that kind of thing."

"Yes, well I didn't kill myself and that's a huge difference: I'm here. She didn't stab me or get someone to drive me into the canal."

"No, she was a wonderful mother. And I'm sure your father would have drawn the line at honour killing."

"Why are you so down on my mother all of a sudden? She's over eighty and she plays on the floor with the children. She runs into the freezing cold Atlantic like a kid. She brings gifts and sends cards and prays for us constantly and thinks you're wonderful. At least *my* mother's not a snob."

Hil just looked at her.

"I'm sorry," said Mary Rose.

Hil got up and went into the bathroom, quietly closing the door behind her.

"Hil? Hil, I'm sorry. Hil?"

Patricia wasn't a snob. Yes she was, but a nice one. At least Mary Rose hadn't said "drunk."

The bathroom door opened suddenly and Hil came out. "Get out."

"What do you mean, what are you talking about?"

Mary Rose knew it was bad because Hil was not crying and she herself sounded like a guilty robot. She felt numb, she knew most of her brain was shut down—she even wondered what an MRI would show in terms of which areas were lit and which were in darkness. Where was the switch? Words issued from her tin mouth. "Don't get hysterical, Hil."

Hil smacked her fist into her own mouth—"Hil," said the robot, "don't bite your hand."

The robot attempted to remove the hand—*thwack!* "Don't touch me!"

"Hil, don't scream."

Hissing, eyes wide, through her fist, "Get out, get out, get out—"

"I'll go. I'm going now."

She spent the night on Matthew's trundle bed and woke up feeling as though someone had swung a cat inside her. It could have been worse. It could have been *What did you get for Christmas? Divorced.*

Mary Rose having successfully held off Maggie's nap until this afternoon now steals into Matthew's room and lays out all his new Baby Gap outfits on his bed, arranging them in action poses, before fetching him up.

He stares. "Who are they?"

"They're your new clothes."

"Where's Bun?"

"He's right there." She points to where she has nestled the stuffed bunny in the embrace of a striped rugby shirt.

He solemnly retrieves Bun from the phantom "child" on the bed and pops his thumb in his mouth.

"Matthew, it's not thumb time, sweetheart. If you're tired, you can have a nap."

"No, I can't. Those kids are on my bed."

"Matthew, they're clothes." She scoops them up and starts folding and putting them in his drawers.

He watches her. "Matt, honey, right now you're showing me you're too tired to do anything but suck your thumb."

Silence. The stare.

"Hey, sweetheart, I forgot to show you the best thing. I fixed your unicorn."

She draws his attention to the window ledge where the tiny glass creature stands, a milky cicatrice at its neck the only indication that it was ever decapitated. She winds it and it commences its slow pirouette, tinkling out its query. He stares at it.

"Why don't you snuggle down with Bun and I'll call you when Diego's on."

He abruptly withdraws his thumb, drops Bun to the floor and casually treads on him on his way out the door.

"Matt?"

"I'm not tired," he says without turning.

Maggie wakes up, Mary Rose changes her, then gets her into her boots and jacket, then waits while Matthew gets himself into his own, then she gets them out the door and down the street then and then and then she wades through conjunctions all the way to the park, over Maggie's protests, "I do not want to go to the park, Mumma. No park. No, no, me no park!"

The mud has frozen into welts. Two or three other toddlers are at play while a couple of nannies sit auditing the sandbox, alongside an actual dad whose tempered enthusiasm and steady pace peg him as a stay-at-home parent. He displays neither the compensatory jubilance of the divorcé nor the studious distraction of I-happen-to-be-working-from-home-today. He displays nothing, even his coat is a version of Mary Rose's standard-issue quilted down, so thoroughly has he donned the drab feathers of the female. Mary Rose is the only mum. "Hi," she says. The dad nods, the nannies regard her warily, as though she might be an immigration officer. The children play Sand-in-Eye. *Howls.* Five tranquil minutes of Montessori-minded categorizing of shovels and sieves, followed by shovel-whack-on-the-head. *Screams.* "Maggie, come help Mumma with the sandcastle." Cat poo captured in sieve. Matthew assembling trucks and backhoes from differently scaled universes. Fifteen minutes. Maggie on the slide, Maggie on the swing, Maggie falling on the concrete of the empty wading pool. "Five more minutes, guys." Matthew not ready to abandon his road-works. Maggie nowhere in sight! Found in orange sliding tube. "I do not want to go home, Mumma. No home. Me no home, no! NO!" Feet going like a circular saw as Mary Rose picks her up.

"Matthew, please leave the truck in the sandbox, it doesn't belong to you, sweetheart."

He throws the truck. "Why can't you buy me a brother?"

At home, she helps them off with their outdoor clothes and then makes hot chocolate and then wipes it up from off the over the out from under before and after and thenandthenandthen creeps in this prepositional pace from day to day . . . What day *is* it? What month, what year? Behold the foot calendar, breeding tulips out of the dead . . . April. Thursday. The fifth. She blinks . . . this week is hurtling by. Right, Hil is previewing tomorrow night.

A text from Gigi.

Mister, did you get my message? It's even better the second day—can I come over?

She'll have to go through the skipped phone messages and find out what Gigi is talking about before replying. On the other hand, she has to head her off—

Love to, but early bedtime tonight, scratchy throat.

xomr

It isn't a lie, she *will* have a sore throat if she doesn't go to bed early tonight—the missing morning nap has begun to take its toll on her if not Maggie.

She dials.

"Hi, Mum."

"You're there! Did you get the—"

"No, the mail is suspended."

"Still? What about Hilary?"

"She's in . . ." If she tells her mother that Hil is actually in Calgary, not Winnipeg, will that start a whole new loop? But her mother can't even remember that Hil is away, so she may as well adhere to reality. "She's in Calgary."

"What's she doing there?"

Sigh. "I thought I mentioned, she's directing *The Importance of Being Earnest.*"

"You said she was doing that in Winnipeg."

". . . Did I?"

"That's where your sister was born."

"Maureen was born in Cape Breton, Mum."

"Not Maureen, Other Mary Rose!"

It is difficult to determine which is more arresting: her mother's sudden reference to "Other Mary Rose" as "your sister" or the stage-farcical tone she has employed.

"Oh right, thanks, Mum."

"She was born dead."

"I know, Mum, is Dad there? I need to know when you're arriving." *Stop.* For God's sake, Mary Rose, listen behind the tone, the woman is elderly, drifting into dementia, her manner may be offhand but the words, the words . . .

"Let me get my purse."

"Mum? Mum, before you get your purse." Go for it, robot. "That must have been a hard time."

"What time?"

"When you lost Other Mary Rose."

"Oh . . . Well, you know, I popped into the Hudson's Bay store on my way home, I didn't get into Winnipeg that often, and the saleslady said, 'When're you due?' And I said, 'The baby's dead,' and she started crying, and I said—"

"Did you hold her?"

"Hold her? No, no."

"What . . . did they do with her?"

"Oh, I think she was incinerated, listen now, we're stopping over at eleven on the seventh, have you got a pin?"

Mary Rose pauses while her neocortex tries to sort out the difference between the two halves of the sentence her mother has just spoken, for Dolly's tone has given no indication that they are anything but twinned, when in fact they are as different as . . . Winnipeg and Calgary.

"Are you still there?"

"Yes—"

"We're getting on the train today."

"Today?!"

"We arrive on the seventh."

"Okay, wait—" Where is her datebook? "Maggie, sweetheart, where is Mumma's big book?"

"Hi, Maggie!" Dolly yells in Mary Rose's ear as behind her there rises a clatter, and a cry from Matthew.

"Maggie!" she yells before she has time to turn around.

But it is Daisy—usually so dainty around toys and toes. Is she dragging her left hind paw slightly? Dolly bursts into song, "... *seven eight, lay them straight, nine ten, a big fat hen . . . !*" Maggie grabs at the phone.

Where is her datebook? Her whole life is in there. What was she doing before her mother called? "When does your train get in, Mum? The seventh?"

"That's it, or wait now, the eleventh."

Matthew is crying.

"Seven, two, one, two, two, two!" yells Maggie, trying to open the dishwasher—Mary Rose pulls her back, and grabs a pencil from the telephone drawer—the lead is broken. She grabs another, it is new and yet to be sharpened. She snatches a scented marker from the craft table.

"Okay." She turns to the foot calendar and writes *7* in the square marked *11* in root beer Smencil.

"That's right," says Dolly, "seventh at eleventh."

". . . Do you mean seven o'clock on the eleventh or eleven o'clock on the—"

"Eleven. Will we see Hil?"

She writes *11* on the *7* square.

"No, Mum, she's out west—"

"We'll see you on eleventh, then."

"The seventh—Maggie, don't touch! Matthew, hush for goodness sake."

"I meant to give it to you last summer."

"Give me what?"

"It's a small little thing. I think you were looking for it."

"You mean the packeege?"

"I better hang up now, Daddy's got lunch on the table."

"He does?" Is she dreaming? Is she dead? "Dad made lunch?" Her father can barely boil water.

"Bye, doll."

Click.

She stands for a moment, in the rubble of the phone call. Then rallies and puts on a *Teletubbies* DVD for the kids on a portable player at the craft table and they squeal with joy at the sight of the big baby face in the sun. Something about the face makes Mary Rose uneasy, it is . . . slurry. In the kitchen she turns on CBC radio while she tries to think what to make for supper—a woman in Yellowknife can play "Jingle Bells" on her dentures and the Catholic Church has just made another large payout but no admission of guilt to victims of sexual abuse.

"Dipsy, Laa-Laa, Po and Tinky Winky!"

It was two days after her sixteen-hour personal power outage on her father-in-law's couch in Halifax—where she had listened to the sounds of Maggie's second birthday party below—when they pulled into the driveway of her parents' comfortable condo late. Every year, she formed the intention of setting out early enough to arrive before sundown, and every year they drove the final gruelling two hours in darkness on a stretch of road she'd come to think of as "Night Danger Highway" for the number of warning signs illustrated with leaping deer and charging moose. The first leg of their journey back home to Toronto was done, and they would stopover for a few days with Dunc and Dolly in Ottawa.

They carried the sleeping children from the car and the warm night air hit them with the force of frangipani. Her parents were back-lit at the open door, "Hello-hello-hello!" Daisy shot like a bullet from the back of the station wagon, pausing on her houseward trajectory to squat and pee in the grass. Dolly woke the children with kisses, Duncan managed an end run and succeeded in carrying in the bags.

The dog went straight to Dolly, whose late-onset affection for the species might be another sign of cognitive decay—dogs were vermin where she had come from. "Is he hungry, do you think?" All dogs were male for Dolly.

In the kitchen, Dolly said, "You'll have a cup of tea." And ushered them to a table full of food. She was disappointed they hadn't brought any dirty laundry.

Mary Rose, Hil and the kids spent the following day at a wading pool followed by a trip to the Museum of Science and Technology. When the lovely afternoon was finally over, she gratefully accepted her father's offer of a "libation" and waited in the kitchen while he went to his "medicine cabinet" to make a selection.

Maggie was sitting on the floor eating a packet of high-fructose chemicals in the shape of Dora and Boots that Sitdy had just given her a half-hour before supper—not that there's ever a good time. She wondered if her parents had remembered Maggie's birthday—there was no sign of a cake. She decided not to say anything—one birthday party was enough, and besides, at two, Maggie was too young to know. Sitdy stumbled over Maggie on her way from the fridge to the counter with a pot, but neither seemed to notice. Mary Rose considered moving the child out of the path of Hurricane Dolly, but Hil was close by, dicing onions—she derived pleasure from the sight of her blue-eyed partner towering over her little brown mother. Dolly shoved the pot at Mary Rose—"Hold this"—and proceeded to clear space on the stovetop. Her mother had always kept a kitchen with a degree of what other people would call clutter. The difference these days was that she had got into the habit of using her glass stovetop as an extension of her counter space, and at present it was heaped with *TV Times* crosswords, bills, scrap paper and several issues of *Living with Christ*. "Mum, your stovetop is not an extension of your countertop."

Dolly replied, "Where's the kettle?"

They'd be living with Christ soon enough if her mother burned the house down. Her father reappeared with two generous drams—"You sure you won't join us, Hilary?"

"No thanks, Duncan, I'm sous-chefing for Dolly."

"Then you'd better keep your wits about you." He chuckled, adding, "I got some of that fancy French water too, what's it called, Perrier?" The way he said it rhymed with "terrier," and the twinkle in his eye attested to his self-mocking intention. Hil laughed, and Mary Rose watched as she brushed her hair back from her eyes with her wrist and turned her best Natalie Wood smile on him . . . Is my wife flirting with my father? Is my father flirting with my wife? Is it okay that I like it?

Dolly, having plunked the pot on the stove, was now safely anchored at the small kitchen table with Matthew and a deck of cards. Mary Rose followed her father over to the spacious living room area and sank into a gold-upholstered bucket chair.

"Slainte," he said, and they drank—he had taken to using the Gaelic expression.

The ice snapped in her glass and she breathed a sigh. Daisy was passed out in a patch of fat afternoon light—she looked appetizing, like a side of cured pork. "Your soft pop station in the nation's capital," was playing Ferrante and Teicher's "Bright Elusive Butterfly of Love" on what her parents still called the hi-fi.

"There is such a thing as genetic memory," he said. He was in his armchair next to her, a side table between them. "I think we remember not only our ancestors' experience but our cellular experience." His blue gaze was directed toward the glass patio door where an orange X was taped at eye level owing to a recent mishap involving his nose; he blamed Dolly for having cleaned the pane without telling him. "I think it's possible we could trace our origins to a deep-time spaceship wreck."

She thought of the surprise cheek-swab kit even now winging its way to him from Texas, and hoped it would not be a letdown; evidently he was after bigger game than a handful of hairy chieftains. She paralleled his gaze through the glass, past the railings of the back porch that gave onto the patio and the retreating perspective of lawns, differentiated by umbrellas, barbecues and the occasional sprinkler lazily combing the light, tossing its tresses, sending up wet sparks. She sipped.

"Aliens crash-landed here," mused Duncan. "And their genetic material dispersed among the cells that were already percolating in Earth's primordial soup."

Waiter, there's a family tree in my primordial soup. She swirled the spirit in her glass. "Dad, what do you think time is?"

"It's four thirty-seven!" bellowed Dolly.

"That's why, as a species, we yearn to travel into space," continued Duncan. Had he not heard her question? "It's not just that we want to explore. It's that we want to go home. It's why we situate 'Heaven' up there in the sky, and why so many of us believe that one day we'll return. And until now we couldn't think of any way to 'go home' and be reunited with 'the Father' except to die."

Her mother bustled over, cup and saucer rattling in her hand, "I just poured you some hot, Dunc, don't burn your mouth on it."

They were drinking Scotch, not tea, but Dolly placed the cup and saucer on the side table at his elbow, returned to the kitchen and burst into the theme from *Carmen*. *"'Toreador-ah don't spit on the floor-ah, use the cuspidor-ah, that's-ah what it's for-ah!'"*

Quiet conversations had always worked like a red flag on her mother. Ditto the sight of anyone reading a book. It was possible Mary Rose had become an author in self-defence.

"You have a beautiful voice, Dolly," said Hil.

Her father got up to put on a CD. Cape Breton fiddle music filled the air as he returned to his chair. "That young gal picked up a fiddle when she was three years old and never looked back." He spoke in the tragic tones of Scottish high praise.

"If the Father is up there, then where's the Mother?" Mary Rose asked.

"Mother Earth."

"So she's down there. So is Hell."

"Well." He winced. "We call it that, but it's really just a reflection of our fear of mortality."

"Then why don't we talk about being reunited with the Mother?"

"Hm. I guess we don't have to reunite with her because she's always right here. Holding us up. Feeding us. Tucking us back in when we die."

"What's the Father doing while she's busy doing all this?"

He laughed. "Good question."

"He's above the fray."

"That's an old management trick." His tone was conspiratorial. "It's why the boss has his office upstairs."

Her gaze strays up to a corner of the ceiling.

"Maybe we associate our power of higher thought with the sky because it's been closest to our head ever since we started walking upright," he said.

"The Egyptians believed the heart was the organ of thought. They threw the brain away."

"And now science has discovered neurons in the lining of the heart."

"And the intestines."

"Exactly, that's where you get 'gut feelings.'"

"And a broken heart."

"Yuh." He aspirated the assenting syllable in a manner as characteristic of his East Coast roots as it was inimitable—a means of rendering even a simple *yes* fatalistic. She watched his eyes close and his head nod in barely perceptible time with the reel.

She heard Matthew ask, "Sitdy, what's for supper?"

In Mary Rose's day, her mother would have barked, *Chudda b'chall!* Shit and vinegar! Masculine form. But she heard Dolly reply gently, "We're having a smorgasbord, Matthew, do you know what that is?"

She looked over her shoulder to see Matthew shake his head no.

"It's a little bit of everything." Sitdy smiled and dealt a new hand. "Habibi." *Darling*: masculine form.

Mary Rose wonders how young Dolly managed to go against "Puppa's" wishes and enter nurses' training all those years ago. Maureen once told her that their mother had experienced "a nervous breakdown" at seventeen. The statement was like a title with no book; another fragment that she had accepted as though it were whole. Another stranded station of the cross. *Dolly breaks the first time.*

The reel ended and a jig began. Her father opened his eyes, reached for his glass, encountered the teacup and it sloshed in his grasp. He looked bewildered, then vexed. Mary Rose moved to help, but he made a calming gesture with his hand that rankled her slightly—it wasn't as if she was "paneeking"—and used his hanky to mop up the spill.

"I'm only putting onions in half!" her mother hollered from the kitchen.

"Put them all the way through!" Duncan hollered back.

"Oh Dunc, you know what'll happen!"

"What'll happen?!" He sounded annoyed. He must be deeply content. "'Time' . . . now that's tricky," he said, picking up the thread. "Time is an illusion. A way of keeping track of change."

Spare a quarter for a loony? "The only constant," said Mary Rose.

"A way of keeping tabs on the tricks that energy and matter get up to. If I was auditor general of the universe, I'd separate those two."

She smiled in appreciation. "I don't know if you can."

"When I reach for this glass, what keeps my hand from passing right through it?"

"Maybe the fact you haven't drunk enough to be seeing double."

He chuckled. "There's that. But there's also 'the swerve.'"

"The what?"

"Haven't you read your Lucretius?"

"Not . . . recently."

"What're they teachin' you in school these days? *De rerum natura.* In which the poet invokes 'the necessary flaw,'" he said with a magical mystery tour flourish.

"Flaw in what?"

"Everything."

"Why is it 'necessary'?"

"You just answered your own question."

"What do you mean?"

"Well. Here we are."

She paused. "I feel like I'm remembering the future."

"I wouldn't be at all surprised," he said.

Had her father ever smoked marijuana?

"Dad, have you ever experimented with—"

"I'm not going to cook this kibbeh," Dolly announced from the kitchen. "I watched the butcher cut the meat and grind it and I made him sterilize the blade beforehand."

Mary Rose shuddered. Food standards were no longer what they had been in the golden age of government regulation. Her family was going to eat a dish the principal ingredient of which was raw beef; the children and the old people were going to die, her mother was going to kill herself and them. Hil and Mary Rose would see out the rest of their shortened, miserable lives as names on a waiting list for kidney transplants. Mary Rose, with her O negative blood type, was likely a goner. She wondered, would Andy-Patrick give her a kidney? Had she been nice enough to him since they'd grown up? *Your sister is being held prisoner in a dialysis machine on the Planet . . .*

She turned to see her mother scrubbing her hands and holding them up to drip-dry like the O.R. nurse she had been, before plunging them into the big old enamel bowl, where she began kneading away, adding salt, pepper and cinnamon to the meat, folding in the onion and the softened bulgur wheat.

Hil said, "I'm watching carefully, Dolly, I want to be able to make this at home."

"Well, ysallem ideyki, dear. That means 'bless your hands.'"

The aroma of eggplant, garlic, tomatoes and pine nuts wafted from the oven—a dish infelicitously named "shucklemushy." At least that was what her mother called it. Recent Lebanese immigrants had different names for things and different ways of preparing food, as Dolly had been astonished to discover. For example, she had yet to meet any Lebanese in Ottawa who ate *kibbeh nayeh*—raw kibbeh. Mary Rose was willing to bet Dolly hadn't met any child brides either.

Also on the menu, Dolly's cinnamony roast chicken with green mashed potatoes called *hushweh*—*try them, try them!* Baked with herbs and juices from the bird. She began to relax regarding the E. coli, if not the mad-cow . . . whatever happened to that, anyway? Perhaps it was implicated in the epidemic in dementia—unless the spike was simply an effect of mass longevity. No doubt it would soon have its own ribbon. A grey one.

"Do you want the other wing?" Duncan asked, indicating their glasses, half rising.

"Sure. I'll get it."

She rose and carried their glasses over to the kitchen.

"I *bought* the chicken," Dolly announced balefully.

"You're falling down on the job, Missus," said Duncan, mock stern.

"I better watch out or he'll fire me." Dolly winked at Hilary, who was crouched before the open fridge. "What are you looking for, dear?"

"The olives," said Hil.

"They're in a Becel tub."

Hil stayed staring.

"It's Yoplait on the bottom."

There ought to be a sign over her mother's fridge: *Abandon all hope, ye who enter here.* Dolly had reused and recycled long before it was fashionable or urgent. A tin of Hershey's chocolate sauce might contain solidified bacon fat; raw egg yolks nested in a Cool Whip tub, and God knows what's in the Nutella jar; she would have purchased the original products exactly once. By the time you got through the decoys, you'd forgotten what you were looking for.

Mary Rose asked, "Matthew, what are you eating?"

He had a chocolate moustache.

"Nutella on a cracker," said Dolly. "It's healthy, they eat it in Europe."

"So that's what was in the Nutella jar."

"What else would it be?"

Maggie was now surrounded by the contents of Dolly's purse, which was capsized like a tugboat amid bobbing cargo. Mary Rose was about to step around her when she noticed the child was playing with a plastic pill container—the rectangular kind with the days of the week stamped on the compartments. She bent and took it from her.

"Mine!" objected Maggie.

A whistling from the stove. Dolly poured boiling water into a waiting bowl of pink Jell-O crystals, picked it up and swung it with its scalding contents from counter to table. Mary Rose scooped Maggie from the floor—"Here, Hil"—and thrust the thrashing child at her.

She moved to rejoin her father with the drinks but Dolly was right on her heels. She groaned, saying, "I'm going to go take a suppository."

"I now know that," said Mary Rose. "And cannot now unknow it."

"You're saucy." Dolly pretended to slap her. "Have you heard from your brother?"

"Not recently."

"When's he coming home?"

"I don't know."

Dolly smiled mischievously. "Do you think he and Shereen will have a baby?"

"I don't know." She meant to sip but gulped and coughed.

"When're we going to play Scrabble?"

"We can play now. Do you ever use the German Scrabble game I gave you?"

"Do you remember what you said when I told you we were going to call him Alexander—"

"Yes, Mum, I—"

"Hilary, do you know what she said, dear, when Andy-Patrick was born? I said to her, 'Mary Rose, will we call the baby Alexander?' And she said, '"Don't call him Alexander. If you call him Alexander, you'll have to put him in de gwound!"'"

Hil shot Mary Rose a questioning look—she didn't know it was a funny story. *Don't even try, Hil.*

"I'm surprised you remember that, Mary Rose," said Dolly, "you were only, how old were you?"

"Five."

"I mean when Alexander was born."

"Oh, I . . . I guess I actually don't know."

Dolly was suddenly shouting again, firing the words past Mary Rose's head. She felt them graze her scalp—"Dunc, how old was Mary Rose when Alexander-Who-Died was born?!"

"What?" he answered irritably. "What're you worried about that for?"

"I'm not 'worried,' Dunc!" And to Hil, "She would have been, let me think now . . ."

"Where's that picture, Mum? The one of us visiting his grave."

"Was there a picture?"

"Dad took it, remember?" She looked over at her father for corroboration but he appeared to be dozing off. She set his drink down at his elbow and removed the cup and saucer. She returned to her mother, speaking quietly. "It's of me and you and Maureen. It was cold, you gave me your sweater."

"It wasn't cold, it was April."

"See, you do remember."

Matthew piped up, "Jitdy, can I have some ice cream?"

"Shh, Matthew."

"Sure," replied Dunc, rallying, hands on the armrests, about to rise.

"No, Dad, not yet, please."

He winked at Matthew. "She's the boss. Come here, Matt, and keep me company while the women finish making supper. Did you know all the best chefs in the world are men?"

"I was going to do something, now what was it?" said Dolly.

"Solve Fermat's Last Theorem?"

"I was going to take a suppository, come."

"I am not going into the bathroom with you."

"You're saucy, come with me now, I want to give you something."

She topped up her Scotch again and followed her mother into her bedroom where Dolly started going through her jewellery box. Mary Rose braced herself—what was her mother about to bestow upon her? A diamond? A dime-store bracelet? Would she be able to tell the difference?

Dolly had moved on to a bottom drawer in her dresser and now she threw something at Mary Rose with a flapping sound. A calendar. "He painted the whole thing with his foot!"

"Really. What happened to his arms?"

"What was I going to give you?" Dolly dropped her arms to her sides with a jangle of bangles. "Golly Moses, Mary Roses, your mother's losin' 'er mind."

This was not different. The confusion, the juggling act. There was no new ingredient, just an old one missing: anger. Like a maze without a minotaur.

"It's okay, Mum."

From the living room came the velvet tones of Nat King Cole posing the age-old question to Mona Lisa. As though summoned, Dolly left the room. Mary Rose followed to see her father dancing a slow, bouncy circle with Maggie in his arms—the child had one hand on his shoulder and the other fastened round his thumb. She was gazing at him with a gravity and contentment that Mary Rose recognized, and she paused, held, too, by the evening light that had inhabited the room. Splendid. Impossible to believe that light could be anything but particulate, so thick and honey-sweet it was, light reflecting light, pouring through the glass doors, suffusing the room with an aching loveliness, rendering the moment at once immortal and irretrievably lost. The song ended, he set her down, and Mary Rose watched as Maggie made a run for the sun.

"Maggie!"—Mary Rose caught her round the middle before she could bang into the glass, and the child screamed in protest.

"Gently!" cried Duncan, his voice reedy with alarm.

Mary Rose set Maggie down and tapped on the glass to show her the door was closed.

"Is she all right?"

She turned. Her father was white as paper.

"She's fine, Dad."

"Don't be getting after her now." His voice had splintered to a whisper.

"I'm not, Dad, I'm not angry at her."

"All right, then, no paneek." He turned to his CD tower.

"Are you okay, Dad?"

He cleared his throat. "Oh I'm fine, it's just you've got to be careful when you grab hold of a child like that."

"Golly Moses," said Dolly. "I thought she was going to run right off the balcony."

From the hi-fi issued sounds of impending battle, a massed drum roll heralding a blast of bagpipes.

Duncan taped an orange cross on the glass at toddler-eye level. Dolly turned the raw kibbeh onto a serving platter, mounded it smooth and imprinted a crucifix with the edge of her hand. "In the name of the Father!" she intoned, raising her other hand in the sign of the cross and looking like the conductor of an orchestra. Duncan lowered the volume on "The Massacre at Glencoe" and they gathered round the dining table, Matthew on his booster seat, Maggie in her high chair.

She watched as Dolly, in accordance with long custom, stood and dismembered the chicken by hand, tearing a wing from the bird and offering it to her. "You don't want the wing? No—Maureen's the one who likes the wing, Hilary, do you like the wing?"

"Sure, Dolly."

She plopped the wing onto Hil's plate.

"Einmal wein, Fraulein?" said Duncan, graciously pouring Liebfraumilch into Hil's glass—a medium-sweet German white wine to accompany raw kibbeh to the tune of muted Highland outrage.

The table was groaning, Dolly had somehow managed to make tabbouleh along with everything else. Now she was pouring powdered milk for the children from a recycled tomato sauce bottle.

"Mum, there's real milk in the fridge, I brought some—"

But Matthew drained his glass and held it out for more, while Maggie sucked hers back two-fisted from a sippy cup.

"Is that what happened to your arm?" asked Dolly.

Mary Rose felt her stomach drop. "What do you mean, Mum?"

"Where's the chow chow?" asked Duncan, looking up suddenly.

"What do you want chow chow for?" asked Dolly.

"For the kibbeh."

"You don't eat chow chow with kibbeh," cried Dolly, "that's a desecration!"

Duncan gave his grandson a crafty smile. "Eat it all up now, Matthew, it'll put hair on your chest."

Mary Rose caught Hil's eye. Had her father not heard what her mother had just asked her? Mixing up a balcony with a patio door in a moment of fear was understandable, but for her mother to forget that

Mary Rose had had bone cysts . . . Unless he was in denial. Or keeping something from her and her siblings—a diagnosis . . . *Alzheimer's*. She felt the old gluey sensation stir in her esophagus at the mere thought of speaking the word. But if she allowed her mother's question to be derailed by her father, she would be enabling the family dynamic of denial and suppression.

"I had bone cysts, Mum. Remember?"

"Of course I do, dear, I'm your mother."

Relief. No need to ask her father anything point-blank, they could stick to neurology and the cosmos. She reached for the Liebfraumilch. Her parents' wineglasses were small, in keeping with their genera-tion—having grown up during the Great Depression when a whole family shared one pair of shoes, a china cabinet full of 1950s stemware must have looked like Versailles—thus she calculated she was really still on her first glass of wine.

Maggie had green potatoes in her hair, Matthew was somehow already in possession of a bowl of chocolate ice cream. Duncan was regaling Hil, "I remember Gordie Howe's last game at the Montreal Forum . . ."

Was it the familiarity of the story her father was telling? Or the conflation of a patio with a balcony door, slabs of time jammed up against one another like ice on Lake Ontario . . . They were eating at the very table at which she had sat so often while her mother cursed her and her father sat by, eyes on the ceiling. It had served as the kitchen table back before her parents downsized. Light being what it is, those scenes were still being played out somewhere . . . Only time separated those events from this one. Twenty years ago, in this very seat, she was shell-shocked.

". . . The place was packed to the rafters, and Howe was going full tilt down the ice . . ."

Hil was smiling with the blank politesse of the good daughter-in-law.

"Dunc," said Dolly.

"And he started passing the puck from his stick to his skate, then from his skate to his other skate, then back to his stick, and he kept this up without breaking stride . . ." His blue eyes were hot, his smile taut.

"Duncan, dear—"

"And that crowd—now you have to understand, Montreal was a tough crowd, still is—well, that crowd got to its feet and gave Howe a standing ovation."

Mary Rose saw his gold tooth, but he did not have long to savour Howe's triumph, for Dolly broke in, "Dunc, was it the Rh factor?"

He blinked as though surfacing from a nap. "Was what?"

"Mary Rose's arm."

"No, no, no, you're confusing the two. The Rh factor has to do with blood type."

"Then what caused the bone cysts?"

"Nothing, you're born with them." He tipped the bottle over Hil's glass but it was empty.

"I wasn't good at having babies."

"Mum, that's not true."

"Does your arm ever bother you now?"

"No, Mum."

"Mumma was good at having babies."

"Dad, is that why you got scared when I went to grab Maggie by the arm?"

He appeared to consider this. "Now that would make sense. Knowing what we know now, about how your arm would have been fragile all along . . . I guess I had that in the back of my mind." He looked up with a chuckle. "Tell you the truth, though, she's so much like you, I was worried she was going to run right out onto the balcony and keep goin' over the side."

Mary Rose exchanged another look with Hilary. She ought to stop obsessing over every little slip-up of her mother's and accept the fact that both her parents were damn old and had every right to be forgetful.

"Was it before or after Mumma died that you gave me the moonstone, Dunc?"

"I think it was before," he said casually, applying himself to the vigorous rearrangement of his mashed potatoes.

"Did she die before or after we lost Alexander?"

He set down his fork and employed the soft-pedal version of the expository tone. "It was *before*. I gave you the moonstone when Alexander was born. Afterwards, I took you for a few days to the Alps and that's when we got word about your mother."

"Doesn't that mean it was . . . after?" asked Mary Rose.

"After what?" he asked.

"So . . . what year would that have been?" Was she drunk?

"It was after the Missile Crisis, so—no. Sorry, my mistake." His tone was meticulous but good-natured. "I'm confusing it with the Bay of Pigs."

Dolly turned to Hil. "We went up the Zugspitze on a cable car and there was no toilet at the top, can you imagine that?!"

"I don't have to imagine it," said Duncan with a rueful grin, "I was there."

Hilary said, "Dolly, it must have been terribly hard to be so far away from your own mother at that time. And then to lose her too."

"Oh it was, dear, it really was! And Hilary, you would know, wouldn't you, doll, you must miss your mother terribly."

Hil nodded.

Dolly continued, "She was a lovely lady, I was right fond of Patricia, and you know how proud she was of you, Hilary. I think Maggie looks a little like her, do you see it too?"

Hil began to cry. Mary Rose made a move to take her hand but knocked over her wineglass. Dolly rose and embraced Hil. "She's with you, dear." She spoke quietly. "She's looking after you. And you know, you might find she's taking care of you now in ways that she couldn't when she was here." Hil buried her face in Dolly's shoulder.

"Mummy, what's wrong?" asked Matthew. He now had a full chocolate beard.

"Nothing, sweetheart." Hil blew her nose on her napkin. "I'm fine, I just miss Gran."

"Gran misses me too," said Matthew, tears filling his eyes.

Duncan reached over and stroked his head—not a bonk, no shingle, a soft pliable hand.

Dolly smacked both hers flat on the table, making the plates and the children jump. "Dunc, tell a funny story, put on some happy music!"

"You're the boss," he said, rising.

The room filled with the sexy, plaintive tones of Fairuz, backed by a Middle Eastern nightclub orchestra *circa* 1955. Dolly had fled the table—the suppository doing its work, surmised Mary Rose. Duncan returned, holding aloft several bright bottles by their necks like the spoils of war. "How about a liqueur, Hilary? You name it, I've got it, do you like crème de menthe?"

From "offstage" they heard Dolly burst into "Happy Birthday." Duncan grinned conspiratorially and joined in as Dolly entered carrying a pink cake ablaze with a single fat candle in the shape of a 2. Maggie screamed in joyous comprehension that this was her *second* second birthday party. Dolly set the cake down and Maggie blew out the candle. "Hurray-hurray!" cried Dolly and Dunc, clapping, and breaking back into song.

At around two a.m., Mary Rose woke up in the basement guest room, surprised by pain. Her arm felt hot. She did not recall having bumped it, but she had been somewhat inebriated by the time she joined her parents in the TV room and passed out in front of *Murder, She Wrote*. She turned to look at Hil slumbering next to her, a sweetly perturbed expression on her beautiful face. She had begun to get lines. Just because she was younger than Mary Rose did not mean time stood still for Hilary. Would they still be together when they were her parents' age, or would Mary Rose have wrecked it by then? Hil would become a regal old lady, Mary Rose a wizened jester. That's if they made it through the first great winnowing—the mid-life cancer disaster that was stalking their generation.

She sat up carefully so as not to activate the comedy springs that set the bed to rocking like an on-ramp in an earthquake at the slightest twitch. She crept between Maggie, asleep with her bum sticking up in the Pack 'n Play and Matt on the fold-out IKEA chair-bed. She slipped out, closing the door carefully behind her, and into the bathroom, where she braced herself for the stab of light and looked at her arm.

No bruise. She popped an Advil—as much for the hangover she hoped to forestall as for the pain. She became aware of another feeling, in her chest . . . the old guilt-shame brew, as though she had done or said something obscene at the supper table—which she had not.

She killed the light and went upstairs.

From the broad staircase she emerged into the airy expanse of her parents' home. Moonlight poured through the kitchen window and overflowed the sink.

A low pony wall defined the kitchen from the dining and living area where a set of big glass doors looked out onto the patio. Pleasant oil paintings and framed photos graced the walls and dotted end tables— Dolly and Dunc's children, grandchildren and now a great-grandchild. Her parents had streamlined and updated, but here and there were objects that resonated at a cellular level: their honeymoon photo. Dolly beaming, waving from the train, eyes saucy with life and laughter. Duncan, amused and movie star handsome in a double-breasted suit. The air force plaque from RCAF Gimli outside Winnipeg. The cuckoo clock from the Black Forest with its rather scrotal pendula in the shape of pine cones. And Dürer's *Praying Hands*, its smooth wood the colour of Dolly's skin. *Ysallem ideyki.* Mary Rose did not have to look to know that stuck to the underside of every object was a Post-it Note with a name. Dolly was determined to head off squabbles among her grieving offspring, and it was a good idea provided they were able to read her writing.

She turned to the fridge, its door thick with snapshots and clippings, including an old bestseller list featuring *Escape* in the number one spot—it was affixed with a Virgin Mary medallion. Next to it was a picture of the Pope blessing a party of Masai warriors. She opened the freezer. Slotted between a tray of buckling ice cubes and a lump of something that looked to be swathed in surgical dressings was a zip-lock bag—a silty envelope of a yellowish substance. It resembled something you were more likely to find in a lab than a kitchen. She pressed it to her arm. The cold felt heavenly.

She took a seat at the table that was already set for breakfast—winsome hens-and-rooster placemats. Through the open window the night was humid and heavy with stars that looked ready to fall like fruit, and a fragrant breeze found her. Ottawa could be like that in summer. On the counter, beneath a glass dome, sat the remains of Maggie's pink birthday cake—her *second* second birthday cake—its half-melted 2 candle making it look like a dilapidated gravestone. Mary Rose shook it off—*Think nice thoughts.* She was reaching for a newspaper when her mother shuffled in.

Arms lax at her sides, Dolly led with her belly, which in the past was Napoleonic but now was toddler-like. Her dusky cheeks were mooshed with sleep, her white hair steepled in an old-lady mohawk.

"What're you doin' up, doll? Y'hungry?" Sleepy contralto tones.

"Sorry I woke you, Mum."

"Get out, you didn't wake me. Here, gimme."

Mary Rose flinched but Dolly merely took the bag and tossed it into the microwave.

"My arm is sore," she said, lest her mother feel hurt by her reflexive withdrawl.

"Your arm?"

Dolly raised her eyebrows; she had a perfect clown face.

"You said it doesn't bother you anymore."

And before Mary Rose could draw back, Dolly pressed her fingertip to the top of the twin scars, and ran it down the stripe. It was such an unexpected gesture—not painful . . . but eerie, scar tissue being at once ultra-sensitive and numb.

Dolly said, "I remember when I was small, if I had anything that was bothering me, or even a sore throat I think it was one time, Mumma would say to me, 'That's your badness coming out in you.' So I knew not to complain."

The word was red and released a pong such that Mary Rose could smell it. *Badness*. "That's what you used to tell me."

"Did I?"

"You said that about my arm."

"You had bone cysts—"

"Mum, how old were you when your mother said that to you?"

"Let me see, was I five or six? I was a dark little thing."

"You couldn't possibly have been bad."

"Oh, I was." A mischievous light entered Dolly's eyes. She giggled. "I always had candy."

"Why was that bad?"

"Well, this was during the Great Depression, no one had candy then, who was I to have candy? It made Mumma so mad, she'd grab a hold of me and holler, 'Where'd you get the candy, demon?'"

"Where *did* you get the candy?"

Dolly got up suddenly and squirted a white stream into the palm of her hand from the recycled Jergens bottle by the sink.

Mary Rose watched her mother rub the cream into her hands. They took on the sheen of polished wood; finely veined, deeply lined.

The microwave beeped. Dolly poured the contents of the bag into a bowl with a *plop*. Chicken soup. She put it in front of Mary Rose, who took a spoonful. Turned out she was hungry.

"Mum, you weren't bad."

Dolly guffawed. "Tell Mumma that! She had twelve of us to cope with and never raised her voice."

"You said she hollered at you."

"Well I was a little demon! She had to slap us and, you know, keep us in line somehow, and then my sisters did a whole lot of the upbringing, my sister Sadie did a whole lot, that's just the way it was in those days."

"Who gave you the candy?"

"His pockets were always full of candy."

"Whose?"

Dolly's brow furrowed. Mary Rose waited. Her arm throbbed.

"Let me see till I get hold of it . . ." Dolly blinked a few times in quick succession. Then her face cleared and she turned back to Mary Rose. "I guess it's gone. What'll we do now, you want to play Scrabble?"

Dolly went down to the rec room and came back with the German edition of Scrabble that Mary Rose had given her one Christmas, having lugged it all the way from a book festival in Munich. It was still in plastic—Dolly unwrapped it and they played with *ü*'s and too many *z*'s.

Dolly won.

Her datebook is in the dishwasher. Mercifully unwashed. She opens it to the current week on two pages, then refers back to the foot calendar and is about to transcribe her parents' arrival information when she stalls. It takes her Executive Function a moment to process what she sees on the foot calendar: April seventh does not fall on a Sunday. She looks back at her datebook: yes it does. What is happening? Her vision begins to constrict. Today is Thursday, you know this to be true. *Hi there, and happy Thursday.* Her heart levitates, sheds weight within her chest and begins to flutter. *Breathe.* You have not entered a parallel world, you are not dead behind a soundproof time-plate, you are not suffering amnesia pursuant to a psychotic break; the foot calendar is a year out of date. April is the foolest month . . .

"All aboard, Teletubbies!" *Woo-woo!*

Chicken, broccoli and quinoa. Successful bath time. Successful bedtime. She successfully downloads the form from the Canada Post website. Prints it. Signs it. Hears Maggie. Heads upstairs, stepping over Daisy flaked out on the landing. Matthew's beloved unicorn is still playing its tune—he must have rewound it—she can see the sound spiralling, a crystal crown of thorns. Before she reaches the end of the hall, however, she realizes the music is coming from Maggie's room. Anger fizzes even as she understands it to be unfounded; impossible for Maggie to have climbed from her crib, seized the unicorn, then scaled the bars upon her return. Matthew must have placed it there—such a sweetheart.

She enters Maggie's room to see the unicorn revolving on the windowsill, and Maggie asleep. Her face is like a flower—as though in answer to the question posed by the first line of the unicorn's song. Mary Rose is surprised by an ache in her upper respiratory tract. She reaches down and strokes the baby brow. How can someone so small wield such power? The discomfort in her chest abates just as Mary Rose identifies it as love.

•

She got very hungry the night of the surgery. Next to her on the bed lay a button on an electrical cord. It was a bell. She waited a long time before pressing it. When she did, nothing happened at first. After a while the night nurse came and Mary Rose asked her for some food. The night nurse said it couldn't be done. Mary Rose asked her for some toast—she had never felt such hunger, it may have been the painkillers. The nurse said no. Something took over, and Mary Rose insisted, offering to make it herself. The nurse may have thought she was being sarcastic, because Mary Rose could not get out of bed on her own. The nurse left, exasperated.

After a while, she returned with a plastic plate of buttered toast and a cup of apple juice. Mary Rose thanked her, intensely grateful. The nurse left and she devoured the toast and drank the juice, then immediately vomited it back onto the plate and covered it with the napkin. She pressed the button. The nurse came and saw what had happened. Mary Rose apologized. The nurse cleared away the plate and left without a word. Mary Rose did not know if she rang the bell again, but she needed more drugs. The nurse did not return.

She was in her red flannel nightgown with the zillion tiny yellow flowers. Pain came on. Shocking, no time to put up a hand. Pain claimed her. Obliterated her. She was no one.

Suddenly the ceiling was gone. High above and all around was the night, black prairie overarching and stubbled with stars. She felt suspended, and yet so Held. The pain was far below and she knew everything would always be all right. The universe loved her.

·

Just after 1:00 a.m. she gives in and gets out of bed, tired but not sleepy. It is an hour earlier in Winnipeg, Hil's final dress rehearsal will have just wrapped up—now is an ideal time to call. She gets voice mail and leaves a message. "Hi darling, just phoning to say hi, hope you had a great final dress tonight."

She should start working—Alice Munro did some of her best work while her kids were sleeping. She sets her laptop on the kitchen table, creates a new document and, after some considerable thought, entitles it "Book." The cursor blinks.

She calls again in case Hil hasn't heard her phone. "Hi, you've reached Hilary. Go ahead and leave a message." Hil's musical voice, something caressing in it yet forthright.

"Hi, sweetheart, it's me again, everything's fine here just maybe give me a call when you get in." It's after midnight out there, where is she?

She calls a third time. "Hi Hil, I'm just getting a tad—I'm wondering—" She presses *3* and re-records her message, "Hi babe, just to let you know, I'm up working so any time you want to call is fine, I love you."

She starts decalcifying the espresso machine. For that matter, the dishwasher could use a good sluicing too. It's late, she can run both machines economically. She watches the brownish water gush from the espresso head into the waiting glass bowl.

Hil is probably out for drinks with the cast and can't hear her phone in the noisy bar. If Mary Rose weren't married to Hil she would probably be living alone. She wouldn't be a mother. She would likely have finished the trilogy by now and have started a new series. Maybe she'd be a single mother with a full-time nanny. And a hot girlfriend. She has unscrewed the fridge filter, but stops with it in her hand; Hil never goes for drinks with a cast until after the first public preview, and that is not till tomorrow night. She checks her datebook to make sure, yes, there it is in the box marked Friday: *Hil 1st public preview*. She could be out for drinks with someone else . . . what was that guy's name? The fly guy. Unless she has met with an accident . . . the shot of worry works instantly on her GI tract and, like her mother heeding the call of a "suppository," she hurries to the bathroom. No sooner is she seated than she hears the phone ring—Hil, thank God.

She returns to the kitchen and the welcome blinking of the message light. "Hi Sadie, Daisy, Maureen, Mary Rose! I'm callin' from the train, do you believe it?!" Her parents are on the move, a toy train seen from the sky, inching across the map, *woo-woo!* . . . "We'll look for you on the seventh, the eleventh . . . What?" Muffled gregarious sounds. "Aren't ya nice! Not you, Mary Rose, the little gal who just handed me a cuppa—not that you're not nice too! You're the nicest, Mary Rosest! See you Sunday *muffle rustle click*." The skipped messages start to play, "Hi, Mister, it's Gigi—"

She redials. "Hi, you've reached Hilary—" *No, I have not reached Hilary.* "Go ahead and leave a message." Hil's beautiful voice . . . Where is the rest of her? In someone's arms? Or dead in a ditch? Fucking Winnipeg. Does she have ID with her? Fucking wheat fields and whiteouts.

"Hil, please call me when you get in, I'm just a teensy bit concerned, no problem, just, hope your day was great."

She grinds her left hip into the edge of the counter, seeking to zap fear with a shock of pain. *Please let Hil be having an affair, please let her not be dead.* Does she have Mary Rose down as next of kin? Of course she does, they are married. As long as Hil is killed in Canada, Mary Rose will be the first to hear—although she might hear if Hil were killed in Vermont too. How long will it take the authorities to call with the news? She is freezing cold. She cannot get on a night flight because she cannot leave the children. She could phone Gigi to come over, then fly to Winnipeg—but that would prove Hil is dead. Or it would prove that Mary Rose is in the grips of a panic attack.

This knowledge does not stem the neural cascade. Her veins are running with dark chemicals—cortisol, vasopressin. The fact that she has the names of these neurotransmitters at her fingertips tells her something but not enough to make a difference. She has been triggered and there is no one she can call—her brother cannot help her, Gigi cannot help her, Santa Claus cannot help, no one can—crazy, crazy but it must be recorded, the only person who might help is her mother, sweeping into Mary Rose's hospital room in a leopard print coat and tam—she is falling down through nothing, scrabbling air for purchase—*Don't move.* This needs to run its course and Mary Rose needs to keep very still because it is very dangerous to start fleeing or fighting in the middle of the night when the children and the dog are sleeping and you cannot see what is after you. As long as she does not move, nothing bad will happen.

Calgary.

It is *two* hours earlier there. She lets out a breath she did not know she was holding, and resets her internal clock back one panic hour. When you are lost in the Black Forest, stay in one spot or you will end up going round in circles because you cannot see the sun. There will be time enough to thrash about in the underbrush if Hilary fails to call in an hour.

Hilary fails to call.

Mary Rose has not moved from the big black windows. Now the real fear can begin, the other was merely a rehearsal. The phone rings and, as though released by the sound, the penny drops.

"Hi, Hilly, I was just calling to see how your preview went!" She wedges the phone between ear and shoulder, unpins the foot calendar from the corkboard and thrusts it into the recycling bin. She inspects her datebook for further contagion from the out-of-joint calendar.

"Oh thank you, sweetheart, I thought maybe you forgot."

"You didn't get the flowers?"

"No, oh you're so sweet, you didn't have to send flowers."

Mary Rose has lied with no warning and the greatest of ease—*am I a psychopath?* "How'd it go?!"

"Well, it went fine," says Hil, her tone cautiously optimistic. "It hasn't quite lifted off yet, but the beats are there, the laughs are there, and we finally got a decent wig for Maury—"

"He must love you for that." Her smile feels leathery, stretched across her face like a cobbler's last.

"Oh, and you know Paul?"

"Paul?"

"The tech director, you know how he told me no one has used the flies in years? Well, he was so happy he took me up and showed me the rigging."

"He showed you his what?" She coughs.

"You sure you're not coming down with something?"

"It's just a cough. Don't worry, I won't get sick the minute you get home."

"That's not what I meant—"

"I'm not feeling great, but that's normal, I spend my day with toddlers, they're germ bags."

"I know, that's why you should call Judy."

"I'll google my symptoms."

"Don't google!"

"I think my mum is losing it."

"Really?"

"She's so forgetful now and . . . jovial. The other stuff has kind of gone . . ." She is suddenly choked up. Mourning the loss of her mother's rage? *Golly Moses.*

"I don't know how much is really gone," says Hil.

"What do you mean by that?"

"I love your parents, they're sweet."

"'Sweet' like what? Like sweet old Nazis?"

She hears Hil sigh.

Don't pick a fight on the phone in the middle of the night. "I'm sorry, Hilly."

"It's okay, I'm going to go to bed soon, I've got an interview at seven."

Is Hil going to take refuge in an affair? I'll know she is having an affair if she is extra nice. Or extra mean. Or if we have sex as soon as she gets home. Or if we don't.

"It's like she needs endless attention, even negative attention," Mary Rose says. "Maybe she's in her 'second childhood.'"

"Maybe she never came out of her first one."

"Oh yes she did, you didn't know her in the rage years."

"Children rage," says Hil. "They just don't usually have children of their own when they're doing it."

Mary Rose is suddenly craving bed. "I think I better crash, Hil, the kids'll be up in a few hours."

"It must have been a really hard time for you and your mum back then."

"When?"

"In Germany."

"I don't remember."

Silence.

"I'm sorry, love, we don't have to talk about it."

"We can talk about it, it's all *she* ever talks about, everything's a dead baby joke."

Silence.

"She was incinerated."

"Who was?" asks Hilary.

"Other Mary Rose." She is surprised at the sullen note in her voice. "She told me today just like that, like we were talking about the weather."

"I'm so sorry, sweetheart."

"What for?" *Temper down, now.*

"Why don't you call Gigi?"

"Why would I call Gigi?"—she hears the ultra-expository tone taking hold—"I merely wished to tell you what my demented mother told me, if it is not too much to ask."

"Of course it isn't, tell me what she said."

"It doesn't matter." She is being ambushed by her own words that feel cool and reasonable in the fish tank of her head until she opens her mouth, at which point they show their fangs. Hil is not the enemy. "I'm sorry. It's like my mother has opened the lid on a big trunk of freaking tragedy and it's all flying out in a jumble 'cause it's not weighed down with emotion anymore, her emotion lobe is—"

"Slow down."

". . . I'm having déjà vu."

"That's because you already knew what happened to your sister."

Your sister.

"I did?"

"You must have, you've written about it."

"I have?"

"Isn't that what the Black Tears are?"

Mary Rose calls to mind the scene in her second book—second in a supposed trilogy. Is this what all that expensive therapy has done for Hilary?

"Really?" Mary Rose has meant to sound withering but winds up whiny. "I thought they were a plot element in a highly successful book for young adults."

Pause.

"Hil? Don't be mad."

"I'm not, but I think I better go to bed now."

She needs to segue to something safe before hanging up. "Hey, I've been dying to tell you, I saw something I want to get for the house. You know how I've always wanted a hanging rack for pots?"

"You have?"

"It would create a ton of space."

"Where would we put it?"

"In the ceiling over the counter."

". . . Where the lights are."

"We'd move the lights."

"So we're renovating again."

"No, it's barely—it's tiny, I can have it done before you get home."

"I think I'd like to be there."

"Okay, I'll buy the rack but I won't install it—"

"Do you need to buy it right away?"

"Why not?"

"You buy a lot of stuff, great stuff, I consider myself lucky—"

"You think it's trivial?"

"It's not essential."

"Flush toilets are not essential, airplanes are not essential."

Hil laughs. "I'll take the toilet over the ceiling rack, Mary Rose."

Hil has used her full name, that tears it.

"I know it's not a huge priority for you that we have a full set of nesting pots, but when you reach for one, it's there. *You* don't *have* to care because *I do* and now you're saying that my concerns are *trivial*, well go back to your rusty old wok and see how you like it—"

"Mary Rose—"

"Or maybe *Paul* can hang one for you from the *flies*—"

"*Stop it!*"

She remembers.

A seared silence. The living room in Germany. In black-and-white, as if she were looking at a picture in the old photo album. This one is taken from the balcony doorway, looking in. There is the coffee table. There is the couch. There are no people, but there is a presence. A powerful sense that something has just happened. The air is pulsating. The air is shocked.

Hil breaks the silence, her voice calm. "I won't do this anymore, Mister. I'm going to bed now. Good night." She hangs up.

Mary Rose pounds her fist onto the inlaid cutting board but it's a half-hearted blow which fails to whet her appetite for self-battery.

She slumps to the table and googles "stillbirth." Hundreds of sites offer themselves up, she is taken aback by the very abundance—resources for counselling and support, page after page . . . She wonders what, if anything, was available in her mother's day . . . Apart from *you'll have more babies.*

She comes across an online photo gallery. Dozens of infants, dressed sweetly, some are holding stuffed animals. All are dead. There are names, and dates. There are messages from bereaved parents, family and friends. Some of the babies look to be sleeping the cosmic sleep of the healthy newborn. Others have discoloured faces, features slurring, foreheads awry in contrast with little toques and pompoms. She scrolls down the silent wailing wall, past name after name after name . . . Beloved. Mourned.

Other Mary Rose died and began to decompose in utero, her cells undoing themselves, undertaking the journey back to potential. But she had a face. Darkening perhaps, skin melting to the touch, distorted by forceps—*don't look*. Look. A baby. Was she cradled, swaddled before being dispatched? Was she sealed in a bag, was the bag placed in a receptacle? Or tossed? At what point did the bag lose specificity amid the hospital waste—did the janitor know the difference between it and the weight of other sealed bags with their contents of diseased tissues, discarded organs, limbs, surgical dressings, all the things that were neither sharp nor flushable? Was she compacted amid catheter tubes, uneaten hospital food, swabs, tongue depressors, paper cups, before being shovelled into the incinerator? Unbaptized, therefore unnamed, therefore no one. Or did she end up on a dissection tray before a medical student? There would have been no need to ask permission of the parents—don't trouble them with this sort of thing, it cannot harm, can only help.

She had a face. Even if it was slipping away, no longer adhering. She had a name, even though it too did not quite stick. She dreamt. She moved. She was someone.

Your sister.

Book Two: Escape from Otherwhere

Impossible to say whether it is day or night, a perpetual overcast has blocked the sun's rays or trapped them here to grow stale. The ground is pitted and pocked—it could be the asphalt of an abandoned parking lot or schoolyard, except that no weeds are sprouting through the holes. It is unlike any place Kitty has ever seen on Hoam, where around each bend and over every hill is to be found a yet more perfect place for a picnic.

She resists the urge to retrace the stepping stones across the viscous stream and return to the thicket where she left Mr. Morrissey nursing his hindmost foot. She would gladly carry him all the way back through the Forgotten Wood rather than take another step into this drear place that has no name. But the Ebony Elf, though crafty, does not lie. If she says this is where Kitty will find two Black Tears, then she must press on. She fingers the vial on its silver chain around her neck and steps further into the gloom.

Kitty has seen marvels aplenty, not always pretty, so it is not the sight of the doll walking stiffly toward her across the pitiless ground that is perturbing, but the state of it. Not only is it naked, bereft even of hair, but half its moulded face appears to have melted then reset in shiny welts—the poor thing must have been thrown into the fire. Kitty waits and fights off a sense of approaching doom—after all, it is nothing but a harmless doll, lame and small. It stops in front of her. She can hear its laboured breath. It looks up at her with painted eyes that are scuffed but still discernibly blue.

"Hello, Kitty."

Kitty freezes. How does it know her name?

"Don't you remember me?" the thing wheezes.

Kitty shakes her head, suddenly reluctant to leave any part of herself behind here, even the sound of her voice.

The doll is sad but insistent. "Why did you send me away, Kitty?"

Kitty's voice is barely a whisper. "I didn't do anything to you."

"Do you know what they did with me?"

What is this place? Is this Hell?

Suddenly it hisses, "I was incinerated."

Kitty backs away.

"Don't leave me," whimpers the doll.

Suddenly its eyes flood black from lid to lid, and liquid night trickles down its damaged face. The tears! Kitty fumbles for the vial and makes a grab for the doll, but it evades her grasp, surprisingly agile.

"Not until you promise!"

"I'm not promising you anything."

"I am not a bad thing," rasps the demon. "But I will not give you your precious Black Tears until you have granted my wish."

Kitty shivers. "What do you want?"

The doll tilts its head. "Don't you remember me, Kitty?"

"I've never seen you before in my life."

"I am yours."

"No . . ."

"I am Susie."

"Go away."

"Hug me."

Kitty is rooted to the spot, transfixed with horror and loathing. She longs to grab the fiend and hurl it, smash it against the cindery ground.

"No."

"That is my wish."

Kitty almost sobs with anger and revulsion, "I can't."

"Hold me, Kitty," the thing wheezes, and stretches out its plastic arms.

"Never."

"Never is what will happen to your brother, Jon. Never was, never will be."

Kitty is gagging as she steps forward, bends down and picks it up. She squeezes her eyes shut and hugs. The doll makes a sound—small but terrible. She hears a rustling, feels a tugging. And then it is over.

She lets go with a shudder, as though she has just been sick to her stomach, and the doll drops to the ground. Kitty's eyes are still shut when she says, "Now give me my tears."

When the doll does not answer, she opens her eyes and beholds the most remarkable transformation. The doll's face is smooth and unblemished, its eyes merry blue, its mouth a rosebud. No longer naked, it is clad in a blue satin robe, fastened snugly about the waist. Kitty cries out and reaches for her. "Susie!"

This time she hugs her tenderly; her doll feels so soft, just as she used to when Kitty was much younger, before she put her down one day and never picked her up again. Her tears are warm against Kitty's shoulder. She cradles the beloved doll and looks lovingly into her sweet eyes where the tears are flowing—crystal clear.

She flings it to the ground. "You said you would give me the tears! You lied! What am I going to do?! Now Jon will never wake up, he will never have been, and I'll never get home!"

Kitty begins to cry. Susie takes the vial from Kitty's hand and catches the tears as they roll from Kitty's cheeks in fat ebony drops.

FRIDAY

Remembered Pain

She feels remarkably unscathed, considering how little sleep she has had. Last night she got to the bottom of something she did not know had been bothering her; and that can be better than sleep. She stayed up till three googling postpartum depression, ultimately ordering a book on the subject. Knowledge is power. The more she understands about her mother's traumatic history and its effect on her own mothering, the better off her children will be. And it is nice to know that the coffee in her mug is completely decalcified. She rubs her arm and places a bowl of porridge in front of Maggie in her high chair and one for Matthew on his booster seat.

"Matthew, it was so kind of you to lend Maggie your unicorn last night."

306 | ADULT ONSET

She will send flowers to Hil for real—freesia? Something that says "I'm sorry" without saying "I'm only sending you these because I'm sorry." Daisies?

"I didn't lend it."

He is gazing up at her steadily.

"You didn't?"

How, then, did Maggie get hold of it? There is something uncanny in the question, evoking as it does the spectre of a demonically nimble toddler, dropping to the floor, padding across the hallway . . .

"I gave it," says Matthew.

"Matthew, it's yours. Mumma gave it to you."

"I know." He looks down.

"Mine," states Maggie.

"Do you still feel bad about dropping it?"

Tears flood his eyes. "I pushed it."

"Oh . . . Matthew, why?"

He cries.

"Oh sweetheart, it's okay." She strokes his head. "Matthew? Matt, honey? It's all better now, I fixed it."

"I didn't want you to fix it!" He smacks away his tears.

"Gentle with yourself, Matt."

"No!" he roars.

"No!" seconds Maggie.

She has an insurrection on her hands. She crouches before him. "Don't you like it anymore?"

He is suddenly calm. "I did never like it, Mumma."

She swallows. Smiles. "That's okay, sweetheart. It's a sad song, isn't it."

"Maggie likes it."

"I like it," says Maggie, in oddly adult tones.

She leaves the porridge pot to soak and they walk Matthew to school. Past Archie's Variety. "'Archie's Variety,'" she says. The weather has aligned with the season, older children are off to school on bikes, music thumps from the open window of a passing car—Maggie is overdressed in her snowsuit, it is going to be a lovely day. There is a darkness in Mary Rose's stomach. "'Grapefruit Moon,'" she says. It is good that Matthew was able to tell her the truth about the unicorn, she is a good mother. The cute guy from the bike shop is setting out his sandwich board. "'Early bird tune-up special,'" she reads aloud. She smiles at him; he is the type of young man she hopes Maggie will bring home one day— although why does she assume her daughter will bring home a boy not a girl? *People who hate themselves are dangerous.* "'Freeman Real Estate,'" she says. Would she know if she had stomach cancer?

"Mumma, why are you saying all the signs?" asks Matthew.

The school bus is waiting when they arrive—the field trip to the Reptile Museum! She had meant to book Candace to babysit Maggie so she could take Matthew up there by car so he wouldn't be killed in a crash. He boards the bus, overjoyed.

Keira smiles, one hand on her big belly. "We have too many volunteers already, Mary Rose, don't worry for a second!" She watches the pregnant young woman board and a doom opens within her, surely the vehicle is marked for death. Sue is waving to her from a window—she is seated between Matthew and Ryan. Sue is not the sort of person to be killed in a bus rollover. As long as Sue is on the bus, Matthew will probably not die. Mary Rose breathes out, then smiles and waves with the other parents as the big yellow bus pulls away. Her heart pounds as she watches a multitude of mittened hands in the rear window waving back.

At home, a message from Gigi, "Hi, Mister, offer's still good, call me."

What is she talking about? Much as she loves Gigi, her old buddy is among the ranks of those child-free friends who have time to go to movies mid-week and sit around leaving cryptic messages for people. She unbundles Maggie from her sweltering snowsuit and goes about rustling up a healthy snack. The late night is catching up with her, she is dying for a nap. *You're not twenty-five, you know.* Twenty minutes is all she needs. She has committed to eliminating the morning nap and she will stick to it. Quit googling and go to bed early tonight.

Craving sleep the way a vampire craves darkness, Mary Rose wills herself to the craft table, where she does a Ravensburger puzzle with Maggie. When claustrophobia becomes acute, she slips away and checks her e-mail.

> Hi Rosie,
> Mummy and Daddy will be arriving in Toronto on Sunday at 11:00 a.m. They had a wonderful time out here and I think they're in good shape for the trip. I know they're looking forward to seeing you. You're doing such a hard job right now, Rosie-Posie, no one knows unless they've been through it . . . and then they forget! I've probably forgotten how hard it was too, but at least I know that I've forgotten. How's that for logic?
> How's Daisy? You can ship her out here if they order her destroyed. I'm serious, we will be a station on the underground pit bull railroad!
> Love,
> Mo

There is one from Andy-Pat: a link to a site where an elephant is painting a watercolour. He is so far out of the loop, she is going to yank him back in—why should she have to go down to the train station of the cross all by herself this Sunday?

> APB all fraternal units: Mum and Dad stopping over by train on seventh at eleven hundred hours. Mustering for coffee and confusion at Union Station.
> xomr

On the other hand, why should she facilitate his relationship with her parents? That's what daughters have always done. What is the point of having lived a brave countercultural life if she is going to do the womany thing now and make her brother look good? The prodigal son: all he has to do is show up and a calf dies.

Delete.

Hi Mo,

Thanks, I'll keep you posted on Daisy. I'm going postal today to pick up the "mystery package"—I hope it's there. I can't bear the thought of Mum finding out that whatever it is she wanted to give me might be lost in the great shuffle called life. Maybe she "mailed" it into the garbage—you know, one of those complicated bins with a different opening for every kind of waste

She deletes the last bit and sends it.

Dear Dad,

I

She did not save the registered letter from her father. It arrived at her basement apartment more than twenty years ago on legal-size fools-cap a week after she came out to her parents; she read it once then tore it up, aware of neither anger nor sorrow, only a belief that, while they were merely paper and ink to her, the words might hurt him terribly one day when her real father came back—how sad for Dad should he ever have to know what he had done to his daughter. It strikes her now that if she had spoken this thought aloud to a friend at the time, she might have recognized it as denial. Perhaps that is why we keep certain things to ourselves; so that we may also keep them *from* ourselves.

One day, a year or so into the fatwa, she phoned him from the home she had recently made with Renée. Renée concurred that, of Mary

Rose's two parents, Duncan was the sane one; she had met them, Mary Rose having smuggled her home as a "friend" in the early days. Mary Rose felt sure that, but for her mother, her father would be able to refer to Renée as her "friend" and turn a bland eye on their shared bedroom. He would visit their home and take them for lovely lunches. He would never need to name—or curse—a thing. After all, he had seen it in her. Groomed her. He nicknamed her Mister and trained her to be better than a boy, never to take a back seat to one. Mary Rose and Duncan were signatories to the secret pact between certain lesbians and their fathers: Notwithstanding her overt feminism, the daughter, in exchange for throwing women under the bus as the inferior sex—along with any competing brothers—is granted honorary-son status. For his part, not only is he seen to be the enlightened father of a high-achieving woman, he gets to keep his throne because his lesbian daughter is neither a man nor in danger of bringing one home. All of this could have continued without anyone ever having to say the L-word. Perhaps it wasn't too late. Why should father and daughter be kept apart by a cruel, crude mother? So one spring day, she phoned and asked him to come see her . . . She has not thought about that conversation in many years. She may have torn it up along with the letter. She types . . .

Dear Dad,

I wonder if Mum's problems with postpartum depression informed the fury with which she responded to my coming out years later. She may have been consumed with guilt and anxiety because of all she had been through, and perhaps she believed she had damaged me somehow—especially during the very sad aftermath of Alexander's birth and death when she would have been hard-pressed to focus her attention on an energetic toddler—and that this was how the damage was coming out . . . as it were

Delete.

She closes her laptop, scrubs the porridge pot, calls, "Maggie!" and experiences an audible *click* as a logical conclusion in the form of a question arrives in her consciousness after a journey of forty-three years: *If I thought Andy-Patrick would have to be put in the ground if he was named after a dead brother, where did I think I was, having been named after a dead sister?*

Scour, scrub, scrape, "Maggie!"

She is going to go down to Postal Station E and give some petty bureaucrat a big thorny piece of her mind. Why seek out bad drivers upon whom to vent one's spleen when there is a Crown corporation to hand? Fucking posties, fucking pensions and benefits and backaches. She swings round with the pot and almost clocks the child on the head. "Maggie! Thank you for coming when Mumma called, sweetheart."

Her daughter looks extra pretty today for some reason, like a little candy apple blossom. "Hey, cutie-pie, wait'll Mummy comes home and sees how much you've grown!"

They will have a nice walk to the post office. They will take Daisy. They will show the postal people what a nice dog she is. Mary Rose will submit the form like a good citizen. The post office will release the mail. The suspense will end, her mother will shut up. They will stop in the park. They will have a nice time. She is a nice mother. See Jane put on her boots.

Maggie sits on the step. Mary Rose stations herself below and takes hold of one little foot with one hand and one little running shoe with the other.

"Boots," says Maggie.

"No problemo! Do you want the ladybugs?"

"Yes, Mumma."

Mary Rose turns to the crowded rack and spots a single shiny red boot wedged at one end. She frees it—the left one, where is the right one?

"Where's your other ladybug boot, baby-girl?"

She starts hunting for it. It is not in the basement. It is not in the backyard. It is not in the bottom of the stroller, it is not in the car.

Where oh where is Jane's other boot? *Other Boot, Other Boot, fly away home!* Mary Rose sighs. Where does a boot go? Does it walk away on its own? Fiendishly skipping off to Hell? It is still not in the boot rack. Where the fuck is it? She kicks through the jumble of footwear that Maggie has obviously ransacked in an effort to be helpful, and with every kick she feels the tide of anger rising—*do not fill above this line.* Relax, it's a boot, not a priceless heirloom.

"Mumma can't find your other ladybug boot, Maggie, you'll have to wear these ones."

The Bean boots with safety reflectors.

"No, Mumma, I will wear Sitdy boots."

"I'm so sorry, sweetheart, I can only find one." This is a grammatical infelicity, it ought to be *I can find only one*, otherwise *only* is modifying *find*—

"I can find one, Mumma."

"You're such a good girl!" With that, she takes Maggie's right foot and, gently but firmly, begins to pull the ladybug boot off it. Maggie goes rigid, shoots out her leg, and her heel finds her mother's left nipple. Mary Rose releases her hold. She smiles, unruffled. *It really does get better.* "Okay, sweetheart, you can wear one of each." Pleased with her patience, she hands Maggie a Bean boot. Maggie throws it at the wall.

"STOP IT!" roars Mary Rose, corralling the bucking ankles, "NO!" grabbing the flailing hands, wrists, arms, "DON'T YOU FUCKING HIT ME!" She is sobbing the words with a force of violence she is diverting from her hands, "I'M GOING TO *SMASH* YOU!" *Stop.*

Maggie is still struggling. Is that a good sign? Mary Rose's hands are still around her daughter's arms, her knees imprisoning her daughter's knees, angry Madonna and child. Maggie is whimpering now, wriggling more than fighting.

It is not that sound has deserted the air, it is that each sound issues briefly from a void into which it promptly returns. Dead. It is as though Mary Rose were hearing everything from behind glass. The air itself has changed such that time cannot pass through it, must go around it instead. It is separate in here. Sterile.

Her hands are still around her daughter's arms. Her hands can feel the small bones within their sleeves of flesh, bones like flutes. She watches her hands as, without warning, they pulse. Maggie screams. The hands loosen their grip but do not let go. They remain like manacles, encircling the arms. Like paper chains on a Christmas tree. She watches the hands: what will they do next? Something is going to happen, she cannot remember what.

A bark from upstairs, a thundering descent followed by clacketing across the kitchen floor. The dog appears at the top of the steps, stops and looks at her.

"It's okay, Daisy, it's just Mumma." Mary Rose hears her own voice as though it belongs to someone else, someone who has arrived just in time. The dog growls. She lets go of Maggie. But the dog remains planted, ears pricked, eyes fixed.

Maggie is staring up at a corner of the ceiling. Mary Rose understands she is feeling fear when she hears herself cry, "Maggie?!"

The child is in a trance.

"Maggie!" Is she breathing?

She lowers her gaze and looks at Mary Rose, her expression blank. She is not breathing. Mary Rose picks her up and, as though kick-started by the movement, breath rushes back in the form of a gasp and a scream. She clings to Mary Rose like a monkey, so hard. She hangs on and cries so hard, hanging on to Mumma.

·

How do you heal time?

·

Mary Rose watches Maggie climb into the stroller and do up her own buckle. She is wearing the ladybug boots. The child was right when she said, "I can find one." She *had* found it, buried in the boot rack all along, she had even been attempting to put it on the correct foot. Mary Rose feels bad as she watches her child patiently manipulate the buckle, her little face tear-stained but content now, and she feels something else too: love. She closes it promptly—like a laptop. She is sufficiently aware to know that accessing love on the heels of rage is not right, it is part of an abusive dynamic. Having ticked that box, she gets on with the day.

The day the daytheday the day is too bright. there are sequential actions that add up to sanity going for a walk to the post office is one of them just do these correct things no one needs to know that you are untethered maybe everyone is. and then andthenand then prepositions grafting one thought to another if they take you have continuity if not you have fractured bits

They go out by the back gate, down the driveway, onto the sidewalk along the peterpiperpickedapeckofprepositions what if she just keeps walking? *One day I'll walk out of the house and never come back.* Daisy lifts her leg and pees on the corner of the fence where the indestructible cosmos will soon spring back to life. Mary Rose sees Rochelle getting into her Tercel. "Hi, Rochelle!"

Rochelle does not immediately return the greeting.

"Isn't it an amazing day?" chirps Mary Rose.

"It's nice." Rochelle sounds wary.

"We're going for a hike. We've got snacks, we've got juice, we even have our sled dog in case it snows again! We're all set, aren't we, Maggie, can you say hi to Rochelle?" Something is wrong with Mary Rose's face.

"Hi Wochewwe."

"Hi."

"I know she looks like me, but I adopted Maggie, but all babies look like me, and if all babies look like Winston Churchill, then I must look like Winston Churchill." A smile has landed on her face like a space alien.

Rochelle says nothing.

Perhaps that's because she knows she is talking to a crazy lady. "We're going to walk all the way across town to Postal Station E and then drop off a form because Daisy almost bit the mailman, she didn't bite him, she bit the box with the Christmas tree stand because I was writing an e-mail to my dad, and now they're coming on the train and my mother sent me a packeege but I didn't get it yet." Has she said all this with an English accent? Mewwy Wose is going to start waffing. She sucks her cheek between her teeth, bites down, and tears flood her eyes. *We shall fight on the beaches . . .* Has she said it out loud?

Rochelle says, "I can take the form in for you."

"Really? Are you going by there?"

"I work there." Voice like a canvas mailbag.

Don't laugh. One day you may start laughing and never be able to stop. "Thanks." She hands the form to Rochelle.

Rochelle gets into her car. "Need any stamps?"

"Ha-ha-hahahaha—" She bites her cheek. "I don't think so, no, hahahahah. Thanks, Rochelle."

"You're welcome."

They go to the park. She pushes Maggie on the swing. They play in the sandbox. They do all the things that can be expressed by sentences suitable for a beginner reading level. Three other toddlers are there. One goes hysterical. His mother has no nice snacks. Mary Rose has nice snacks. Mary Rose opens her bag and offers a fruit strip.

"Thanks!" says the woman. "I feel like such a terrible mother!" And she laughs.

Matthew is alive.

"Hi, Sue, thanks."

"What for?"

The bus did not roll over—at least not in this world. There is a world in which this same crowd of parents is gathered in front of the school, keening. A world where a spot on the highway is heaped with flowers and teddy bears . . .

"Have a nice weekend."

As the day progresses, a parallel reality plays itself out, as though the world were bifurcating with every move Mary Rose does not make. When it turns out the cap on the Thermos of chocolate milk she is shaking has not been fastened. When she sees from her driveway that she has missed the recycling truck by one second and the driver ignores her. In another world, the Thermos cracks the window, a crazy woman pelts down the street pushing a big blue bin on wheels, shrieking obscenities.

She does not swat Maggie on the head when the child shoves her bowl to the floor, she does not grab Matthew's ear, cheek, hair, she does not tell him to "shut up and quit whining or I'll give you something to whine about!" She does not hit his head or his little hands, and then she does not seize Maggie by the arm and yank, does not yank her down the hall and up and over the side of the crib, *IS THAT WHAT YOU WANT?!* She makes lunch and then she cleans up andthen she does not smash them.

"Thank you, Mumma."

"You're welcome, sweetheart. Would you like to watch a video?"

"Yes!"

For all that she abstains from doing, the capsule bursts in the pit-drip of her stomach and she feels the dark chemical release, re-blazing neural trails. It will pass and so can she; as normal in a world where she might lose touch with reality in ways that would never land her on a psychiatric ward or even on antidepressants. She would not be arrested or even questioned for any of the raging she did this morning, or even the squeezing. She has committed no crime. Yet she knows that she is full of crime.

"Would you like to watch *Bob the Builder* now?"

"Yes!"

Play all.

By late afternoon, the undone possibilities cease to flash like old-fashioned Kodak cubes in her peripheral vision, and their place is taken by a movie that begins running in her mind. It is of herself and Maggie on the steps this morning. But it does not end with her letting go of Maggie's arms, it continues, the movie of what she did not do: She does not let go, she gets up. Shegetsupshegetsupshe *jerks* Maggie up by the arm, hauls her up the steps and across the kitchen; close-up on raw wing tip, straining, toddler feet fill the frame, scrabbling for purchase as though in an attempt to become airborne . . .

Somewhere, someone is watching this, providing commentary—it is the mother's own voice, but the voice has been left behind on the steps, the mother is now merely a motor function, a set of impulses moving through space—who will stop this? Again and again, like a scene untethered from a movie, Mary Rose sees the thing she did not do, the thing she knows so well how to do, as if she had done it already many times, as if she had trained for it. She looks down at her hands. They know something. But, like a child who won't reveal who it was that gave them the candy, they are not telling. They can taste the tang of it, though, and they are craving satisfaction. They clench and unclench. She slips into the powder room, leans against the door and lets them batter her head as hard as they want to while she watches herself assault her two-year-old over and over again.

Out in the living room, the children know nothing of this, they are watching a different movie.

•

He loved her into language. She would curl up with him and "read" the newspaper. They read the funnies together. His body was safe and gentle. His hands were patient and precise, his voice calm. Within the circle of his arms—around the newspaper, around the steering wheel, around her when he held her on the balcony—was all the time in the world.

"Do you hear that? That's the cuckoo bird."

Huge egg yolk sun streaking the sky red. So free out here. So safe.

"Good night, sweetie pie. See you in the morning."

•

Everything will look better in the morning. She was sleep deprived when the whole boot kerfuffle happened earlier today. She ought to have had a good cry last night over the stillborn baby pictures. Suppressed sorrow for her mother and her "inadequately mourned" deceased sister was bound to surface as rage—if it had been anyone else up till all hours googling grief, Mary Rose could have told them what would happen if they failed properly to discharge their feelings. Reassured by this insight, she heads upstairs with a mug of Sleepytime tea. She overreacted today, but it isn't as if she battered her child.

She looks in on Matthew, curled asleep with Bun in his arms. She kisses his forehead—is he a little hot?

In Maggie's room, a subdued *thwack-thwack* tells her Daisy is lying on the floor in front of the crib. "What are you doing there, Daisy?" she whispers. She leans over and looks into the crib by the dim light from the hallway. Her daughter is breathing evenly, baby lips puffed with sleep, lashes stirred by a dream.

She bends to pat Daisy. The dog lifts her eyes and regards her from beneath a furrowed brow and Mary Rose understands as plainly as if the animal had just spoken: Daisy is protecting Maggie. From her.

Remorse rides in like the cavalry, too late. All the unknown crimes are upon her now, the ones that draw no distinction between doer and done-to or wanted-to and did-do.

Big tears roll down her face as she watches her beautiful baby. Something threatens to pierce her heart, like a shard of glass. She stands weeping and loving her child, but it is the love of a remorseful devil, it is not a safe love. She withdraws as quietly as possible, and smacks the tears away.

Children are forgiving, yes, and resilient, so long as you don't try the evil spell of "nothing happened" on them.

No one knows, no one sees. But the body will tell. Act out in illness or in violence.

She brushes her teeth, this woman of forty-eight who has everything. Mary Rose MacKinnon puts on kissy boxer shorts and a tank top.

It is when she turns out the light that she becomes aware of the pain. Like the sound of a fridge humming, it isn't until all else is still that she "hears" it. It is just present enough to disrupt sleep and she needs her sleep, tomorrow is another day; another day another pair of boots . . .

In the bathroom, she switches on the light, opens the mirror and reaches for the Advil. There is nothing wrong. It is merely memory lodged in her arm. *That's your badness coming out* . . . She knows what "badness" means. She knew at age five. Badness was hot, as her arm so often was. Badness had to do with what were called "impure thoughts": sins you committed with your mind whether you wanted to or not. Sins you committed with your hand by touching yourself "down there." The constant pain in her arm was not only a punishment, it was a beacon of her badness. Throbbing red light of badness, its pulsations occupied the same frequency as sexual excitement. Best keep that sort of pain to oneself.

She closes the cabinet with a prickle of fear lest the devil appear behind her. She relaxes suddenly and looks directly into the mirror—if Satan is there, let him show his face. But there is only her own face, sheet-wrinkled and bloodshot. *Hi there, and happy Friday.* She swallows two pills.

Pain blooms in her arm like a time-lapse hothouse flower. What is happening? It's okay, you know what this is. "Remembered pain." Phantom pain. Back-from-the-grave pain—

"It hurts."

She has said it aloud and scared herself—she sounds too young, as though a child has spoken through her mouth . . .

Get a grip.

Am I having a panic attack? No, because there is still an "I," a rind of self around the pain. Cancer. *I see no indication of that.* But that was six months ago. Throbbing now. The cysts have come back. *I know of no research to support that.* Electrical pain signal, pinging from a transmission pole in her arm up to her back teeth, shorting-out her vision. She ought to have filled the prescription for Tylenol 4s when she had the chance. *You want fives? We're talking bone pain, right?* She swallows another Advil and chases it with two regular Tylenols. She holds the mirror in a staring contest; pain is something she can do. *You get an old pathway that kicks up* . . . A pathway overgrown with vines. It has slumbered for decades, but someone is hacking open the entrance. Where does it lead? There is no glimpse of a castle, just a tangle of thorns . . . Mary Rose steps away from the mirror, and into the path of an oncoming narrative.

Downstairs, she opens the freezer and presses a bag of frozen organic peas to her arm. She retains sufficient self-possession not to start with "bone cancer." Still, her hands are cold as she googles "pediatric bone cysts."

BOSTON CHILDREN'S HOSPITAL

Smiling doctors in white coats, soulful children gazing into the camera. This is the real world, not just the world in her head.

What is a unicameral bone cyst?
A unicameral bone cyst is a fluid-filled cavity in the bone,
lined by compressed fibrous tissue. It usually occurs in
the long bones of a growing child, especially the upper
part of the humerus.

Check

They affect children primarily between the ages of 5 and 15.

Check

They are considered benign. More invasive cysts can
grow to fill most of the bone's metaphysis and cause what
is known as a pathological fracture.

See Jane fall.

What are the symptoms of a unicameral bone cyst?

"It hurts. That's your first clue."

Unless there has been a fracture, bone cysts are without
symptoms.

"How many times did your mother make a sling for you out of an old scarf?"

THE NATIONAL HEALTH SERVICE DIRECT WALES
A bone cyst is a benign (non cancerous), fluid-filled
cavity in the bone which weakens the bone and makes it
more likely to fracture (break). It occurs mostly in
children and young adults.

It is not known what causes bone cysts.
They are twice as likely to affect boys than girls.

"*As* girls," not "*than*."

If the cyst causes the bone to fracture, it is likely that
your child will experience additional symptoms, such as:
pain and swelling, inability to move or put weight on the
injured limb or body part.

"How could we know? You never cried."

You should always contact your GP if you or your child
experiences persistent bone pain.

"If you'd had a broken leg, we'd have taken you to a doctor."

Further testing is usually only required if:

"**Required only** if," otherwise *only* is modifying *required*.

- The cyst has developed on the end of a long bone
that is still growing (an area of the bone that is known as
the growth plate).
- The cyst is so large that the affected bone is at risk
of fracturing (breaking).

See Jane fall the second time.

Curettage and bone grafting
During this procedure a surgeon cuts into the bone to
gain access to the cyst.

While the pills have distanced the pain, they have not doused it. Of course not, it is phantom pain! *"When I reach for this glass of Scotch, what stops my hand from passing right through it?"*

> The fluid inside the cyst is drained and the lining of the cyst scraped out using a tool called a curette. The resulting cavity inside the bone is filled with chips of bone, either from other parts of your child's body or from donated bone tissue.

"A piece of someone's kneecap."

> . . . carried out under general anaesthetic, which means that your child will be asleep during the surgery and will not feel any pain.

Thanks to the Tylenol, someone is feeling pain, but it is not me. Not-Me is feeling it. "Mary Rose, do you read me? Come in, Mary Rose, this is Armpain, I am being held prisoner on the Planet Zytox . . ."

> **MEDSCAPE REFERENCE**
> Reoperation—subsequent operation required due to recurrence.

A view of the hospital smokestack, as seen from Dr. Sorokin's window, captured in a calendar of beautiful watercolours painted entirely with the artist's foot.

> Should pathologic fractures of the long bones be treated via immediate flexible intramedullary nailing?

Jane is crucified the first time.

TEXTBOOK OF PEDIATRIC EMERGENCY MEDICINE
page 357:
. . . injured when the arm is forcefully abducted, for
example falling and grabbing a tree branch . . .

See Jane swing like an airplane.

If the pain is chronic . . .

Even Andy-Patrick respected her sore arm . . .

Pressure may produce exquisite tenderness in this area
so palpation would be gentle.

"You can stop massaging it now, Dad. It feels better."

What causes a unicameral bone cyst?

Nothing, you're born with them. Her feet are freezing and sweating
inside her slippers. The pain is gone. Cancer does not behave like that,
is not vanquished by over-the-counter analgesics—she is either neu-
rotic or among a minority of normal people who experience neurological pain feedback loops. If she met herself now, she would not want
to be her friend. It is time to go to bed.

Theories have been proposed but none have been definitively proven.

That should read, "none *has* been definitively proven," not "have,"
because the subject of that clause is the collective noun "none," not the
plural noun "theories."

Some speculate that repeated trauma puts the bone at
risk for developing a bone cyst. This, however, has not
been proven.

Wait. Bone cysts cause repeated trauma, yes. Wait.

Some have theorized that bone cysts are the result of
repeated trauma, but this has not been proved.

Wait. She tries to turn the information around in her head, like a
midwife reaching into the uterus when a baby goes breech.

It is necessary for primary care physicians to proceed with
caution, to avoid unfounded charges of child abuse.
However, in cases where differing accounts of an injury are
given, or medical attention has been unduly delayed . . .

Dr. Ferry scolding her mother in the front hall . . .

Always consider the possibility of abuse in young children, especially if the injury is unexplained, the history is
implausible or inconsistent between caregivers, or the
seeking of medical care was delayed unreasonably.

She follows the thread through a labyrinth of websites, and at 1:48 a.m.
meets the Minotaur in New Zealand.

SKELETAL RADIOLOGY, VOLUME 18, NUMBER 2
Post-traumatic cysts and cyst-like lesions of bone
Abstract: They describe two patients with cyst-like
lesions of bone that developed at the sites of healed or
healing fractures.

Case 1
A 9-year-old girl . . .

Case 2
A 6-year-old boy . . .

At 2:00 a.m. she is shocked to see it laid out frank and unfreighted:

Simple or unicameral cyst can be caused by trauma.

Surgery is the best option.
Curettage and grafting most often indicated.
Prognosis is generally good with treatment.
Bone cysts are more common in young dogs.
These cysts can cause lameness and pain.
Any breed can be affected, dogs are usually less than 18
months of age, both males and females can be affected.

Lameness is the most common sign.

She scans the banner at the top of the page: **VET SURGERY CENTRAL INC.**

She gets up and puts the kettle on.

Even assuming the fractures caused the cysts, anything at all might have caused the fractures. She may have rolled off the couch, climbed over the bars of her crib and fallen. A two-year-old can break their arm without an adult realizing it. It is called a green-stick fracture: the bone bends then heals, perhaps not perfectly. Or a mother grabs her toddler by the arm to prevent them touching the stove, the handle of a boiling pot—grabs the non-dominant arm, likely the left that lags behind its mischief-making twin—and, with the force of her fright, she wrenches. The small bone breaks more easily the next time. And the next.

If the fractures caused the cysts, then what caused the first fracture? If the airplane swing was a pathological fracture, there must have been at least one before it. Before Canada. An accident of some kind. If so, why is it not part of family lore? "Mary Rose's first sling." She can easily believe her mother was too depressed to see what was right in front of her, but what about her father? Where have all the fathers gone? To work. The mothers stayed home at the epicentre of that mid-twentieth-century invention, "the nuclear family." Alone with a crying baby in the crib. And one in the grave . . . and one up in flames.

A mother alone in the mundane light of day in the middle of the week in the middle of the living room where nothing ever happens and keeps on happening, no one there to take her child, even for a moment, into the safety of their gaze where she can see how she loves it. Banal trauma, drained of drama . . . mondaywednesdaytuesdaywednesdaythursdaythursday no one sees. No one tells. The body tells on itself. Mary Rose broke and mended a number of times, broke the growth plate—broke time.

That's your badness . . . Badness requiring surgery. Badness tattooed on flesh in the form of a scar. Two, one for each dead baby. Badness that, decades later, can be touched off like a siren at the brush of a passerby, then dilate to a traffic-parting wail at the drop of a ladybug boot.

Her mother asked, "Is that what happened to your arm?" But was she forgetting? Or remembering.

The marks on a body are marks on a map, trails blazed in flesh, they tell you where you have come from and how to get back again. Her scars can take her home. Down through time to an apartment building at the edge of the Black Forest. Down to the racketing funnel, the tornado in the living room, beating of sound, strobing of light. Step back—not too far or you will be out on the balcony. Observe the room around the commotion. There is a coffee table, a couch. And at the centre, a column of swirling darkness. Is it possible to slow it down? To see what is there? . . . But the column becomes a scrawl like a crayon wielded in the fist of a child, and it blacks out the picture.

The kettle screams.

She leans against the counter, before the big black windows.

"Did I wake you?"

"It's okay, what's up?"

"Nothing, it's just, I'm a bit, I've been googling . . ."

"Oh no. Oh Mary Rose, you do not have cancer, there are not spiders living in your face."

She laughs. "I know, I just called 'cause I'm afraid I'm going to kill myself when I was twenty-three."

"What's wrong?" Hil sounds wide awake now.

She laughs again. "I don't know why I said that—"

"Are the children okay?"

"Everything's fine."

"You said you wanted to kill yourself."

"When I was twenty-three—"

"I'm calling Gigi to come over and be with you."

"It was a weird thing to say, okay? It runs in the family, a flaw which neither of our children stands to inherit."

"I'm coming home."

"You do not have to—"

"Don't kill yourself, Mary Rose, don't kill yourself in our house with our children sleeping—"

"Don't worry, I'll wake them up first, I'll go to a sleazy motel out on the Lake Shore and order a mai tai and jam the cocktail umbrella up my nose into my brain—it's possible. You can make anything into a weapon, I learned that in the militia."

"You learned that from your mother."

"Sorry to bother you, I'm going to hang up now."

"Why do you need an enemy?"

"What are you talking about?"

"Something is wrong with you. Find out what is wrong with you, Mary Rose."

Mary Rose is abruptly aware that it is possible for her not to say another word or to make another voluntary movement for the rest of her life. She does not even need to breathe. Nothing is happening. It is that easy. Eventually you forget where the switch is, then you forget there is a switch, then there is no one to forget anything . . .

"Mary Rose? Mister? I'm calling 911."

"I almost hurt her."

She tells Hil about the boot incident. She makes it sound unprecedented, her voice sounds flat but not crazy. "I think I had a short wick 'cause of the pain in my arm."

"You've always had a short wick."

"You're implying that I'm abusive just because I told you something lots of mothers experience but never admit to—lots of parents—not to mention I didn't actually really do anything to her."

"Okay. I believe you, but I still think you need help."

"Please don't pathologize me! I really will go crazy if I can't express the slightest twinge of frustration without you calling in the white coats."

"I mean help with the kids."

"Oh."

"I think we should schedule Candace to come full-time for a while."

"And what am I supposed to do while she does my job?"

"Finish the trilogy."

"God, Hilary, I don't even know if it *is* a trilogy." She punches her head.

"Don't punch your head."

"How did you know?"

"You've already started the book."

"I have?"

"It doesn't have to be perfect, it just has to be true."

"I write fiction."

"Fiction is not the opposite of truth."

Hate is not the opposite of love.

"I can't."

Fear is.

"Then go on a trip," says Hil.

"You want me to go away?"

Silence.

"Hil? Are we breaking up?"

"We're married. Married couples don't 'break up,' they divorce."

Mary Rose's voice sounds robotic in her own ears, which is how she knows she is telling the truth but from a distant galaxy. "I googled 'bone cysts.'"

". . . Why?"

"My arm was sore."

Big sigh. "I asked you if it was and you said—"

"It wasn't sore then, okay? It doesn't hurt on cue, it's not a singing frog, it's called 'remembered pain.'" Mary Rose is suddenly stung with humiliation to be caught whining over something so flaky and Freudian, her precious little psychosomatic "owie" exposed to the glare of Hilary's mature gaze. "I'm sorry it's not a nice neat tumour to tell you about—"

"Mary Rose, I won't continue like this—"

"Like what?! Stop it, stop being so fucking healthy and listen to me, get off your high fucking horse and listen, then get the hell out of my life, you're out of it anyway!"

She is shaking.

"I'm listening."

Her palms are moist. "It sounds dumb, but maybe the thing with my arm happened 'cause of something that happened." Where have all her words gone? She is an empty Scrabble board. Maybe she should try saying it in German. "Because it could be possible that bone cysts are caused by repeated trauma. I feel unreal, I feel like I'm making this up, are you there?" Her voice sounds dead.

"I'm here."

"So it's possible it broke before I was four. At least once. Are you there?"

"I'm listening."

Her feet are warm, Daisy is lying on them.

"It's just, it's upsetting to think my arm might have been broken that early on and no one noticed even then."

"Why is that more upsetting than the times you already know about?"

"Because—because—because something happened, right? If this is even correct, if the cysts were caused by a fracture or more than one, then—then . . . And then if that's true, then something must have happened and no one knew." andthenandthen

"Maybe they did know."

"It would've been part of family lore, I would have had a sling, 'Mary Rose's first sling.'"

Silence.

"Hil, are you still there?"

"Why do you think it isn't part of family lore?"

"I know what you're saying, I've already thought it."

"What?"

"She broke my arm in a fit of rage and that's why he took her to a shrink."

Now her voice sounds cut and dried in her own ears, cavalier even—that's more like it, *The Importance of Being Ironic*.

"Is that what you think happened?"

332 | ADULT ONSET

"It could have happened when I was running for the balcony, I can totally picture that."

"She broke your arm while saving you."

"It's possible."

"Then why don't you know about it?"

"Hil? I wonder if that's why she was so harsh when I came out."

"'Harsh' is kind."

"Because she felt guilty. If I was a lesbian, it must mean I was damaged and . . . if she knew she had damaged me . . ."

"Do you think he knew?"

"Of course he did, he was sitting right there at the kitchen table staring at the ceiling while she tore into me."

"I mean back then."

"Oh. No. It was nineteen sixty-one, he went to work, he came home and read the paper, he was a man. He didn't have to know anything."

"You said he took her to a psychiatrist."

"He didn't have to catch her breaking my arm to know she needed help. I know you think he was an enabler, but he's also the reason I'm alive, he's why I've been able to achieve anything at all, he saved me."

"He didn't save you from her," says Hil.

". . . Which time?"

"You just answered your own question."

"You sound just like him."

"I know you adore him."

"So you do think she battered me."

"That term is outdated," says Hil.

"How do you know?"

"I'm on a website."

"I love you, Hil."

"A sign of abuse is 'when there is delay seeking treatment.' It's called medical neglect."

Silence.

"There's no proof she broke my arm."

"Why do you need proof?"

"Because if I knew for sure, I could forgive her."

"I don't know if it works like that."

"You're saying I have to forgive what I don't remember?"

"You don't have to forgive anything. I don't forgive them."

"I don't even know if there's anything to forgive."

"You have your scars, you have your chronic pain, you have your broken heart at twenty-three, what more do you need?"

"You think I'm greedy? I'm a trauma glutton, ha-ha—"

"Just believe what you already know."

"What do I know? Bad stuff happened and my parents didn't get me help in time but I'd like to know if the original cause was accidental. Or not."

"You're obsessing over one event."

"It's a critical—"

"But you started by telling me about 'repeated' trauma—"

"Yes, but there would have been a 'first' trauma and I want to know if she did it on purpose."

"Do you want it to be true?"

"I want something to be true."

"There's loads."

"I'm just trying to do what you told me to, I'm just trying to"—here she does a high-pitched, simpering caricature of Hilary—"'Find out what is wrong with me!'"

"I'm going to hang up—"

"See?! You can't take it, no one can."

"Take what, your self-loathing? You're right, I've had it."

"Don't hang up."

Silence. Is it her own heartbeat she hears or Hil's through the phone?

Finally Hil asks, "Why did you say it was nineteen sixty-one?"

"I don't know, I would have been walking, running—two, two and a half, that's when accidents happen, that's when . . . mothers lose it."

"When did your brother die?"

She sighs. "I don't know. Jesus Murphy. I'm two or three in the picture. I went to the grave."

"It must have been devastating."

"Even Maureen has blanks from around that time, she doesn't even remember hanging me over the balcony. Oh my God, Hil."

"What?"

"It could have happened when Maureen yanked me back onto the balcony, it's called 'forcible abduction'—"

"When was this?"

"Around that time, springtime, grave time—"

"So she was how old?"

"Seven?"

"How is that even possible?"

"Well it happened. Maybe my mother caught her in the act of dangling me and she's the one who yanked me back to safety and that's when it broke."

"Then why are you the only one who remembers any of this?"

"Okay, so it was Mo on her own, all the more reason she would've had to yank and twist to get me back over the railing, it must have hurt like hell which is probably why I don't remember that part, and she forgot the whole thing 'cause she felt guilty, and she never told my parents so why would I even get a sling—"

"That's just one event."

"Yes, but it sets up all the others."

"But you already know there was 'repeated trauma,' 'neglect'—"

"The balcony is something I can hang on to—literally, okay? It's something I can point to, it's a picture, I can frame it, I can say, 'See? That's what happened. My mother didn't do the first one.'"

"The first what?"

"Assault! Accident, whatever."

"You're fixated on your arm, when it's just part of—"

"It's the key to the whole thing."

"It's just one aspect of a pattern of—"

"How can you not know it matters?! I'm talking about a series of events, you're talking about a disco ball."

"A 'disco ball'?"

"'Aspects,' little bits, shiny busted mirror spinning on the ceiling—"

"I don't understand—"

"I don't want the *everythings*, I just want to get my hands on a *something*!"

Hil's voice is calm. "Even if you could prove your mother broke your arm in a fit of rage, you'd justify it with how much she suffered."

"My mother did suffer. I don't know if we can actually imagine what she suffered."

"I don't have to imagine it. I live with you."

"Is that supposed to be funny?"

"I'm sorry, I mean I live with some of the results of how your mother dealt with her suffering. And I'm not talking about one event. So you have to decide. Do you want to come out of the closet? Or do you want to prove that it wasn't so bad by raising your own children the same way?"

"Hil? . . . I'm afraid."

"What are you afraid of?"

I'm afraid of my hands.

In the aftermath of the swirl, a seared silence. But not stillness. The air is in motion. It is as if sound had just now been torn from the room. What remains is the aftershock of sound. The air throbs. Thickens, takes on the sheen of a fresh bruise. What has just happened? Empty does not equal safe. Quiet does not equal peaceful. Something has retreated. It will be back, you cannot know when. And strangest of all? There is no one in this picture. *Where is the Me?*

"I'm afraid that it's true. And I'm afraid that it isn't."

"Sweetheart. It's right in front of you."

She looks at her face in the big black window. Shock of white, gaunt and shadowed. Like an X-ray.

"Mary Rose? What you're telling me is very sad, I'm sorry."

"How was your preview?"

"We got a standing ovation."

"That's great."

"Mary Rose—"

"I'll get some friends over tomorrow, I'll get some help. Don't worry about the kids."

"I'm more worried about you."

"I'm fine."

"I love you."

"Love you too, good night."

"Mister?"

"I won't hurt them."

"Don't hurt yourself."

"I promise."

.

She hangs by the wrists, looking down over the bright green grass where her father is playing catch. If he looks up, what will happen? What will she have to feel? What will she have to know?

.

She goes upstairs and looks into Maggie's crib. Bone cysts are not genetic, but they are hereditary. Today she did not pass them on to her child. What about tomorrow? She can get help with her anger. She can get help sorting out what happened and did not happen to her and who's on first, the chicken or the egg? She can hang on to the balcony for dear life until she grows strong enough to haul herself back to safety. But, she wonders, is there a surgical procedure to open the heart? Because right now, she would give anything to be able to feel—without the kick-start of anger—the love she knows she has always had for her child. She can see this love. Behind glass. Sleeping. With a fragment of poisoned apple lodged in its mouth.

SATURDAY

Swerve

At eight a.m., she calls Sue.

"Want to get together with the kids? . . . No, everything's fine . . . Exactly! . . . Ha-ha . . . Perfect, see you then." Sue has seen through her already, and this early morning shout-out just confirms what a mess she is. What if the unthinkable occurs and she cries in front of Sue? But Sue is as close as she can get to Hil right now, and she needs a Hil.

She lets Maggie colour in her datebook but draws the line at handing over her entire bag. She leaves the breakfast mess and gets down on the floor with Matthew and a mountain of Lego. Today is a different world. A house fell on her last night. Her whole mother fell on her, yet here she is playing in the rubble, and wearing a macaroni necklace. She sings, *"It's a beautiful day in this neighbourhood, a beautiful*

day for a neighbour . . .'" She is pain free and, not exactly dizzy, a bit off
to one side—as though she were sticking out of herself at an angle.
Normally she would try to stuff herself back in, but today she is going
to let it be.

Matthew takes a block from Maggie. Maggie hits him with the
datebook. He screams. Mary Rose makes peace without yelling—
without wanting to yell. She has a sense of reprieve. Something has
withdrawn . . . The catastrophes flash in her periphery just as they did
yesterday, but depleted of force—perhaps she could learn to live with
them the way some people learn to live with voices. Indeed, her sobri-
ety is intoxicating as she goes about motherproofing her home.

At 8:10, she calls Candace. "Can you do Monday morning?"

"I've got my cake decorating class."

"Okay, thanks."

"Are you stuck?"

"No, not at all. Yes. I am stuck."

"I'll bring Maggie, she'll enjoy it."

If the thing comes back, the children will be safe. It is as though
she were getting her affairs in order in the event of her sudden
disappearance.

What about tomorrow? She can bring the children to the train
station for the hour-long stopover, her parents will enjoy that, and
then . . .? The vacant sun-pressed plain of a Sunday afternoon . . .
Think: you know hundreds of people, Toronto is seething with family
entertainment, go paint some clay pots, jump on a trampoline in a
cavernous facility north of the 401. Or maybe just a quiet day at home
with the kids—

"Give it back!"

"No!"

"Mumma-a-a-a!"

She calls Gigi and leaves a message. "Hi, want to go to the zoo
with me and the kids tomorrow afternoon? And then stay for supper,

actually can you come for supper tonight too?" Does that sound like a cry for help? She recalls it is all of 8:15 of a Saturday morning and hopes Gigi has her ringer turned off—unless she has spent the night at the home of her latest "lady friend." The doorbell rings just as she hangs up. Daisy does not go crazy—tuckered, perhaps, from her crib-side vigil. Who can it be at this hour of the morning? Animal Control? She peeks through the window. Gigi is standing on the porch with a pasta pot and her motorcycle helmet. Mary Rose opens the door.

Gigi is built something like a pasta pot herself. Her coal-black curls are slicked fresh from the shower, she sports a leather jacket, a vintage bowling shirt and her signature sly smile. "I was in the neighbourhood with a batch of meatballs on the back of my bike, so I thought I'd drop by, see who's hungry."

Maggie tackles Gigi's legs, Daisy lumbers from the landing, Matthew saunters up and informs his godmother with professorial *gravitas*, "I have a helicopter that goes underwater and fights snakes."

"Awesome."

"Here, let me take that," says Mary Rose.

Gigi is born and bred Toronto, a genuine St. Clair Avenue Eyetalian. She called herself a dyke back when you could still get beaten up for it on a Friday night, she called herself a dyke when you could be censured for it by lesbian feminists, she called herself a dyke when lesbian feminists reclaimed the word, and she still calls herself a dyke now that "queer" has rendered the term quaint. "I'm a dykosaur," she likes to say.

"What are you doing up this early on a Saturday?" asks Mary Rose. "Or did you not go to bed?"

"Oh, I went to bed." The slightest gleam enters her eye.

"The kids have gymnastics at nine, want to come?"

"Does a bear defecate in the woods?"

She has known Gigi for twenty-five years. She is a serial monog-amist whose sexual appeal for straight women from every walk of life is as mysterious to Mary Rose as it is irresistible to said women, and is either evidence of Gigi's internalized homophobia combined with fear of commitment, or simply evidence of Gigi. Mary Rose makes room in the fridge for the pasta pot and reflects that longevity is nine-tenths of friendship—you can't know, when you're twenty-three, which friends will be there for the duration.

They walk down to the Jewish Community Centre, where Gigi watches Maggie's Kid-tastics class in the gym, freeing Mary Rose up to watch Matthew's swimming lesson. They stop at the park on the way home and play tag, jackets flying open and Sue arrives, a vision of waffle-knit loveliness with her perfect baby and rambunctious sons.

"Sue, this is my friend Gigi."

Mary Rose watches them shake hands and sees Sue blush. How does Gigi do it? Matthew finds a bird's nest, Ryan steps in dog poo, Maggie runs after the big-brother Colin and repeatedly face-plants in the sand.

Her cellphone rings. "Saleema, hi . . . You're a mind-reader . . . Perfect."

Gigi has joined Ryan and Matthew, pushing them on the round-about. Colin is running around it in the opposite direction with Maggie in hot pursuit. He stops short, causing her to run smack into him and they both fall.

"Colin, be gentle!" cries Sue, making a move, but Mary Rose stops her with a hand on her sleeve, calling, "Maggie, be gentle!"

Sue laughs. Mary Rose says, "He's a great kid, both your boys are really nice."

Sue bursts into tears.

"Oh," says Mary Rose stupidly, and fumbles a gently used tissue from her sleeve.

Sue takes the tissue and blows her nose. "I'm so glad you called this morning, Mary Rose, I don't know what I would've done." Then she throws her arms around Mary Rose and hugs her. Mary Rose instructs her arms to hug back and waits to find out what is going on. Sue squeezes her and says in a voice taut with emotion, "I don't know how you do it."

"Do what?" Mary Rose sounds in her own ears like a shell-shocked Bob Newhart.

"You're always so calm."

Over Sue's shoulder she sees Ryan and Matthew chasing Colin through the climbing structure with its multiple levels and lookouts while Maggie, stranded on the ground, ululates in frustration at the base of a metal platform which is just above her reach. Colin suddenly leaps from the "crow's nest," lands on the platform with a clang and reaches down over the bars of the railing for Maggie. His toes are almost off the platform but he manages to grasp her by the wrists in an effort to pull her up and over the railing. Mary Rose watches. He is not hurting her, nor is Maggie in danger should he let go—her feet are inches from the sand—no, here is what has caused the warmth to leave her hands, and the breath to stall in her chest. He can't do it. Colin is not strong enough to pull Maggie up over the railing and onto the platform. He is seven. She is two. It's right in front of her.

Sue has released her, is saying something.

"No, no, come to my house for lunch," replies Mary Rose—evidently she has heard and processed what Sue has said. Gigi rejoins them, Sue discovers that Gigi knows her brother-in-law from the film industry, and "I love your jacket, Gigi, it looks so authentic." Mary Rose smiles, strolls over to spot Maggie on the slide. *Then who was it?*

"Bum down, Maggie, bum down, that's right."

Her mother. Caught Mary Rose just in time as she climbed on an overturned bucket, reached up and went over the railing. *Then why isn't it part of family lore?* Caught her just in time—*Then why is Mary Rose hanging, facing out with her back to the bars?* Caught her turning over a bucket in a bid to reach the railing, "I'LL TEACH YOU!" By the wrists, up and over the side, "IS THAT WHAT YOU WANT?!"

344 | ADULT ONSET

"Good job, Maggie! Go again?"

Unless it didn't happen at all.

Back home, spelt animal cookies and strawberry milk. Sue nurses the baby. Mary Rose puts on Raffi and they all dance. Her macaroni necklace breaks. They make a fort in the dining room with three-hundred-thread-count sheets. Colin bodysurfs headfirst down the stairs, Ryan and Matthew follow suit—tears.

Unless it was her father.

Matthew's hamster gets loose, Maggie sticks a macaroni elbow up her nose, Ryan finds a tube of lipstick, Daisy corners the hamster under the bathroom cabinet, Gigi coaxes it out with peanut butter. Lunchtime. Matthew sneezes and tomato sauce comes out his nose.

No, her father is down there, playing catch with a version of himself . . . what is this memory made of? What is any of them made of? Did she situate him down there in order to exonerate him? Or to reassure herself that he would catch her if she fell? But in the dream—memory, rather—her fear is that he will look up. And see . . . what? That she is in danger. That she is . . . in pain. And she will know that he knows. And she will fall . . .

Saleema and Youssef arrive with cupcakes—Saleema can't stay, okay maybe a cup of tea. Her head scarf is a study in strobing houndstooth. "You might want to post a warning," says Gigi. Mary Rose takes her aside. Gigi says, "Sorry, did I offend her?"

"What? I don't know, I was going to ask if you could stay over tonight."

"Sure," she says, and doesn't ask why.

She knows Gigi will have to arrange doggie care for her black Lab, Tanya—the dog can't come here because Daisy would eat her. Mary Rose glances at Daisy's dish—she hasn't touched her breakfast. The doorbell rings.

"Here's your mail."

"Thanks, Rochelle."

A glut of bills and flyers.

Rochelle doesn't budge. Is she waiting to be asked in? Does she wish to join the merriment? "Would you like a cup of tea?"

Mary Rose has thought Rochelle socially awkward, but it dawns on her now that Rochelle may be that rare personality type, the Fearless Pauser.

Finally the woman speaks. "Are you all right?"

". . . Are you checking on me?"

"Yes."

". . . Thank you."

"When's your next book coming out?" Rochelle turns purple.

"I don't know."

"There was no package."

"That's okay."

"Say 'hello Dolly' for me."

Mary Rose chuckles, but Rochelle's affectless expression suggests a joke has been neither intended nor registered. "I will do that."

"Your dog didn't bark."

Mary Rose looks up at the landing. *Thwack, thwack.* "She's tired."

"You're welcome," says Rochelle. And leaves.

Mary Rose turns, about to regale her friends with the absurdity of her spectrumy neighbour, when it arrives like the mail in her hands, delayed but dogged: what her mother meant when she said, "Here we are": Mary Rose is alive. Her mother didn't kill her. She sets the mail down on the front hall table.

"I'm going out to buy flowers," she announces. "I'll be right back. Let's go, Daisy."

Daisy's tail twitches politely, but she remains curled on the landing.

Mary Rose is walking alone; no dog, no stroller, no child by the hand, she hasn't so much as a bag. Unaccommodated woman.

"Hi, hawney."

"Hi, Daria."

Daria is on her porch as usual. "Kids okay?"

"Great, thanks, *grazie.*"

Daria sees everything. If something were to happen to Mary Rose, Daria would be able to tell the police exactly when she left her house—it has shaped up to be a nice day.

Passing the park, she notices a cluster of crocuses in the bruised turf—they weren't there this morning. Her children are safe. She has made them safe. Hil is right, it doesn't change anything; time to let go of the balcony.

Archie's Variety. Should she buy the flowers now or wait till after she's had a walk? "Hello, how are *you*?" Winnie practically sings it.

"Hello, Winnie." Mary Rose smiles back. Classical music is playing. What is Winnie's Korean name? Would it be rude to ask? Maybe it is Winnie.

"How is your mummy?"

"She's fine, Winnie, thank you for asking."

Just inside are several tubs of tulips, red, white, and only one yellow bunch. She takes it and places it on the counter.

"You pick yellow, pretty."

Mary Rose reaches into her pocket but comes up empty. "I'm so sorry, I forgot my wallet, I'll be right back."

But Winnie will not hear of her leaving without the tulips, saying, "You trust me."

Out on Bathurst Street once more, Mary Rose is a bit light-headed but that is unsurprising, she keeps forgetting to breathe. She looks down at her feet to steady herself as she walks. This sidewalk could be anywhere, this could be any time in the last hundred years. Speed up the frames and see all the feet through time, hers among them, her mother's appearing alongside for a moment, likewise her children's, and all the others, feet like schools of fish, her own recurring but less frequently until they fail to reappear, then fewer feet. Then disintegration, ash, grass, forest, sand. She will still be part of it, though unimaginably diffuse. She looks up. Bathurst is a dingy glare, Saturday traffic zooming in a spray of grit. Without her wallet, she is without ID; were she to be killed today how long would it take for the information to reach her friends at home with her children? This is why it is important never to just "pop out" and leave one's child alone in order to track down the source of a car alarm . . . of course one might just as easily die in one's own home—best, really, never to be alone with a child who cannot yet dial 911.

Nothing has ever been hidden, she is merely putting the bits together. Like a dinosaur skeleton at the ROM; not all the bones come from the same animal, still you get an idea of what the beast looked like. Unless it was mythical and none of it ever happened. Unless it was mythical and something like it is always happening.

She could ask.

"Dad, did you know? Is that why you took her to a psychiatrist?"

"I took her because she was blue."

"Did you see her do it?"

"Did I see her . . . what, break your arm? Of course not."

"No one sees what happens between a parent and a child in the middle of the deserted day."

"I would have known."

"No one can know."

"You just answered your own question."

The day has dulled. Poetry is gone from the sky, nothing is like anything else, everything is merely what it is. Did it happen?

An ambulance is parked outside the subway station, silent lights flashing, a streetcar squeals past. She feels oddly light, her limbs seemingly in a process of distension; without pain to staple her to the present, her head is floating upward. It is as though the whole of her has only ever been held together by a string, slackening now like a faulty puppet. All of it happened, none of it happened, it is still happening . . .

The package is somewhere. Other Mary Rose is somewhere, when I die I will be everywhere . . . She needs an angel to carry a message from the top of her mind way down to her darkness where words waver and go out or else ignite the air. What angel, what bird of pray or ebony elf will volunteer to carry this message? Which of them is small enough to squeeze between yet bold enough to go behind the lines, below the words—down, down to the bottom of the well with the message: "War is over. Peace now. I'm coming for you"?

Victim of a victim . . . Crime continues to be played out until it is understood, at which point, like a spinning chunk of kryptonite, it slows, ceases mid-air and drops to the ground with a harmless *klink*. Is that all there is to a trauma? A sad mother, a father who wants everything to be okay. Damage bred in the bone; a bone with holes, like the stops on a flute doomed to sing the truth. Depressed mother. Crying baby. Closed door. Why is it not a truth universally acknowledged that an absence of trauma under these conditions is remarkable? Why is it anything but ordinary that Mary Rose's mother might have injured her, then sought to bury it along with the dead babies? And why is it surprising that truth makes its way out through the body like a vine invading from within? What you mistook for sinews now revealed as sprouts from a seed swallowed long ago, creeping, pushing, straining toward the light, ensnaking arteries, choking heart and lungs; vines disguised as veins, forcing blindly out, *I'm going to smash you!*

Or that truth should sing like a flute fashioned from a bone whose holes determine not only its tune but its nature as an instrument of song? It does not mean you are crazy if you can hear the song, or read the entrails. And suddenly the spell is broken. No fairy-tale vine, no magic flute. An injury, sad and small. *It hurts.*

At the corner of Bathurst and Bloor, so many people. Flowing past and amid one another, human currents adhering to the laws of physics, not tripping into turbulence—how do we do that? How do birds know when to turn as one in flight? She watches all the people, all the people, and sees them collapsing one by one like expertly demolished buildings, disintegrating from the inside; all the perfectly normal people falling down inside their nice coats. And the coats stay standing. Knowing a thing is not the same as believing a thing—they are twins but not identical, parallel thoughts that can veer apart like a cartoon train track . . . She stands still, letting the crowd break past her, risking turbulence. The feel of people's coats brushing her shoulder, her cheek, the smell of hair, chattering of words and motion, if she unfocuses her ears she can imagine she has just arrived here and does not understand the language. Where is everyone going? *Wohin gehen sie?* They are all on the way somewhere, on the way to work, on the way to the store, on the way to a friend, on the way, on the way, on the way home . . .

A bridge is the way to do it if you are going to be sure. Also, it is simple and inconveniences the fewest people. Netting has been erected along the bridge over the Don Valley, but there are others. There is the Skyway bridge in Hamilton, forty-five minutes away. She does it in her mind's eye, and perhaps this means it really happens somewhere— just as, somewhere, Maggie's arm was broken yesterday morning, and somewhere else, Mary Rose's never was. She mounts the railing at the crest of the bridge. Far below is Lake Ontario, great slab of water. She leans forward and commits her body to the air. The wind bears her up at first, then gives way and she falls headfirst—the water will be like concrete—on the way on the way down her heart breaks open like the palms of two praying hands to reveal her children cupped within; they were there all along. Too late, she knows she loves them.

On the other side of the intersection, Honest Ed's winks and flashes. *Only the flowers are crooked!* Secrets from Your Sister is having a sale. *I'm not crying, don't you cry.* The light turns green, she stays still. People bump past, one or two look back irritably over their shoulder— hint of turbulence. This is how it starts. If you survive, you return with swollen ankles and a shopping cart full of plastic bags, another spare loony. What is the difference between me and them, the marginal ones? Streetcar wheels rattle past, car tires hiss, the difference between slicing and crushing, slicing is better. It is important not to have hit her children or cast them out. But, standing at the corner of Bathurst and Bloor across from Honest Ed's, here on this tide-deserted beach, pocked with shells, scribbled with seaweed, is this what is left? It has caught up to her, her mother's curse. She cannot see a future. She sees what is right in front of her, the traffic, and she craves it. Not so much death, though that is a by-product, but injury, and with it something certain. Pain. She tastes the impact, yearns for the relief of it, metal slamming into her, smashing her. It has been on its way to her for her whole life. The light is yellow.

Everyone knows it is better not to abuse their children; that it is worth everything to change the habits that perpetuate abuse. The world depends on it. But Mary Rose has discovered the hidden cost. It is so steep as to bankrupt the best intentions, and the worst part is that payment is due the moment the change is named. This is because to enact the change is to experience by contrast the shocking nature of what preceded it. It is to de-normalize violence; unwrap it like a dangerous gift and see it glowing, hear it blaring like a siren, feel it beating like a heart. For Mary Rose, it means betraying her own mother by mothering differently. Better.

It is possible to know all this, and yet have no place to put it. It is possible to be outside on a sunny day, but trapped inside a cave.

She looks down. Her hands look older now than her mother's do in memory. Something needs to change. The light is red.

Good night, sweetie pie. See you in the morning.

She is looking in the window of Secrets from Your Sister. The chopstick girl sees her and waves. Mary Rose waves back and that is when she realizes she no longer has the flowers. Where have they gone?

She had them before she crossed the street. She retraces her steps east along Bloor until she reaches the corner of Bathurst. A streetcar rumbles past. She scans the busy intersection for a glimpse of yellow. But the flowers are not in the street, they are not right in front of her, they are gone. At least they weren't run over. She stands amid the crowd waiting to cross at the lights, and experiences an odd sense that, along with the tulips, she has lost a piece of time; as though it has slipped between the tracks and been swallowed up—because, come to think of it, she cannot recall having crossed the street. She remembers standing on the other side, waiting for the light to change. And she remembers being on this side and looking in the window of Secrets. So, clearly she did cross over. Because here she is.

She walks back up Bathurst. She will pick up a second bunch from Winnie on the way home, then pop back and pay her for both—they'll have to be red or white this time.

"Hi, Winnie."

Winnie does not look up at first and Mary Rose is seized with an uncanny dread, one that, before it can be clothed in words, is dispelled when Winnie responds, "Hello, how are *you*?"—singing it as enthusiastically as if she had not just seen Mary Rose a scant fifteen minutes ago.

It is a cultural thing, Mary Rose reflects, the super-politeness. She surveys the tubs of tulips just inside the door. "Oh, there was another yellow bunch after all."

"You pick yellow, pretty."

She places it on the counter, "Can you hold on to these for me, Winnie, I'll be right back with money for two bunches."

"No, you buy one."

"I haven't paid you for the first one yet."

"You buy only one."

"Okay, thank you so much. I'll be right back with money for one!"

Winnie laughs. "No, no, you take, you take."

"Really?"

Carmen is blasting through the speakers, *Toreadorah!* Mary Rose smiles and says, "Thank you, Winnie."

The house is quiet but for the sound of Looney Tunes from the basement. At the kitchen table, Sue, Saleema and Gigi sit intently, each bent over a hand of cards. Gigi is teaching them to play poker. They grunt in greeting like a trio of 1960s husbands as Mary Rose enters the kitchen with a cheery, "I'm back," proving once again that gender is a construct.

She fills a vase with water for the tulips and places them on the kitchen counter in front of the windows that are suddenly fuzzy with rain. In the centre of her visual field there appears a splotch. It grows. Sickly yellow orb, blocking her view. It is not anxiety, she is feeling none, it has to do with the high pressure system. Low pressure? She goes to the powder room and pulls up her sleeve, positioning her arm so as to see it around the big indoor sun. The scars are still there. Does the fact that she checked mean she is crazy? She feels dizzy again, but that is likely the result of having to peer around an orb. Laughter from the kitchen.

Her guests are leaving—all except Gigi, who is not really a guest but a member of the Chosen Family. Maggie hugs Colin who responds by lifting her a full four inches from the floor before toppling backwards against the wall. Sue harnesses her baby to her chest where it blinks and beams like a second head sprouting straight from her heart, and Mary Rose suddenly misses Hil with the acuteness of a thorn to her own heart. Saleema hurries downstairs from what Mary Rose is coming to think of as "the prayer room" and rushes Youssef out the door but not before he flings his arms around Matthew and gives him a kiss. Gigi helps Mary Rose pry Ryan, sobbing with middle-child rage, from the train tracks in the living room. He punches Matthew, Matthew punches him, Ryan apologizes, Matthew gives him Percy, Maggie punches Matthew, Matthew cries. Sue hustles her children out the door then turns and, taking Mary Rose's hand in hers, says quietly, "You saved my life today."

Mary Rose seats herself at the kitchen table behind the newspaper and runs her eyes back and forth across a column width so Gigi won't wonder if there is a big yellow sun in her way.

"Are you okay?" asks Gigi.

"Yeah, I'm reading the paper."

"The business section, who knew?"

"Stop hitting on Sue, she's married."

"I didn't hit on Sue."

"You flirted with her."

"I flirted with Saleema too."

"At least she's divorced."

"They'd be insulted if I didn't flirt with them."

Mary Rose lowers the paper. "You know how that would sound if you were a man?"

Gigi shrugs and smiles. "It would sound like it sounds."

"Hil is sick of me."

"She loves you."

"I used to be the successful older man, now I'm a frustrated housewife."

"You're a woman, Mister. Face it."

"That's what Hil says."

"We never thought we'd be able to get married. We thought we were out in the cold, so we made the cold into a party, but cold is cold and family is family and you guys are mine. I'm not a writer, I can't say it pretty."

"Thanks for coming when I called."

Gigi leans down and puts an arm around her—Gigi favours butch attire but is in fact quite bosomy behind Vince's Bowlerama. "I was coming anyway," she says.

Mary Rose nestles into the hug. ". . . Hil called you."

"Yeah."

"Good."

"It's gonna be okay, Mister."

Mary Rose goes upstairs and, as quietly as possible, throws up. She remains on her knees, embracing the toilet bowl—white dignity of the Virgin Mary. Our Lady loves you no matter what. She loves lesbians and lepers and leprechauns. "Dear Our Lady, please make the yellow sun go away." Our Lady does. She brushes her teeth, no longer obliged to peer around an orb in order to see that she has burst blood vessels in her eyes with the force of retching.

She returns to the kitchen and checks the google history on her laptop. The bone cyst sites are there, she didn't dream it, she didn't google it in a parallel world. There is an e-mail from Maureen, in the subject line: "Found it!" She opens it to find a link to a government website. She double-clicks and a page comes up with a Maple Leaf flag on the banner and the heading CANADIAN POSTWAR MILITARY AND DEPENDANT GRAVES ABROAD. On the sidebar, a menu: *What's new? Browse by name. Browse by location.* At the centre, filling the screen, is a photograph of a gravestone. Flush against the grass. It is more grey than white—no doubt with the passage of years. There is a name. *Alexander Duncan MacKinnon.*

"Who's that?" asks Gigi.

"My brother."

And there are dates. *December 18–December 23, 1961* . . . no wonder Christmas is sad. She was two. Maggie's age.

"Is Gigi still there?" asks Hil.

"She's staying over, the kids are in bed, we're in the basement watching *Mamma Mia!* again. Do you want to say hi?"

"I believe you. How are you doing?"

"I'm fine, it's all pretty banal." Hil is silent. Mary Rose adds, "Not in the Hannah Arendt sense of the word."

"Call me from the train station tomorrow."

"I will, what're you eating?"

"Perogies, I'm on a break."

"Winnipeg's got the best perogies. I'm surprised you could find them in Calgary."

"I love you, have a nice evening."

"Have a good preview." She holds the phone out. "Say hi, Gigi."

"Hi, Gigi," calls Gigi at the phone.

Daisy levers herself up onto the couch and wedges between them, next to the popcorn.

Winnie is smiling down at her, as if Mary Rose were much smaller and unable to see over the counter, saying, "You pick yellow." Winnie's voice deepens demonically, her smile undertows to a frown as she adds, "You put him in de gwound." Mary Rose wakes in a sweat, her heart pounding. But there is another sound behind it—and she realizes it was this other sound that woke her. A thud-thudding accompanied by a kind of guttural clicking. It is a completely new sound. She gets up. It is coming from the landing. She goes to the top of the stairs and looks down.

"Daisy?"

Daisy appears very old and grey under the fluorescents of the Veterinary Emergency Clinic, but she is panting affably, cold-nosed and alert, huddled between Mary Rose's knees. If Gigi hadn't been sleeping over, Mary Rose would not have been able to rush the dog to the clinic—it is almost as though Daisy waited till it was safe.

"Good girl, Daze."

Sometime after 2:00, the vet examines her and listens, unfazed, to Mary Rose's account: she got up to find Daisy lying on her side on the landing, limbs spasming, mouth foaming, eyes rolled back.

He says, "Best not to let her sleep near the stairs from now on." And writes a prescription for anti-seizure medication.

"Does she have epilepsy?"

"In a dog of her age, it's more likely to be a tumour."

"You mean . . . a brain tumour?"

"We can't say without an X-ray."

He tells her an X-ray would require that Daisy undergo general anaesthetic, which poses its own risks.

"And what if it does turn out to be a tumour? Can you operate?"

"I'm sure if you look hard enough, you'll find a vet who's willing to operate. Personally, I wouldn't."

Fucking prick. Mary Rose is blanched with rage, can barely get out the words. "Because she's a pit bull?"

He looks bemused. "Because she's old."

He has freckles. He is pale. Younger than she first thought. "What would you do?" she asks.

"Take her home and love her."

She puts Daisy's bed in the living room and closes the baby gate at the bottom of the stairs. She gets down on the floor, spoons around the dog and cups the old helmety head in her palm, feels the warm weight of it. "I'm here, Daisy," she whispers. "I'm here."

SUNDAY

A Long Follow-Up

At ten-thirty on Sunday, April 7, Mary Rose MacKinnon gets off the subway and walks the underground maze to Union Station. She passes a Laura Secord candy store and pauses. Laura Secord was a Canadian farm girl who tipped off the British that the Americans were about to attack across the Niagara River in the War of 1812. Somehow she came to be synonymous with candy. Maybe that was her reward for saving the British Empire. In the window is a chocolate Scrabble game. Mary Rose hesitates, then resists buying it for her mother. She has been a crusader against Dolly's sugar addiction, why become an enabler now? "Who gave you the candy?!" "General Brock. His pockets were always full of it." She buys a coffee at the Croissant Tree from a woman burdened with life-altering beauty, and waits in the stray subordinate clause of Arrivals.

She is early. She steps into a bookstore. Soon she will be able to walk into bookstores without a pang. Eventually her books will go out of print and no one will ask, "In the third one, will Kitty do this/see that . . .?" She buys her father a book. *Payback*, by Margaret Atwood. Now she has nothing for her mother.

She has left Maggie and Matt with Gigi, the three of them doting on Daisy, plying her with treats, encircling her with train tracks and towers and totems—both Elmos were going. Hilary will be home Thursday. Mary Rose needs to remember to send flowers for her opening. She needs to remember to buy eggs on the way home; they are going to decorate them for Easter. An echoey announcement darkens the fluorescent air, "Train incomprehensible from incomprehensible is now incomprehensible."

She is here to meet her parents. She has known them all her life, what if she does not recognize them? What if they do not recognize her? Maybe she is the imposter. Maybe she really was killed in the street yesterday and she will see them but they will not see her. She will follow them frantically into the PATH all the way to the Tim Hortons, screaming unheard at their retreating backs. She looks up at the light in the ceiling high overhead and wills her vision not to constrict—tunnelling is a sign of an anxiety attack. She is not aware of feeling anxiety. Which is perhpas a sign.

Where are her parents? Their train has arrived. *To lose one parent may be counted a misfortune, to lose two . . .* The crowd balloons past her.

"Golly Moses, Mary Roses!"

"Hi, Mum."

Hug. She dreamt it all, none of it ever happened. It was all a midlife childhood abuse fantasy born of the desire to make sense of her own bad behaviour by pinning it on her parents. Baby Boomers, unite!

Bonk on the head. "Hi, Dad."

"Where are the kids?!" Dolly looks around, alarmed, as if Mary Rose had only moments ago abandoned them.

"They're home with a friend."

"Why didn't you bring them?"

"I'm sorry, I just . . . wanted to . . . not."

Dolly is resplendent in leopard print beret, velour hoodie, gold bangles, an eighteen-karat Holy Mother round her neck and stretchy pants. "Oh, doll, you're exhausted."

"I'm not—"

"You're not twenty-five, you know."

"Daisy had a seizure."

"What's that?" says her father. Bright red peaked cap, yellow windbreaker.

"You got a new freezer?" pipes Dolly.

"No, yes, well, I want a new freezer," says Mary Rose.

"Dunc, buy your daughter a freezer!"

"What kind do you want?" says Dunc.

"It'll be your birthday present and your Christmas present for the next three years!" Dolly, mock fierce, slicing the air with her hand, setting her jingles to bangling.

"Better get one with a balcony in that case!" Duncan grins.

Mary Rose smiles. He looks good, good colour in his face.

"Where's Maggie?!" says Dolly, looking around, alarmed.

"Mum, she's home with Matt and my friend Gigi—"

"Where's Hilary?" asks Duncan.

"I told you, Dunc," says Dolly. "She's in Winnipeg."

Mary Rose says, "She's . . . out west."

"Did I tell you, I slept right through the prairies?!" exclaims Dolly.

"How's big Matt? You got him up on skates yet?"

"Not yet, but—"

"There's no rush, Gordie Howe didn't own a pair of skates till he was twelve—"

"Shall we head for the Tim's?" says Mary Rose.

They pass a flower shop—winged Mercury is stamped on the glass, the messenger god with his meek bouquet.

"Oh look, would Maggie like that?" Dolly's attention has been snagged by a sparkly arrangement with a heart-shaped balloon: *Forever in Our Hearts*.

"Mum, not that."

She shepherds them toward a sign that says Eatery with an arrow pointing down and nudges them onto the escalator.

"Mum, hang on to the railing."

They make it to the food concourse. It could be worse: the bolted chairs and tables are of blond wood, the lighting is good. Her father treks over to the Tim Hortons counter between the sushi bar and the Pita Pit while she guides her mother to a banquette. Duncan rejoins them with a tea, two coffees and, tossed genially onto the table, "A whole bunch of junk."

"Danke schayne," says Dolly, flirtatious. She tips a packet of Splenda into her tea and bites into a doughnut with sprinkles.

"Mum? Why do you bother with Splenda?"

"So I can have a doughnut."

"I don't think it works that way."

"'By your children be ye taught!'"

Faux slap.

"The gal behind the counter," says Duncan appreciatively, "she was speaking Japanese or Swahili, I'm not sure which."

Dolly smiles. "So many Orientals in BC nowadays."

Her mother does not remember, her father needed not to know, and Mary Rose is left holding the bag. Of bones. And reading them . . . This is how crazy ladies are made. Best drop it.

"They're taking over," says Duncan, "and that's probably good news for the rest of us. If you really want to be bilingual nowadays, learn Mandarin." He bites into a crueller, his eyes boyish blue.

Dolly digs into her purse and comes out with a paperback copy of *Journey to Otherwhere*. On the inside cover, a Post-it Note specifies the inscription: "For Phyllis, My Best to You." Phyllis is getting married again.

"Your mother should be getting a percentage," says Duncan with a wink.

Dolly finds a Best Western pen in her purse and, as Mary Rose signs the book, chants, "I used to be Abe Mahmoud's daughter, then I was Duncan MacKinnon's wife, now I'm Mary Rose MacKinnon's mother!"

"Mum, how come you never say 'I used to be Lily Mahmoud's daughter'?"

"He was head of the family."

"She did all the work."

"He came to this country with nothing and—"

"I'm just saying—"

"'If I say black is white, it's white.'"

Duncan laughs. "Look out, Mister."

"Mum, that is meaningless."

Duncan says, "It was meaningful, all right, it meant he was the boss." *Don't kick the football.* "I know, Dad, and look at the result."

"What 'result'?" says Dolly. "You're the result, I'm the result, and we have Puppa to thank—"

"Exactly."

"What're you getting all worked up for now?" says her father in his innocent-bystander tone.

"I'm not worked up, Dad." *You kicked the football.*

"In the old country—" says Dolly.

"Please don't tell me about good slaps."

"No one can tell me Puppa didn't love Mumma—"

"I never said—"

"His pockets were always full of candy!"

Duncan laughs.

Mary Rose says, "Mum? Is that who gave you the candy?"

Dolly's brow creases. "What candy?"

". . . Nothing. It's okay." She hands the copy of *Otherwhere* back to her mother and it disappears into the purse.

Duncan marshals a gruff tone. "How's the new book coming?" Tone of high esteem.

She does not want to hurt his feelings by telling him that she is not going to write it. "Well, in a quantum sense, it's already out there just waiting for me to look it into existence."

"That's one very sophisticated piece of procrastination."

They laugh.

On the other hand, why does she assume it will hurt him if she does not write the third? Is she self-sabotaging in order to punish him? Is she still willing to do—or not do—anything to get his attention, including fail miserably?

She gives him the Atwood book. He frowns, pleased. "What're you spending your money for?"

"You'll get it back, Mary Rose," says Dolly good-naturedly. "You're getting the silver tea service when I go."

"Go where?" says Duncan.

She chats with her father about the fascistic tendencies of the federal government and the roots of the current economic collapse. "Bush, Cheney, Rumsfeld, Rove and the whole lot of them should be tried for crimes against humanity," he says. "And that goes for Milton Friedman too."

"Milt Friedman," says Dolly. "Did we know him in Germany?"

"Like the fella says, 'Those who don't remember history are doomed to repeat it.'" He takes a newspaper from the pocket of his jacket.

Dolly opens her purse again.

"What are you looking for, Mum?"

A number of objects surface: the folded tartan tote bag, collapsible hairbrush, packet of jam from the train, the rosary, the *Living with Christ* pamphlet—the brown "Sunday Offering" envelope still tucked in its pages, perhaps her mother is holding out on the Church—the small grey velvet box . . .

"Is that it, Mum?"

"Is what it?"

"Your moonstone ring."

"Yes, in the box."

"Is that what you wanted to give me?" Her mother has been carrying it around the whole time . . . Mary Rose prepares herself to be moved. This is what difficult mothers do in the end: bestow upon their embattled daughters a token of their love. Roll credits.

But Dolly says, "Why would I give you that?"

"Because . . . Dad gave it to you when Alexander was born, and . . . it was a hard time, and I was . . . kind of there."

. . . a fuzzy Chiclet, pussycat change purse, plastic pill container, the rosary again, mini address book from a hair salon . . . bits and pieces, concrete counterparts to the tiny words that have beset Mary Rose and murdered meaning in a hail of prepositions. She looks away.

This is what you get in the end. Fragments. Parts of speech. Her mother has gone to bits. Her father is on a saner-seeming loop. He knows how to make lunch. Supper cannot be far behind. Don't ask for the moon—or even the moonstone. Her mother has said "sorry." Her father has said, "Some things really do get batter." *Dear Dad, I.* Maybe that was it—the whole of her reply to his touching e-mail, maybe she finished it after all. The sense of "something missing" simply comes with the existential territory. Somewhere inside she is still wailing, damp, toothless and tiny against his bare shoulder. Snap out of it, you're forty-eight years old. Leave them alone.

Her parents will be re-boarding the train for their home in Ottawa in less than an hour. Their home, in which they are independent and ask nothing of their children except that they visit. They have just crossed the country as they have done so many times, two little old Canadians traversing the vastness—west to east this time. When the Rockies gave way to the foothills and the forests thinned to prairie, when the train crossed the North Saskatchewan

River and rolled through the outskirts of Winnipeg; past the Walmart and the McDonald's where once there was a tavern, an arena, a rutted highway that led out onto the prairie . . . did her father's hand give her mother's a squeeze? Before she dozed off and he returned to his paper, did they think of Other Mary Rose? Did Dolly say a prayer?

Is she in the sky over the prairie? The vault of the heavens that holds us all, cherishes us all. Energy energy everywhere, endlessly returning love in the form of life, even mineral life. In the guise of time. Is the train part of her? Is the grass part of her? The sound of the horn, the cattle ignoring the rude blast, the car parked at the level crossing, family inside waiting to drive safely on, all part of her? She is everywhere now. Like God.

Dolly looks up from the depths of her purse.

"Give me your postal code again, Mary Rose."

She hands back the Best Western pen and Dolly writes it in the mini address book.

Duncan says, "I see where they're touting the new head of the IMF as a woman, as if that's her only claim to fame."

"I think Andy-Patrick is seeing someone."

She sees her father contract like a salted oyster, while Dolly compresses her lips and stares out over the tabled expanse.

Duncan is pained but polite. "What about . . . what was her name? Nice gal . . ."

"Renée," states Dolly.

"Shereen," says Mary Rose. "They broke up."

"We haven't heard from your brother."

"We didn't hear from Andy-Patrick the entire time we were away," says Duncan, his voice reedy.

"He's been super busy," says Mary Rose, feeling some compunction.

Her parents will be reassured to know that she and her brother have seen one another, so she makes the recent contact sound like the norm. "He was over playing with the kids, having supper with us the other night."

Duncan disappears behind the business section.

Dolly polishes off her doughnut and asks, "Have you heard from your brother?"

Mary Rose decides that it might indeed be wise to learn Mandarin—it could be a way to stay neurologically spry.

"Did you get the packeege I mailed you yet?"

"Mum . . . No, not yet."

"Dammit, what in the name of time is going on?" She is getting worked up.

"Mum, the mail has been—"

"Duncan, do you remember the packeege I had for Mary Rose?"

"What packeege?"

He is getting cranky too—time for their afternoon nap.

"Forget about it, now," he says.

"Forget what?"

"The packeege."

"I did forget it, that's the problem!" Tears in Dolly's eyes, a candy sprinkle at the corner of her mouth. *Oh Mum, please don't cry at eighty-one in the Tim's, I can't bear it . . .*

"Relax now, throttle back," Duncan instructs his wife, making a calming gesture that makes Mary Rose want to bark like crazy. Like Daisy.

Dolly goes to say something, bites it back, sighs elaborately, and suddenly the sun comes out. "Look who's here!"

It's Andy-Patrick, strolling toward them in hair-tipped splendour.

"Well, hello, stranger!" says their father, gripping the table, rising, whacking him on the shoulder. Andy-Pat leans down to his mother, who hugs him tightly then pretends to slap him.

He gives her a chocolate Scrabble game.

"Where the heck did you find something like that?" Duncan smiles broadly.

"Let's all play, come on!" cries Dolly.

"I don't know if you have time before your train," says killjoy Mary Rose.

"We've got time," says Andy-Patrick.

"Wait now," says Dolly, unwrapping the game, "I thought this was—oh, I'm all confused. I thought this was, this isn't the, this is, this isn't in German, or isn't it?"

Sister and brother hesitate in unison, as though syntactically stalled in the effort to sort out which of their mother's questions is answerable.

"Why would it be in German?" asks Duncan, as though trapped in a play by Ionesco.

"I gave you the German Scrabble, Mum," says Mary Rose.

"What's the difference?" says Duncan.

"There are umlauts in German," says Mary Rose, "as well as the classical extra letter—"

"It's German *chocolate*," quips Andy-Pat, helping with the plastic wrap.

"You gave me a German Scrabble, didn't you, Mary Rose?"

"That's right, for Christmas one year."

"Why?" asks Dolly.

"Because . . . we lived there."

"I know we lived there—" Dolly sounds petulant.

"Temper down now," says Duncan.

"Don't tell me to temper down."

"Would you like more tea, Mum?"

"Tea nothing, listen to me now."

For a moment, Mary Rose's mother is there. The one who cast her out. The one who always walked faster than she could, who got an extra ten percent off everything and always had room for one more at the table. The one who swept into her hospital room in a leopard print coat and hat and turned the figure on the bed back into Mary Rose with one bold look.

"Mum, I gave you the German Scrabble game because I was born there."

"No, Mary Rose, you were born in Winnipeg."

Andy-Pat glances up from the chocolate game board.

"No, Mum. That was Other Mary Rose."

Dolly's eyes narrow, her mouth forms a small *Oh.*

"I'm the second Mary Rose, Mum. The first one died."

"Did she?" Dolly's face slackens. Not quite sad clown. Perplexed. "Why? What did I do to her?"

Mary Rose watches darkness opening up behind her mother's face; not the rolling thunderhead of days gone by, but a steadily oncoming darkness, close to the ground. "Mum, you didn't do anything. It was the Rh factor, do you remember what that is?"

"Of course I do, dear, I'm a nurse."

Andy-Patrick says, "Who wants to play?"

"That's what happened to the others too," says Mary Rose.

"And what happened to you, Mary Rose?"

". . . I don't know, Mum. Did something happen to me?"

"I did something to you, what was it now?"

Dolly's brow contracts, the corners of her mouth turn up with effort, like a toddler on the potty. Mary Rose stays very still, lest she startle her mother off the scent of whatever memory is nosing onto the path. In the Black Forest. Dolly's lips part. Then, finally, "I guess it's gone." She leans back in her seat and chuckles. "Your mother's losing her marbles, Mary Rose. Dunc? Dunc're you asleep, dear?"

"I musta bin." He blinks, but does not meet her gaze.

Andy-Patrick places chocolate tiles on chocolate trays.

Her mother has so much unmoored guilt, she is ready to believe she baked her own children into pies. Truth is not going to come this way. Will not yield to direct inquisition. Is unspeakable. The whole fabric of

Mary Rose's life is stained with the dye of what can never be stated, a skein from which she spun stories while she still could—fee-fi-fo-fum, ready or not here I come, can you guess my name? If you are going to forgive, you have to forgive what you don't know. What you can only half see. The rest is dark matter, exerting a pull, making itself known only by the degree to which you wobble off course. Because you don't get the whole story.

Love is blind. Forgiveness is blind in one eye.

"I don't remember, Mum."

Dolly reaches out and places a hand on Mary Rose's cheek. Gentle. Warm.

"I love you, Mary Rose."

Your mother is leaving. Learn her face.

"I love you too, Mum."

She has said it from the Tim's and from the concourse outside the Tim's; from the PATH and the train station above it, from the top of the CN Tower and out beyond transmission range. She has said it from a story long ago and far away across an ocean; from a living room with a coffee table and a couch and a balcony. And she knows, across the miles of underwater cable, through mists of anaesthetic, behind walls of glass and within a cave on a sunny day, from before she was born and after she died, as the message rises from one side of the bolted Formica table, ascends to the blue, the black, the forever, and descends to the other side where her mother sits, that it is true.

"Why are you crying?"

"Because I'm grateful to be here."

"I know what you mean."

Andy-Patrick is staring at the game board. Duncan's hand is resting on Dolly's; his, parchmenty with age and pale with a dusting of freckles, the tip of his ring finger gone; hers, light brown and lined like seasoned wood. *So many miles . . .*

It occurs to Mary Rose that this is the first time, outside infancy, that she has cried in front of her father. Then it occurs to her that it is the second time, because there was that time in the bathtub . . . It is not that she forgot—it is more a trick of filing; as though she had tossed the bathtub memory on the hall table along with the mail twenty-three years ago and there it has lain, unregarded, like Poe's purloined letter.

Suddenly Dolly looks straight at her.

"I know about your mail situation, Mary Rose." She opens her purse, and withdraws the *Living with Christ* pamphlet. "How do you like that, I never mailed it at all. I've been carrying it around this whole time." She takes the brown "Sunday Offering" envelope from between its pages and hands it to Mary Rose.

Mary Rose opens it. A creased black-and-white photo.

"I meant to frame it before I sent it to you," says Dolly.

In the photo, Mary Rose stands between her mother and her sister, looking down at the stone, flush against the grass. It is etched with letters and numbers that are fuzzy and will be likely fuzzier under magnification. Mary Rose's dress is white like the stone, while draped across her left shoulder is her mother's sweater. And resting there, offering comfort along with the warmth of the sweater, is her mother's hand. It strikes her suddenly: the sweater is covered in a floral pattern. Tulips.

"Thank you, Mummy." Mary Rose is more surprised by this word that has slipped out and shown its tail, *Mummy*, than by the photograph. After all, she already knows what is written on the stone.

"The dates'll be there," says Dolly, putting on her reading glasses, leaning forward to look. "Although you might need a magnifying glass."

"It's okay, Mum. I'll look when I get home."

"What've you got there?" asks Duncan, putting on his glasses, reaching for the photo. Mary Rose hands it to him. He looks at it and nods slowly. "Well, well. I remember taking that."

"What time of year was it, Dad?"

"We placed the stone in springtime," he says, and closes his eyes.

Dolly pipes up. "I found it in my jewellery box! What was it doing there?"

"Did you take it from the photo album, Mum?"

"I must have. Unless—Dunc. Dunc, dear, did you take this photo out of the album?"

"Why would I do that?" he asks, his voice a little husky.

"Because it's . . . a sad picture?" says Mary Rose.

He doesn't answer.

"Dad, Maureen sent me a link to a site . . . Canadian military graves abroad, I'll forward it to you. Dad?"

He opens his eyes, his brows elevate congenially, his lips compress in a good-natured upside-down smile. "What's that, sweetie pie?" He turns his blue eyes to her.

I love you, Dad.

"How's the genealogy going?" Her heart is shredding.

He sits forward. "Well now, there's a fella in Boston, name of Jer*ome* MacKinnon, he's an ac*count*ant with *Del*oitte, and it turns out he and I share a marker on the *Y* chromosome, which puts us *right* back to the *Clearances*."

Dolly's eyes narrow, she speaks slowly. "You know, that must have been a hard time, when I think about it."

"Don't think about it," says Duncan.

Andy-Patrick helps himself to a chocolate tile and offers the tray to his mother.

"Mmm, ever good," says Dolly, her mouth full of vowels.

"Let's go, Doll Face, we got a train to catch." Duncan helps his wife to her feet and she steadies herself on his arm.

"Did you want the moonstone, Mary Rose? Here, you have it."

"That's okay, Mum, I'm really happy to have the photograph, thank you."

"I'll take it," says Andy-Patrick.

"What do you want with a lady's ring?" says Duncan.

"He can give it to Mary Lou," says Dolly.

Andy-Patrick opens the velvet box and slips the ring on his pinky. Duncan rolls his eyes and shakes his head, but grins and slaps Andy-Patrick on the shoulder.

"Bye, Dad," says Mary Rose.

He bonks her on the head. "Thanks for coming to see us off, Mister."

The redcap greets them by name and laughs at something Dolly says. Duncan beams with pride, and they mount the narrow escalator up to the platform. Two little old people in bright clothing. Near the top, they turn and wave, then disappear.

Somewhere, a train has disgorged a tide of commuters that washes past them now. She goes to slip the photo back in its envelope.

"Can I see?" asks Andy-Patrick.

She hands it to him.

"What's that you've got on?" he asks.

"Mum's sweater."

"Looks more like a scarf."

She looks over his shoulder.

It's a sling.

Because she fell, or was pushed, punished, rescued. Or it was a cold day. Or it was warm.

"What's the matter?" he says.

She speaks before she is aware of formulating the words. "You helped me."

"What do you mean?"

"That time when Mum called and asked you to come for supper? You said, 'I can't, Mary Rose and Renée are here.'"

"Yeah?"

"And then . . ." We can't know which words will undo us. She waits until she can trust herself to speak. "It was over. The whole bad time."

He hands her a hanky. "It's clean."

"I'm sorry."

"At least you're not crying and driving."

"I mean I'm sorry for being a shit to you, A&P."

"You've never been a shit to me."

"Yes I have."

"I've deserved it."

"I'm bored with being a shit to you, I'm bored with you deserving it."

"Okay."

"I'm amazed you carry a hanky."

"Chicks love it."

"You carry it because you cry."

"Chicks love it."

She puts the photo in her pocket.

He says, "Can I ask you something? Don't be mad."

"What?"

"Would you call me Andrew from now on? Or at least Andrew-Patrick?"

"Sure."

The streetcar rattles up Bathurst Street past Toronto Western Hospital and she notices Balloon King is gone, in its place a Starbucks. At the corner of Bathurst and Bloor, she glances out the window for a trace of herself—this happens quickly, such that it slips into consciousness as "normal." Is that all there is to insanity? Slow it down: she has just turned her head, looked out the window and searched the crowd at the intersection to see if she was among them holding a bunch of tulips. She was not. She pictures swift faeries, a legion of puckish creatures chuckling as they trip through the regions of her mind. Is this what happens when you stop being angry for a moment? The light turns green.

Someone saw what happened to the flowers. There is always a witness. She shared a moment of her life with the people and pigeons at this corner yesterday, now they have dispersed and what is to say it mightn't have been an important moment?

She gets off the streetcar at the subway station and continues on foot up Bathurst. "You pick yellow," Winnie said. And she said something else too . . . "You buy only one." Mary Rose goes cold. What if she never had the first bunch of yellow tulips at all—what if she hallucinated them? But that could have been the language barrier, Winnie may have meant, "I want you to pay only for this bunch, not the previous bunch." She stops outside Archie's Variety—the voice of Kiri Te Kanawa soars out, *"Swing low, sweet chariot . . ."* She could pop in now and ask, "Winnie, did I leave with yellow tulips the first time I came in?" What if Winnie replies, "No. You come only once"? Would that prove Mary Rose went missing for . . . the amount of time it took to buy tulips? Has she lost a piece of time? It is one thing to speculate as to the existence of parallel worlds, it is another to realize you may have entered one. That is not science fiction, that is psychosis. Unless the other worlds are real . . . indeed, they are more mathematically probable than she herself is. Was the whole episode an especially vivid déjà vu? Winnie might be mistaken—forgetful, like the best of us. How can Mary Rose know for certain? Winnie waves to her from inside the store. She waves back, and keeps going.

Hil comes home. They hide Easter eggs for the children. She finds the costume that Mary Rose hid behind the brogues.

"Put it on."

"I meant to return it."

Hil pulls off the tags and tosses the confection at Mary Rose.

"Hil, no, it's like I'd be in drag, it's more your thing."

"Mister? You have to remember something. I like women. Now put it on and get back in here."

". . . Can I have a back rub?"

———

The faeries cease their daylight raids and resume their dream haunts. Rage is in remission. The kitchen is clean but not too clean. A storm has passed, Kansas-sized, but Mary Rose feels the prickle of renewable force, can see it in the way leaves rustle in the absence of wind, in the livid quality of evening light, smell of electricity in the air. Glimpse of old pathways, vines parting, brambles beckoning . . .

The psychoanalyst is in the same building as the hypnotist. Different floor. The pneumatic drills are gone. Maybe this is who her accountant was visiting—that is more disturbing than a hypnotist; Mary Rose can accept that her accountant might grind his teeth at night, she has a harder time accepting he has a subconscious.

On one side of the room, two upholstered swivel chairs face one another. On the other side is a couch—halfway down its cushioned surface she makes out the imprint of someone's bum. She takes a chair. The analyst sits opposite.

Mary Rose says, "I'm here because everything is fine."

It is time to make a fresh incision through the scars; allow sections of Time to bleed afresh, then re-graft them. *After* seeks *Before*. She will be her own donor this time . . . She clicks on the blank document called "Book" and types . . .

> *December in Winnipeg, 1956. The sky was huge and grey. The regional bus groaned, its exhaust thick with carbon . . .*

Daisy dies in May. It is almost as though she waited until it was safe.

"Where *is* she, Mumma?"

"Mumma, where is *she*?"

Like a magic trick, the city is suddenly in full leaf.

The lady at the counter smiled and said, "Oh, when're you due?"
"The baby's dead," she said. And the sales lady started crying.
"Don't cry," said Dolly. "I'm not crying, don't you cry."

She phoned to invite him to visit her home on his own. She was in the bedroom she shared with Renée; mauve walls, a Georgia O'Keeffe print of an iris, it was the eighties. It was around four or five o'clock on a Saturday afternoon. Renée was puttering in her workroom, turning something into something else. Mary Rose dialed her parents' number. Her father answered. She knew her mother was out at choir practice.

"Mum's out at choir practice."

"That's okay, Dad, I wanted to speak with you."

"Oh yeah? What's up?"

She asked him to visit her home. He said no. She realized she had been unclear, she tried to be more specific. "I know you can't come with Mum because Mum won't come here, but you could come."

No.

"You could come on your own."

No.

"Please come."

No.

"Please."

She started to feel unreal, saying things she had not planned to say, things that were bypassing her head-traffic controller, the more laconic he was, the more she unravelled. "You're my father, you could come see me, Dad, please Dad, please see me." She sounded to herself like a robot. "I'm begging you, Dad, please, please, please come and see me in my home, Dad please. It doesn't matter what Mum thinks, you can do what you think is right."

"I do think it's right." He spoke calmly.

Dear Mary Rose, You have chosen to go down a path that we, as your parents, cannot follow . . .

She heard herself moan, she hugged herself with her free hand and started to undress. She went into the bathroom because she was not safe. She needed to be in a place where she could know she existed. She ran the water.

"I'm your daughter, and I am telling you that you are doing a terrible thing, Dad, a terrible thing to me, please stop doing it." She was saying things no one in her family said, not even people in movies said these things, people in books did not say them. She sat in the tub, hot water lapping about her hips, she hugged her knees, felt her breasts soft against them, stroked her head, her shoulder, rocked, it's okay. Water is real, it holds you, tells you you are there, *there, there, Daddy's got you.* "You're saying you hate me!" She screamed it.

"I'm not saying that to you. That is what you are saying to me." His tone was detached, reasonable. *Your lifestyle is opposed to the values with which we raised you, and by insisting upon adhering to that lifestyle, you have turned your back on us . . .*

"When you have had enough, perhaps you'll come home."

"I have, I visit your home all the time, why won't you come to my home?"

"That's not a home."

"It is so!" She screamed it. "It's my home!" She screamed it. "I have friends who would refuse to visit you and Mum because of what you're doing, is that what you want?" She was shaking. Renée came in, Mary Rose waved her out.

"That's up to you."

. . . our door cannot be open to you in the way that it was in the past.

"So if I stopped visiting you in your home, you would not seek me out."

"That's up to you."

"You could let me go."

"You let yourself go."

"You would let go of me, and you would never come after me."

"You've turned your back on us."

If you had a broken leg, we would take you to a doctor. In this case, it is your mind that is broken, but you kept it from us . . .

"My heart is breaking, Dad, it is breaking right now."

He was implacable.

"We are prepared to come see you when you decide to take the help we are offering."

He was glass.

"What help?!" She shrieked it, shocking herself, yet even amid the sense of unreality, another sense was emerging, a deep recognition. Naked and shrieking, she made a decision to listen to everything he had to say so she would have all the information. Get him to say it. Don't tear up the letter this time. "I'm your daughter," she said.

"Not this part of you."

"No 'part'!" *Bang!* on the glass. "Only one Mary Rose!" *Bang bang!* "I am the same one you loved and were proud of, I am the same, I am the one you carried, I am the one!" Sobbing, deciding, knowing this sorrow was already in the past.

"The Mary Rose I know does not choose to live the way you are living now."

"You said, 'Do it your way.' I am brave."

"You are sick."

She cried into the phone. Renée returned with a glass of wine, set it on the edge of the tub and withdrew. He didn't hang up. Was that a good thing? Or was he determined to show he was impervious? As long as she was the crazy one, he was the sane one.

"I love you, Dad, why don't you love me?" Calm now.

"I didn't say that."

"But if I don't change, you will never welcome me or come into my home." No more banging. Just hand smears.

"You have chosen to go down a path that—"

"You don't want me to have love."

"What you have is not love."

She curled over her knees. "What if someone had said that to you about Mum?"

"There's no comparison."

"I love Renée, she is my family."

"She's not my family."

"What if you hadn't been allowed to marry? You were considered to be different colours in those days."

"Don't be silly."

"You want me to be alone for the rest of my life."

"*Being* homosexual is not wrong. *Practising* homosexuality is."

"Oh. I'm supposed to become a nun?"

Silence.

"Wow. Okay, you're wrong. That's a bad reason to become a nun or a priest. What you're doing to your own daughter now is a sin. You want me to hate myself."

"I don't know what happened along the way to pervert the normal course of your development. I'm in the dark about that. If you had let us know early on that you had these tendencies, we would have been able to help you. But you shut us out. If you'd had a broken leg—"

"I had a broken arm, and you didn't do anything."

"We didn't know it was broken."

"Why didn't I get an X-ray?"

"No one thought your arm could possibly be broken."

"It hurt. All the time."

"We're getting off topic here." *topeec* "If you were a drug addict, I would not be doing my job as a father by giving you more drugs when you beg for them."

Absurdity can be a balm. She splashed her face clear of mucus and tears, and spoke calmly. "If I had told you when I was a teenager and still living at home, you would have taken me to a psychiatrist."

"That's right."

"And you would have had me hospitalized and treated. Electroshock, maybe."

"That's one option, but you never gave us the chance. You hid your disorder from us."

She cried again, but not in anger. "I haven't believed in God since I was fourteen, Dad, but I believe in Good because I have been looked after and I believe in Love because somehow I knew enough not to show anyone, not even myself, who I was while I was still in your hands. I am so scared when I think of what you would have done to me, and when I think of that, I think that what you are doing to me now is something I can handle because I'm twenty-three and all you can do to me now is hate me." She was shaking when she got out of the bath, but she had the information.

The next time she saw her parents, it was as though she and her father had never had the conversation. Her mother did her laundry. Her father poured her a Scotch and asked about her work. They ate, they chatted, she and Dolly played Scrabble. At some point, the three of them found themselves at the kitchen table. Her father's gaze drifted to a corner of the ceiling as the crazy light entered her mother's eye and it began again.

When Odysseus finally makes it home, he is much changed, but his loved ones know him by his scar. Will she make it home? Will she recognize herself?

Grafts leave scars on the skin, yes, but on bone too. Scars make you stronger, and they help tell a story; like striations in igneous rock, a story of eruptions and epochal inches. Her scars can take her home. Down to the bone, into the marrow, down among the stem cells where the stories germinate.

It will all go back to carbon one day, back to gemstones and crystals and star stuff. She has a vantage point for the moment. An "I."

Pinhole aperture, like an old-fashioned camera. All she can do is try to bear witness. Writer, write thyself . . .

> *It must have been the pill they gave her that made the bus*
> *ride into something that slipped time and space, because that*
> *bus is still lumbering, big-eyed and heaving, over the ruts of*
> *the road . . . Dolly is there still, in her kerchief, forehead*
> *vibrating against the glass, staring out at the gaping sky, her*
> *belly a grave . . .*

Mary Rose has a picture of Alexander's grave. She knows where his physical remains are, she could go there. Everything is somewhere. She could go to Winnipeg, to the hospital, and find the smokestack. She could place her hands against the warm bricks. *My sister.* And she could say her name: *Mary Rose.*

She can go to Kingston and look up at the windows of the General Hospital—two of them were hers. She can say a prayer for her bone donor. And she can say a prayer for herself: the child of ten, immobilized on the operating table. And the girl of fourteen, standing next to her mother in the surgeon's office. *They've come back.*

You cut me to the bone, Dr. Sorokin. Laid bare my humerus, riddled with history; tamped in cadaver bone, and I grew. Thank you. Four years later, you cut through the scar, raked the fallen leaves, drained strange fluid and returned it to the earth. Cut my hip, harvested the hill of bone; transplanted it to the valley of my arm and filled in the shadows. Bless your hands.

Pray for the baby who stands pounding the glass. Pray for the mother lying on the couch. Pray for the young woman immobilized at the kitchen table, *I would rather you'd been born dead.* Pray for her, and all others who have been whipped from the door so they will know they are loved.

Pray for the children in the sunroom at night, where the table is set for supper beneath the big black windows, and the brave damaged toys care for one another. They are there, still. Like the big blue city bus that rolls and dips and labours on. Pray for the young woman in the kerchief at the back, her belly big and lifeless, *you'll have more babies . . .*

The marks on a body are the marks on a map. They tell you where you have been, and how to get home again so that you can stop going round inside yourself. Look down at the map. Look up at the sky. Where is the sun? Now walk. Make a new pathway, walk out of the forest.

She can go back to Germany, land of horror and sweetness, where a *Mädchen* in white waits, a person of two and a half. Together they can look down at the stone, flush against the grass.

> *Ask me whatever you want, I will answer.*
> *Your arm hurts because it is broken.*
> *No, he does not need to breathe down there.*
> *No, you did not do this.*
> *That is what remains of his body, his soul has left it.*
> *His body has returned to the earth to make more grass*
>   *and food and air and rain.*
> *That is where all the flowers have gone.*
> *But you will always have one in your name.*

Maggie is drawing hieroglyphs in Mary Rose's datebook, which she has looted from her bag. Mary Rose tips the contents onto the kitchen floor and sits cross-legged next to the child.

"Purse," says Maggie.

"Bag," says Mary Rose. "That is a lesbian word for 'purse.'"

Hil says, "I'm a lesbian and I have a purse."

Mary Rose looks up. "Did you feel that just now?"

"What?"

"Happy."

Re: Some things really do get batter

Dear Dad,

Sometimes things need to get worse before they can get better.

Love,

Mary Rose

End

ACKNOWLEDGEMENTS

Thank you. Without whom . . .

Beatrice Ahad

Katherine Ashenburg

Bill Bolton Women's Hockey League

Tracy Bohan

Susan Burns

Sarah Chalfant

Trudy Chernin

Anne Collins

Trish Convery

Louise Dennys

Jerry Doiron

Margaret Anne Fitzpatrick-Hanly

Margaret Gaffney

Ken Girotti

Mary Giuliano

Robert Gordon

Janet Hanna

Kendra Hawke

Kate Icely

Honora Johannesen

Sarka Kalusova

Wendy Katherine

Sharon Klein

Eleanor Koldofsky

Melanie Lane

Amanda Lewis

Mary Paula Lizewski

John-Hugh MacDonald

Malcolm MacDonald

Mary MacDonald

Isabel MacDonald-Palmer

Lora MacDonald-Palmer

Jackie Maxwell

Nancy McKinnon

Clare Meridew

Gordon Meslin

Rowda Mohamud

Deirdre Molina

Montana

Cassandra Nicolaou

Mara Nicolaou
Arland O'Hara
Alanna Palmer
Alisa Palmer
Marven Palmer
Pam Plant
Maria Popoff
Lisa Robertson
John Robinson

Harriet Sachs
Matthew Sibiga
Olivia Smith-Lizewski
Stormy
Lillian Szpak
Sister Walsh
Maureen White
Andrew Wylie

PERMISSIONS

Bensahel, H., Y. Desgrippes, P. Jehanno, G.F. Pennecot. "Solitary bone cyst: controversies and treatment." *Journal of Pediatric Orthopaedics B* 7, no. 4 (October 1998): 257–261. Used by permission of the publisher.

Lyrics from *Won't You Be My Neighbor?* by Fred M. Rogers, © McFeely Rogers Foundation; used with permission.

Unicameral Bone Cyst. Boston Children's Hospital. http://www.childrenshospital.org/health-topics/conditions/unicameral -bone-cyst. Used with permission.

Bone Cyst. NHS Direct Wales. http://www.nhsdirect.wales.nhs.uk /encyclopaedia/b/article/bonecyst/. Reproduced by kind permission of the Department of Health, © 2014.

Mehlman CT. Unicameral Bone Cyst. *Medscape Reference.* Updated May 10, 2013. Available at: http://emedicine.medscape.com/article/1257331 -overview. Used with permission.

Fleisher, Gary R. and Stephen Ludwig. *Textbook of Pediatric Emergency Medicine*, 6th ed. Philadelphia: Lippincott Williams & Wilkins, 2010. Used by permission of the publisher.

ANN-MARIE MacDONALD is a bestselling, award-winning novelist, playwright, actor and broadcaster. Her works include *Goodnight Desdemona (Good Morning Juliet)*, *Belle Moral: A Natural History*, *Fall On Your Knees* and *The Way the Crow Flies*. She lives in Toronto with her wife, Alisa Palmer, and their two children.